# WINDMILL HILL

**Lucy Atkins** is an award-winning author, feature journalist and *Sunday Times* book critic. She has written for newspapers including the *Guardian*, *The Times*, the *Sunday Times* and the *Telegraph* as well as many UK magazines. She teaches on the Masters in Creative Writing at Oxford University.

Also by Lucy Atkins

*The Missing One*
*The Other Child*
*The Night Visitor*
*Magpie Lane*

# WINDMILL HILL

# lucy atkins

QUERCUS

First published in Great Britain in 2023
This paperback edition published in Great Britain in 2024 by

QUERCUS

Quercus Editions Ltd
Carmelite House
50 Victoria Embankment
London EC4Y 0DZ

An Hachette UK company

Epigraph © *The Complete Andersen*, Jean Hersholt,
The Hans Christian Andersen Centre, University of Southern Denmark
Illustration on page viii © Nicola Howell Hawley

The moral right of Lucy Atkins to be
identified as the author of this work has been
asserted in accordance with the Copyright,
Designs and Patents Act, 1988.

A CIP catalogue record for this book is available
from the British Library

PB ISBN 978 1 52940 794 5
EBOOK 978 1 52940 795 2

10 9 8 7 6 5 4 3 2 1

Typeset by CC Book Production
Printed and bound in Great Britain by Clays Ltd, Elcograf S.p.A.

Papers used by Quercus are from well-managed forests and other responsible sources.

*In memory of my beloved mother,*
*Beryl T. Atkins (1931–2021),*
*whose last words were*
*'Don't patronise me'*

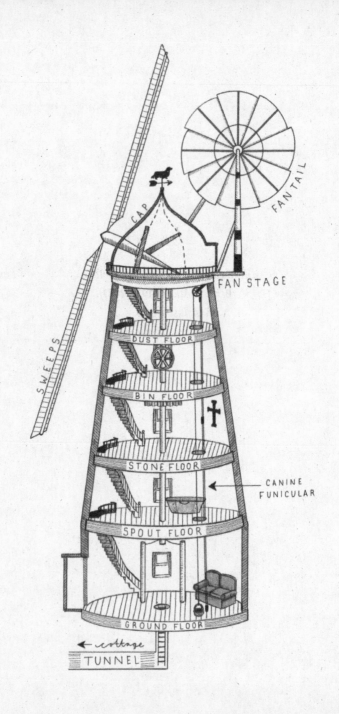

SWEEPS

CAP

FANTAIL

FAN STAGE

DUST FLOOR

BIN FLOOR

STONE FLOOR

CANINE FUNICULAR

SPOUT FLOOR

GROUND FLOOR

*cottage*

TUNNEL

'The other day I wisely let the father and his helpers examine my throat and the hole in my chest. I wanted to know what was wrong, for something was wrong, and when you're out of order it's well to look into yourself.'

HANS CHRISTIAN ANDERSEN, The Windmill

# Author's Note

The windmill, the characters and all the events in this novel are pure fiction. My windmill was, however, inspired by the beautiful Jack windmill at Clayton in East Sussex, near to where I grew up, which has a little chapel on the stone floor, and a very spooky tunnel.

F. Layton Burgess, Chairman
Claycombe Parish Council

22nd June 1921

Dear Lady Battiscombe,

I write in the strongest possible terms having received complaints from several Claycombe residents about depraved and ungodly goings-on at your windmill on the evening of 21st June.

Two of your guests, dressed in pagan robes and trailing foliage, accompanied by an inebriated young lady wearing a swan costume, caused a scene in the Chalkman public house. Later that night, a member of the parish council, whilst innocently airing his Jack Russell, noticed individuals of both sexes cavorting in a state of undress through the churchyard. Among them was a man in a bishop's costume playing what appeared to be an oboe.

As well you know, we in Claycombe pride ourselves on our quiet, pious and respectable village. I therefore ask you most emphatically to refrain forthwith from these wanton and antisocial activities.

Should you choose to ignore this letter, I can assure you that there will be consequences of a most serious nature.

Yours sincerely,

F. Layton Burgess (Mr), Chairman, Claycombe Parish Council

# Chapter 1

Hendricks had eaten both her hearing aids and her wrist was on fire. Those were Astrid's two most pressing problems. She was also alone, truly alone, for the first time in years, without Mrs Baker, without the dogs, and she simply wasn't used to it. She felt rather bewildered, in fact, as if a great hand had reached down, plucked her from the windmill and dumped her in security. She had jolted her sling against the corner of the passport machine and deep inside the bone there was a burning now, so intense that everything around her seemed to wobble at the edges. Her lower back felt jagged from the interminable walking and standing, and the terminal felt airless; she was already exhausted from all the corridors, some of which had moved beneath her feet, trolleying her along in a strange, weightless state, powerless and transcendent, movement without effort towards an unwanted unknown.

She had expected to feel a bit more gung-ho about the whole plan when she got to the airport, but the opposite seemed to be happening; she felt simultaneously invisible and exposed. What on earth was she playing at? She came to a standstill at the end of a long queue for the baggage scanners. It struck her that this trip was, very possibly, an enormous error.

For some time now, when things became difficult like this, an odd whirring feeling would start up in her chest, as if everything inside her was revving up and threatening to spin out of control. She had been made to understand the physical cause of this sensation, of course, but she certainly wasn't going to think about that – thinking about the body was the quickest way to make it misbehave. She hadn't said anything to Mrs Baker about this because Mrs Baker would only insist on going back to the doctor. Astrid had had almost no need for doctors in her eighty-two years and had absolutely no intention of starting now. Her main problem wasn't her body, anyway, it was the dogs; or more precisely, their absence. Gordon, particularly, would be very distressed, back at the windmill without her. Juniper and Hendricks had each other, but Gordon would feel so abandoned, he simply wouldn't understand where, or why, she'd gone. And Mrs Baker would be no comfort to him, none at all. She might not even notice his distress, and if she did, she wouldn't be able to alleviate it. She probably wouldn't even allow him to sleep under the covers – if she even let him sleep in her bed. The sensation in Astrid's chest intensified. She felt odd, now, liverish. She wondered if she might, in fact, be about to pass out.

Fainting in public really would be ghastly. She straightened her shoulders and took a few deep breaths, expanding her diaphragm and trying to push Gordon's anxious little face, his pointy snout, curly beard and sensitive brown eyes to the back of her mind. She felt, suddenly, that she was being watched, and she turned to look at the queue zigzagging behind her, certain that she was about to find Magnus's face among the strangers: the puff of white hair, the pale, Celtic eyes. He'd tracked her for decades now, popping up at weak points like this, glimpsed before vanishing. It would almost be odd if he wasn't here.

These thoughts made no sense, she did know that. *S.O.B.* She straightened her spine. *Silly old bat.* Magnus was not in the queue behind her. Magnus was in the Scottish Borders, dying. The spinning feeling became so fierce for a moment that she had to lean on the handle of the carry-on case to catch her breath.

It didn't help that she and Mrs Baker had parted at the drop-off point on such awful terms, squabbling about money – money, of all things! Now that really *was* absurd. The truth was that over the past eight months, ever since the Awful Incident, they'd both become a bit unhinged, prone to bickering and flare-ups, and odd sightings. Finding Magnus's interview in the *Sunday Times* had only worsened their nerves, and then when Nina came to the windmill – sweet, kind Nina – everything had somehow escalated so that now, just a week later, she was here, in a security queue, at Gatwick airport.

Usually, Mrs Baker would step in to kibosh Astrid's more impulsive or impractical plans. It had long been Mrs Baker's job to provide containment and restraint; she was the cling film over the madder notions, the paperweight on Astrid's fluttering mind. But this time, she hadn't intervened. Mrs Baker really wasn't herself at all at the moment. She was seeing Constance Battiscombe regularly now – and not just in the windmill, but inside the cottage too. Everything really must be getting out of hand if Mrs Baker was seeing ghosts. It struck Astrid then that she should just pull out – get out of the airport, go back to the windmill. It was very possible, she realised, with a mixture of surprise and dismay, that Mrs Baker needed her.

The thought of Mrs Baker back at the cottage with the dogs, the windmill towering darkly above them, the November wind roaring over the Downs, slamming into the aged bricks, tugging at the rotting sweeps and rattling the fan stage made

Astrid very uneasy indeed. As they'd driven away down the hill that morning, she'd turned to look back at the tower, and it had seemed to teeter, as if this time it really would collapse onto the cottage. Thin charcoal clouds had moved fast behind it, tilted phantoms making their escape, and for a moment Astrid had felt as if her presence alone had been holding the windmill up all these years. She simply didn't trust it not to topple without her.

The notion that the windmill might collapse was not, in fact, outlandish. Pieces of it were definitely coming loose. The next big storm could rip off the sweeps, perhaps even take off the fantail. She pictured the iron star wheel spinning through the sky and slicing through the cottage roof. The villagers would be up in arms. They'd roar up the hill, raging about irresponsibility and nuttiness and public safety. Or perhaps they wouldn't. They didn't get agitated about the windmill the way they used to; it was almost as if they'd given up caring. In the old days when she used to go down to the village for her newspapers and milk and bread, people would stop their conversations to stare as she entered the shop, and then, as she left, she'd hear mutters and tuts beneath the tinkle of the bell. It was quite a thrill. Once, as she paid for the *Guardian* and a loaf of granary, she'd noticed a small child goggling at her and heard its mother hiss, 'That's the windmill woman. Don't stare or she'll have your . . .' Astrid didn't catch what – bones for breakfast? Guts for garters? The child's eyes had widened and it had buried its face in its mother's side, plainly terrified; Astrid had been delighted.

'They probably think we're a couple of lesbians,' Mrs Baker had said, when Astrid told her. 'It's naked prejudice, that's what it is.'

'Or the weird sisters.'

'Well, you're a bit peculiar but we don't look anything like sisters.'

'Shakespeare, Mrs Baker, the Scottish play. The witches. Though there were three of those, of course.'

The hostility and suspicion had been there long before Mrs Baker came to the windmill, though. It had been there when she was with Charlie, whose ex-wife was a stalwart of the local Women's Institute, but it wasn't just that – even before she'd met Charlie there had been antagonism. The problem was that when she bought the windmill, people had recognised her from all the newspaper reports; they thought they knew what kind of person she was, and consequently, from the moment she arrived on the hill, they had wanted her off it.

She rather missed being noticed, disapproved of, gossiped about. They never really had occasion to stop in the village any more; the shop had been closed for over ten years now, and when they needed a newspaper or a pint of milk, they had to drive to the petrol station where nobody noticed, or knew them, or cared whether the windmill stood or fell.

She did feel guilty about the state it was in, of course she did, but it was a personal rather than a public guilt, the sense of having failed and neglected it. It had not always been this way. She had tried, for many years, to deal with its numerous problems, to fix the bits that fell off, to shore it up and do the right thing, but she had never been one for order and maintenance, and even if she had been, there was no money, now, for that.

The man in front of her had edged forwards, so she tugged the handle of the carry-on case and took a step or two after him, doing her very best to ignore the hysterical objections of her lower vertebrae. There was no sense fretting about collapse. Fretting wasn't going to keep the windmill upright any more than her presence would. She must put it out of her mind. In general, Astrid found, it really was best not to think too much about the windmill – it was simply there, a battered and draughty adjunct, moaning and complaining, home to spiders and rodents, a lifetime of ephemera, a demented barn owl and a fallen altar.

She reminded herself that her decision to go to Scotland was not rash or deranged, it was entirely necessary. She must tackle Magnus – put a stop to his destructive lies once and for all. Nobody else could do it. Mrs Baker must have seen the logic of this, even though she hadn't been able to bring herself to admit it. If she hadn't seen the logic, then Astrid wouldn't be standing in the airport, because there was no money for this trip, none whatsoever.

The idea of going to Scotland had come to Astrid the morning after Nina's visit. Her wrist had kept her awake all night – there had been no way to get comfortable, even with the tablets – and she'd lain awake with the cast propped up on a pile of pillows. The bone felt fuzzy and odd, both painful and numb, which didn't quite seem possible, but was. Eventually, she'd gathered her strength to sit up, and as she did so, she'd experienced an unfamiliar moment of clarity: she would go to Scotland and confront Magnus. She would force him not to publish his memoir. Nina couldn't do it. Nobody could but her.

It was still dark outside, and as she felt around with her good hand for the bedside lamp, she knocked a box of tissues onto the floor, then the alarm clock, and then a full glass of water. At last, she found the light switch. Juniper and Hendricks were illuminated, melded on the eiderdown into a little curly mound, noses tucked into each other like the flaps of envelopes, differentiated only by their knitted bed jackets: powder blue and cerise. Gordon, who always slept under the covers, ideally with his nose shoved into Astrid's armpit, crawled out, blinking anxiously, but Juniper and Hendricks didn't bother to move. She needed to pee, but first she had to find the painkillers because the wrist had suddenly dropped the numbness and opted for agony. She located the pills, but it was going to be near impossible to pop one out one-handed, she was going to need Mrs Baker for that. She didn't know what time it was as the clock was now gone. She managed to sit up, her back howling objections, and got her legs off the bed. She tried to hold the pill packet with her teeth and extract one with her good hand. Gordon, handsome in his bottle-green cable knit, watched intensely. 'You're no help,' she said. He wagged his stubby tail and looked hopeful.

The bedroom was freezing. She could already feel her toes going numb, the tip of her nose too. Gordon wiggled onto her lap and poked the pill packet – it fell. Bending to retrieve it was unpleasant. The room seemed to whirl, and for a moment she felt completely drunk – and suddenly she remembered Magnus teetering on the porch roof of the rented cottage outside Stratford declaiming Tennyson. *To strive, to seek, to find and not to yield!* He'd had a long session in the pub and was trying to climb in the bedroom window; as he gestured, his foot slipped – a brief comical look of shock crossed his face and he toppled backwards into a clump of rhododendrons. His leg was in a cast for weeks and he had to be replaced on stage, though fortunately, he was only playing First Lord in Arden. He'd sulked in the rented cottage for a week or so and then had gone back to London while she wowed and dazzled as Rosalind. The RADA tutors had constantly warned them that their careers would be gruelling and difficult, but hers really hadn't been. She'd been terribly lucky, always working. The whole thing had been bliss – until it wasn't.

She extricated herself from the ancient, sprigged eiderdown, the blankets. Her knees and ankles creaked and snagged as her feet felt around for her boots. Gordon jumped off the bed, then Juniper and Hendricks slid off, *thud*, *thud*, and they all made their way to the toilet. It was tricky to get her leggings and pants down with one hand. The dogs watched, mildly curious. The pain in her wrist and back made her dizzy again, and slow. 'I'm doing my very best,' she said. 'Don't judge.' They wagged in unison. When she'd managed to get her clothing back up, they all made their way past Mrs Baker's closed door to the top of the staircase. It was a palaver to get them into the Dickinson with one hand and lowering the basket with the dogs inside felt extremely precarious; she had to secure the rope with her feet and let it out incredibly gradually whilst trying not to imagine them plummeting to the hall below. Luckily, they were patient and sat still. She had invented two different pulley systems: one for the spiral staircase in the cottage, another for the ladder staircases in the windmill, but she'd never anticipated the day when she'd only have one working arm. At some point, she was going to have to install something clever and mechanical, in the cottage at least – an electrically powered dumb waiter perhaps. But of course, there was no money for that, either.

The kitchen light was on already and there was clattering. Mrs Baker was at the sink, furiously scrubbing. Her bottom swung from side to side. 'What on earth . . . ?' Astrid glanced at the Kit Cat clock which twitched its tail and slid its eyes to the window, to the door, and back to the window again. 'It's not even half past six!' Mrs Baker had rolled up the sleeves of the fisherman's jumper that she never really took off in the winter months and her hair was flattened at the back, grey curls tangled then shooting up, electrified, at the crown.

Astrid went over and handed her the pill packet. 'Could you . . . I can't seem to . . .' It was Constance's silver coffee pot in the sink, its spout crested like a peacock's head, entwined flowers around its belly and a frond curling round its handle – a devil to polish. 'Why are you doing that? The horse has rather bolted there, surely?'

Mrs Baker put down the cloth and took the pill packet, peering up briefly. 'You look tired, Astrid.'

'A tired look is an old look,' Astrid sang in her mother's voice. 'You are old. No sleep?'

'I slept like a baby, thank you.'

Mrs Baker popped out two pills. 'You'd better sit down. I'll make you a coffee. You look peaky.'

'I'm positively blooming, Mrs Baker.'

Mrs Baker held out a hand with a pill, palm flat, as if medicating a horse.

The dogs were waiting to be lifted onto the sink. Astrid bumped her shin on Tony Blair and as she leaned over to wrench open the kitchen window her back howled. A blast of freezing November air rushed in. She was glad she'd kept the dogs' knitted jackets on – or were they tank tops? Jerkins? Body warmers? If she was to start selling them on the web, she was going to need the right terminology. Jargon was everything in the world of marketing. She'd also need a computer, and seed money – wool was frightfully expensive. There was a fortune to be made in canine knitwear, she felt sure of that, but the problem was how to get started when there were no funds. She sensed the wind changing direction and the windmill, proud, redundant, let out its low and plaintive groan.

Mrs Baker leaned past her to fill the kettle. The tap clanked and rattled, and brackish water juddered out. Astrid gestured at the waiting dogs. 'I don't think I can . . .' Mrs Baker bent down. Though only eight years Astrid's junior, and somewhat broad in the beam, she had the strength and flexibility of a young shot-putter. She lifted the dogs, one by one, onto the sink and they wobbled off down the plank, swallowed by the fog: Hendricks first, ears pricked, alert to squirrels or foxes, with Juniper wad-dling benignly after him. Gordon cowered on the windowsill where Mrs Baker had put him, and Astrid had to lean over and gently push him after the others with her good hand. She closed the window then, shivering, and went to get the jar of kibble, congratulating herself for remembering to step around Tony Blair. Mrs Baker was back at the coffee pot, half of which was shining like a silvery Aladdin's lamp. *It should be back in the windmill*, Astrid thought. *It definitely should not be inside the cottage.*

'I've decided to go to Scotland and confront him. I must stop him writing this book.' She hooked the kibble jar with one arm. 'I really have no choice.'

Mrs Baker's large hands stilled. Astrid waited to be told that she did have a choice, that this was a ridiculous idea, that she couldn't hope to influence what Magnus did or didn't publish, that they didn't have the money for a ticket, but – and this was highly unusual – Mrs Baker held her tongue.

'I can't let him ruin my life for the second time,' Astrid said. 'I won't.'

Mrs Baker rubbed the pot's fat belly.

'You could come with me. We'll go in Gloria.'

'That car wouldn't make it to Scotland, Astrid. It can barely make it to Asda.'

'Gloria? Of course she would – Charlie always said a

Mercedes-Benz lasts a lifetime. It's why all the taxi drivers have them.'

'Charlie's been dead over twenty years, and that thing wasn't new when he got it. Also, it'd cost about a thousand quid in fuel.'

'It could be a holiday.'

'A holiday to Scotland in November to confront your dying ex-husband?'

They looked at each other.

'Perhaps not.' Astrid's wrist began to throb, suddenly and violently, as if all the emotions of forty-five years were trying to get out via the fractured bone before it sealed itself over. She closed her eyes and waited for the moment to pass. When it had, she said, 'But I have no choice, I have to go. We simply can't have that kind of exposure. You know that as well as I do.'

'Exposure?' Mrs Baker turned again. 'What are you on about now?' Her face was crumpled, ruddy and baggy, but her eyes, as always, were alert, assessing where this might be going, and what she should do to contain it.

'Exposure, Eileen! We can't have it! You know why.' It had only been eight months since the Awful Incident and Mrs Baker hadn't put it behind her any more than Astrid had. She was being wilfully obtuse.

Gordon was back at the window already, nose sponging the glass to come in. Had he even got to the bottom of the plank? If he did his business on the kitchen floor again, Mrs Baker would be furious, but Astrid couldn't bear his 'Cathy, I've come home' look, those plaintive eyes looming at her through the condensation. She put down the kibble, leaned over, unhooked the latch and let him back in. 'So, I shall need you to drive me to the library this morning.' She looked at the kibble jar. 'I need to get onto the web and book a plane ticket. Nina said you can get terribly cheap flights now, not like the train. Do you know she paid over a hundred pounds for her train ticket from Edinburgh? I shall have to stay overnight, of course.' Mrs Baker wasn't looking at her, she was back to polishing. 'Perhaps I can stay with Nina in the gatehouse. I'll phone her before we go to the library.'

Mrs Baker put down her cloth and took the kibble jar from Astrid. She wrenched off the lid then went and shook some into the dog bowls. Juniper and Hendricks were coming back up the plank now, Hendricks first, still agile despite his years, his sister close behind him, slower, fatter. 'We'll have to get a new credit card, I suppose.' Astrid tossed this in and waited, but Mrs Baker said nothing. She went to the sink, lifted Hendricks down, then hoicked Juniper after him. Hendricks was already shoving Gordon off the kibble. 'So rude!' Astrid scolded and toed Gordon's bowl aside. She suddenly felt exhausted, even though the day had barely begun.

She went over to her chair by the Rayburn. Various bits of her were fizzing and buzzing: her wrist, her lower spine, her breastbone. She felt like that board game, Operation, where body parts light up, electric, at the slightest touch. Her knitting was in the basket by the chair. She'd almost finished the striped dog jacket. She'd been trying to crochet a grinning mouse that would look like a jockey on the dog's back, but the snout had come out warped; it had been too fiddly even with two hands, and there was something demonic about the eyes – pink embroidery thread had probably been an error, but of course, she couldn't remedy that now as crafting would be out of the question for a while.

Mrs Baker was scrubbing the coffee pot with the blackened cloth again, so vigorously that her breath was coming out in little huffs. Below her, Tony Blair seemed to cower. Nina had bumped her shin on him too when she was washing her wound. She'd looked down. 'Is that a stoat?'

Astrid had struggled to explain to Nina why they had a tax-idermised stoat in the kitchen. He'd been there for years, and she genuinely couldn't remember, but Mrs Baker forgot nothing. 'There's a hole in the tiles for the stopcock, goes all the way to the foundations. The base of the stoat fits the hole, stops mice getting up.' Astrid had noticed that when Nina smiled two sweet dimples bracketed her mouth.

She'd once had the idea of taming the kitchen mice: training them, using cubes of cheese, to perform little tricks – she'd read an article saying that mice were surprisingly intelligent and biddable, positively eager to please. Then she'd come down one morning to find a beheaded corpse. A dog – probably Sloe, Sloe really had been a dreadful savage – had had other ideas. They'd put Tony Blair over the hole in the floor for the mice's protection, as much as anything else.

Astrid tugged the scalloped frill of the mouse ear. 'At the very least, I have to make him take me out of his memoir. I can't be in it, don't you see? The whole ghastly scandal will be dredged up again, and the reporters will find out I'm still alive and then they'll come up here, poking around and asking questions about Magnus – and of course, they'll want to know who you are, too, and we can't have that, can we? We can't have strangers poking around the windmill. Certainly not now. Dear God!' She covered her mouth with the crocheted mouse. 'Imagine!'

'Reporters?' Mrs Baker turned, leaning her bottom against the sink. 'Why would reporters come up here? What *are* you on about?'

'The ghastly scandal, Mrs Baker! It'll be all over the papers

again, they'll want to know what became of me, and then they'll
come up here demanding answers, and that's just . . . well . . . we
can't *possibly* allow that, can we? The intrusion. People coming
up here. Not now – my God – not after what we've done.'

'*What we've done*?'

'Yes! Good Lord, Eileen, I should think that was obvious!'

Mrs Baker looked at her for a long moment, and then went
back to polishing. 'I hate to break it to you, Astrid, but he's the
famous one, not you.'

Astrid straightened her spine. 'You don't know what they're
like, Eileen, you have no idea. You've never been in the public
eye – you've never been the subject of an international scandal.
They're merciless. One whiff of Magnus and they'll be up here,
I'm telling you, and then what will they find out? They're like
bloodhounds, they won't rest until they've torn us to pieces.'

'Bloodhounds don't tear, they just sniff.'

'Well, we don't want any sniffing either, do we?' Astrid felt her
chest tighten at the thought of people writing things about her.
The old shame loomed in the anteroom of her conscious mind,
so she closed her eyes and tried to think of something more
pleasant. Knitted fruit – a fruit basket dog jacket, studded with
strawberries, apples, bananas with tiny little black lines down
the yellow. She must make more dog jackets as soon as her wrist
was healed. Perhaps Mrs Baker could help. But Mrs Baker wasn't
a knitter. Her needle skills were focussed on damage limitation:
mending, reattaching, strengthening.

Gordon was trotting over now, wagging his little tail. 'There,
my darling.' She patted her lap. 'Was that nice? Come here,
now, hup.' She helped him up with one hand and felt instantly
calmer as he nestled onto her. She pushed the rusty curls out
of his eyes. He'd look wonderful in a fruit basket. He could be

the model. They could have professional photographs done. She felt rather pleased with herself then. She'd always been good at distracting herself from unpleasant thoughts, but lately she'd elevated this skill to an art form.

'Listen, Astrid.' Mrs Baker tossed the cloth into the sink and turned again, rubbing her hands down her apron. 'If this is the only reason you're going to Scotland, then I think you should forget it. No one's coming up here. No one's interested in you any more. You're an eighty-two-year-old woman, nobody cares what you did or didn't do forty years ago.'

'Forty-five. The scandal was forty-five years ago – almost forty-six.'

'Right. Ancient history.'

'But they do care about Magnus. They care about *him*! Don't you see? Anything to do with famous people, they're all over it. They'll come here, I'm telling you, they'll be crawling all over the windmill asking questions, and we won't be able to stop them. We simply can't allow it – not now. You know that as well as I do – I really don't know why you're being so obtuse!'

Mrs Baker rolled her eyes. 'Don't be so dramatic. I can't take it at this time of the morning – I haven't even had my coffee.' She picked up the silver pot which was gleaming now, its curving spout catching the light, its ornate belly reflecting a small, warped version of Mrs Baker with stretched-out cheeks and a Mohican hairdo. For a moment Astrid wondered if she was intending to fill the pot and serve them from it, as she had when Nina visited – had she lost her mind? – but of course, she wasn't doing that, she was just looking for somewhere to put it down.

There was nowhere, of course. The kitchen surfaces were jumbled with papers and *things*, all sorts of things: rusted keys and cracked plugs, dog leads and knitting needles, broken picture frames and the crocheted hats, each shaped like a strawberry, that she'd made last winter for the refugee babies but didn't know where to send; a table lamp without a shade, a fractured Toby jug, a clock whose hands had detached from its face and lay like toothpicks along the rim. Mrs Baker, who had long ago given up trying to declutter, carried the pot out of the kitchen. Juniper flopped into the dog basket, gave a sigh and began to lick her bottom. Hendricks came over, and Gordon, in Astrid's arms, watched them both, warily. Then Mrs Baker was back, crossing the kitchen. As she reached for the mugs on the shelf above the kettle, she said, 'Listen, Astrid, if it'll make you feel better to see him one last time, then that's what you should do.' The draining board rattled as she plonked the mugs down.

'Make me feel better? Don't be ridiculous! That's not why I'm going. Seeing Magnus won't make me feel better. I'm going because I must stop him, why can't you see that? I cannot – I *must* not – be in this memoir. Media interest would be a disaster – a catastrophe – for both of us!'

Gordon leaped off her lap. She knew she sounded shrill, but she didn't care. In the month since she'd found Magnus staring at her from the masthead of the *Sunday Times*, it had, on some level, been a constant struggle even to stay moderately calm.

8th May 1919

Dearest W,

I am still waiting! This windmill consumes my thoughts. I am having such difficulty sleeping, and when I do sleep, my dreams are all of windmills. I cannot stop thinking about its sorry state of neglect – of abandonment. There was still flour dust on the upper floors and in one corner I spotted a small pile of grain, tipped out by the miller when he closed the door for the last time. It is unbearably sad.

Miss Jones tells me that I have grown pallid with 'over-imaginings' and makes me drink her revolting beef tea, but there is nothing wrong with me, nothing physical at least. It is simply that I cannot stand this infernal waiting.

On my instruction, our Mr King has been in touch once again with the owner's representative, a Mr Banks, who says that the owners are about to sign the papers and assures us that there is hope of the tenants moving out by early summer. Why this Mr Banks cannot simply insist that they leave I do not know, I think he must be soft-hearted. I may not have mentioned this to you, but I must take both mill and cottage because the two are joined by a tunnel (the cost is £580 for both, a sum to which I have already agreed, Walter, so please do not fuss). I shall let you know when the sale is complete.

But how are you, dear? Do send more news of life there. Do try to keep warm, I know how your chest can be, and winter in Washington certainly sounds bitter. What progress is there with your great 'Battleship of Tomorrow'? I feel sure that it will be magnificent, this innovation of yours.

Your loving C

# Chapter 2

As she looked at Magnus's face on the front of the *Sunday Times Magazine*, Astrid felt a surge of habitual and complicated loathing, and then – another reflex – she leaned over to toss him into the fire. As she did this the words *much anticipated memoir* caught her eye. She whisked him from the flames just in time.

She must have cried out because Mrs Baker appeared in the snug holding a potato ricer. 'What the devil . . . ? Are you all right, Astrid?'

Astrid held out the singed colour supplement and gave it a shake. 'Devil,' she said, 'is the word. He's writing a memoir. He's talking about it here, in the *Sunday Times!*'

'Hang on, I need my glasses.' Mrs Baker put the ricer down on a pile of ancient *Radio Times* magazines and felt around in her apron pocket.

Gordon was standing by the fireplace, his stubby legs quivering beneath his chartreuse jerkin. 'Come here, come back, darling, it's all right.' She held out her hand, but he didn't move. Mrs Baker took the newspaper and scanned it.

'Read it out loud,' Astrid said. 'Come on!'

Mrs Baker cleared her throat.

*We are seated on the terrace of Magnus Fellowes' stunning Georgian home in the Scottish Borders. Fellowes, who turned eighty-one last year, may be terminally ill but his famous blue eyes are undimmed –*

'Blue?' Astrid cried. 'They're pale grey. See what I said, these reporters simply twist the facts.'

*. . . For a moment I find myself genuinely starstruck –*

'Starstruck? Where *do* they find these fools?'

'Do you want me to read this or not?' Mrs Baker looked sternly over her glasses.

'Yes,' Astrid said. 'Read it! Go!'

*Fellowes moved into this magnificent house, which belongs to his son, after his cancer diagnosis last year. When I insist that he must tell me if he feels tired, he brushes me off with the sort of foul-mouthed geniality that suggests genuine irritation: 'I'm not a fucking invalid, son.' I believe him. He is grizzled, thinner and more haunted-looking perhaps, but his craggy face – familiar now to a whole new generation thanks to the Marvel franchise – is handsome still, albeit partially concealed beneath a bushy white beard left over, he tells me, from his Olivier award-winning* King Lear *last year. The cricket commentary is on the radio, Fellowes is a lifelong fan, and as he gazes out at the land, he looks almost regal –*

'My God, this is unbearable!' Astrid shouted. Gordon left the room, claws skittering on the wooden floor.

Mrs Baker's eyes skimmed the text. 'He's going on about some charity thing he's supporting, child poverty . . .'

'Nothing about the memoir?'

Mrs Baker held up a finger.

*Fellowes' hellraising exploits in Hollywood in the late seventies and early eighties are the stuff of legend. He partied with Hollywood royalty – Jack Nicholson, Warren Beatty, Martin Scorsese – but gave up alcohol in 1985 and, as he puts it, has 'lived like a fucking monk' ever since. I'm not sure I believe him. At the height of his fame his name was linked to several very famous women, and he has been married three times, but he is a notoriously private man (this is his first interview in eight years) and has always refused to discuss his private life. That will change next year, of course, when his much-anticipated memoir,* But Then Again, *hits the shelves –*

'*But Then Again*?' Astrid threw up her hands. 'What sort of a title's that?'

'Regrets, Astrid.' Mrs Baker grimaced. 'Let's just hope you're one of them.' She went back to the article. 'Child poverty, doing his bit for this campaign, knows what it's like to grow up poor, youngest of five, alcoholic dad dead, single mother, poverty, begging scraps, all the old pity stuff, blah, blah ... Ah, right, here we go:

*As our interview comes to a close, I tell him that I'm a huge fan of* I Am Me, *the 1977 film directed by genius auteur Jack Rohls, for which Fellowes received a Best Actor Oscar, and Rohls a Best Director nomination. The film was recently voted eighth in a British Film Institute poll of Top 100 Films of the twentieth century. I expect him to be pleased, but his smile evaporates. 'We're talking about fucking child poverty,' he growls. 'Not that.' Flustered, I point out that people find his career fascinating, not least his famously intense relationship with Rohls. The two reportedly fell out during the filming of* I Am Me, *and never spoke again. But I'm flailing under his ferocious gaze. 'You're a national treasure,' I blurt, hoping to mollify him. 'That's just fucking meaningless,' he roars. I babble that I*

*Am Me is iconic, and he gets crosser. 'Why can't you people fucking move on? Leave all that alone.' When I ask why, if he wants us to leave the past alone, he decided to write a memoir he shoots me a withering look. 'I didn't.' He gets to his feet. 'Now I am fucking tired, son.' He glowers at me, and out of nowhere his actual son appears, a tall, heavy-set American in his fifties, who looks nothing like his father, and who smiles, but not with his eyes, bringing our interview to a close.*

Astrid snatched the colour supplement and scanned the last paragraph.

*Fellowes does soften a bit as we say goodbye, perhaps regretting his outburst. 'You know,' he says, 'the things that feel most real to me now, the things I fucking lie awake at night thinking about, are the things I didn't do. But people don't write memoirs about those, do they?' He taps his temple and stares into my eyes, suddenly intense. '"Nothing is but what is not."' He gives me a meaningful nod. 'Get that in your article, son, okay?'*

This quote was for her, there was no doubt about it. An outrageous dig. Oh, he was monstrous, always had been. *Monstrous man!* She scrunched up the magazine and hurled it at the fireplace. She watched it melt, blacken, then catch and flare, expanding into a huge multicoloured hand, fingertips stretching and flexing, reaching for her, then crumpling to ash.

Mrs Baker pulled the fireguard across, startling Juniper and Hendricks in their basket. She took off her reading specs, folded her arms and looked down at Astrid, assessing the extent of the damage. Astrid closed her eyes. She felt the snug spin gently. She tried to find something nice to think about but couldn't. He'd done this before, sent her Shakespearean messages via interviews, but never so blatantly, never so pointedly and cruelly; such gloating. She opened her eyes again. Mrs Baker was kneeling in front of her now, cherry-cheeked, concerned. The snug, the fire, a blanket slung over her knees, she was suddenly hot.

'Are you breathing, Astrid?'

'What? Of course I'm breathing. Where's ... where's ... Gordon?' The words came out staccato.

'Stay there, I'll fetch you some water.'

'Make it a Jim.'

Mrs Baker came back a moment later with a glass of water. 'Do you want to lie down?'

'No Gordon – no Jim?'

'Gordon's gone and I'm not giving you bourbon. It's not even lunchtime. Drink the water.'

'I'm perfectly ... I'm really all right,' she said. 'No need to fuss. Where's Gordon? Where did he go?'

Mrs Baker got up with a sigh, pops detonating inside the flesh of her knees.

*Nothing is but what is not.* They'd had a terrible fight about that line. Magnus had insisted that it was simple: Macbeth's fixation on something that has not yet happened but should, could, must, will – the power fantasy more real than the present. Astrid, though, had felt that the line was more nuanced; Shakespeare is saying that what we perceive, this thing that we call reality, might not be real after all – that perhaps nothing ever is. She went to the line before it, *smothered in surmise.* Imagination is everything, she argued, it smothers both reason and reality.

It was the only real fight of their marriage – soon they were screaming at each other across the kitchen table.

*It's there on the page, Astrid, right there – simple. Why do you have to complicate everything all the time? It must be fucking chaos inside your head.*

*Well, your ego's so massive you can't see the nuances in the poetry, but I can – that's why I'm the better actor.*

She remembered how his chin jerked up at this, the shock and hurt in his eyes. They both knew it was the truth, but she should never have spoken it.

He yelled that she was being a petulant child and perhaps to distract from what she'd just said, she picked up the teapot and threw it. He sidestepped and it bounced on the tiled floor, shattering, and spraying tea up the wall. They both stared at it and then, after a moment of silence, he started to laugh. Magnus had an amazing ability to redirect from fury to mirth in an instant, to move on, offering genuine forgiveness. He stepped over shards of teapot and kissed her face and neck. *You're right. You're better than I am, so much better – at Shakespeare anyway. You're brilliant. I love you.*

Astrid felt the snug spin. She mustn't keep going back like this – it really was ghastly. The complexities of regret, pain and anger were multiple and exhausting. She must stay in the present. She allowed her eyes to travel from object to object in the snug, like a climber finding footholds up a rockface: the leather-bound Keats, the barley spindle side table, the fringed yellow lamp, the fire tongs, and on the rug, a chicken thigh bone that the dogs had picked clean. She decided to put all the objects in the room in alphabetical order, but couldn't work out whether the chicken bone should go under B or C. She felt Magnus's hand close over hers and her eyes filled with tears.

This sense of inhabiting a life that had never happened, but also somehow had – a life that was, in fact, still playing out somewhere alongside this one – was beyond logic; it was inexplicable, lonely and vivid, simultaneously real and unreal – positively Shakespearean in its contradictions. Like so many of life's deepest truths, it made no rational sense whatsoever.

Some of the books, she noticed, were still not sitting right on the shelves. A few spines jutted at angles. She had an image, suddenly, of Mrs Baker slamming the sliding bookcase back over the tunnel hatch with such force that the castors shook, the books juddered – some tumbled out. But she absolutely must not think about the Awful Incident – not on top of Magnus and his memoir. It really would be too much to bear.

Gordon still hadn't come back. She called out in a high and tremulous tone, 'Where did that dog go?'

'Listen, Astrid.' Mrs Baker was calm and pragmatic. She came and sat on the footstool, her knee caps popping again. She smelled of rosemary and onions. 'He either will or won't put you in this bloody memoir but there's nothing you can do about it either way, so don't go getting yourself worked up like this. It's not worth it. You know that.'

'Where is that dashed dog?' She made a feeble effort to stand, but her legs were too weak.

'Don't get up or you'll pass out. He'll come back in his own time when you calm down. He'll be hiding somewhere – crapping on the kitchen floor probably.'

*Nothing is but what is not.* As Astrid stood in the queue at Gatwick the words rolled across her mind. Perhaps it was deluded to imagine that Magnus was sending her messages via a national newspaper's colour supplement. Why on earth would he bother? His life had been a monumental success. He had married again after her, twice more. He'd had affairs with the world's most beautiful women. He'd known great directors, artists and authors, presidents and prime ministers. The thing he'd said to Nina, that little scrap of nonsense, could be dementia or cancer drugs, or perhaps just nostalgia, triggered by latent guilt. He might even, at the end of his life, want exoneration. But what did Magnus know about pain? He had never experienced the dreadful emptiness of losing everything he loved, never known what it's like when your life collapses and you must seal off the old, shamed self and start again as if there is nothing wrong with that, as if nothing is absent or damaged or broken or lost – or worse, playing out in parallel in some secret hidden place, illogical, undiscoverable; really quite unhinged.

She'd spent so long despising him for what he'd done to her but then, eventually, Charlie had come along, and she'd managed to shut it all away. She hadn't allowed herself to think about Magnus for years but the *Sunday Times* interview, and then Nina's visit, had opened it all up again and it was as if no time had passed at all. She had no idea how she was going to face him in Scotland, not really. This whole trip was madness.

It was probably the tablets she'd been given for her wrist that had made her decide to go – *some sweet oblivious antidote* – not to the weighed-down heart but to good sense. She simply wasn't in her right mind. But no, if that was the case, then Mrs Baker would have stepped in. Nina too. Nina was clearly a sensible person. Nina would be there at the airport to pick her up and drive her to Northbank where they'd have tea with Magnus, and the next day, when it was all over, Nina would drive her back to Edinburgh again and send her home. The idea of Nina waiting at the airport felt comforting and solid, the stage mark to aim for, which was odd since they'd only met once.

Nina was a composed and thoughtful person, though, that much was clear; competent and not easily ruffled. She'd demonstrated this when she'd come to the windmill for tea and it had all got a bit out of hand and she'd ended up having to stay the night. She wasn't tough, though. Far from it. There was a sort of vibrating sensitivity inside Nina – Astrid had tuned into that and then found it hard to ignore. She seemed like a solitary soul – solitary, but not, perhaps, lonely. Astrid felt, oddly, as if she'd known Nina for years. Perhaps this had something to do with Nina's response to the windmill; she'd been almost shaken in its presence, and Astrid had recognised this, because it had been her own reaction when she took the keys over forty years ago, and let herself into the tower for the first time.

Standing on the threshold that day, peering into the dark, circular room at Lady Battiscombe's scattered possessions, Astrid had felt the abandoned tower rising above her, felt its power and resilience, its intelligence, and its potential instability. A mixture of trepidation, anticipation and perhaps awe had pressed down on her – she couldn't move for the enormity of it. Then rooks cawed in the oaks behind the windmill and a gust of wind came round the side of the tower – and she was released. She stepped inside. It would be her home for the next seven years, until the Great Storm brought Charlie to her door.

The cottage had been derelict in those days, and she'd had no money to restore it, not that she'd wanted to. She had only wanted the windmill. She'd moved right in. She only had a couple of bags, and nowhere else to go and she'd simply slotted herself into Constance Battiscombe's footprint, sleeping in the ornate iron bed, treading on the moth-eaten rugs, browsing liver-stained volumes of Keats and Shakespeare, the photograph album, the tin of letters. From the very start, she'd felt a profound connection to the unknown woman whose life she had adopted, not because of these objects, but because of the tower that housed them.

The ground floor was the bedroom, since that was where the bed was, and there was no way to move it on her own. With the rugs, a Calor gas stove and Constance's old tapestries hung over the windows against draughts, it could be quite cosy. She wintered on the enormous horsehair sofa with blankets and quilts piled on top of her, napping, reading or daydreaming. In retrospect, it was possible that the stove was mildly gassing her, but in the spring, she threw open the door and emerged unscathed into bright daffodil-shaking days and the wind came in and swept out the dust, bringing scents of chalky turf and trees in bud, the faintest traces of sea salt, and she felt alive for the first time in years. There were sleepy summers, too, long, sweet-scented days when the windmill was a cool refuge, and then damp autumns when the leaves blew in and circled the tower, rain poured off the cap in waterfalls, and the moisture from the earth seeped back up the walls.

There was a tap on the Spout floor, and she had a butler's sink installed up there to make a simple kitchen. The next floor up, the Stone floor, was where she received her Letters from Beyond clients. It needed almost nothing done. The altar stone made a writing table and the crucifix, the torn velvet curtain and the gold-edged bible were excellent props. The top two floors, Bin and Dust, were empty and she rarely climbed up to them because the floorboards, even in those days, had an unreliable, faintly spongy feel. The wind whistled oddly through the gaps in the cap, and there was a barn owl in the rafters which flew at her once, a terrifying sight, talons out.

A week ago, as they'd sat in the garden waiting for Mrs Baker to bring out the coffee and cake, Nina had noticed that the iron cladding on the windiest side of the tower, which was mottled and streaked with coppery rust, caught the autumn sun so that the windmill seemed to glow. She couldn't keep her eyes off it. 'It's glorious,' she said, and Astrid recalled that the young millwright, Joe Dean, had used the same old-fashioned word. It was possible, Astrid realised, that Nina had made the journey from Edinburgh not so much to talk about the memoir as to worship the windmill.

'I've been a bit obsessed with windmills ever since I was a little girl.' Nina gave an apologetic smile. 'My dad was an enthusiast. We lived in Holland for a while, we used to go and look at them together at weekends.' She looked up at it again. 'They have such personalities, don't they?'

Astrid definitely didn't want to think about the windmill's personality, so she decided not to encourage this line of conversation. 'Well, it's rather a liability, I'm afraid,' she said. 'Decrepit, and really quite unpredictable.'

Nina looked round at the cottage and the tangled garden and, beyond it, the Downs. Gentle undulations, turning khaki now, fell steeply to the Weald. Clusters of sheep clung to the folds beneath the chalk path which ran along the ridge. A seagull surfed slowly overhead, circled back. Some strands of hair flicked across Nina's face and as she pushed them away, her eyes went up to the tower again. 'It sort of dominates everything, doesn't it?' She laughed, then, as if she'd revealed something about herself and was embarrassed; the dimples on either side of her mouth deepened. Astrid peered up at the rusted tower, the peeling cap with its little globe at the top, the lopsided fan stage and dirty, cracked windowpanes which, if you looked too long, would inevitably produce a shadowy face. From this angle the tower seemed to be leaning to the left but that could not, surely, be the case.

'The whole cap turns towards the wind, doesn't it?' Nina said.

'Well, it used to. That fan, there on the back' – Astrid pointed – 'catches the wind and turns it. But it's all rusted in place now. Nothing moves any more – nothing that's supposed to, anyway.'

Nina looked eager. 'I was reading that these tower mills were a great innovation once. Didn't they replace the old wooden post windmills where the whole body turns, not just the cap?'

'Yes, that's right. It was fancy and new-fangled once, believe it or not. It was the centre of the community for miles around – people would be coming up this hill bringing grain, taking flour, and the millers would be rushing up and down inside the wind-mill, hauling sacks around, fixing things, keeping it going. There would have been such a hubbub, lots of dust and clanging about.'

They both looked up at the silent windmill. Then Nina took a breath. 'I don't suppose . . . I mean, I hope this isn't intrusive, but I'd really love to have a look inside, if that's at all possible?'

Astrid felt a jerk of alarm. 'What? Oh no . . . no . . . we don't go in there.'

Nina's face fell. 'You don't?'

'Well, the front door's broken, you see. It's completely blocked.'

'Yes, I saw some sort of stone slab there. What happened?'

Astrid gave a helpless shrug and looked at the back of the cot-tage, hoping to see Mrs Baker, who, she knew, would definitely not want her to be discussing this. 'The altar stone fell down two floors and broke the door.'

Nina leaned forwards, frowning. 'The altar stone?'

'The previous owner, Lady Battiscombe, installed an altar on the Stone floor in the twenties – I believe some of her friends dug it up from the village churchyard. It's probably medieval, buried after Henry the Eighth clamped down.'

'On altars?'

'Yes, yes, because of the relics in them. Altar stones have small pieces of saints sealed inside them. Henry the Eighth found that awfully threatening.' Astrid cleared her throat, rather wishing that she hadn't embarked on this. 'Anyway,

the altar stone fell down the stairs last winter and did rather
a lot of damage – it's wedged itself across the door so we can't
get in any more.' She waved a hand. 'And even if we could,
we wouldn't want to since it's really quite dangerous in there
now, with a hole in the floor and a broken staircase – it's an
absolute death trap.' She looked away, hoping that this would
be the end of the discussion. 'There's also a very territorial
barn owl living in the cap,' she added. 'Descended from a long
line of absolute psychopaths.'

Nina laughed and her eyes crinkled so nicely that Astrid felt
herself relax a bit. She'd been expecting somebody much less
congenial. What on earth, she wondered, was this lovely young
woman doing stuck in the Scottish Borders writing Magnus's
awful lies for him?

Nina's first letter had arrived only a week after they'd read
the *Sunday Times* interview. It was rare to receive anything
in the post that wasn't a bill or a threat and Astrid had felt some
trepidation as she opened the envelope. The tone was formal,
and she'd pictured a dragon lady in horn-rimmed specs bashing
at the keyboard.

*Dear Ms Miller,*

*I am helping to prepare Magnus Fellowes' forthcoming memoir
for publication and there are one or two things that I'd like to
clarify, if I may? I will be coming down to London next week for
some final research, and I wonder if it would be possible to meet?
I would be very happy to come and see you in Sussex – I'm sure
you're busy and I will take up as little of your time as possible.
I know this is short notice, but I could come next Thursday, if at
all convenient?*

Astrid had put her toast and marmalade aside. Somehow, her brain couldn't quite process what she'd just read. 'I expect she's an Audrey Hepburn fan.' She handed the letter to Mrs Baker. 'People get funny about Audrey. She probably wants to touch the hand that touched Audrey's.'

Mrs Baker read the letter silently, munching buttered toast, then looked up. 'What's Audrey Hepburn got to do with it? She wants to talk to you about the memoir, Astrid, she says it right here, she's fact checking. She'll be' – she looked at the letter and turned it over, as if the answer might be on the back – 'one of those ghost writers. All the celebrities have them. None of them write their own books any more. She'll want to talk to you about that old scandal, I expect, get the facts.'

'What? But I can't possibly discuss that with a complete stranger!' The notion made her feel panicky, not just the thought of going over what happened in the Tudor hunting lodge all those years ago, but the aftermath. This stranger, this ghostly writer, would want to know about the end of the marriage, the shame, humiliation, betrayal. It was out of the question.

'You could put the record straight,' Mrs Baker had said. 'Tell her what really happened.'

'And you think he'll let her write the truth? Of course he won't. He's lied about that night for forty-five years, he's not going to come clean now.'

Mrs Baker looked at her for a moment, chewing slowly, then wisely let it go.

Three days later, another letter arrived. Astrid read it out loud over their elevenses. It was a little less formal. In fact, a whiff of desperation rose from the page.

*Dear Ms Miller,*

*I am so sorry to bother you again. I have no phone number for you, or I would have phoned and tried to explain myself a bit more clearly. I've been hired by Magnus's son, Desmond Fellowes, to finish the memoir, somewhat urgently. Magnus has, until now, had no involvement in the book. Desmond is very much spearheading the project, which it seems has been long and complicated (there have been several writers before me). It has recently become clear that Magnus hasn't actually seen or approved the draft that I've been working on. It also seems that there could be some fairly major discrepancies when it comes to an event that took place at a Tudor hunting lodge in Wiltshire in the 1970s, between you, Magnus, the film director Jack Rohls and the American actress Sally Morgan. The version which I have inherited from the previous writers paints you in a somewhat negative light. I recently had the opportunity – for the first time – to talk to Magnus and he was very distressed when I described how the events of that night are currently portrayed in the book. Apparently, this is not how he described it to the previous writers. Unfortunately, we were interrupted before I could get more information. Desmond has now instructed me not to speak to his father again. He is too fragile to discuss the book (I don't know if you're aware, but Magnus is very ill). Desmond insists that I keep the account as it is – he is my employer, not Magnus, and so, as you can probably tell, I'm in a difficult position. I thought that I should ask you for your account of that night, in the hope that this might clarify the situation and give me a sense of how best to proceed. I only want to do the right thing!*

Astrid closed her eyes and felt Mrs Baker ease the letter out of her hands. 'You should talk to her, Astrid.'

'Too sick to discuss his own memoir?' Astrid opened her eyes, suddenly furious. 'What rot! He's not too sick to talk to the *Sunday Times*.' She felt something catch in her throat, started to cough and took a swig of coffee. 'I think I might go and have a lie-down.'

'I think you should let her come,' Mrs Baker said in her no-nonsense voice. 'You want the truth told in that book, don't you?'

'The truth? Magnus won't tell the truth. Why would he? He's lied about the ghastly scandal for forty-five years – ever since he threw me to the lions, the coward. The man has no conscience, Mrs Baker, no decency. He's only ever thought of himself!' She started to cough again; she felt hot and struggled to take in air, as if her lungs were shrivelling inside her like chestnuts tossed on the fire.

'But he's dying, now, isn't he?' Mrs Baker persisted. 'People see things differently at the end of a life. Maybe he wants to put the record straight.'

Astrid couldn't understand why Mrs Baker was taking his side like this. 'Of course he doesn't! Why on earth would he?'

Mrs Baker picked up the letter. 'Well, this Nina person sounds all right, doesn't she? She says she just wants to do the right thing. It can't hurt to tell her your side of it, can it? Let her come here for tea. I'll write and tell her yes.'

Standing in the security queue at Gatwick airport, all this felt a bit surreal now. Astrid really wasn't sure how, in the space of just a few weeks, she'd gone from spotting a newspaper interview to a looming confrontation with the man who had ruined her life. By teatime she'd be sitting in his palatial home. She imagined a polished Georgian table laden with Swiss roll, his favourite, and scones and jam, shortbread biscuits, bone china teacups rattling in fine saucers – he always did have a sweet tooth, unless Hollywood had knocked that out of him. It probably had. He wouldn't be the man she used to know. She remembered his childlike delight long, long ago in Sicily, somewhere by the sea, Catania perhaps – he'd called it Catatonia – a sweltering place, horns blaring, the smell of donkey dung, espresso-coloured eyes watching them everywhere they went. Their honeymoon? Yes, it must have been. Magnus had discovered ice cream sandwiched in a brioche, and, like a little boy, he'd stuffed his face, three in a row, then grown queasy, and she'd had to take him back to the hotel and nurse him with iced water and cool towels on his forehead until he felt better and then they'd made love, slowly, with the curtains billowing in the hot salt breeze, offering glimpses of the bluest sky, their skin slick, sliding against one another, and afterwards, the feel of his chest rising and falling under her cheek, damp whorls of hair and his musky scent, something like tree bark, strongest at his throat, just beneath the ear – it had been a brief heaven. Perhaps she'd be unable to control herself when she saw him again. Perhaps she'd simply reach across the table and throttle him while kind, decent Nina looked on, aghast. It was, after all, no less than the man deserved.

8th June 1919

Dearest Walter,

Miss Jones and I returned to the windmill on Saturday and were greeted by Mr Banks himself. I was envisaging an older gentleman, but he is forty at most and, although taciturn, there is a quiet liveliness about him that I found awfully pleasant. He opened a hatch on the ground floor of the windmill and led me down a short ladder into a tunnel (Miss Jones declined to follow). The tunnel is awfully spooky – low and damp and garlanded by spiders' webs, impossible even to stand up straight in. It links the windmill to the granary (which the current tenants are using to house a pig) and the cottage.

The cottage itself is a sorry place. It is tiny and in great disrepair and I have no interest in it, I simply want the windmill. On the day we visited, lots of sweet, grubby children were running in the yard, some barefoot despite the drizzle, laughing and chasing a goat, with hens and dogs everywhere. A barn cat was tapping at a captive mouse, and the sound of bleating sheep and children's laughter filled the air: happy chaos. Mr Banks stopped to joke with the little ones, who seemed to know him – they were delightful and cheeky. As we left, he handed each a coin and they were in raptures.

I found Mr Banks terribly interesting – so unlike people we know. He told me he is a Fabian, and a pacifist. You'd disapprove, I know, but I rather think you'd like him anyway. I wrote to him the next day to tell him that I shall not mind if the family stay in the cottage for a while (though I fear they would make rather noisy neighbours). I must confess that I was almost disappointed when he wrote back by return of post to reassure me that the family does intend to leave.

The windmill really is perfect, though the bricks need a fresh coat of tar and the wooden cap is peeling. Inside, it just needs a good clean. It stands at the top of a steep chalk path, close to the ridge of the South Downs. It looks so sad now, so alone; it can no longer grind – both mill and granary have been used to house prisoners of war, and Mr Banks explained that much of the mechanism was stripped out to make room for their beds. The sweeps – Mr Banks instructs me that in Sussex they are 'sweeps', not sails – are secured by a brake wheel up on the 'Dust floor', which is at the top, beneath the rotating cap, and is very prettily shaped like a beehive with a little globe on top, as if the windmill is holding up the world. Mr Banks assures me the sweeps would still rotate, even though they have been tethered for thirteen years now. However, they will need attention from a millwright first. The windmill is longing for release, I feel that strongly, and I plan to be its liberator.

I shall feel better when I have signed the contract. In my imagination I am already clearing out the floors and placing my furniture inside. I know it is only to be a summer bolthole, but somehow I feel as if my whole existence was for this windmill – as if I've been looking for it all my life. The idea of going back to the drawing rooms and teapots of London is unbearably claustrophobic for me. I cannot explain it, but I feel called to the windmill – you will laugh at this, I know, and tell me that a tower is far more claustrophobic than a grand London house.

You must write and tell me your news too, dear. I feel so awfully distant but I trust all is well.

Your C

P.S. The chalk soil up here will be perfect for a lavender garden – you know I have dreamed of one for years, since we saw the fields in Provence. The earth is scattered with flints and chalk, entirely untamed.

# Chapter 3

There was some kind of fuss going on up ahead, but Astrid couldn't make out what it was. Officials were zipping about and there was an air of unease. The terminal seemed at once too quiet and too loud. She wished for the mobile phone so that she could call Mrs Baker. The outburst at the drop-off point was such a horrid way to part. It was rare to see Mrs Baker genuinely angry – unsettling, really.

If Mrs Baker had been herself, she surely would have quashed the trip – said that it was a ludicrous idea, that they couldn't afford it, that it would be futile – but she hadn't. A new thought settled in the back of Astrid's mind: perhaps Mrs Baker wanted her gone. The previous night, as Mrs Baker was serving up the shepherd's pie, Astrid had made a final attempt: 'Are you absolutely sure you won't come to Scotland? We could easily get another plane ticket.'

'There's a notice under there.' Mrs Baker nodded at the kitchen table as she picked up their plates of food. 'Says they're cutting the electric off if we don't pay by the end of the month.'

'Oh, that.' She waved her good hand. She felt that she should be able to provide a solution but unfortunately none sprang to mind. She put Gordon down in the basket with Hendricks and Juniper. He sat on the edge, looking up at her with quiet desperation, as if she'd dropped him into a hole and was about to shovel earth on top of him. She smoothed her nightdress, ready for the supper tray. The day had passed, and she hadn't got dressed; she often didn't. Mrs Baker had given up objecting.

Mrs Baker flopped into her seat on the other side of the Rayburn. 'Why do you think I've polished that thing up?' She gestured at the table and Astrid saw that the coffee pot was back, balanced on a pile of newspapers and gleaming at them, ostentatiously. The curling bits of silver coming out of its top and handle looked perkier, quite flamboyant – wildly out of place. 'The pot? But you can't sell that – it belongs in the windmill!'

'Remember what we got for the captain's ceremonial swords?'

'But those were different!'

Mrs Baker picked up her fork. 'It's that, or no electric.'

'Couldn't we sell Tony Blair instead? It would be sad, but we could take him to the Lanes. Or to Lewes – people will buy anything in Lewes.'

'If nobody on the whole of eBay wants a taxidermised stoat, I don't think the antiques dealers of Lewes will be begging for it.'

It was, Astrid realised, a relief that Mrs Baker was being this proper version of herself, grumpy and solid, dealing with things, objecting. Mrs Baker's fork pierced the potato crust of her shepherd's pie and steam puffed out. When she looked up her eyes were kind. 'You'll be all right, you know,' she said. 'It's only one night.'

Astrid felt her throat tighten – suddenly, she was close to weeping. Mrs Baker chewed for a moment, staring at her plate. 'And I expect you'll feel better if you see him before he dies,' she continued, 'patch things up or whatever.'

The tender moment vanished. Astrid put down her fork and

stared at Mrs Baker, who glanced up, then shoved anther hefty forkful into her mouth. The notion that things could be 'patched up' with Magnus was ludicrous, and Mrs Baker knew it. It was positively inflammatory of her to say so. Squabbles could be patched up, jacket elbows, grazed knees, but not abandonment, not betrayal, not four decades of silence. Astrid opened her mouth, but her throat was still too tight to release any words.

She looked down at her plate. She mustn't rise to this sort of provocation – she simply didn't have the energy. She searched frantically for a pleasant thought. The helping of pie looked neat on the chipped plate, its potato topping perfectly browned. The tomato, lentil and carrot filling would be delicious, it would almost pass for lamb mince. Mrs Baker's economies were awfully clever.

Astrid watched her chomping away with an innocent air, and suddenly she understood what Mrs Baker was doing: bickering would offer a diversion, much better than contemplating whatever lay ahead – or worse still, talking about it. But Astrid felt far too exhausted to squabble. She sat back and her gaze met the round plastic eyes of the Kit Cat clock above the Rayburn as they flicked sideways, and back again, and its tail marked another second, and another. It really was a ghastly thing, with dark vertical slits for pupils, a jaunty bow tie, a disturbing grin. Mrs Baker had presented it to Astrid as a sixtieth birthday present on the Millennium eve, when they barely knew each other; the night when all the clocks were supposed to stop, or go backwards, or reset themselves or something catastrophic – the night when it became clear that neither of them had anywhere else to go, or anyone else to celebrate with. It had been watching them ever since, its sly eyes ticking off their squabbles and jokes, chats and silences, stand-offs and alliances, their witness and, perhaps now, their judge.

Why on earth hadn't she thrown it out? It really was an awful piece of tat, but she couldn't imagine their life without it.

Mrs Baker was up again. She'd devoured her pie already, and was after a second helping. 'Who'd look after the dogs if I came?' she was muttering. 'No kennel would have them, not with Juniper's bowels and Gordon's nerves and Hendricks' ... well, just Hendricks. No kennel would keep that dog for more than five minutes, even if we could afford to send him to one.'

Astrid looked at the three little curly heads, three pairs of eyes fixed on her plate, three dear bodies snug in their little knitted tank tops. They always made her think of the Wombles when they were grouped like this. 'We can bring them with us.'

'You can't take three miniature wire-haired dachshunds on a plane, Astrid, for the love of God, and I don't know where you think we're getting the money for another ticket. We can't just bung another eighty quid on a credit card. Not without consequences.'

'Then we'll drive!'

Mrs Baker puffed out her ruddy cheeks. 'Honestly, Astrid, I don't know what's madder, the idea that the car could make it to Scotland or this notion we've got the money for another ticket when we haven't even got enough to put mince in a shepherd's pie.' She turned, niftily bypassing Tony Blair, and dumped the empty pea pan in the sink.

She should eat, Astrid knew that – she'd not really eaten all day. She sat up straight. 'Do you know, this smells delicious,' she said, brightly. 'Who needs mince? It's terribly bad for the planet. I read an article saying we must all become vegans.'

'We practically bloody are,' Mrs Baker said, grimly, sitting down again and digging in.

Mrs Baker loved her hotpots and roasts, her chunks of ham,

her toad in the hole, her bacon sandwiches. Suddenly Astrid felt as if she'd let her down. 'Do eggs count?'

Mrs Baker looked up, frowning. 'For what?'

'For vegans? Are eggs vegan?'

'Vegans can't eat animal products, Astrid.'

'But hens are birds,' Astrid objected. 'Not animals.'

Mrs Baker stared at her with small bright eyes. 'Birds are animals.'

'But are they?' Astrid said. 'I'm not so sure. They have beaks.'

Mrs Baker put down her fork. 'Who said an animal can't have a bloody beak?'

It was possible, Astrid thought as the queue inched forwards, that Mrs Baker really was planning to vanish, that right now she was back at the cottage, packing her bags, tidying the kitchen, leaving down kibble for the dogs. She'd done it before, after all – bolted from a life, gone incognito, assumed a whole new identity.

She felt things start to tilt and pictured herself crashing forwards into the man in front of her who was sturdy and short and hunched, balding with a lot of white neck hair. She imagined how wiry the hairs would feel poking up her nostrils. But no, she wasn't going to pass out. She was being very silly, she knew that – an S.O.B. of the highest order. Mrs Baker wouldn't bolt. For all her blunt bossiness, and her unsettled past, she wouldn't leave. They were in this together, and not just because of what they had or hadn't done. Mrs Baker would stay because she was a loyal and steady friend. She might have abandoned one identity, but that had been entirely necessary and a very long time ago. It certainly did not make her a bolter.

The real problem, Astrid decided, was not their silly tiff outside the airport, but the sleep deprivation – it made everything feel precarious and unstable. When she turned her head, the whole terminal swayed. This instability was nothing new, of course. At the hospital, when the doctor had asked her if she had any 'visual disturbances', she'd laughed so much he'd wanted to know if she'd hit her head too. It was rare, she told him, to find an edge that didn't waver.

Just that morning, as they'd driven down the hill towards the village, she'd turned to look back at the windmill and its sides had seemed to ripple, as if she was looking at it through a desert haze rather than the clear, cold November air. She'd felt the wind shoving through the gaps in its oak cap, thumping the iron-clad bricks, circling the defunct core, licking the rusted joints and cogs, shaking the fettered sweeps, causing them to strain against the brake, to quake and screech and moan. Then she pictured everything coming loose: the sweeps spinning out of control, the whole thing wobbling until the cladding tore and black bricks rained onto the cottage, onto Mrs Baker and the dogs, forking up the chalky earth, obliterating everything. She had turned to face forwards but as they chuntered down the chalk track, she felt acutely aware of the hillside sloping down to Tangled Wood.

Gloria's fumes were worse than ever that morning, vapours gasping through the vents, as if the old car was about to explode. Astrid had to crack open the window and then, inevitably, she looked at the ditch, then over the hawthorn, and down to the wood. It was little more than a scraggly clump perched above the village, knots of yew, beech, ash, sycamore, holly, briars, gorse, and in there somewhere the hollow holly tree, its roots entwined with ivy and dog's mercury that must have been trampled by all the strangers in their plastic hazmat suits.

She could not imagine how cold, impaired or afraid you must be to take refuge in a hollow holly tree, with all the scratching and puncturing that would involve. And Alan had been injured, badly. He must have been in dreadful pain. She forced herself to look forwards again at the potholed chalk track. Mrs Baker's hands were braced on the steering wheel, her eyes fixed forwards too, as they always were nowadays when they passed this particular point on the hill.

They reached the village and a man with a walking stick dragging his portly Jack Russell past the church stopped to stare as they chugged past. Astrid perked up. It was nice to be noticed. In the old days, she'd rather loved the feeling that her presence was noted in the village – even if it was with disapproval. The corner shop was long gone; her namesake pub, The Miller's Arms, and the post office too, all closed. Some of the hostility had been territorial – on some level, the villagers felt that the windmill was theirs, and resented Astrid for owning it. There had been various incarnations of the 'windmill committee', all marvellously theatrical. She rather missed all that drama. Everyone who had harangued her about the windmill seemed to have moved or died or given up caring. The only one who'd really cared, though, was Jack Dean, the millwright. Poor man, so young – lung cancer. He'd left a wife and three little boys.

Total collapse was a very real possibility now – it had, after all, been thirty years since Charlie's renovations – but there was no money to pay for repairs, even if they'd been in a position to get someone in. This didn't stop the young millwright from trying, though. Just the other day he had been back. From the kitchen window, Astrid had noticed his woollen hat bobbing up the lane. His dog, a black Labrador, saw a rabbit and bombed under the gate towards the windmill – soon it was sniffing round the fallen altar. The millwright paid it no attention. He was peering up at the tower as he came through the gate and crossed the courtyard. Astrid froze when he knocked. The dogs went wild, shot down the hall, snapping at air.

They didn't answer the door, of course. In the months since the Awful Incident, they'd instigated a policy of never answering the door to unsolicited callers, which, since all callers were unsolicited, meant never answering the door. The dogs yapped and bounced beneath the letter box as the millwright pushed through a handwritten note – he was lucky Hendricks didn't take his fingers off.

'Desperate.' Mrs Baker held up the piece of paper. Astrid snatched it. The note was nice and polite and he had lovely, cultured handwriting, even if his words weren't terribly encouraging. He just wanted to help, he said. He was very attached to the windmill, it meant such a lot to him. He listed things that needed attention: the cap was in urgent need of repair, the mortar should be replaced and the grass growing out of the bricks removed; the fan stage was unstable, the sweeps loose and rotten, there might be dry rot inside, too, which meant potentially weakened floorboards and ladders which could, he said, be 'lethal'. The front door should be fixed up and put back on, and the big stone slab that had smashed the staircase to bits and knocked it open from the inside would really need to be removed because rain was getting in, and wildlife, too. He'd love to have a look if they'd give him permission. He could even just come back and fix up the front door if they'd let him.

'I suppose he has to tout for work,' Astrid said. 'I mean, who needs millwrights these days?'

'We do,' Mrs Baker said, darkly.

'Perhaps we should offer him a cup of tea . . .'

46                          LUCY ATKINS

But Mrs Baker had already walked off down the hall with the
note crunched in her fist.

Through the gap in the kitchen curtains, Astrid could see him
waiting patiently in the courtyard. Mrs Baker was right: even if
they could afford it, they couldn't possibly have him examining
the fallen altar or poking around inside the tower. The Labrador
was still there, digging at the stone in a very focussed way. There
could be traces of blood still. What's more, only one slipper had
been found on Alan, tucked into his belt, which meant that the
other had to be up here somewhere – and if found, that slipper
would link them all, decisively. The notion that the young man
had been looking at the windmill, even from a distance, was
quite unsettling.

He went away eventually, but he didn't give up, and a week or
so later he was back. This time he left a longer, more emotional
letter. He didn't want to intrude, he said, he just wanted to *offer
help to restore your glorious windmill. She looks a bit poorly and sorry
for herself right now, a bit sad and unloved.*

'Sad and unloved? Poorly? Sorry for herself?' Mrs Baker rolled
her eyes. 'Bloody millennials.' They began to snigger then, trying
to be quiet, clutching each other's forearms but escalating despite
themselves – knowing he was out there, probably listening – and
that set the dogs off and Hendricks started baying, turning in
circles, and it was a while before they could all pull themselves
together to read on.

He fully understood, he said, that it might feel financially intimidating to embark on structural work, but the windmill was a vital
landmark, a precious piece of local heritage and he could help
them to raise the necessary funds. He mentioned preservation
committees and English Heritage grants, and said he'd work on
a voluntary basis, if necessary. Then he told them about himself.

*You could say windmills are in my blood. You might remember my father, John Dean, who worked on this windmill back in the 1970s and early 80s? My grandfather, Harvey Dean, was also a millwright, and his father, also Harvey Dean, helped your predecessor, Lady Battiscombe, to turn the abandoned windmill into a dwelling in 1919.*

Astrid turned to Mrs Baker. 'Good Lord, Eileen, I knew him!'

Mrs Baker let the letter drop to her side. 'You're old, Astrid, but not that old.'

'No, not the Harvey Deans – John. John Dean. Charlie hired him to repair the storm damage in 1987, 1988 and he . . . we . . . well, he was a terribly sweet man.'

She remembered the summer night when Charlie was in Ireland, and John had been working on the sweeps all day, and they'd drunk Sussex ale, watching the sun swell and fatten as it slid, a deep cerise ball, into the smooth crevasse of the Downs, and then they'd gone together to Constance's creaking bed. She felt her face heat up at the delicious memory, and turned away, calling to the dogs, hurrying back down the hall to the kitchen. She peered through the gap in the curtains. The young millwright was sitting over by the water butt now, looking at his boots. She couldn't see his face, but he had a nice stance, broad-shouldered, peaceful, chalky boots crossed. It was unusual to see someone young doing nothing like this, not staring at a phone. Astrid felt that she would rather like to invite him in. She wanted to know, for a start, why he'd choose such a dying and outdated profession, but she knew it would be unwise to talk to him. Mrs Baker would – rightly – stop her.

She'd never told a soul about John Dean, least of all Charlie. She should have felt guilty, but she never had, even at the time. That night belonged to the part of herself that continued to inhabit the windmill long after she was living with Charlie in the renovated cottage; the part of her that belonged to nobody. This part of her existed still, in fact, inside the windmill – it had stayed in there when the rest of her moved into the cottage to be looked after; to forget. Perhaps its continued existence, in some obscure way, explained why she had been able to accept Charlie so unquestioningly.

Charlie had built two small bedrooms above the snug, picture windows with a panoramic view of the Weald – all the dotted villages and fields, the silent railway line cutting through them and the Ouse snaking towards the coast. He'd installed a little loo on the landing between the two bedrooms and put in new plumbing, actual radiators powered by the bottle-green Rayburn, which was elderly now, of course, clanking and temperamental and, bafflingly, liable to turn cold if the wind came from the west.

As Mrs Baker passed the dog basket, she dropped the letter – in a flash Hendricks was tearing it to pieces and Juniper was eating the bits, while Gordon, resplendent in powder-blue alpaca, watched them, looking puzzled. If there was a canine autistic spectrum, she thought, Gordon could well be on it.

The windmill's screeching and scraping and moaning and rattling could certainly be intimidating but Mrs Baker had probably been right to feed Joe Dean's letter to the dogs. They certainly couldn't have a stranger poking around the windmill, not now, and even if they could, the days of grants and committees, trusts and millwrights were over. It was silly to worry about it collapsing in her absence. The windmill had stood on the Downs since 1862, it had made flour, housed prisoners and bohemians, seen births and deaths, sorrows and joys; it had been struck by lightning – some links in the break chain were still fused into a scar – the sweeps had been torn from its body more than once;

it had been decapitated, it had spontaneously combusted, it had fed and sheltered humans – imprisoned some, killed others – and it was still standing. It would be standing long after she and Mrs Baker and the dogs were in the ground.

Who would have it then, though? Astrid would leave it to Mrs Baker, of course – being eight years younger, Mrs Baker would be the one left behind. But Mrs Baker had nobody to leave a windmill to, no family to speak of. She'd once divulged that there had been an older sister, in Kent, long gone. There would, presumably, be nieces and nephews somewhere. Would they get the windmill? This thought was unnerving. Mrs Baker wouldn't talk about her family but over the years, Astrid had gleaned details of tight-knit Baptist parents, appalled when their twenty-year-old daughter was impregnated by her boss, a married shoe shop owner, stalwart of the Freemasonic lodge – there had been recriminations, hellfire, a near-enforced adoption, then painful estrangement. She didn't want to discuss any of this, and Astrid knew not to push or pry. Mrs Baker chose to keep her pain inside, to deal with it in her own way. Opening things up and talking about them was not an option. Astrid had understood this, intuitively, from the very beginning. She had never asked questions, or allowed herself to be nosy or intrusive. She hadn't even pressed Mrs Baker for her real name even though she'd felt from the very start that Baker had to be an alias. And this, perhaps, was the reason Mrs Baker had stayed.

They could leave the broken windmill to the village, perhaps. Over the years there had been various accusatory attempts by 'windmill committees' to take it from her. Men in anoraks would appear with thermos flasks and poke around, flagrantly trespassing, whilst lecturing her on local history. Perhaps she or Mrs Baker could bequeath the windmill to the parish council – the ultimate act of revenge.

She might have laughed out loud at this idea because the man in front of her in the security queue jerked his head up and glanced over his shoulder as if she'd shouted something inappropriate or obscene – as if an old woman alone in an airport had no right to laugh, no right to make any sound; no right, in fact, to exist. 'What?' she said. 'What?!' She felt other eyes on her, the swivelling of heads; irritable, anxious people forced to wait too long in a queue, not knowing what was happening, why the delay, now ready to turn, in need of a target. This, Astrid thought, was the sort of situation in which ordinary, decent people were overtaken by their animal instincts. She'd felt it once before – the villainising mob.

She could feel her mind growing lawless now. She kept coming up against her younger self, that was the problem, all the confusion and anger, the dreadful public humiliation. She'd felt, forty-five years ago, as if a freight train had been driven through her core. The hollow feeling had lingered for years, worse even than it had been as a child, after her father took his own life. There was betrayal then too, though of course her father had harmed himself while Magnus had done the opposite. Magnus had protected himself. It struck her, for the first time, that the two men she'd loved most in her life, the two men she'd adored and trusted, had both abandoned her. They'd done it in very different ways, certainly, but their legacy was the same: shame – hers.

Suddenly, it all felt unbearably present, as if time had swept backwards, erasing the decades so that she'd only just staggered out of the National Theatre, deranged and deluded, almost naked, with shaking, bloodstained hands.

3rd July 1919

Dearest W,

But of course I shall stay inside the windmill. I assure you it will take very little to make it comfortable. There are a few windowpanes to repair, some planks in the cap must be replaced, iron cladding fixed on the wind side and bricks tarred, but when I put down rugs, and hang my grandmother's tapestries against draughts – I have already measured for hanging rails – it will all be perfect. (The tapestries, along with the carpets, are currently in storage in Bath. I have written to arrange their despatch to London and will transport them to Sussex whenever the time comes.)

There is no need to worry about cold or damp. I am considering ingenious ways to stay warm. I thought perhaps of constructing a chimney like a 'spine' inside the body of the tower – I am confident that it will be possible to come here all year round. And yes, Walter, gas lamps can easily be hung from the rafters; I have discussed all this and more with Mr Banks, who is terribly genial. It turns out that the poor man lost his wife recently, to the influenza (on which matter: I shall be much healthier here than in Smythe Square, trapped in overheated drawing rooms, breathing the whole of London).

I plan to make a bedroom on the 'Spout floor'. Mr Banks told me, when we met again last week (I could not stay away), that the windmill is warmest on the lower floors because the cap, being mobile, creates draughts. As for your question about water: rain runs off the cap, is captured and passed through a charcoal filter and collected in a tank. There is a hand pump, perfectly serviceable. So yes, dear, it will be more than habitable. It will be a sanctuary.

*In answer to your second question, I do understand that you enjoy your social life in London. We shall find a compromise when you return from America. We can perhaps discuss this on your visit home. Do you have a date for that yet?*

*Finally, as for your question about the cottage, I can only repeat that I have no interest in it. It is a dismal little single-storey hovel, two rooms, plus a scullery, not enough windows. The granary, which is attached to the cottage, might be useful, though. Mr Banks, who has entered into the spirit of things (he is a man of energy and vision as well as interesting ideas – I recently discovered that he knows George Bernard Shaw!) has pointed out that the granary could be divided by putting in a ceiling/floor to make a bedroom for Miss Jones, with a kitchen below. Miss Jones wants me to install servants' bells on each floor. She suggested this somewhat dryly, but I think it is an excellent idea and plan to adapt the grain bell.*

*I am terribly sorry there is so much frustration for you, Walter, with all the engineering problems you outlined so fully in your last letter. The Americans do sound difficult, but what it must be for you to contemplate holding so many lives in your hands, I cannot imagine. Still, small battleships will, I feel sure, be the brilliant innovation you envisage.*

*Your C*

# Chapter 4

It was important to get a grip. Nobody was looking at her, not really, nobody cared. The feeling of exposure probably had something to do with the way they'd parted at the drop-off point. If they'd said goodbye amicably, it might have felt all right to be leaving, but the quarrel had been so unexpected – it had come out of nowhere and, in truth, Astrid was still rather reeling from it.

It was Mrs Baker who had pulled the trigger. As they drew up outside the terminal, she'd turned and narrowed her eyes. 'You look half dead, Astrid.'

'You woke me up at two o'clock in the morning, how do you expect me to look?'

'What? Sorry, but you woke *me* up.'

'You came into my room. You stood over my bed screaming!'

'What are you on about? You were the one screaming. You woke *me* up. And look at you now – you're white as a sheet, you haven't eaten properly in days, weeks probably.'

'I've never felt better!' Astrid shouted. She unbuckled her seat belt with her good hand and struggled out. Mrs Baker got out too and they faced each other across Gloria's seagull-spattered roof. Mrs Baker's face had taken on the fixed, unreachable look that signalled genuine conflict. 'Listen,' she said, tight-jawed,

'I've been going along with this for your sake. I've shut my mouth about the cost because I thought you needed to see him one last time but I'm not going to let you bloody die up there in Scotland, leaving me with three dachshunds, a load of credit card debt and a broken bloody windmill.'

Astrid glanced at the dogs, who were lined up and staring through the window. It was a bit late for cold feet. 'But it was *you* who told me to go, you said I should confront him.'

'What? I did not.'

'Yes, you *did*!'

Mrs Baker leaned an elbow on the roof, her fist around the keys. 'You're not well, Astrid, look at you. You look like a ghost. You can't get on a plane, not in this state. Get back in the car.'

'But – *what*?'

'Just do what you're told for once in your bloody life!' she bellowed.

'You seem to have forgotten, Mrs Baker, that I employ *you*!' Astrid heard herself with dismay – a high-handed stranger. She had no idea what corner of her psyche this voice had been lurking in. Then she realised that it wasn't a stranger – it was the voice of her own mother, the way she used to talk to the housekeeper, or the maid. 'I'm sorry, I didn't—' she began, but Mrs Baker cut her off.

'Right.' Her cheeks were burgundy. She pushed herself away from the car and went round to the boot. 'Fine!' She wrenched it open and lifted out the carry-on case, dumping it next to the bollard. 'There you go. There's your bloody bag. My name isn't Mrs Baker, so it's about bloody time you stopped calling me that, and just to jog your memory, Astrid, you haven't paid me in twelve years, so I really don't think I work for you any more, do I?'

Before Astrid could apologise again, Mrs Baker marched back to the driver's seat, got in, tugged the door, which shrieked, stuck, then slammed. She gunned the engine; Gloria belched, stuttered, gave a throaty roar and departed, far too fast, smoke billowing from the rattling exhaust, three pairs of startled brown eyes at the back windscreen receding.

Astrid stood by the concrete bollards, shaken. She really hadn't a clue what had just happened.

It occurred to her now that this awful outburst might have been nerves: not hers, but Mrs Baker's. It was very possible that Mrs Baker did not want to spend the night alone at the windmill. A bizarre, unprecedented and yet strangely plausible notion squatted in front of her: Mrs Baker was afraid.

The Awful Incident had been the very worst thing to happen to Astrid since the night at the Tudor hunting lodge forty-five years previously, but it must have been far worse for Mrs Baker, who certainly hadn't been herself in the past eight months. It was no coincidence that she had started to see Constance Battiscombe shortly after it happened. Since neither of them could cope with examining the oddity of this, they'd largely avoided discussing it.

This first sighting took place the evening after the police officers had knocked on the door, wanting to know if they'd seen anything 'untoward' on the hill. Mrs Baker was scraping dripping off the roasting pan while Astrid filled in the previous Saturday's *Times* crossword with the published answers, when Henricks started baying and shot down the hall. She managed to grab Juniper and Gordon, who were on her lap, and hurried after Mrs Baker, who was trying to get to Hendricks before he got at whoever was on the other side of the door.

The police officers, faced with two flustered old ladies and their yapping little dogs, became terribly reassuring. Nothing to worry about, but had there been any disturbance up here, about a week ago? Any strangers? Any unexpected vehicles?

The officers were positively grovelling by the time they left, insisting that it was 'a criminal element' that had strayed up from Brighton – nothing for the ladies to worry about at all. These men were no danger to the public, the individual concerned was 'known' to them – it was just bad luck he'd come this far up, probably fleeing his attackers. The incident bore all the hallmarks of organised crime – an isolated revenge attack; there was no threat, absolutely none, though if they were to see anyone, they shouldn't approach them, they should call in. In fact, if they had any concerns, anything at all, they should call. Astrid clutched Gordon and Juniper, while Mrs Baker, who had Hendricks pinned savagely against her bosom, knitted her brows and accepted the Sussex Police business card.

They watched the officers retreat down the hill, then hurried across the courtyard and stood in the freezing drizzle, looking at the flashing lights below. White blobs, people in plastic suits, tramped across the sheep field. Some kind of pale bivouac had been erected in Tangled Wood.

They were shaken, of course. They hurried back inside, wordlessly, double locked the front door, poured stiff Jim Beams. They switched on *Countdown*, and after that they watched several recordings of a garden makeover programme back-to-back, which made them feel quite deranged. Mrs Baker didn't even cook, they gnawed on crackers and cheddar and Marmite. All evening, the dogs squabbled and whined and paced and yapped.

A south-easterly gale blew in from the Channel that night, hurling fistfuls of rain across the swollen backs of the Downs, slamming against the windmill, tearing at the sweeps, which wailed and trembled in their sockets, causing what remained of the mechanism inside to convulse and strain against the brake. But Astrid was woken not by the keening of the windmill but by a thud against her bedroom window. The dogs shot out from beneath the eiderdown, spilled onto the floor, Hendricks ahead, giving his loudest hunting cry.

Her first thought was that Alan had returned.

She jerked up, picturing his face – the wild, jaundiced eyes and lopsided mouth, the fat tongue stuck out, waggling at her. It took a moment to realise that he wasn't out there, clinging to the drainpipe. She flipped the switch on her bedside light, but nothing happened. The light in the hall was off too. Perhaps a sweep had been ripped off and had hit the electricity wires. The sweeps had been torn off before, in the Great Storm of '87 – the night that brought Charlie to her door. But it wasn't a sweep hitting Astrid's bedroom window, it couldn't be – the bedroom faced away from the windmill, across the Weald. Perhaps the crashing sound had come in a dream; Astrid's dreams, in the week since Alan smashed his way through the kitchen door, had teetered on the edge of violence, with flashes of teeth, maniacal laughter, tunnels and wagging tongues. But the thudding noise had woken the dogs too: all three were at the window now, yapping and spinning in circles like small tornadoes. The disturbance was real.

Her heart bounced inside her chest, and she pressed her breastbone with her hands as if she could still it manually. She got up, felt her way to the door and onto the dark landing. The dogs flew out after her – Mrs Baker opened her own bedroom door at the same time and blundered into Astrid who toppled backwards, flinging out a hand to grab the rope of the Dickinson and missing, but Mrs Baker seized her by the arms just in time to stop her plummeting backwards down the staircase.

'What the hell's happening out here? Are you all right, Astrid?

Are you okay?'

'Me? Yes! You?' Astrid clung to Mrs Baker, feeling the solid fore-arms through her flannel nightshirt. 'Something hit my window.'

Mrs Baker peered down the stairwell and flipped the light switch. 'Power's out.'

'Something hit my window!'

'I heard you. Would you listen to that bloody wind? It'll be a branch ripped off the oak – it might even come down this time.'

'It didn't come down in eighty-seven, it won't now,' Astrid said, firmly.

The dogs were weaving in and out of their legs, yapping insanely. Astrid reached down and managed to grab a handful of fur and wool: Gordon. She lifted him and held him close to her body – he was quaking. The other two were whipping about, thrilled. 'Do shut UP!' she shouted; they ignored her. Mrs Baker pushed through the darkness into the bedroom and, aware of the dark stairwell, Astrid hurried after her.

The gale threw rain against the glass and the cottage seemed to quake and rattle as if it was about to wrench itself from the windmill's grip and take off, at last, across the Downs. As Mrs Baker ran her fingers down the windowpane, Astrid had an image of the back door's splintered lock and cracked glass. She saw Mrs Baker give her head a quick shake as if she was slotting the same unpleasant memory back into its place.

Astrid had always considered perception to be an act of will; reality was optional, a space to be curated with whatever thoughts and memories you allowed yourself. In the week since the Awful Incident, though, she had rather lost her grip on this – thoughts and memories seemed to be popping in and out of her head unbidden and unruly. Hendricks and Juniper were still yapping.

'Dear God!' she cried. 'Stop this dreadful racket!'

They didn't, but then Mrs Baker hollered, 'Shut it!' and they did.

Mrs Baker's fingers traced the crack down to the frame. Astrid stepped back, trod on someone – Juniper – who yelped. 'Oh Lord, Eileen. Don't push it, the whole thing will shatter!'

'It's just a hairline crack. I need a torch and tape.' Another gust slammed the cottage. 'Christ alive,' Mrs Baker muttered and peeled off. Before Astrid could follow her, the bedroom shadows had swallowed her up.

Astrid felt her way to the bed, found her dressing gown and hearing aids, shoved her feet into her boots, and called the dogs who were still yapping at the window. She herded all three into the Dickinson at once – something she didn't usually do as they were quite heavy en masse – and lowered them down, bracing her whole body against the rope. Then she hurried down the spiral staircase after them. Gordon was waiting patiently for her at the bottom as he always did, but the other two were gone. A cold draught shivered along the hall; she could hear their claws faintly recede, but it was pitch dark, she could see nothing. Mrs Baker had vanished too. For a bulky septuagenarian she could achieve remarkable bursts of speed. As Astrid felt her way along the wall, she had a distinct feeling of a presence in the corridor in front of her, terribly still. She forced herself to keep moving forwards, past, onwards.

Then she was at the kitchen door. She could hear Mrs Baker opening drawers. She'd managed to fix the glass in the back door with superglue and a pair of tights after the Awful Incident and, astonishingly, it had held all week. This was a good thing as there was no money for a glazier – or a locksmith for that matter. The door was barricaded now with logs and boots and old dog beds, perfectly secure. The window in Astrid's bedroom was much bigger, though. It could surely not be patched up with a pair of tights.

Astrid held the torch while Mrs Baker flicked fuse switches. Nothing happened. 'Sod you then.' Mrs Baker slammed the metal door, then found the electrical tape. As Astrid followed her rump and torch-lit slippers down the hall she made sure not to look back. Mrs Baker clattered up the stairs, while Astrid grappled with the overexcited dogs, trying to get them all into the Dickinson again, then hauling it up. But of course, up was harder than down, so she had to get Gordon out again. She heaved the two older dogs up, then tucked Gordon under one arm, and climbed the spiral stairs back up to the bedrooms. If they had money, she thought, the first thing she'd do would be to install a dumb waiter instead of the Dickinson. Her design was inspired by the basket that the poet would lower and lift from her window, but Emily Dickinson only had to haul poems or flowers or gingerbread – three overweight miniature dachshunds was a different order of magnitude. Not for the first time, she cursed Charlie for putting a spiral staircase into the cottage – one that her small dogs could not negotiate unaided. In an ideal world, she thought, she'd install a proper lift. But of course, in a power cut a lift wouldn't work anyway, so she'd be back to the manual Dickinson. She paused, out of breath, at the top of the spiral sensing that, not for the first time, her thoughts had led her in a circle.

She was thankful that they hadn't been in their beds on the night of the Awful Incident. Alan had broken through the back door when they were watching TV in the snug. She thought of Mrs Baker shoving him backwards through the hatch and slamming the bookcase across it – the hurly-burly of him going off down the tunnel, his bellowing and bashing receding and then moving up into the windmill. There had been a dead look behind Mrs Baker's eyes that Astrid had never witnessed before. It had been an hour or so of him crashing about inside the windmill before a window on the Bin floor shattered and something flew out. Peering out from the landing, they'd seen it glint in the rain. Then a few minutes later there had been a massive thudding, followed by a terrible crack of wood – and the windmill's door had flown open. That was when they'd made the decision to get the dogs into Gloria and go.

But the Awful Incident – like all awful incidents – had passed. It was over. Alan was not outside, clinging to the drainpipe or throwing things at her window, because Alan was gone, for good. 'Eileen?' she called into the darkness. 'Where are you?'

'Where do you think I am? I'm fixing the bloody window. Come and hold the torch.'

After they'd taped up the glass, they made their way back downstairs again. They knew they wouldn't sleep now, didn't even need to discuss it, and as the wind shouldered the wind-mill – a bit less intensely now – they hunkered in the snug. Astrid lit the candles while Mrs Baker made a fire, and then Astrid fetched the Jim, while Mrs Baker got the biscuit tin. All three dogs piled onto Astrid's lap, trampling each other's noses and paws, wriggling into the warmest spaces, pushing to settle, and despite the moaning wind and the shock of having thought, from a half-sleep where time is not linear and logic is elusive, that it was Alan's fists on the bedroom window, Astrid felt content. There was no intruder, no threat, no menace. They were safe, truly safe, perhaps for the first time in over twenty years. She felt a rush of optimism – almost joy. It was such an adventure to be alive and awake at three o'clock in the morning blanketed by dogs, the fire crackling in the grate and Mrs Baker next to her,

queenly in the candlelight. It struck her that if the windmill did
come down on them, she wouldn't mind terribly much. To be
extinguished by a windmill on a stormy night would, all told,
be rather a splendid exit.

She must have nodded off and while she was dozing, Mrs Baker
heard coughing in the tunnel, got up, tugged the bookcase aside
and squeezed herself through the hatch.

Astrid was woken by the ghastly scream. The dogs flew off
her lap in all directions; Mrs Baker's seat was empty, the bookcase pushed back, hatch open. Astrid cried out, and then as if
it was a game of murder in the dark the lights came back on,
illuminating Mrs Baker just as she emerged, grey-faced, from
the hatch. She heaved the bookcase back in place and motored
off down the hall without a word.

Astrid followed her to the kitchen. 'Good God, Eileen, what's
going on now? What on earth were you doing the tunnel?'

It was a while before Mrs Baker could answer but when she
did, she said she'd heard coughing, gone through the hatch
and seen a woman standing at the end, by the bottom of the
ladder. 'Just staring at me, all accusing – like she was saying, *I
know what you've done.*'

'But you've done nothing. Nothing at all!'

Mrs Baker took her seat by the Rayburn, lips clamped shut,
feet spilling over the top of her slippers. The eyes of the Kit Cat
clock flicked to the door and back again. 'She died of consumption, didn't she, your Lady Battiscombe?'

Constance Euphemia Battiscombe had indeed suffered from
consumption, though she had actually died after falling down
the perilously steep ladder staircase in the windmill – Astrid
always wondered whether she might have had a helping hand
from Miss Jones who, judging from the letters, had put up with

rather a lot in her years of devoted service. But it was perhaps unwise to raise the subject of Lady Battiscombe or Miss Jones when Mrs Baker had temporarily lost her mind. 'You're being very foolish.' She used her best Roedean headmistress voice.

Mrs Baker gazed back at her, hollow-eyed.

It had been so odd, seeing her this way. Mrs Baker had always been wholly, at times stubbornly, attached to reality; Astrid had never seen her flustered or spooked before, even in their Letters from Beyond days – and those candlelit evenings on the Stone floor with the windmill folded in darkness, the only sound the scratching of Astrid's silver pen and the wind moaning through the defunct mechanism, would have challenged even the most hardened realist. Having lived through a genuine and prolonged threat, Mrs Baker was never going to be rattled by some incense and a few candles. But ever since the Awful Incident something had shifted in her; she was coming undone.

For the first time in years, Mrs Baker went up to bed before Astrid that night. Astrid listened to her heavy feet stomping about, the toilet flush, the rattle of the pipes, and then everything was still. The storm had passed now. The night was spent. The feeling of ease and joy she'd experienced earlier, in the snug, was gone, too. She knew she should go up – *To bed, to bed, to bed* – but she couldn't face the shenanigans with the Dickinson and the dogs. Finding the police on the doorstep had been rather a shock. She wasn't going to allow herself to dwell or relive the Awful Incident – she mustn't – but somehow it had left her with an odd, guilty feeling that was difficult to smother; a sense that there had to be some kind of comeuppance. Clearly, Mrs Baker felt this too.

She felt her heart quiver and then pause, and for a second nothing happened, even the Kit Cat clock seemed to stop, as if

interrupted mid-tick. And the wind came back, moaning through
the windmill's cap, half-heartedly rattling the fantail, then dying
out. Astrid felt her heart give a little kick and begin to beat
again. She imagined the iron mechanism – what was left of it –
quivering to stillness once more inside the tower, dust drifting
back onto surfaces, cogs releasing their knuckle hold; the owl
settling back on its perch high up in the cap, its feathers smooth,
its body still but alert, tuned in to the tiniest sounds: the needle
tap of tiny claws, the heartbeat of a hiding mouse.

**8th August 1919**

HUZZAH! CONTRACT SIGNED WINDMILL MINE
C

# Chapter 5

Astrid felt a tap on her shoulder and turned. The airport. She was in the airport. A tall young man, just a boy really, behind her in the queue, pointed ahead of them with an encouraging smile and she saw that people had shuffled forwards – the horrid neck hair man was yards ahead, and she knew that she must move too. There were pains shooting up her spine, but she had no choice other than to go, because there were so many people behind her, impatient. For a moment she rather wished that the windmill had collapsed on them that night, eight months ago. It would have been a quick and decisive end, no time to think, better than dying alone in an airport on the way to confront Magnus. Better, too, than entering the wild west of dementia, or some other uncharted decline, with something waiting at the end that she could not name but feared anyway.

She forced herself to move on, tugging at the handle of her carry-on case. It really did not do to look ahead like this – or backwards for that matter – and certainly not inside oneself. The trick was to avoid looking anywhere at all. She'd always been rather good at that – she'd almost made an art form of it – but lately she was slipping.

She wanted, badly now, to go home to Mrs Baker and the dogs, but there was no way out. The roped queue zigzagged back to the entrance, but beyond that there were automated security gates, and all those corridors, miles and miles of them – getting out would take more strength than she had. She summoned her father's favourite Winston Churchill quote: *Success is not final, failure is not fatal. It is the courage to continue that counts.* Why on earth hadn't her father followed his own adage? Even now, seventy-four years on, there was a hollow pain in her heart when she thought of him. Her childhood had ended at the age of eight. Her adulthood had ended at the age of thirty-seven – or so she'd thought. But of course, she'd been wrong about that, because it had started up again.

She wasn't going to allow Magnus to destroy her for the second time though. That really would be absurd. More importantly, she wasn't going to allow him to destroy Mrs Baker, who had been through quite enough. Mrs Baker deserved to live out the rest of her days in peace, even if Astrid couldn't.

She wasn't looking where she was going, and she felt herself whack into something solid. Pain shot up her wrist – she cried out. The neck hair man spun round, spiteful eyes glaring from a wrinkled, bulbous face. 'How silly of me, I'm so sorry!' She pushed aside the pain, gave her most charming smile. He glared a moment longer, then turned away in disgust, as if hit by an inanimate object, an out-of-control suitcase or luggage trolley. Astrid felt, then, that she'd had enough of men who glared and blamed and turned away, men who kicked their way through doors and took whatever they wanted, men who smashed windows and staircases, who put themselves first, stamped on others to get what they wanted. She'd never been in favour of public confrontation, but a sudden outrage overcame her. 'Oh, do fuck off!' she shouted at his back. 'Just fuck *OFF*!'

She felt taller, then, and rather elated – the pain in her arm simply vanished. The man stiffened but didn't turn. She re-adjusted her sling, straightened her spine, lifted her chin. People really were staring now; she felt the collective shock, as well as the surprise, amusement, alarm. She didn't care. Let them stare – let them! She caught someone's eye and nodded, almost bowed, and she knew that she held them in her hands now, every one of them – they were hers. She felt herself grow taller still, straighter, more purposeful. The fury had gone and for a moment she felt entirely herself: powerful, commanding and free.

And then the queue moved on, and suddenly, she could see the baggage checkpoint. A hefty man was kicking off his cowboy boots, but nobody seemed to care. Astrid saw that the people walking through the rectangle had no footwear either and it seemed to her that they'd all lost their minds, but then she understood that, of course, it was terrorists. Nowadays people hid explosives in their shoes. She felt briefly satisfied, as if she'd solved a fiendish crossword clue – which almost never happened.

She was not, she decided, going to take off her own shoes. They were white trainers with diamante accents and Velcro fastenings, new from Asda, and she couldn't take them off because that would involve bending down or standing on one leg and she wasn't capable of either, certainly not one-handed. She wondered what Mrs Baker would do if she were here but couldn't quite summon an answer. Mrs Baker's world view had, for over twenty years, been pragmatic and consistent, but all that changed when Alan smashed back into her life. Intermittently, throughout the spring and summer, there had been more sightings – faces at windows, figures flitting at dusk, faint coughing, footsteps, wafting lavender. It wasn't until Nina came, though, that Mrs

Baker had started to see Constance inside the cottage, too.

They'd both been exhausted that evening, after Nina left, and while Astrid's mind frothed sweetly with painkillers, Mrs Baker had glued herself to the television. Astrid couldn't hear the programme very well, or make sense of it – people dressed in animal costumes were singing and being judged in some way – and so, with Gordon draped across her chest like a fox fur, she'd dozed. She woke with a start when Mrs Baker heaved herself out of her chair with a strangled cry.

'What now?' Astrid struggled to sit up – found Gordon's legs caught in her necklace, wrestled with him. 'What? What?'

'Waltzing.' Mrs Baker pointed at the door. 'Slippers!' she hissed. 'Out there.'

'Nonsense. I don't hear anything.'

'You haven't got your hearing aids.' Mrs Baker took a ninjalike step towards the door. She looked so absurd that Astrid started to laugh. Mrs Baker straightened then, and marched to the door, flinging it open; she looked mad, her grey curls sticking up. She listened a moment, and then stamped off down the hall to the kitchen. All three dogs followed, thinking it was time for their pee.

Astrid hauled herself up and hurried after them, a bit wobbly. She found Mrs Baker with her back against the sink, clutching a book of Shakespeare sonnets. The Kit Cat clock delightedly informed them that it was just gone midnight. Astrid went over and seized the book, which was open on Sonnet 71, *no longer mourn for me.*

It was one of the leather-bound volumes that had originally been in the windmill with the letters – she'd found it that afternoon, not long after Mrs Baker had left to drive Nina to the station, when she'd wandered up to the windmill with the dogs. It must have been thrown out by Alan and had somehow come to rest under a lavender bush, which had protected it, somewhat, from the elements. A glimmer of its gold-leaf edges had caught her eye and she'd bent to retrieve it with her good hand. *Constance Euphemia Battiscombe, 1908* was inscribed in faded ink, a schoolgirl copperplate, on the inside cover. She'd brought it inside and laid it face open by the Rayburn to dry out. She hadn't said anything to Mrs Baker about this because she felt guilty – not about the book but about the encounter she'd had just after she found it.

She'd come out of the lavender garden and was trying to get the dogs away from the altar stone – all three were frantic, sniffing and digging and clawing – when she heard a man's voice call, 'Hello?' He was over on the footpath, just ten yards or so away, looking over the hedge. He held up both hands. 'Don't worry, I'm not stalking you. I live in the village. I've just been walking my dog.'

He had a friendly smile, a shabby puffer jacket, a woollen hat. 'I've just seen a buzzard.' He gestured at the pink sky above the windmill. The mill stood quiet and self-contained, moisture dripping down the rusted cladding, which glowed copper as the sun sank behind it. Astrid walked over and as she came closer to the smiling man, she was transported back thirty years: it was John Dean, lovely, handsome John Dean, smiling at her over the hedge.

His son. His son, of course. The millwright. Joe. He looked uncannily like his father. 'What happened to your arm?' he said, kindly.

'I took a small tumble.'

'That doesn't sound good. Is it broken?'

'Just a little fracture.'

'That must be painful.'

She felt a bit heady and beamed at him. 'Oh, not at all, they gave me some marvellous pills.'

'Your dogs are trying to move that stone for you.' He pointed behind her. 'A bit of a David and Goliath situation.'

'I do know it needs attention,' she said. 'But I have no money, you see. None at all.'

Joe Dean's eyes lit up. 'But there are ways to find funding – did you read my letter? Honestly, I'd be happy to do anything, in my spare time, just to make it sound for you. No charge.'

'You'd really work for free?' She peered at him over the jagged hawthorn. 'Why would you do that?'

He frowned and rubbed his chin. 'Well, I suppose it's hard to watch it disintegrate when I know I could help. This windmill's been a part of my life – a part of the landscape of my childhood, really. I grew up in the village. I think you knew my dad?'

She felt her face heat up. 'You do look awfully like him.'

He smiled. 'People always say that.'

'I knew him.'

He nodded. 'He worked on your windmill in the late eighties, didn't he, after the Great Storm?' He looked up at it. 'I remember coming up here with him once or twice, as a little kid.'

'I remember you,' she said. Though it could have been his brothers. She really just remembered small boys.

He cleared his throat, nodding. 'This windmill's not just part of the external landscape, it's . . . ' He shrugged, as if he'd reached the limits of language. 'It feels like a bit of my dad's in it, somehow, and the other way round too, maybe. A little bit of your windmill's sort of in my DNA, I think.'

Astrid nodded. In all the years of villagers stomping up the hill and telling her she was failing she'd never heard anyone put it quite like this. It reminded her that, in some inscrutable way, the windmill wasn't really hers; never had been.

'Your father was a good man,' she said. 'I'm sorry he died so young.'

He looked a bit startled, then smiled. 'Yes, me too.'

She felt the windmill above them shift its attention. The fan stage rattled and spun. The sun was lowering fast now, its pinks spreading, saturating the sky. 'I suppose there's not much call for millwrights these days, is there?'

'Well, you'd be surprised. I mean, I have to take work all over the country, but there are only about fifteen millwrights in the UK now, so there's usually a mill somewhere that needs me. I was in Shropshire most of last year, with a beautiful old tower mill, and I've been working on a post mill, recently, near Chichester.'

Astrid thought about all the windmills dotted across the country in hamlets and villages, on hilltops or ridges – there had been over three hundred of them in Sussex and Kent alone. She liked to imagine that the mills, like trees, could communicate with each other through mysterious networks, sending out distress signals, warnings, messages of support, jokes, love. They'd once been the focal point of their communities, the source of daily bread, and now they were vanishing – sucked back into the earth, ivy-slathered, stunted, capless, worm-eaten, crumbling, wrecked. The lucky ones had been repurposed, stripped back and turned into dovecotes or watch towers, while others had been rescued and restored by people like Joe Dean to house families or holidaymakers. A handful had become heritage sites – brought back to life, grinding local grain into flour sold in picturesque packets at exorbitant prices.

'But I do it because I love it, really,' Joe Dean was saying. 'I did try to do something else. I was a secondary school teacher for ten years, believe it or not, in Tower Hamlets, but I felt I was in the wrong life.' He looked up at the windmill which leaned and trembled, very slightly, as if he'd stroked its flank. The painkillers gave Astrid a warm, fanciful feeling, not entirely trustworthy. She knew it was actually quite cold. 'I must go in.' She glanced back towards the gate; soon Gloria would come chuntering up the hill.

'That's not the altar stone, is it?' Joe Dean nodded at the windmill. 'Lady Battiscombe's famous altar stone?'

Astrid felt flustered, then. She called the dogs.

'How did it happen? Did it come through the floorboards? It must weigh a ton.'

She knew that if she stayed any longer, it would all spill out: the Awful Incident, the horror and violence. At school she'd been the girl nobody told secrets to, not because she was malicious or gossipy, but simply because she couldn't hold anything in, she had no restraint, no boundary. 'It's so chilly, I really must go inside.'

'Mrs Miller?' he called after her. 'I promise, I have no agenda, none at all – other than to help.'

She'd said nothing to Mrs Baker about this encounter, but she wondered if there might be a way to let Joe Dean help, just to get the stone away, and fix the door back on. She knew what Mrs Baker would say, though: if Joe Dean lifted that stone, what might he find?

She eased the book of Shakespeare sonnets out of Mrs Baker's hands and closed it. 'It wasn't a ghost that put the book here, Eileen, it was me. I found it in the lavender garden this afternoon. He must have thrown it out when he was smashing things. It's a miracle it isn't completely ruined.'

Mrs Baker stared at her a moment then she said, 'He deserves what he got. We did nothing wrong.'

'No, nothing.' Astrid touched Mrs Baker's forearm, solid under the fisherman's knit, and said, softly, 'He's gone now, Eileen. Alan's gone and he isn't coming back.'

*30th September 1919*

*Walter,*

*The tone of your letter is so upsetting. You call me headstrong, but I am merely trying to live! Would you prefer that I am trapped in claustrophobic London rooms with dull acquaintances, gossiping and complaining? I find a freedom here that I have never had before. Nobody is watching me. I can breathe. I do not have to use table napkins or brush my hair or wear a girdle. But I do not wish to quarrel with you, not with the Atlantic between us, and so much opportunity for misunderstanding. If only you could see the windmill, standing above me in the glorious English sunshine, creaking like a ship, you would understand, I am sure, why I should want to be nowhere else.*

*We have been here a month now and Miss Jones is not, as you fear, pining for 'civilisation'. In fact, civilisation has come to us: I met a London artist when I was in the village last week. She was down to visit friends nearby and was keen to see the windmill. She is to come to tea here next Friday. She studied painting at the Slade School of Art, and knows the Andersons, vaguely. She has a round, open face, and bright, hazel eyes; I liked her instantly.*

*As for Miss Jones, she is never one for displays of enthusiasm, I grant you, but she tells me she is content to 'do her duty' wherever I should need her. And really, she is hardly 'ancient', Walter. She is in her forties! I should have thought that you would be glad to have us up here in the sweet fresh air, with skylarks and butterflies (I thought of you this morning as I spotted a silver-washed fritillary and a ringlet). None of this is 'madness' – it is quite the opposite. Sometimes, Walter, I feel that you disapprove of anything I do. But I will not squabble with you, not like this.*

*Yr C*

# Chapter 6

The only thing about the next twenty-four hours that Astrid wasn't dreading, she realised, was Nina, which was funny, since they'd only met a week ago – and the encounter could hardly be called a success since it had ended in A&E.

She and Mrs Baker had woken ridiculously early that day. When Astrid got downstairs with the dogs, just after six, Mrs Baker was down already, fully dressed, buttering a cake tin. 'Some people are against Battenberg,' she said, as if they were mid-conversation. 'It's the marzipan. People can be funny about marzipan. So I'm making a sponge too. No one minds a Victoria sponge, do they?'

'Except vegans.'

Mrs Baker's hands stilled. 'Bloody hell. Do you think she's one of them?'

The Kit Cat clock twitched feverishly above the Rayburn as Astrid, knocking her shin on Tony Blair, opened the kitchen window and bent to lift the dogs – a zap of pain shot up her spine with each one. She shooed them down the scaffold plank into the soupy mist. 'Watch it.' Mrs Baker whisked a turd from the tiles by Astrid's foot with a piece of newspaper. 'Bloody Juniper. You need to get her out quicker. She's going senile.'

'Aren't we all, Mrs B.'

'Well, you're not crapping on the kitchen floor.' Mrs Baker dumped the balled paper into the bin. 'Yet.' She lifted the kettle.

'I still have one hearing aid,' Astrid said. The tap clanked and sputtered as Mrs Baker wrenched it on and off again.

They weren't used to visitors, that was the problem. There was a sense of trepidation and guilt, too, as if they were about to be searched or interrogated or exposed. Perhaps they were. 'I just don't know why she's coming,' Astrid said.

Mrs Baker poured batter into the cake tin. 'You invited her, Astrid.'

'You did, strictly speaking. And I didn't think she'd actually come.' The Kit Cat clock flicked its tail feverishly, as the dogs emerged from the fog like manifesting spirits, snouts on the window, brown eyes, furry bodies. Astrid lifted them in and down, one by one, despite the howl of her lower vertebrae. She thumped again into Tony Blair, swore and tipped kibble into their bowls, spilling it – bits bounced and spun over the floor tiles. She was overwrought and it was not even breakfast time.

The kettle gave a spark as Mrs Baker flipped the switch but thankfully the electricity didn't cut out. Astrid took her seat by the Rayburn and picked up little fat Juniper, who always finished first. Junie settled immediately, with a small, contented fart, then Gordon hurried over and jumped up too. She felt a little bit calmer, and wondered what to wear that day. The emerald cashmere, with a brooch and a shawl to cover the worst of the moth holes – the embroidered Russian shawl with the fringe, for a touch of mystery. Juniper buried her nose into Astrid's elbow and gave a little sigh. Hendricks had finished his food and had chased down the spilled kibble and was now poking at something under the kitchen table.

Mrs Baker was muttering something about vegans as she dropped a teabag into the Garfield mug. 'What?' Astrid touched her ear, but her remaining hearing aid had vanished. Under the table Hendricks swallowed something, looked at her a moment through shaggy eyebrows, then waddled out, past her, to his basket.

'You look—' Mrs Baker said when Astrid came down, later, dressed.

Mrs Baker herself had not changed out of the fisherman's jumper and navy trousers but she had, Astrid noted, put on a clean white shirt.

'You'll have to shout.' Astrid tapped her ear. 'I can't find either of my hearing aids now.' Hearing aids cost a small fortune, there was no replacing them. Fortunately, she was only mildly deaf, and Mrs Baker tended to speak quite loudly, and didn't mind having the volume of the TV high as her own hearing was far from perfect – not that she'd ever admit it.

At the clanging of the doorbell the dogs went wild. Astrid and Mrs Baker looked at one another. The bell danced on its wire pull and the dogs crowded round the kitchen door, scrabbling, hopping over one another, Hendricks positively baying. They didn't move. It was entirely possible, Astrid thought, that they wouldn't answer the door, that they would simply wait for Nina to give up and go away. But then Hendricks had somehow got his nose round the kitchen door, levered it open, and all three dogs were off down the hall. The Kit Cat clock twitched riotously, as if it might wrench off the wall and answer the door itself.

They heard a woman's voice. 'Hello? It's Nina!'

Mrs Baker seemed to galvanise, and Astrid was suddenly alone. She could hear demented yapping out in the courtyard. She rested her cheek against the kitchen wall, one hand on the neck of her cardigan, which was buttoned too tight. She thought, then, that she heard a human yelp.

After some moments, the footsteps came down the corridor. For a second she looked for somewhere to hide, then she got a grip and straightened her back as the stranger – Nina – stepped into the kitchen, flanked by Juniper and Gordon.

She wasn't as Astrid had pictured her at all. She was quite young, in her thirties perhaps, pleasant to look at in an unshowy, unintimidating way; slim-ish, wearing heavy framed glasses, dark hair pulled into a ponytail, little wavy bits escaping round the ears. She wore jeans and a simple black jumper, a duvet jacket, white trainers. 'Hello!' she called over the dogs' racket. She had a slightly elfin chin, and there were dimples on each side of her smile, which seemed a bit strained. She was also clutching one of her hands at an odd angle.

Mrs Baker appeared behind her then, red-cheeked, Hendricks snarling in a stranglehold. 'He had a go,' she muttered grimly, walking past Nina and shoving him into Astrid's arms.

'It was just a little nip,' Nina cried over the yapping. 'Completely my fault!'

There was blood, Astrid saw. Quite a lot of it. 'You little brute,' Astrid scolded. He growled at Nina as she went to the sink. 'Outrageous!' Nina bumped her shin on Tony Blair and Astrid saw her glance down at him. She somehow had a good-natured air, despite the obvious setback of the hand. Astrid felt some of the panic ebb.

Juniper was losing interest already, but Gordon was still upset, running in circles giving flabbergasted yaps as if he couldn't believe they'd allowed an intruder to get all the way to the sink. Astrid shoved Hendricks under one arm and scooped Gordon up too but he was wriggling so much that Hendricks snapped at his head, and then someone's paw became tangled in her earring, tugging so hard it was a miracle that it didn't rip her lobe off, and it took a moment for her to free herself and separate them. Her head was pounding. It was all, plainly, a mistake. She hadn't driven Gloria in years, not since they were doing the mourning, but she seriously considered bundling the dogs in and driving away, leaving Mrs Baker to deal with their visitor.

Mrs Baker was helping Nina to wash the wound. The tap rattled and lurched and spat and she heard Nina cry out in pain, or perhaps alarm. 'It comes out a bit yellow, but it'll clear in a minute and . . .'

Astrid didn't catch the rest. 'We must take our coffee outside!' she shouted. They both looked round with surprised expressions.

'She's got to wash the blood off, Astrid – he had a good go,' Mrs Baker said, loudly and pointedly.

Astrid moved, without thinking, towards the back door, but of course it no longer opened – they'd still not been able to replace the lock, that was beyond even Mrs Baker's fixing skills, and so it was still barricaded. Astrid had a sudden, unwelcome memory of hearing the lock splinter. It must have been awfully loud for her to have heard it over the television, though of course she'd had both her hearing aids then. She remembered scrabbling for the remote control as they heard the roar, 'Eileen!'

Mrs Baker had shot out of her seat. She'd reached the door in a flash and her solid silhouette had trembled against the hall light.

There were neat puncture marks in the heel of Nina's hand; blood bubbled out of them. Mrs Baker came at her with a tea towel, but Nina whisked the hand away. 'It's okay!' she cried. 'Do you have any kitchen towels? A plaster would be good, though.'

*Skittish*, Astrid thought.

Hendricks started gnashing again, wriggling. 'If we go out,'

Astrid bellowed, 'he'll calm down. He'll be better outside. Mrs Baker will bring us coffee!' She knew what Mrs Baker's expression would be, so she didn't look.

'She's drying her bloody hand, Astrid.'

'It's okay, really, it's fine, I think.' Nina's voice was calm and clear. 'I'd be happy to go outside. It's so sunny today, not that cold really.'

'Almost Hallowe'en and hot!' Astrid had no idea why she was shouting. Nina said something but she only caught the word 'deceptive' because Mrs Baker was opening and closing cupboards, clattering about. Astrid whistled to Juniper then made for the hall, hoping that Mrs Baker would oblige, that Nina would follow, and that nobody would savage her on the way.

The fog had cleared away, a lemony sun hung in the pale blue sky and it was almost windless. As she pushed down the side of the cottage, her jumper snagged on briars and nettles needled through her leggings. Something scurried into the tangled bushes and she felt the windmill staring down at her. Seen through a stranger's eyes, Astrid supposed that the garden might look a little neglected, but these days their energy went, by necessity, into the vegetables.

Nina emerged from the side of the cottage a few moments later. She stopped and looked up at the windmill. Astrid peered up, too, gingerly, not quite sure what she'd see. The windmill stood above the cottage, tall and proud against the pale blue sky. From where they were standing, only the top floors were visible and, perhaps because of the light, it looked strong and fit; solid, useful, important. The sun bounced off the chalky hillside, flinging light at its cap, which seemed to glow, despite the peeling paint.

'We can sit over here,' Astrid called out.

Nina turned and saw the Downs sloping away ahead of them, tawny turf with glints of chalk, and the Weald stretching out, a patchwork of ploughed or grazed fields, dotted with villages. 'What a view!' She looked around at the garden, then. 'This is amazing – are you rewilding?'

'Re-what?'

'Rewilding?' Nina spoke loudly.

Astrid had no idea what she was talking about, so she decided it was best not to engage. She let Gordon down but kept a firm hold of Hendricks, who was still staring intensely at Nina. He gave a low growl. She closed her hand over his snout and walked over to the picnic table. Somehow, she managed to slot her body onto the bench, gritting her teeth against the nasty shots in her lower back. The table wobbled but held. She felt like a gymnast, upright again after a series of improbable moves.

The table was mossy, soft as a rug under her fingers, crusted here and there with seagull spatter. Nina hadn't moved, she was staring up at the windmill again.

'Do sit.' Astrid waved a hand. 'Please. Here.'

'So, I was reading all about it' – Nina slid effortlessly into the opposite bench, which gave a loud creak – 'on the train down.' She smiled, looked up at the tower again, and said something else – Astrid caught the words 'badly damaged'.

She felt herself go cold. It hadn't occurred to her that Nina would dive straight in, with Mrs Baker still in the kitchen. It was too much, too intrusive! She didn't know what to do. She must escape, obviously. It was so rude to be questioned like this, without preamble, delicacy or tact. What had possessed her to allow this stranger to come to the windmill? She couldn't possibly discuss Sally Morgan, Rohls, the ghastly scandal, its hideous aftermath, not like this. Not ever, in fact.

She'd have to ask Nina to leave. Perhaps she could say that the dogs were too upset, they weren't used to strangers. Unfortunately, they all looked quite calm now. Juniper was pootling over by the Shrew Tree, Gordon was at her knee, wanting to come up, and even Hendricks had stopped gnashing.

'The windmill?' Nina said, quite loudly. 'I was reading about it on the train, how it was badly damaged in the Great Storm of 1987? Didn't it catch fire?'

Astrid felt a rush of relief. The windmill! Of course. She was talking about the windmill. The Great Storm. 'Yes, yes . . . yes!'

'It must have been dramatic.'

'Well, it was, rather.' Astrid looked down at Gordon, her thudding heart calming a little. She patted her lap. 'Hup.' He thought about it, then gathered himself, and hopped up onto her lap next to Hendricks, who gave him a dismissive look, but didn't move. Astrid felt much better, anchored by dogs.

'I expect you're too young to remember it,' she said to Nina. 'You probably weren't even born in 1987.'

'Oh, well, yes, I was a little girl, but we lived abroad. My father worked for the Foreign Office.'

'How glamorous.'

'It wasn't really. It just meant I went to boarding school from the age of eleven.'

'I went to boarding school too. Several. Ghastly places. I was sent away when I was eight, after my father shot himself, and my mother ran off with an Italian count.'

Nina's eyes widened, and Astrid wondered whether she'd revealed too much – she wasn't used to social interaction – but then Nina was nodding. Her eyebrows met in an anxious upwards tick. 'I'm so sorry. My dad died when I was fifteen so . . .'

Astrid straightened Gordon's jumper. She had no idea, none

at all, how they'd got onto such a personal subject with so little preamble. She decided to get things back to the windmill. 'It spontaneously combusted,' she said.

'What?'

'In the Great Storm.'

She saw Nina trying to catch up. She had nice, kind eyes, awfully sincere.

'The gale was so powerful that the sweeps overrode the brake, you see, and the shaft started turning against it, and then the friction from that created huge sparks which shot out of the cap, burning holes right through the wood. It could have caught and burned to the ground with me inside it if Charlie hadn't saved me.'

'Charlie?'

'My ... my ... well. He's dead now. But that's how we met. Charlie rescued me.'

Nina looked hopeful. 'How romantic.'

'Well, yes, I suppose so.' Astrid's eyes travelled to the spot over by the pond, under the Shrew Tree, just behind Nina, where she'd found him on that May morning, poor Charlie.

The grass in those days was always neatly mown. Charlie had been a dedicated gardener. She'd spotted him from the kitchen window, on his back next to the pond, as if he'd lain down to listen to the skylarks, only it was very early and quite chilly, and the grass was wet and he wasn't one for lying down outside. The Shrew Tree had seemed to be leaning over him, tenderly. She'd opened the kitchen window and called his name, but she already knew. She remembered kneeling next to him. His face had a strange blankness and looked flatter as if someone had let the air out. His eyes were half open still, his jaw ajar. She saw that a handful of enchanter's nightshade was scattered next to him – he'd been weeding. That was when the toad appeared. She hadn't thought about the toad in years. It crawled out from under Charlie's neck and stared up at her, warty sides heaving, then turned and slid, carefully, regretfully, into the pond, barely disturbing the algae.

She felt the sadness pressing on her heart, and bent over Hendricks to hide it, adjusting the neck of his sweater. Nina leaned forwards and the table creaked under her elbows. 'I'm so sorry,' she said, gently. 'I didn't mean to . . . I didn't realise you'd married again after Magnus.'

'No, no, Charlie and I weren't married.' She wanted to explain, then, that although she'd been very fond of him, she really hadn't missed him all that much, not after Mrs Baker came. It had only been that first few months when she was alone in the cottage and coping with his awful son, and all those murky business dealings, that Charlie's absence had seemed unbearable. There had been a particularly horrid visit from his son one night; he'd appeared with a ghastly little succubus in a shiny suit, trying to get money out of her – trying to get the windmill. It wasn't appropriate to start talking to Nina about this, though. She did know that.

She wondered what was taking Mrs Baker so long. Nina's injured hand was resting on the table. Mrs Baker had found her a plaster, Astrid saw, but the blood was beginning to soak through it already. 'Is that awfully sore?' she said. 'Hendricks can be very naughty but he's not a bad boy. He's always been a protector, you see, and he had a difficult experience not too long ago so he's rather on overdrive, I'm afraid.'

'It's okay, honestly, it's not as bad as it looks, and it really was my fault. I stupidly went to pat him before he knew who I was. He was probably terrified, poor boy.'

Astrid managed not to say that Hendricks did not know fear.
She remembered his teeth sinking into Alan's shin, the awful
thud of the boot against his ribs. He'd picked himself up, shaken
himself off and gone back for more, brave soul. But there was
no need to think about the Awful Incident – and absolutely not
now, eight months on, whilst entertaining a new guest. The sun
vanished behind a drifting cloud and she felt herself shiver. It
was not as warm as it looked. Perhaps she could send Nina to
fetch a blanket from the kitchen and see where Mrs Baker had
got to.

Nina was saying something about getting lost when she got off
the bus in the village. 'I walked up here from the bus stop, and
I was looking for the footpath through the woods. You'd think
it would be obvious, but I had to ask someone.' She articulated
her words clearly. 'And this old man said, "You're not going up
to see that bloody windmill woman, are you?"' She laughed.

'They still call me that?' Astrid was rather pleased. Not forgotten, then, after all.

'I suppose you've lived up here for a long time?' Nina's eyes
had strayed back to the windmill as if it was whispering to her
at a pitch that nobody else could hear.

'An absolute age,' Astrid said. 'The windmill was my fortieth
birthday present to myself.'

This was not, in fact, true. Astrid had never actually made the
decision to buy herself a broken windmill and a near derelict
cottage, but someone had taken her to the auction, and poetic
notions of destiny, thanks to her name, had coalesced and her
hand had gone up, and there it was, one of those small, unreg-
ulated moments that shape a life. If there was one piece of
advice she'd offer a young woman like Nina, it was 'Never go
to an auction when you're having a nervous breakdown.' But

Nina probably didn't need advice, she seemed terribly competent, quite self-contained. Nina, she realised, was the first person
under forty that she'd spoken to other than the boys at the petrol
station in a very long time.

It would have been helpful, when she was Nina's age, if she'd
had an older woman to advise her; things could have been quite
different if she'd had some sensible support. But her mother
had been too preoccupied by whatever charlatan she'd married,
and anyway, if she'd have offered advice, Astrid would have
ignored it for her own safety. Her mother had, in fact, found the
whole thing hilarious. 'It'll blow over, darling!' she'd cried, as she
passed through London en route to Buenos Aires. 'Tomorrow's
chip paper!'

The photographer from the *Evening Argus* had showed up the
day after she collected the windmill keys and 'Windy Miller' was,
predictably, the front page of the next day's local paper. And then
the London newspapermen got hold of it and by the afternoon
they were standing in the courtyard, even though she'd been
out of the public eye for over three years by then. She'd locked
the door and stayed in the tower reading Constance's letters,
eating stale biscuits, drinking a lot of red wine, peeing into a
bucket, and creeping out to the toilet only late at night when
they'd driven off down the hill for a few hours' kip.

'That's brilliant.' Nina was smiling; the fine lines around her
eyes creased, the dimples deepened. Her front teeth were lovely
and white and overlapped slightly. 'It was my fortieth birthday
last month,' she said. 'I gave myself a chocolate brownie.'

'You're not forty!'

'I am.' She smiled, but there wasn't any lightness in her eyes.
Astrid sensed, suddenly, that something horrid had happened
to Nina, that she was wounded inside, her spirit dampened.

88    LUCY ATKINS

There was a rattling sound and they both turned to see Mrs
Baker processing across the grass with a brass tray. Constance's
coffee pot swayed above a stack of shivering plates and cups,
and two cakes. Astrid had quite forgotten about the coffee pot.
It had been under the kitchen table ever since Alan threw it
through the Stone floor window. It was a miracle that it was
still in one piece.

Nina's visit, of course, got out of control before they could even
eat the cakes, and the next day she'd gone back to Edinburgh
with nothing quite resolved, which, of course, had led to Astrid's
plan. It might be a bit impulsive to go to Scotland, but it was
necessary. She had, in a sense, allowed a lie to curtail her for
almost half a century, but enough was enough. It was time to
free herself.

25th November 1919

Dearest W,

Since I have heard nothing from you after my last letter, I assume you are too busy to write, or that a letter has been lost.

I have no news other than my windmill, so at the risk of annoyance, I will tell you about that. I have been frustrated to find that before I can release the sweeps I must replace them, as they were damaged in a storm last winter – it can certainly be wild up here. It is easy to forget that although the sweeps are oak they are over fifty years old, and take such a battering. Mr Banks says the millwright cannot work on them until the weather is more suitable. On the bright side, the exterior bricks are tarred now (I can, as you requested before, forward you copies of the bills for repointing and tarring, but you do remember that I am using my own money, don't you?). Perhaps next year we will clad the more exposed side in iron for better protection against the elements. The cap will be repainted in the spring probably, and then the windmill will be very elegant again.

Mr Banks has also arranged for builders to begin work on the granary in the spring, so we shall be very busy then, if you do come home. For now, Miss Jones sleeps in a little nest up on the Stone floor (so called because it is where the disused millstones lie, one next to the other in order to distribute their weight across the floorboards). As for the 'close quarters' you mentioned in your previous letter – perhaps you could think of the windmill as a ship? It harnesses the wind in its sails, after all; the cap is constructed like a hull, and there is even a deck. Miss Jones and I are shipmates.

*I have worked out a way that the grain bell can be rung from any floor, but Miss Jones has a habit of creeping up and down stairs and appearing, suddenly, in a room looking put upon, or anxious, even though I have not rung for her. The problem is the draught, which sometimes stirs the bell, causing it to tinkle, and she is always so alert. She also tends to shudder whenever the wind changes direction, causing the fantail to spin, which can be quite irritating, as this happens frequently. But still, she is devoted, and cares for me diligently. I shall be very glad, though, when her quarters are finished. Then I shall have the windmill to myself.*

*I hope you feel less cross with me now that you can see how I live when I am here (which is, I confess, almost all the time – I have barely set foot in London in weeks). Daphne – the London artist, I think I mentioned her to you? – is becoming a wonderful friend. She recently took me to a party at the house of a painter she knows, not too far from here, and I met some terribly interesting people, artists and poets and potters and philosophers – a ballerina too, though she didn't dance. We ate pot au feu and the host had somehow got hold of grapefruit, which was bitter, but delicious.*

*I hope that you are taking some pleasure in your great endeavour even though there are so many worries for you. I hope, too, that you have found a way to get more sleep, Walter. You will feel less cross if you do, I'm sure.*

*Your C*

# Chapter 7

The vast automaton jabbed a finger at Astrid's legs, then at the conveyor belt, and barked something she didn't catch. She tried to look defiant. She could not, surely, be expected to climb up there to be scanned? She lifted her chin. 'Are you *mad*?'

Behind her, the line of strangers seemed to tense and flex. Astrid attempted to get a grip. She did know that the official could not possibly expect an eighty-two-year-old woman with one arm in a cast to clamber unaided onto a conveyor belt. 'Can I just . . . Jesus.' A woman pushed past her, causing her lower vertebrae to spark hot little flame-throwers up her spine, and something about the tone brought back the voice from the auditorium all those years ago: *Mad bitch!*

But she absolutely must not start remembering the night at the National again, not now. Absolutely not. It was forty-five years ago, ancient history. *Stop it*, she told herself, sternly. *Stop this nonsense.* She lifted her chin. *S.O.B. Absurd.* The show must go on. It had, and it would.

Astrid knew that lack of sleep and the shenanigans of the previous night lay at the root of this feeling that everything was not just out of control, but somehow mystifying. The previous night had been particularly foolish, even for them. At two o'clock in the morning Astrid had opened her eyes to find an enormous figure in an Edwardian nightgown looming over her bed. She'd screamed, of course, and the figure, clutching its frilled neck, had begun to wail too, a deranged, high sound, and then the dogs were off, and there was bedlam in the bedroom.

Once they'd established that it was just the two of them, and that neither was Constance Battiscombe, they'd started to laugh, and then they couldn't stop, and Gordon yapped so hard that he bounced off the bed and was momentarily stunned on the floor, paws up, and as they bent they banged their skulls together. *An Agatha Christie crime scene*, Astrid thought: *two dead old ladies and a crushed dachshund in a windmill, no weapon.*

When they'd all got up off the floor, Astrid's wrist was in agony so they went down to the kitchen for more painkillers. Astrid settled in her chair, Gordon on her lap, Juniper and Hendricks in their basket while Mrs Baker fetched the tablets and a glass of water. Then she began to make cocoa. She'd put a man's overcoat over the ridiculous nightdress, Astrid noticed. It was an enormous thing in brown windowpane tweed. Where on earth had she found it? It wasn't one of Charlie's. The only coat she'd kept of Charlie's was a mildewed brown shearling, still in the hall. Astrid watched her move around the kitchen, opening and closing doors, collecting the milk, a tub of cocoa powder, sugar and mugs, deftly avoiding Tony Blair. It was almost unnerving the way Mrs Baker veered between this old competent self and the new one: an unhinged midnight ghost-seer.

She heard the windmill let out a faint, plaintive groan and shudder as the wind picked up. Gordon heard it too, and quivered. Perhaps he sensed that she was leaving him the next day. Hendricks and little fat Juniper wouldn't really care, they had each other, but Gordon, a dog of intuition and sensitivity who mostly glued himself to her side, would be alone. He would mind that very much. She stroked his curly ears, wondering if it might be possible to smuggle him onto the plane in the carry-on bag. She could make air holes in it. He got up, turned, lay down, pushed his nose into her hand, licked it. Turned again. Something was wrong. She looked about the room trying to see what it was. The Kit Cat clock was ticking too loudly, that was it. Its eyes and tail twitched from side to side too rapidly; it was definitely speeding up.

Mrs Baker brought over the cocoa, pink pottery cup for Astrid, the Garfield mug for herself. She settled into her seat, legs apart, the daft Victorian nightdress poking up at the collar of the old coat. 'You were howling like a banshee,' she said. 'I thought you'd been murdered in your bed.'

'Howling?' Astrid blew on the cocoa. 'Was I really?' She took a sip. It was ridiculously sweet – was Mrs Baker *trying* to give her diabetes? The bulbous eyes of the Kit Cat clock slid to the door and back to the window. 'What was that about then?' Mrs Baker said.

'I haven't the foggiest. I was dreaming, I suppose.'

'You haven't done that for ages.'

'Done what?'

'Yelled in your sleep. You were choking when I got in, like someone was strangling you.'

'I don't think I *yelled*, Mrs Baker.'

Mrs Baker lowered her mug. 'You don't look good, actually.'

'It's the middle of the night, you don't look good either.' It struck her that Mrs Baker was giving her the out. She could say that she was unwell, that her wrist was too sore to fly the next day. She imagined eating toast and marmalade as usual in the morning by the Rayburn, filling in the crossword while

Mrs Baker soaked beans for the lunchtime soup, or went out to dig up carrots. Another day would pass and then it would be breakfast again, and again, and again – these days, they always seemed to be eating breakfast – and eventually enough breakfasts would have passed that Magnus would be dead, and his memoir would be published and the journalists would either come to the windmill, or not come, and life would either carry on as normal, or detonate.

'You shouldn't go tomorrow if you're poorly,' Mrs Baker said.

'Nonsense, I'm radiant with health.' She felt the irritation building. Mrs Baker looked like a slab of butcher's meat wrapped in brown paper in that ghastly coat. Where *had* it come from? It must have been left years ago by a guest – when there were guests. It definitely had negative associations. Astrid remembered the Last Man then – she hadn't thought about him in ages. It was his coat, she was sure of it. It was seven or eight years ago that they'd stopped the B&B. Yes, she was certain that the coat had belonged to him, their last guest.

He'd been colossal, six foot seven at least, with a face like a ham hock, pellucid, thyroidal eyes, a Welsh accent – was it Welsh? Perhaps Northern Irish. Lyrical, anyway, and far too soft, too high, at odds with his heft. He'd used the idiom of an eighteenth-century nobleman which was unsettling, but he wasn't one of the Letters from Beyond guests. He'd been attending an amateur entomologist society event at Brighton racecourse and soon after he arrived, he'd pulled a red biscuit tin from his satchel. Crawford's Rover Assorted, Astrid recalled (how funny to remember that detail – the pink wafer, the jammy circle). She hadn't thought about the Last Man for ages because, of course, when it came to menacing men rampaging through the windmill he'd been rather overshadowed by Alan.

He had been awfully odd, though. She remembered how he'd opened the biscuit tin to introduce them to his 'familiar', a horned, conker-coloured beetle about three inches long. 'Do not rush to judge,' he said in his curious voice. 'For a tender heart beats inside her gleaming shell.' He said it was a Madagascar hissing cockroach, and offered a Latin name, something *portentosa*, Astrid recalled, which had seemed apt. 'Be not afraid,' he cooed, tilting his head, 'for she is vegetarian.'

It had marked the end of their bed and breakfast days.

The Madagascar hissing cockroach would have been quite enough, but that night the rain was relentless, and the mill's door swelled and pressed into its frame so that even a hulk like him couldn't force it open when, for reasons of his own, he'd taken fright in the small hours and attempted a panic-stricken departure.

They'd been woken by vulpine howls coming from the top of the tower. Out in the courtyard, hanging on to one another, they'd peered up through the rain and seen his anvil head on the Bin floor; he must have smashed the glass. He couldn't get his face out, since it wasn't a large windowpane, just his nose and chin. 'Satan carved messages on the beams!' he roared. 'He's turning the bible pages!'

They'd warned him, of course, as they warned every guest, not to climb to the upper floors, especially to the Stone floor, where the boards were already weakened by the weight of the altar and the millstones. The ladder stairs, with their smooth indented treads, could also be perilous in the dark, particularly if you forgot to come down backwards. One Letters from Beyond client had ended up in A&E with a badly gashed forehead and two broken arms after he took fright midway through a session and hurtled headlong down them.

'I will not be incarcerated with Satan!' the Last Man bellowed from the Bin floor. 'I am not a sinner!'

Mrs Baker had to go down the tunnel eventually, and up through the trapdoor to guide him out. The lilting voice had gone when he burst from the hatch into the snug, barefoot, looming and bellowing about trickery, bible pages, Satanic carvings as he slammed his block fists against the bookshelf. He wouldn't listen when Astrid tried to explain that the carvings on the beams weren't from Satan, they were little messages from millwrights and millers, hundred-year-old graffiti. Then a dog, Gilbert – it must have been Gilbert in those days – had a go, and Astrid had had to pry his jaws off the man's simian foot, while Mrs Baker, her voice at once no-nonsense and respectful, manoeuvred him out of the snug, down the hall and out the front door.

His bellows faded as he lolloped barefoot down Windmill Hill towards the village in the rain. As they locked the front door, they looked at each other. 'That's the last man we're having here,' Mrs Baker said. 'That's it.'

Astrid agreed. They couldn't keep the bed and breakfast open any more, people were simply too mad. They'd have to find other ways to supplement what was left of Charlie's money.

Mrs Baker discovered the empty Rover Assorted biscuit tin upturned on the boards of the Stone floor the next day. She'd given it a scrub, but they never could face using it. It wasn't clear why the man had been so spooked by the carvings. They were on the applewood beams, dotted here and there, carpenters' marks, some initials, a few millers' names and dates. Astrid found her favourite, a little message of maternal love carved on the main beam up on the Bin floor where the setting sun would illuminate it every evening. *My Anemone.*

She pointed it out to Mrs Baker. 'It isn't just the flower, you know, anemone means "wind" – at weather stations they have anemometers to measure the speed of the wind.' Mrs Baker gave her a puzzled look. Astrid went to pick up the bible, which the Last Man had thrown across the room. She dusted it off. 'Constance Battiscombe's poor little girl who died here? Her name was Anemone.'

'So that's a memorial carving then, is it?'

'What? No.' Astrid wondered why Mrs Baker always insisted on seeing the dark side. She'd always seen the carving as a little statement of a mother's joy, not a howl of grief.

Later, as they were sitting in the snug watching a quiz show with Mrs Baker barking out the answers well before the contestants, Astrid thought about the carving and wondered how she hadn't made the connection, in all these years, between it and the cherub in the churchyard.

For a long time after the Last Man left, they'd expected to meet the Madagascar hissing cockroach, or for him to come back to rescue his familiar. Fortunately, neither was seen again.

Mrs Baker must have forgotten about him, though, or she wouldn't be wearing his awful coat. Then again, perhaps she didn't care. She hadn't been afraid of the Last Man. Having lived with a man who posed a genuine threat to her life, she had a heightened instinct about when to be frightened, and when not to be.

'When I heard you screaming earlier, I thought we were being burgled,' Mrs Baker said.

'A burglar would be awfully disappointed if he came in here,' Astrid said. 'Unless he wants a taxidermised stoat.'

'There's all that old stuff still in the windmill, though, isn't there. People might have a go at that now the door's wide open.'

'Who'd want some damp old tapestries and a box of letters?'
'You never know.'

'We aren't selling anything else, don't even think about it.'
Astrid hated taking things out of the windmill. It always felt very
wrong. Charlie had once taken some of Constance's books to an
antiquarian bookshop and she'd gone and got them back. The
windmill had had enough stripped out of it already; it seemed
wicked to remove anything more.

Mrs Baker did sell the ceremonial swords, of course, but
they'd had no money then, absolutely none, and three thousand
pounds had been impossible to ignore. Plus, they'd belonged not
to Constance but to Captain Walter Battiscombe – a man who
had, to all accounts, loathed the windmill, or at the very least
not seen the point of it.

'You could think of it as the windmill giving back for a change,'
Mrs Baker had said, cleverly.

But nobody would want the remaining contents, the mouldy
old fabrics, the horsehair sofa, the rickety bits of furniture and
damp books, the bible, the frightening wooden crucifix, the
torn velvet curtain, the photo album, the tin of letters. None
of these objects had any monetary value, they were a random
collection, life frass. But they were all that was left of Constance –
particularly the letters. There were four bundles: the Walter
bundle, written by Constance to Walter (none of his letters to
her had survived); the Grieving Mother bundle, from the families of the American boys – Astrid had only managed to read
these through once and although a few were polite, thanking
Constance for a condolence letter, most were vicious, accusing
Captain Battiscombe of criminal ineptitude, even murder. Some
of the mothers (it was always the mothers who wrote) gave
heartbreaking details about their sons. One had lost twins, the

ship went down on their eighteenth birthday; another grieved
for the precious only child who she'd given birth to at the age of
forty-six, her 'gift from Jesus'. Then there was the Pious bundle,
from Constance's sister-in-law, Mary, and finally, the Outrage
bundle – from the Claycombe Parish Council, local societies,
mothers' groups. Astrid had organised them into these bundles
when she'd had the idea to write a book. She'd even spent a
day or two in the Imperial War Museum, looking into Captain
Walter Battiscombe's disastrous invention. It seemed that the
Captain had been at the vanguard of a short-lived trend for 'small
battleships'. His design had rather demonstrated why larger battleships were preferable.

There was one letter, though, that didn't fit into any bundle. It
was from a bishop, clearly a family friend, and had been written
soon after Walter's ship went down.

*You must not*, he wrote, *take your husband's errors as your own. Dearest
Connie, it is our tendency to feel guilt by association, to take responsibility for
the mistakes of those we love, but you must distance yourself from Walter's
errors – not outwardly, of course, but inwardly. His mistakes are not yours.
You are blameless, your soul is innocent and unstained.*

Astrid could only assume that the bishop had not heard about
the goings-on at the windmill, or about Constance's illegitimate
child.

In the end, she hadn't made a great deal of progress with the
book. She found that she entirely lacked the focus or diligence
for research and the bundles all went back into their tin.

Mrs Baker was looking at her now, eyebrows raised, as if waiting
for a response. Astrid was about to confess that her thoughts had
drifted to Constance, but stopped herself. The last thing Mrs
Baker needed at two in the morning after a fright was talk of
Constance Battiscombe and all the dead boys.

'Are you listening? That oak construction,' Mrs Baker said, impatiently. 'That might fetch something?'

'What oak construction?'

'The thing inside the windmill, Astrid, for cleaning the grain.'

'Could you mean the smutter?' There was no way Astrid would allow Mrs Baker to remove actual pieces of milling equipment, no matter how much they were worth. She'd rather starve to death. 'Nobody would want a contraption for getting fungus off wheat,' she said, firmly.

'But it's a curiosity, isn't it? It could be turned into a cabinet or something. People go for that sort of thing, don't they?'

'We aren't selling the *smutter*!' Astrid had learned the vocabulary of windmills from John Dean. She remembered him scratching a diagram into the dust with a stick to explain how the shaft and the massive wooden wheels, some of which had cogs the length of his forearm, would transmit the wind energy to turn the millstones, the runner stone circling over the bed stone, concave against convex, crushing the grain, forcing it along the runnels that the miller would regularly dress, honing the granite into clever geometric patterns. There was a name for those patterns, she recalled, something to do with scissoring. No – harps, that was it, the runnels cut into the millstones were called harps.

She remembered John Dean's big blunt fingers tracing the harps as he described how they were calibrated precisely by the miller to give different grinds. Here, you could insert a coin between the stones, and here, a piece of brown paper, and here – he ran his fingertip over the granite – the gap would be so tiny, the grind so fine, that you could slide only a piece of tissue paper between the stones. When she'd asked whether these patterns were called after the aeolian harp, he'd looked at her for a long time, smiling with his lovely brown eyes. 'Maybe so, Astrid, maybe so.' Her belly turned molten as he put down his beer bottle, slowly, and held out his hand.

Some of the words she'd learned from John Dean were meaningful to her still, while others were no longer attached to anything, but she enjoyed them all the same: the star wheel, smutter and wallower, the hopper, shoe and damsel, the worm gear, cap, fantail, fan stage, the sweeps.

Mrs Baker was rubbing her knees, brow furrowed. Her frizzy hair, almost all grey now, was flattened on one side, her face shadows and jowls. She looked old, a tired, portly old person wrapped in the Last Man's coat, and Astrid felt a wave of protectiveness, followed by dismay. Mrs Baker was not supposed to be vulnerable – she was not supposed to be old, either. She felt the clock's eyes flick to her and back to Mrs Baker. Its plastic tail twitched from side to side, side to side, as she sipped the cold cocoa. Everything felt a bit off, muffled and floaty. The painkillers must be kicking in.

'Did you put the whole bag of sugar in this?' she said. 'It's dreadfully sweet. Quite undrinkable.'

Mrs Baker got up. 'Don't drink it then.' She held out her hand for the mug, and she was herself again, solid, huffy, brisk. Astrid felt the anxious, floaty sensation ease. The overcoat swung from Mrs Baker's broad hips as she stomped over to the sink and tipped the cocoa away. She began to wash up the milk pan then, furiously working the Brillo pad around the cast-iron base. Gordon lifted his head and watched as she plonked it upside down on the draining board.

'I'm sorry.' Astrid knew she'd been rude. 'That was ungrateful. I'm not at my best.'

Mrs Baker wiped her hands on a tea towel and turned. Her

voice was thick with concern. 'You shouldn't be up in the middle of the night when you've got to be at the airport tomorrow. You'll do yourself in.' She flipped the tea towel out and folded it in half, lengthwise.

Astrid pointed at the clock. 'It already is tomorrow.'

Mrs Baker looked at her, steadily. 'You don't have to go, you know.'

'Oh, but I do. I have a plane ticket. You said it yourself.'

'It's just sunk costs at the end of the day.'

'I must see him, Eileen.' The intensity of her voice caught her by surprise. She cleared her throat. 'I thought I'd threaten to sue,' she added, though the idea had only just popped into her head.

'Sue who? Magnus?' Mrs Baker's eyes widened. 'Magnus Fellowes the multi-millionaire national treasure?'

'The law does not discriminate, Mrs Baker.'

'Course it bloody does. And it definitely doesn't cover suing your ex for what you think he *might* write about you.'

'And at which university did you do your law degree?'

Mrs Baker tossed the tea towel aside. 'Listen, Astrid, I've gone along with this trip because I thought you wanted to see him one last time, but suing, that's just daft, even for you.'

'Why on earth would I *want* to see Magnus again?'

'To say goodbye, Astrid.'

'Goodbye? Are you mad? I said goodbye to Magnus forty-five years ago when he betrayed, publicly humiliated and abandoned me.'

Mrs Baker's intelligent eyes were steady. 'Did he, though?'

'What? Yes! You know he did!'

'It was you left him, though, wasn't it?' Mrs Baker came back and sat down again, heavily, in her chair. She puffed out her cheeks. 'Not to sound too touchy-feely or anything but I've

always had the feeling you've not really put him behind you.
All this talk about hate, it's two sides of the same coin, isn't it?
If you'd really put him behind you, he wouldn't bother you, not
like this, and he does, always has. Whenever his face crops up
on telly or in the newspaper or whatever you get all weird, like
you are now – no, hear me out, you know what I mean. You go
all daft for ages. Just look at you, you've whipped yourself into
a frenzy, heading for Scotland, screaming in your sleep, talking
about suing. I'm not blaming you, from what you've told me
it was all very complicated and whatnot, and you never sorted
it out.'

'What on earth!' Astrid shook her head. Everything felt outrageous and baffling.

Mrs Baker was still talking, 'That's the only reason I thought
it might be a good idea for you to go to Scotland: to say goodbye
one last time. I thought you might get – what do they call it? –
*closure*.'

'*Closure*?' Astrid had never heard Mrs Baker talk in this way
before. It was absurd; worse than absurd, it was disloyal. She
really *had* lost her mind. '*Closure? Closure?* I had *closure*, as you
call it, four decades ago when he hung me out to dry.' She felt
as if things were coming loose inside her, things that should
very much be nailed down. 'Honestly!' she cried. 'Closure! You
really must stop watching daytime television!'

Mrs Baker leaned forwards, her head on one side. 'Are you all
right? You've gone pale.'

'Because it's half past two in the morning, and you've turned
into Oprah Winfrey!'

There was a moment of silence, then Mrs Baker let out a snort.
Then Astrid began to laugh too, and Gordon stood up on her lap,
wriggling and leaping at her face, trying to lick her tears. Mrs

Baker flopped back first, defeated. 'God Almighty,' she wheezed. 'I'm too old for this.' Her thick, varicosed calves protruded from the awful coat. Astrid stopped laughing and wiped her face. She felt wrung out.

'Listen,' Mrs Baker said. 'This book of his. It doesn't matter. People want to read about the famous actor and his famous friends, Warren Beatty, Jack Nicholson, all that Hollywood malarkey. They don't care about something daft that happened with a nobody they've never heard of.'

'But it was an international scandal – you remembered it yourself when I first told you. You said you did.'

'Only because you reminded me. If I hadn't ended up stuck here with you, I'd have long forgotten about a bunch of bloody actors doing daft things to each other in a stately home forty years ago, believe me.'

'It was a Tudor hunting lodge and it was—'

'All I'm saying is, who's going to remember it now, really? Or care? Nobody, Astrid. That's who.'

'But a young woman died!' Astrid cried. '*Sally Morgan died!*'

'She was famous at the time, I grant you, but no one remembers her now, do they? Or you, for that matter.'

'I was in every newspaper, me, my face, everywhere. I was on the *Nine O'Clock News* twice in a row. You have no idea what it feels like to be villainised like that. Everyone, and I mean everyone, turned against me. They said I was mad, perverted and jealous – and dangerous, too, a dangerous, jealous lunatic with blood on my hands. People screamed abuse at me from the auditorium. I've never felt more alone in my life. I had to leave the country, I had to run away for *three years*. It was ... it was *unspeakable*. And it was his fault. He was weak and selfish, he abandoned me, he stitched me up, him and that despicable predator, Jack

Rohls.' Astrid rearranged Gordon's collar and tried to smooth the curls under it but her fingers, knotted and swollen, were shaking and wouldn't bend.

'It was bad for you, Astrid, I do know that.' Mrs Baker's voice was quieter now, compassionate. 'But it was forty years ago. You've got to let it go now.'

'Forty-five years,' Astrid cried. 'Almost forty-six!' Gordon raised his snout, and Astrid looked into his dear, worried eyes. She felt very cold as if she'd been standing out on the hills. She might as well have been – there was a draught coming down the hall, the November air pushing through the gaps around the front door, which was warping now too, just as the door to the windmill had been before it was smashed open by a hunk of medieval marble. It would be the cottage next, the walls, the floorboards. She imagined the entire structure folding in on itself like damp origami. The wind hustled the brick tower above them, and Astrid heard a ghostly whistle somewhere in the pipes of the Rayburn, or the radiators, or the pockets of air inside the brickwork, between the roof tiles, running through the hollows in the mortar. She was genuinely not sure that they'd make it through another winter. Something had to give.

*22nd March 1920*

*Dearest Walter,*

Well, the millwright, Harvey Dean, came last week with the sweeps he built over the winter – they are vast and so heavy. It took Dean and his men two days to fix them on. The day they finished was clear, bright and cold, and we all climbed up the windmill. Mr Dean is a big, kind, quiet man, who always wears a woollen hat on the back of his head and keeps a pipe clamped between his teeth. His little boy, a sweet chap of about seven years old, was also there, and solemnly helped his father to oil the front and rear windshaft bearings. Then Mr Banks eased the chocks from the brake-wheel spokes and, when he gave the signal, I tugged with all my might on the brake rope.

The windmill creaked and groaned terribly, and then, after fourteen shackled years, the brake released and slowly the fantail caught the breeze, and then the cap began to turn, inching round above our heads. The noise was extraordinary, quite deafening, a scraping, moaning, screeching. Debris and stagnant rainwater tumbled out of the windshaft as the sweeps caught the wind and began to turn, and then it all started to move – inside, the parts rained woodworm frass, little chunks of rust, spiders' webs, dead insects, feathery shards and tiny mouse skulls that the owl had concealed.

When we were certain that all was well, Mr Banks and I rushed back down with Mr Dean's little boy nimbly leading the way and we all stood outside with Miss Jones and the men, watching as the sweeps turned.

As they picked up speed the bearings began to warm, the joints softened, and the terrible screeching lessened. Soon the sweeps were making a gentle whooshing sound as they passed, and although the windmill's body and insides still creaked and cried, there was such delight in the sounds, such power, even though the grinding mechanism itself is gone, and a sense of tremendous liberty. Harvey's little boy called it the 'magic mill' and it really did feel magical – both static and in whirling motion – the most wonderful, exhilarating sight.

I discovered something curious too: the sweeps turn backwards (anticlockwise). This took me by surprise. And as I watched, it seemed to me as if each reverse pass was taking the windmill back through its memories, swooping through past moments which caused it to sigh and weep and laugh and cry out with pain, or regret, or joy, or delight – or perhaps all those things in close succession.

I have a strong sense that it was glad to be liberated after so long alone, neglected, dismissed and shackled. It is content to be useful – useful to us, that is, and loved again, I really do feel that. Even though it can no longer grind, it can offer shelter and harness the wind, and turn its sweeps to delight us, and that, truly, is enough.

I will stop now. I am quite carried away tonight, and I know it is hard to understand, when you are in such a different place, but I do wish you could be here and then perhaps you would understand.

I suppose your silence (I have not had a letter since late January?) is because of the post but I hope you are well and happy, dear, and that there is great progress for you, too. You will build the finest small battleship all the world has ever seen, I am sure of that.

Your C

# Chapter 8

The X-ray tunnel sucked in the bags, one after another. Astrid watched her dull black carry-on case vanish down the belt towards the dark mouth. They'd bought the case for £5 in Help the Aged because Mrs Baker had deemed Astrid's carpet bag 'unusable'.

'What in God's name is that?' she'd said when Astrid brought it out of the wardrobe.

Astrid had been expecting this. 'It was handmade in Tangiers, Mrs B. Timeless craftsmanship. The embroidery, look, and this sturdy leather bottom, still solid as a rock.'

Mrs Baker folded her arms. 'You can't take that thing to Scotland.'

'Why on earth not?' The fabric part of the bag was a little moth-eaten, well-worn from her years on the road, but it was roomy, and perfectly functional if you popped a bin bag inside it.

'It's too big for hand luggage. It's also got bloody great holes in it. Look, there – and there. And it stinks' – Mrs Baker sniffed it – 'like a dead Labrador.' She heaved it out. 'It weighs about the same as a dead Labrador too. How would you even lift it? For God's sake, be practical for once in your life.'

Mrs Baker had won this battle, of course; she almost always did win such small battles, not because she was better at arguing but simply because she cared more about things like this, and also, perhaps, because Astrid, on some level, knew that she needed to be reined in. The Help the Aged case was horribly ordinary, but now that it was in the hands of strangers, she was rather glad of that. She was also glad of its wheels. She'd very much like to phone Mrs Baker to tell her this. She now regretted her refusal to take the mobile phone. 'I don't need a phone,' she'd said, as they got into the car and Mrs Baker pressed it into her hands.

'You will in an emergency.'

'What emergency?'

'Just take it.'

'But if I take it, you won't have a phone. What if *you* have an emergency? Or the dogs?'

'Then I can go down to the village, can't I?' She shoved the phone into Astrid's handbag but when she wasn't looking, Astrid slid it back into the pocket of the Last Man's coat, which Mrs Baker was, bizarrely, still wearing.

She hadn't been wearing it when Nina came, though, thank goodness. She'd had on the sleeveless padded thing she'd got in Oxfam fifteen years previously. Astrid herself had been wearing her silver metallic duvet coat, also £5, and also from Help the Aged. As they sat in the garden waiting for Mrs Baker to bring out coffee and cake, Nina had admired it. When she explained about the Lewes charity shops, Nina said, 'Didn't Virginia Woolf live in Lewes?' And they'd talked a bit about Rodmell and Monk's House and Charleston, which Astrid and Mrs Baker had visited a few times, in the days when they used to go out in Gloria for daytrips. As they talked, Nina's eyes kept straying back to the windmill. 'Could it still grind?' she said.

'The windmill? Oh no, it hasn't done that since 1910. It sat empty for a while, then it was used to house prisoners of war, and they stripped out some of the mechanism to make room for the men. Then it was turned into a home in the 1920s.'

'Yes, I've read about Lady Battiscombe. Didn't she run some sort of artists' colony up here?'

'Oh, not quite. But I believe she may have been on the fringes of the Bloomsbury set – only the very fringes, though.'

Nina sat up straighter. 'Do you think Virginia Woolf came here?'

'I have no idea. It's possible, I suppose. All sorts did.'

Mrs Baker was unloading the tray. The coffee pot looked ridiculous, ornate, tarnished almost black and very precarious. What was she thinking? Astrid hoped that she'd at least rinsed it out. It swayed against the cups and plates, which rattled against the cakes. Nina leaped up to help her, and Hendricks gave a snarl. Nina froze. 'Don't mind him,' Mrs Baker said. 'Just ignore him and he'll lose interest.' Nina reached for the pot. 'I've got it,' Mrs Baker sounded short. The table listed left, and Nina grabbed its edge with her good hand. She reached out again to lift the cups and saucers off the tray, and again Hendricks gave a soft warning growl. 'Leave it,' Mrs Baker snapped. It wasn't entirely clear who she was talking to, but Hendricks stopped growling, and Nina sat back down.

Mrs Baker had a thing about helpers. When she'd first arrived at the cottage, in 1999, she'd swiftly taken charge of almost everything. For a while Astrid had tried to do some domestic things, but eventually, on a day when she'd dropped the cheese soufflé into the dogs' basket, got distracted while washing up and left the sink running so it flooded the kitchen, then forgotten, again, to close the chicken coop, Mrs Baker had put her foot down. 'I'm used to doing things my way,' she said. 'You're paying me to look after you, so you need to let me get on with it.' Astrid, who until that moment had had no clear idea why Mrs Baker was still at the windmill, had stepped aside then, gladly.

It was a golden time, in many ways, those first ten years or so – Astrid's sixties. There was still Charlie's money left, so financial pressures were minimal, and with Mrs Baker taking care of things around the house, Astrid had passed her time doing things she enjoyed – reading poetry aloud, listening to radio plays, taking long daily walks on the Downs, knitting small animals and canine jerkins. It was around this time that she'd had the idea of writing up the history of the windmill and had organised the letters, but she really was a useless historian. She was no good at ordering information and libraries filled her with gloom – a harsh reminder of everything she would never know. She had no aptitude for research and would get muddled by her own notes. She also had a tendency to go off on tangents. This was how she'd revived her interest in the *I Ching*. And then taken up Tarot. She'd called herself 'Madame Savoy' and put a notice in the paper, mainly for something to do on Saturdays when Mrs Baker was up in London with her daughter. She spent a lot of time scouring charity shops, putting together elaborate outfits which she'd accessorise with Bedouin jewellery and kohl around her eyes. Word of mouth spread, and soon Madame Savoy was doing weddings and hen nights and balls and corporate events. She met so many interesting people. Many were bereaved, or troubled, sometimes by odd things: one woman at the chartered accountants' annual ball, a plump, shy, frightened little person, awfully ordinary looking, whispered that she kept waking in the night to find the ghost of a Bichon Frise on the pillow next to her.

Mrs Baker plunged a knife into the Battenburg – everything wobbled. Nina steadied the table and glanced down at its legs, which were uneven, with long fissures in the greyish timber, aged like elephant skin. Diplomatically, she accepted slices of both cakes, saying that while she loved marzipan, she also had a soft spot for jam sponge. She even asked how Mrs Baker made it so light. 'It's fresh eggs.' Mrs Baker's cheeks pinked. 'Proportions too. You weigh two eggs, put in the same weight of flour and sugar.'

Astrid felt buoyant as she watched Mrs Baker pour from the coffee pot, which seemed to have come into its own; it appeared almost to preen, despite its tarnished coat, as if it was delighted to rediscover its proper purpose. The table looked festive, too, with the cakes, a blue-sprigged jug of milk, all the crockery, and their nice appreciative guest. It was so uplifting, so very unexpected. She'd quite forgotten how much she enjoyed meeting new people. She had no idea now why she'd felt so panicked in the kitchen when the doorbell rang. Lack of practice, probably, and perhaps also the fact that the last person to come into the windmill had just been released from prison.

Holding up the cake knife, Mrs Baker squeezed onto the bench by Astrid. The whole structure shuddered, there was a terrible creak and a gentle cracking sound and for a moment it seemed sure to collapse. *Two old ladies under a table*, Astrid thought. *With a knife.* But Mrs Baker moved her weight just in time, just the correct amount to counterbalance the sway, and somehow it all righted itself. Nina's brows were knitted. Hendricks gave a panicky squirm and Astrid let him down. Gordon spread himself out, resting against her torso like a baby, front paws curled to his chest. Nina said, 'He's adorable.'

'Gordon? Isn't he? He's terribly insecure, though. Unlike Hendricks and Juniper.'

'I love their names. I'm guessing you're gin lovers?'

'Not really. I called my first dog after a gin and it sort of spi-ralled,' Astrid said. 'The truth is, we only drink bourbon, Jim Beam – Mrs Baker got a taste for it when it was on special offer once at Asda. We could have called Gordon Jim, of course, but it might have been confusing, and he'd have felt even more like an outsider.'

'So, are they all siblings?'

Astrid put her hands over Gordon's ears. 'Juniper and Hendricks are, they're the children of my previous dogs, Sapphire and Gilbert, but Gordon was a rescue. I got him at a funeral. His owner died, and he'd been abandoned – forgotten entirely, left to die in a shoebox, can you believe it.'

'More coffee?' Mrs Baker shouted.

Astrid hadn't said Sapphire's name in ages. It had been twelve years, but she still felt a wave of pain at the thought of poor Sapphy lying in her basket, with tiny Juniper and Hendricks wriggling and mewing at her dry teats – she'd had to bottle feed them afterwards. Losing Gilbert had been agony too, obviously, but of a different kind – less shocking than Sapphire's sudden, unexplained death. Astrid knew, of course, that Alan had done something to her when he came to the windmill that very first time – tracked them back, after Mellie's funeral. He must have slipped Sapphy something, though she had no proof of it. At least Gilbert had escaped. By the time he went, aged fifteen, he was blind, paranoid, incontinent, demented and scrofulous, the dear old soul.

Nina peered down the spout of the coffee pot and the sun went behind a cloud. Astrid thought of all her dead dogs, buried behind the windmill, each one beloved, lost and mourned. She felt the chill of winter enter her bones. 'Why did you come here?' she said to Nina, who looked up, startled. 'What is it that you *want*?'

*29th June 1920*

*Dearest Walter,*

*I am very sorry that you find my accounts of the windmill so infuriating. You must understand that it is hard for me to know what else to write about – or even what to ask you – since I have had so little information about your life in America. You could be in Timbuktu for all you tell me. But I do not wish to squabble. I do understand that your work is secret and that it is hard to find time for letter writing. However, you must, in return, understand that this is why I tell you so much about the windmill. It is my life.*

*I could tell you how we have managed to install a stove. Or that Miss Jones is now in her new quarters, or that there is a female barn owl living in the cap, a sort of pallid ghost that I sometimes glimpse, wings outstretched, hunting in the dark; or that I feel safe and protected here, even as the wind slams against the tower. I could tell you that Daphne, my artist friend, has brought people to see me at the windmill – colourful, exuberant people – and that she has been taking me around with her, too; that a fortnight ago, we attended a party at a country house not far away where there was a séance and one man strongly felt the presence of his beloved Great Dane; or that next week we are up to London for an exhibition of the oddest works, by a 'Surrealist' painter Daphne knows from her time at the Slade School.*

*However, since my life is such an irritating subject for you, I must send accounts of other things instead.*

*I know you'd like me to give you news of London society, so I will try. Eleanor Jarvis had a baby last month – or perhaps it was*

Sophia Jarvis, I cannot remember. I also received news that Daisy Simpson, who you remember rejected poor Sheridan, is engaged to be married (sadly I do not remember her fiancé's name, I believe he is not somebody we know). Hetty Anderson was unwell but has fully recovered. Other than this, I confess, I am somewhat out of touch.

I shall bring better news of people you know soon. Next week I go to Oxfordshire to visit Sheridan and Mary, and Mary, as you know, always has so much to say.

Your C

# Chapter 9

She needed to phone home before she got on the plane. Specifically, she needed to know that Mrs Baker was still at the windmill. Usually, she found their daft bickerings and stand-offs rather entertaining. Even when they were genuinely furious with each other, and they often were, one of them – almost always Astrid – would give in soon enough, say something funny, offer the other a dignified exit. The way they'd parted outside the airport, though, with Mrs Baker's bitter words ringing in her ears, was unnerving. Her own comment about payment had been ludicrous. She had tapped a deep, suppressed high-handedness, the product of her childhood. She had no idea that even a tiny part of her was infected by her mother still – she certainly did not think of Mrs Baker as staff. The last time the two of them had had a row about money was when they were doing the funerals, and even that wasn't really about the money, as such.

She'd given up being Madame Savoy by then, having run out of tolerance for demanding, drunk clients, groping men and mockery. They'd given up the bed and breakfast too, and had been trying – increasingly desperately – to think of other ways to make money. It was Mrs Baker who'd come across the advert in the *Evening Argus*. She came into the snug one afternoon brandishing the pages. By then she'd let go of the quaint notion that employment needed to be respectable.

'Are you sensitive, versatile and over seventy?' she asked.

'I certainly am.' Astrid tossed aside the crossword.

Mrs Baker peered over her specs. 'You're the least discreet person I know, Astrid, and as for sensitive and versatile . . .' She grimaced. 'But they're asking for trained actors in their seventies.' She held out the paper.

### Discreet Mourners
#### – Their loss is your gain –

Astrid looked at her. 'Whose loss is my gain?'

'Funerals, Astrid. Fake mourning. You pretend to be a grieving relative. I remember reading about it at the dentist that time when you had to have your extractions. You can earn fifty to a hundred quid per funeral, plus travel.'

'The dentist is hiring mourners?'

Mrs Baker stared at her. 'No – what?'

'Are you saying Mr Singh wants to hire me to *mourn him*?'

'God Almighty, Astrid. Forget Singh. This has nothing to do with dentists. It's the relatives of dead people, they hire the mourner agency, and the mourner agency hires actors.'

Astrid, out of her depth, began to feel irritable. 'What on earth are you talking about?'

'A job, Astrid. I'm talking about a job as a fake mourner.'

'The theatre?'

'God Almighty, Astrid! Real funerals!'

'But why on earth . . . ?'

Mrs Baker shrugged. 'Nobody wants an empty church.'

'But that's . . . that's *dishonest*.'

'They do it in other cultures. It's normal in China.'

'A lot of things are normal in China that I wouldn't dream of doing.' She tried to think what the Chinese might do that she wouldn't, but knew nothing about China and could only come up with eating monkey brains and persecuting Uyghur Muslims.

'In other cultures, it's normal for professional mourners to wail and crawl behind the coffin. It helps other people get their emotions out, sort of thing, you know, lose their inhibitions and cry or whatnot. It's perfectly respectable. Quite helpful, really.'

'My crawling days are over, Mrs Baker. You know what my knees are like.'

'There's no crawling involved. You just have to grieve.'

'No one would know I'm an actor?'

'Exactly. You could do it in your sleep. All you have to do is put on a black dress and look sad for a few hours, and you get a hundred quid. Plus travel.'

'But what sort of person hires *mourners*?'

'Who cares? There's no shame in sending a loved one off with dignity, is there? All funerals need criers.' Mrs Baker looked down at the newspaper. A shadow seemed to pass over her, and her shoulders slumped, and Astrid knew that she was thinking about Mellie's funeral.

It had been six years since Mellie died and Mrs Baker still hadn't talked about the funeral. Mellie's friends had all come down from London, about twenty of them, bringing pan pipes and drums and dogs on strings. They wore colourful knitwear, had piercings and tattoos, and had mourned openly, with full hearts. The crematorium smelled of patchouli, alcohol, stale cigarettes, marijuana, damp dog, woodsmoke, unwashed wool. They were demonstrative, and so terribly kind. A tiny, thin, sprightly Irishman in a military overcoat with brass buttons seemed to have appointed himself as the officiator. Someone explained that he was a shaman. He showed them to their seats at the crematorium and asked if they'd come to the ceremony in the woods after. Mrs Baker muttered that they'd probably just go home. Everyone was weeping and holding each other. Astrid hadn't seen such deep collective emotion in one place since her theatre days. She was glad that Mrs Baker's daughter had had so much love in her life, even if she hadn't had a proper home. It struck her then that the only mourners at her own funeral would be Mrs Baker and the dogs.

There was only one person in the crematorium who was not weeping. Astrid spotted him at the back and knew instantly who it was. She had no idea how he'd found out about Mellie since Mellie had cut off all contact with Alan at the age of eighteen. He was sitting very still, watching Mrs Baker with a dead-eyed stare that made the hairs on the back of Astrid's neck stand up. He was not a big man, she saw, but he was thickset, with a broad face and small darting eyes that rested on puffy eyebags. His black, open-necked shirt stretched across his shoulders and his skin was tanned, far too tanned for England; Mrs Baker's theory that he had been living in Spain ever since the Slipper Robbery might be correct. His hair was cropped to the skull.

Mrs Baker, thankfully, hadn't noticed him. For once, she wasn't alert. Her eyes were down, and she clasped a wadge of tissues. Astrid reached out and folded both hands over hers, holding them tight while the Irishman spoke about Mellie in a husky, booming voice that gave his slight form substance, made him taller – Astrid saw that he would be a fine actor. Mellie's troubles, the shaman said, had never dimmed her spirit. He talked about her two loves: her dog, Bennie, and her mum. He fixed bright eyes on Mrs Baker. 'You were always her hero, Mrs Stonehouse.

She knew what you'd sacrificed for her. You couldn't save her, none of us could, but you tried, and you loved her more than anything in the world – she knew that.'

Astrid sat up straight. Stonehouse? She stared at Mrs Baker's profile, her bowed head, her reddened nose. She had always known that Mrs Baker wasn't really Mrs Baker – in an odd way, this was why she'd kept on calling her Mrs Baker; it had always felt like a nickname – it *was* a nickname. Astrid had never challenged her about her real name; to do so would have felt intrusive, even confrontational. Mrs Baker had very good reasons for being Mrs Baker, she did know that, but hearing the unfamiliar name, Stonehouse, in the crematorium, on the tongue of a shaman, had been, momentarily, a shock. Then she realised that perhaps Stonehouse wasn't her name either, perhaps it was Alan's.

Mrs Baker gave the *Evening Argus* a little shake under Astrid's nose. 'Think of the money, Astrid.'

So, Astrid phoned Discreet Mourners. She mentioned her time at RADA, the RSC and the Audrey Hepburn film. 'It was a very small part,' she admitted. 'I only had a few lines.'

'Oh. My. God. You knew Audrey Hepburn?'

'Well, I only—'

She wanted to know what Audrey was like. 'Was she nice? Was she as lovely in real life? How did she stay so skinny?' Astrid mentioned that Audrey had let her borrow her make-up artist. Audrey Hepburn had, in fact, been the least important thing at the time because it was on that silly, boring shoot in the south of France that she'd first encountered Magnus. Initially, she'd avoided him. He was too charismatic, too popular with the other girls, not handsome in a classical way, exactly, but more devastating because of that – solid-featured, broad-shouldered, with intense, pale grey Celtic eyes and that big laugh; a terrible show-off. All the girls fell for him, and he showed no restraint. Astrid made up her mind to loathe him, but they ended up travelling through France in the same car, crammed into the back seat with a girl who talked all the time, and their bodies had fizzed against each other, electric. After that, they were never apart. Until, of course, they were.

It was a risk to mention the Royal Shakespeare Company, and RADA, but the Discreet Mourners woman failed to link Astrid Miller, Audrey Hepburn's Friend One, with the Astrid Fellowes who had been at the centre of a scandal in the 1970s and had gone mad on stage at the National, midway through a matinee of Macbeth.

A few days later, a package arrived containing the Discreet Mourners welcome pack. There were 'Tips for Preparation', the first of which was 'DO YOUR RESEARCH!!!' It was important to know 'everything' about the deceased. A checklist was provided, including 'middle name, pet names, nicknames'. There were also 'Ten Rules for Decorum', the first of which was: 'Never fraternise with other Discreet Mourners. The temptation to share your stories will be overwhelming.'

A week later, the woman called with details of a booking in Chichester. 'How's your American accent?' she said. It was a seventy-five-year-old golfing agent who had fallen out with just about everyone he'd ever known before dying of pancreatic cancer. His favourite nephew, the only relative he'd not disowned, feared an embarrassingly low turnout and wanted to honour his uncle, whose considerable estate he was inheriting. The nephew suggested that Astrid play the part of a cousin from Ohio. He would be happy, she said, to brief her himself, over the phone.

Astrid's American accent was, in fact, variable – there had been little call for American accents at the RSC. She spent most of the golfer's funeral trying to work out which of the guests were real and which were fellow Discreet Mourners. She concluded that those who gave too much detail about the deceased, who threw in middle names or hobbies, and who ate greedily at the wake, which was lavishly catered, were Discreet. She made sure to say little and eat almost nothing; she channelled the grief so effectively that it almost overcame her, physically, and at one point she had to step out of the room. She found herself in a small drawing room where she heard a distraught, faint, high-pitched keening. For a moment she thought it was inside her head, but it kept on – it was real. She searched the room and eventually found a shoebox under a side table. Inside, was a tiny, starved puppy, a miniature wire-haired dachshund, a little scrap, lying on sodden newspaper, its fur matted with excrement. It looked up and gave a faint wag. The nephew appeared in the doorway. 'What the hell are you doing? I'm not paying you to sit in another bloody room!' Astrid turned with the shoebox, and the man, seeing her horror, grew suddenly shame-faced, and hung his head like a naughty schoolboy. 'The neighbour was going to have it but she's allergic. I meant to get rid of it, but the funeral . . .' Astrid took off her scarf and wrapped it around the stinking, shaking pup who nestled close to her, whimpering. He was so small and tremulous, a quiver of sparrow bones. 'I'm leaving now,' she said. 'And I'm taking him with me.'

She was so shaken that she had to be helped to the car by a man who claimed to be the deceased's golfing buddy – clearly Discreet, though, gratifyingly, he obviously believed her to be real.

The next day, the Discreet Mourners woman rang. Astrid expected a reprimand but the woman said that the client had been so delighted that he'd offered a £50 bonus – to Astrid alone. 'We've never had that before.' She sounded excitable. 'It must be your classical training.' Astrid, who'd been up all night feeding Gordon with a pipette, was so surprised that she agreed to a heart attack in Basildon the following week.

The mourning was, in fact, trickier than it sounded. It wasn't just a question of stagey weeping at the back of a church. The acting required significant research, sometimes several phone calls with the client for background information, and then a dramatic performance sustained over many hours. Astrid had never thought before how funerals are primarily social events. Much of the job involved making suitable conversation, for which she had to have answers, convincing anecdotes – details, dates, names – all whilst conveying the subtle instability of grief, whether mournful nostalgia, deep fragility, deadened shock or simply a dignified, dour solemnity. It was vital to get the tone right.

Each funeral took on an energy or personality of its own, influenced by the mourners, both real and Discreet. Some were demonstrative occasions, calling for a more open style of mourning – sobbing, volume – while others were almost silent, requiring a stiff upper lip. They weren't all Christian ceremonies, either. One was Buddhist and Astrid, despite a lot of research, had struggled to keep up with the quick, irregular tonal shifts, the jags of crying, then silence, then prayer. There were physical hazards to contend with too. At a natural woodland burial she stood in the rain for an hour and came down with a bad chill; she was in bed for a week, with Mrs Baker bringing her broth and paracetamols.

It was difficult not to be swept up in the sad poignancy of a life's end, and Astrid came to see her role less as a deception than a service. She noticed that, just as it had on stage, her performance would unlock emotion in others – the Chinese, it turned out, were on to something. Guests would gravitate to her, sharing secrets about the deceased. Often, she found herself comforting people as they spoke of guilt or regrets. This stopped the role from feeling too grubby but even so, as she drove home, she would feel herself deflate a bit and sometimes this flat sensation would last for days.

The deceased were never terribly old, that was part of the problem. A limited number of mourners would, after all, be normal at funerals for the very elderly. Most were for people who were younger than her, only in the hinterlands of old age, and each booking told its own sad story of grudge-holding, misunderstandings, lost opportunities, dysfunction or vitriol. She began to recognise fellow Discreet Mourners too; subtle nods were exchanged. Outside a harrowing suicide in Wiltshire the deceased's carer grabbed Astrid's arm and hissed, 'I just got his fucking name wrong and that man there, that major with the red face, thinks I'm a con artist. He's threatening to call the police. You've got to back me up.' Astrid broke away, appalled, but at the wake she found herself standing next to the suspicious red-faced major, and made a point of praising the carer's devotion.

Later, the major followed her to the loos and seized her arm, his eyes pink with unshed tears. He tried to speak, but couldn't.

'*Give sorrow words*,' she said. '*The grief that does not speak knits up the o-er wrought heart and bids it break.*'

He looked confused.

'Shakespeare,' she added. '*Macbeth*.'

'Yes.' His fingers tightened on her wrist. 'God. Yes!' And then he leaned closer and, in a strangled voice, said, 'He was the love of my life.' He wept, then, and she took him in her arms and held him, until he had gathered himself back up.

The desire to exchange stories with the fake carer in the car park afterwards was, as the Discreet Mourners woman had warned, almost overwhelming.

The driving was the hardest bit of all, though. Astrid had never been comfortable at the wheel of a car. She couldn't entirely remember whether she'd ever actually taken a driving test, and Gloria was a cumbersome vehicle, emitting mysterious sounds and disquieting smells of burning oil, rot, halitosis. The power steering was long gone, if it had ever existed, so parking was hellish and the fumes, after a long day, could be soporific. After one particularly gruelling drive back from Basildon, where she re-entered the M25 in the wrong direction and found herself near Cambridge, Mrs Baker became the chauffeur.

The car journeys after that were better, but it wasn't long before Mrs Baker was arguing that she, too, should become a Discreet Mourner. 'I might not be seventy but I'm discreet, and I'm coming anyway, aren't I, so there's no point me just sitting out in the car when I could be earning cash in there with you.'

Astrid found the economics of this difficult to argue with. She felt she might even rather enjoy showing Mrs Baker the ropes, having company inside the churches and crematoriums and pub rooms. Sadly, this turned out not to be the case.

Mrs Baker told the Discreet Mourners woman that she had years of amateur acting experience, which was, in a sense, true. Their first joint booking was a wealthy pigeon fancier from West Wittering who'd devoted his life to his birds. He had sat alone in his detached home for decades sewing beautiful, intricate pigeon costumes, which he kept in small oak wardrobes. Some of the garments were displayed at the wake: little knights and princesses, goblins and faeries. He had suffered a slow and painful decline after a locum GP, unaware of his pigeon obsession, misdiagnosed inflammation of the alveoli as late-onset asthma. He'd alienated most of his family by then, and had no friends, but his only son was devoted, and couldn't bear the idea of an empty church. 'Dad's only crime,' he told Astrid on the phone, 'was that he preferred pigeons to people.'

There was a handful of genuine mourners in the church that cold spring day, plus a few distant, but hopeful, relatives and at least ten moirologists, possibly more. Astrid was an old school friend over from Australia while Mrs Baker, unwisely in Astrid's view, had opted to be a pigeon fancier. She'd spent long hours on the library computers beforehand, and in the car her conversation had circled around rollers, tumblers and tippers. Astrid, sitting in the passenger seat with all three dogs shedding hairs onto her black dress, had a bad feeling. 'If you go too far,' she said, 'people are going to smell a rat.'

'No one thinks about fake mourners, Astrid.'

'"If you're not judicious, they get suspicious."' Astrid quoted the Discreet Mourners welcome pack. 'People have heightened instincts at funerals.'

Her doubts, as it turned out, were misplaced. Mrs Baker pitched her act brilliantly. She sobbed in the church and sang hymns in a bracing soprano. Astrid had never heard her sing before, or sob like this, and she felt that she was seeing a hidden part of Mrs Baker, a part capable of deceit, which had always, until that moment, been theoretical. She ate too many sausages at the wake, which was both irritating and reassuring, while offering well-chosen and convincing anecdotes underpinned by an impressive fact-based knowledge of pigeons. She was so convincing that even Astrid found herself sucked in, and when she overheard Mrs Baker saying to the vicar, 'It's not just pigeons, it's parakeets, cockatiels, poultry, even budgerigars have been implicated,' she had the uncomfortable feeling that she was being upstaged.

As they walked across the car park, she felt more overwrought and upset than usual, and she had no idea why. They drove a little way and then pulled over in a layby to let the dogs sniffle and pee. Mrs Baker talked the whole time without drawing breath, and Astrid recognised post-performance adrenalin. 'That son, though, are they always like that? In the church he kept hissing at me to cry harder. Did he do that to you? I was bloody bawling by the end.'

Astrid said nothing. Her own tears had been perfectly pitched. No relative had ever offered her stage directions. She really was exhausted. They got back into the car.

'Stupid bugger, anyone could have overheard him. *Cry harder. Cry more!*' Mrs Baker laughed, and Gloria veered towards the verge. She was driving like a lunatic, entirely out of character for a woman who, as far as Astrid knew, had never so much as broken a speed limit.

'They get nervous,' Astrid said. 'Would you slow down?'

'I suppose grief takes people in different ways.' Mrs Baker attempted to overtake a coach just as the dual carriageway funnelled to single lane. She pulled back in, just in time, straightened her arms against the steering wheel and blew out through her mouth. 'All I could think about was those poor bloody pigeons, with their little costumes. Gassed by the council, the vicar said.'

The engine roared as Mrs Baker pushed Gloria onwards, round corners and roundabouts. It was getting dark as Arundel Castle reared up against a priestly purple sky. 'What's the matter with you then?' Mrs Baker turned to her. 'You've gone quiet. Are you all right?' But a fox was in the road. It saw their headlights and froze, eyes luminous, fathomless, facing down its doom. Astrid screamed, seized the door handle, as if she might fling herself to safety and Mrs Baker swerved without braking, missing the animal by a whisker, spilling the dogs sideways from Astrid's lap onto the gearstick. And then Hendricks was in the foot-well, scrabbling at Mrs Baker's feet, and there was a moment of frenzied grappling as the car swerved. 'Get him out!' Mrs Baker bellowed. 'Get that bloody dog out!'

'You've turned into a maniac, Eileen!' Astrid shouted when she'd got all the dogs back onto her lap and Mrs Baker had regained control of the vehicle. 'You're drunk with power! You dominated that funeral!'

'I – what?'

'You were neither discreet *nor* sensitive!'

'What? Me? Why?' She turned her head and, for a moment, looked genuinely hurt.

'Keep your eyes on the road, dear God, look where you're going.'

'Stop shouting.'

'It was shattering.' Astrid felt suddenly tearful. 'Keeping tabs on you all day. It was draining. Dreadful!'

'What are you on about? That was the most fun I've had in years.'

'You were a stranger to me.'

'Yes, well, I thought that was the point. I was pretending to be a bloody pigeon fancier.' Mrs Baker's cheeks had gone very pink. 'You were pretending too.'

'I wasn't pretending, I was *acting*.'

Mrs Baker glanced at her, crossly. 'What's the difference?'

'Sausages.' Astrid flailed. 'You ate far too many sausages!'

'You *what?*'

'I warned you about that, didn't I? I said, don't eat too much at the wake. Fake mourners can never resist the free buffet, and what did you do . . .' Astrid felt quietly vindicated then, and felt herself calm down a bit. Mrs Baker might be able to produce tears on demand, she might be able to dissemble and she might possess an above average recall of facts, but that did not make her an actor.

The agency woman phoned the next day to say that the son had been very happy, but Astrid's heart was no longer in mourning, if it ever had been. She told Mrs Baker that she was done with moirology. There would be no more funerals.

Mrs Baker was not ready to quit, though. The money was too good, she said. Where else would they, together, earn £200 for a single day's work, and have a free, all you can eat buffet thrown in? They bickered about this as they drove back from the petrol station the next day with two pints of milk, the *Radio Times* and an extravagant box of Lindor truffles.

Astrid was still rattled, on some level, by the previous day. She couldn't quite get over seeing Mrs Baker as a pigeon fancier. It was as if a barrier had sprung up between them, one that, perhaps, had always been there, but had only just made itself known. Ever since that first day, when Mrs Baker had stood in Charlie's study and Astrid had seen the look of relief on her face, it had been clear that she was haunted. Over the years, small details of her past had emerged, and Astrid had felt nothing but admiration for the strength it must have taken her to endure all those years, not to mention the courage to vanish, change her name, start a new life. She particularly admired how Mrs Baker had managed, for ten years, to see Mellie, even though Alan could at any moment have come back from Spain, tracked Mellie down and ambushed them both.

It was clear that Mrs Baker had endured a great deal of pain, both physical and mental, but this was the first time Astrid had been forced to confront exactly what it must have taken for her to survive in that house in St Leonard's. She would have had to act all the time; to calibrate, precisely, the reaction she needed from her audience of one in order to keep him under control, as much as she possibly could.

'What about the money?' Mrs Baker said, as they pulled into the courtyard and Gloria sputtered to a halt.

'Not everything's about money.'

'Only people with money say things like that.'

Astrid turned her head, crossly, but Mrs Baker didn't. Her profile, with her double chin, ruddy cheeks, wiry curls, exuded dismissal. 'I don't have any money!' Astrid shouted.

Mrs Baker did turn, then. Her eyes had a no-nonsense look. 'Because you gave it all away.'

'But I gave it away for you! For us!'

'And a fat lot of good that did anyone.' Mrs Baker wrenched the key out of the ignition and started to get out.

'Most people would accept sixteen thousand pounds to go away for ever,' Astrid shouted at Mrs Baker's bottom.

She turned and leaned back in. 'What do you know, Astrid? You grew up in Hampshire, your dad was landed gentry, you bought yourself a bloody windmill. What do you know about poverty?'

'It wasn't Hampshire, it was Berkshire, my father drowned himself, and my mother gave away all his money.'

'Runs in the family then. People like you think if you give someone enough money, you can control them.' She gave a bitter laugh. 'With Alan, that's like giving a hungry dog a biscuit and waving a big juicy bone. He's going to eat the biscuit, he isn't going to turn that down, but he won't leave you alone till he's got the bloody bone too.'

'But I gave him the bone! You know I did. I gave him everything I had.'

'I know,' she said. 'But Alan doesn't, does he? All Alan sees is a posh old lady in a bloody windmill, a cash cow. We're just lucky he got himself arrested right after Mellie's funeral, that saved us, but you know the first thing he's going to do when he gets out of prison is come up here and—'

'But we've talked about all this, Eileen. He's not getting out for years, so we don't need to worry about it now, do we? He could die in jail. He could find God and reform. He could go senile, get cancer, anything. Plus, you still have the slippers, don't you? Isn't that the whole point of the slippers? While we've got them, he can't hurt us. We control *him*, not the other way round.'

Mrs Baker looked at her for a moment, resting both hands on the rim of the door without saying anything. Her eyes were almost glazed. Then she straightened, shut the car door and went inside.

Astrid sat for a moment, holding the milk, the *Radio Times*, the Lindor truffles. She felt shaken and confused. They were entirely at odds, for the first time in years, perhaps ever. A wall had sprung up between them and she didn't know how, but she felt it was her fault. And that seemed unfair. The argument wasn't about money, not really. She didn't know this version of Mrs Baker, granite-eyed, accusatory. It was hardly Astrid's fault that Alan had found out about Mellie's funeral and tracked them back to the windmill. It also seemed a bit unfair that by giving him every penny she had, she'd be accused of displaying an upper-class desire to dominate.

Mrs Baker wasn't in the kitchen. Astrid went and got the dog basket, the biscuit tin and some blankets, and stamped across the courtyard and up to the windmill, where she ensconced herself for the rest of the day. Mrs Baker didn't come out to get her, she never did when Astrid took herself off to the windmill like this. As she sat on the horsehair sofa, carpeted by dogs, listening to the creaks and groans and scuttlings, the intermittent thud of the wind against the tower – sounds which she knew as intimately as those of her own body – she felt herself settle. The noise of the wind, when she was inside the windmill, always reminded her how tiny, insignificant and fleeting life was. She was a speck blown in, and one day, she would be blown out again. But the wind itself was so much bigger – omnipresent, ever-changing, timeless. Neolithic settlers on the Downs would have felt it the same way she did – gusts that thudded against the body; gales that flattened the grass like an invisible hand; soothing, soft breezes stroking bare skin. After a while, she went and got Constance's letters out of the trunk and reread them all. Then she dozed. When she woke up, she was cold and stiff, and it was getting dark. High above her in the cap, the barn owl screeched at the coming night, and she heard all the evening movements in the tower, the rustlings and creaks, the activity of wood, insects, rodents, dust. She was hungry now, and dying for a cup of tea. Or a Jim. She felt that perhaps she'd never known Mrs Baker, not really. The fact that for the first eleven years she hadn't even known her real name suddenly felt monstrous.

'Why *did* you call yourself Baker?' she'd asked, the night after Mellie's funeral.

'It just came to me.'

Astrid left it at that, but she always wondered if there had been an element of irony about this choice, Baker and Miller, as if they were cards in that game she used to love as a child, Happy

Families: Mrs Baker the baker's wife, Mrs Miller the miller's wife. Only there was no Mr Miller, no Mr Baker. How unfashionable that card game would be now that nuclear families were out, and women were no longer defined by their husbands. The other game she'd loved as a child was Old Maid, where you had to avoid the dreaded spinster card. She remembered asking her mother why there were eligible bachelors, but not eligible spinsters. Her mother had looked at her for a moment, deeply serious. 'Being alone, darling, is the worst thing that could happen to a woman.'

She'd always assumed that this, or something like it, was why Mrs Baker had married Alan. Perhaps she'd thought that even a violent criminal was better than nothing. The night of Mellie's funeral, Astrid had asked her about this too. They were in the kitchen at bedtime, letting the dogs out for their last pee.

'He wasn't a violent criminal when I met him.' Mrs Baker shut the door. 'He was only nineteen, just a kid.'

'But I thought you were twenty when you had Mellie, and he's not her father?'

'He's not, and I was. He's five years younger. He was no angel, but he hadn't got into anything bad then. Mellie was still very little when I met him, and he wanted to look after us – us against the world, he said.'

'So, you simply didn't notice that he was a monster?'

'That's what I'm saying, Astrid, he wasn't. I mean, he had his moods, but he had a terrible childhood, and he was good to us at first. I'd been on my own a few years, don't forget. A single mum. My family wouldn't have anything to do with me.'

'But when he first hurt you, didn't you ... I mean ...'

Mrs Baker let the dogs back in and locked the door. 'It was gradual, wasn't it. He felt bad, said sorry, all that. I'm not stupid.' Mrs Baker looked at her without blinking. 'And by the time I realised it was never going to stop, I had no choice, did I.' She turned and went up to bed without waiting for the dogs, or washing the mugs, or turning off the lights, or even saying goodnight.

Remembering this, as she sat alone in the cold windmill, it struck Astrid that it had been distressing to witness Mrs Baker's capacity for deception at the pigeon fancier's funeral not because she'd seemed like a stranger, but because her ability to dissemble spoke of the unspeakable things she'd endured. For over two decades, she'd had to play the obedient, devoted wife. She'd had to maintain that convincing persona day in, day out, stay calm, recall facts, show appropriate emotions under pressure, succumb to Alan's body, his whims, his fists. These were skills she'd had to develop to survive, and to keep her child safe.

Astrid suddenly needed to go back to the cottage.

The smell of cooking, a soupy sweetness of sautéed onions and warm bread, wafted down the hall. Mrs Baker was at the kitchen table, listening to Radio 2, specs on, fixing the hands onto the broken clockface. She'd cleared a space on the tabletop; she often did this when she was cross – claiming territory. But then she'd obviously calmed down because there was a warm loaf on the countertop, a pot of soup simmering on the Rayburn and a plate of shortbread cooling on the windowsill. The Kit Cat clock flicked its tail as Astrid entered and Mrs Baker looked up; Astrid saw the anxiety and hope in her eyes, and felt a flood of overwhelming love and protectiveness. If Mrs Baker had been a hugger, she'd have gone over and thrown her arms around her, but Mrs Baker was not a hugger, she was far too self-contained for physical affection and always had been. She was a complicated person, a survivor, but there was a big, tender, courageous heart buried inside the hard-won defences.

'There's soup,' she said, gruffly. 'I kept it warm for you, figured you'd be half frozen up there in your windmill.'

'It *is* a bit chilly in there.' Astrid went to find the kibble jar, stubbing her toe on Tony Blair. 'I dozed off, I'm afraid. You'd better not have eaten all the Lindor without me.'

'Haven't even opened them.' She put down the clock – the hands were back on. 'Go and get yourself warm by the Rayburn. It's leek and potato. I'll feed the dogs.'

They didn't argue about money again. Nor did they do any more mourning.

F. Layton Burgess, Chairman
Claycombe Parish Council

31st July 1920

Dear Lady Battiscombe,

I am writing to you following a most unsatisfactory exchange this morning with your guest, who informed us that you were out buying a 'suckling pig'. I, and my fellow parish council members, have never in our lives been spoken to as rudely and offensively as we were by this foreign gentleman and his young male 'friend'. The noise alone, from those beagles, is a public menace, and we certainly did not appreciate being, quite literally, hounded off the hillside. That gentleman's gypsy caravan, moreover, is blocking the lane.

My fellow parish council members and I were most dismayed to see positively perilous wire constructions coming off the windmill, not to mention clear signs of debauchery. As we made our way down the hill we spotted what looked like some kind of spiritualist ceremony taking place in the wood. There was chanting. Had there not been a lady in our group, we should have intervened directly. By the time the Watch Committee got up there, your friends had dispersed.

I do not know what sort of establishment you are operating there, but the village will not tolerate it. Should your foreign gentleman's 'canine circus' not depart forthwith, you can expect a visit from PC Butcher.

Yours sincerely,
F. Layton Burgess
Chairman

# Chapter 10

A jolt on the shoulder and a shot of pain brought Astrid back to the present. A man had shoved past her as she stood at the scanner. Behind it, she could see someone emptying her suitcase: she recognised her Bedouin scarf, then she saw her denture cream, a pack of moist toilet tissues, her shampoo. 'What on earth are you doing?' Astrid called over and then covered her mouth with her good hand. The security official by the carousel explained in a well-trained voice that everyone had to remove liquids from their luggage before it went through the scanner. 'But that's ointment!' She pointed at her Anusol tube, which had been hurled into a tray for anyone to see.

'You'll get it all back on the other side, madam.' The official articulated each word. 'You need to go through now.'

'To the other side?' Astrid felt panic rising. 'That's not liquid,' she shouted over to the official with her case. 'Put it down! Stop that!'

Everyone seemed to have lost all sense of what was reasonable and what was not. The floor swayed. She felt antagonism massing behind her. 'Excuse me!' a woman barked, nastily, shoving past, and something about the tone pinged a tripwire to the past again – the voice ringing out from the upper circle: *Mad bitch!*

A rational portion of her mind that night had remained aware of the audience, the position of her body on stage, the stances of the other actors, whose collective energy shifted to vigilance when the woman shouted. With that cry the boundary – always permeable – between herself and the character she was playing had vaporised so that her internal world mapped itself onto Lady Macbeth's. She was no longer acting, but inhabiting, and the anguish of all the unspeakable acts, the tremendous guilt, coalesced in her, plugging up her heart, her mouth, her mind until she could no longer breathe, think, speak or reason.

The tall, kind boy was bending down, speaking to her in a clear, audible voice, his face close. 'Are you okay? Can I help?'

'What?' she said. 'What's happening?'

'You just need to go through the scanner now, over there.' She followed his finger, saw a woman in uniform waving what looked like – surely was – a gun.

The suspended rectangle made a high-pitched bleeping sound as she walked through it. She wasn't surprised. The woman began to run a scanner over her body as if driving out spirits and she felt that perhaps the noise was internal. For some time now, somewhere deep inside her, high-pitched alarms had been sounding intermittently, just like this one. They were asking her to remove her jewellery, holding out a tray, impatient. With her one hand she unlooped her amber necklaces which clacked and skittered into the plastic tray, but there was no getting the rings off, not with one hand. Mrs Baker had had to put them on for her that morning and now, with the suffocating airport heat and all the waiting, her joints had swollen, knotted bone ends throbbing – they'd have to chop her fingers off to get them. She let her hand drop. 'I can't . . .' She heard her voice wobble. 'It's just not possible.' Her vision blurred.

Then, somehow, they all seemed to accept that the rings weren't coming off. 'If you'd just like to step over here, madam, this way.' She was guided aside.

'Really!' Astrid cried. 'Is this absolutely necessary?'

An official said something she didn't catch.

She decided then that she would do nothing more. It was too absurd. Did they really think a one-armed eighty-two-year-old woman wanted to blow up an easyJet flight to Edinburgh? It struck her then that they might expel her for non-compliance. It wouldn't be the first time. She'd been thrown out of four successive boarding schools until, at the age of fifteen, her mother had sent her to live with her godmother in Switzerland so that she might at least learn French. It had been the wrong part of Switzerland, though, so she'd learned some German, with a smattering of Romansh and, since her godmother was mostly away, some other things too, which had led her to the ghastly Formica table in the city. It was more than sixty years ago now, and she still remembered the smell of bile and detergent, and the pain, too. There had been a crucible of dried blood by her face, and a grim-faced woman between her thighs, sleeves rolled up, snapping in French, which she was very glad not to have learned.

She felt herself sway. 'I feel a little faint,' she said, but nobody heard. She really must get a grip. *S.O.B.* She took a deep breath. *S.O.B. Pull yourself together.*

It was lack of sleep, nothing more. *Horrible imaginings.* But no, she definitely wasn't going to think about what the doctor had said at A&E.

'Madam? You can go and collect your bags now.'

She opened her eyes. 'Do you know,' she said, 'you're quite rude.' She waved a hand in a sudden flourish. 'All of you!' Someone pushed the tray of necklaces at her, she grabbed them with her one good hand and walked away with dignity, shoulders back, chin lifted. Deportment was everything.

The officials moved on to another problematic traveller. Astrid hooked her necklaces back on and spotted her handbag sitting open at the end of the conveyor belt where anyone could have taken it, anyone at all. She went over and was about to walk away with it when she realised there was still the carry-on case to come. The original official was opening a leopard skin case. Hers had vanished. Had it been confiscated? She tried to concentrate as bag after bag floated past. She had no idea what to do. She very badly needed to sit down. Her lower spine was agony now, and a headache was beginning to seriously consider its options. Perhaps if she just sat down and waited, then somebody would eventually send her home. But of course, some people lived in airports for years, unnoticed. She walked delicately towards a line of seats and lowered herself into one. It took all her effort not to cry out.

'Hello? Sorry?'

She opened her eyes. The tall kind boy who'd been behind her in the queue was standing over her again. 'Is this yours?'

She gazed at the carry-on case, then at him. She wondered if he'd put all her things – her pants, pills, denture cream, ointments, vests and socks and wet wipes, far too many things for just one night away – back inside it. 'No,' she said.

He blinked. 'Oh, right. But I think . . .' He was terribly sweet, such a nice kind face, the sort of grandson you might invent for yourself, except for the fact that he had headphones dangling from his ears. 'I remembered this . . .' He lifted the acid-yellow luggage tag. Astrid squinted at it and made out the words, *Excuse Me, Not Your Bag.*

Mrs Baker had bought the tag that morning in the petrol station. 'In case you get confused.'

'Confused?' Astrid was offended. 'I've hitchhiked solo to Syria, Mrs Baker, I've lived in a cave with a Bedouin lover, ridden the Magic Bus to Kathmandu – I think I can negotiate a short hop to Edinburgh.'

She snatched the handle from the boy, who looked startled, then loped off. 'Thank you!' she called after him, but he didn't seem to hear. Perhaps he'd put his headphones back in.

She watched him disappear down the escalator then looked at her hands. There was the ring that Mohammed had given her the day they met. She'd been looking at it on his jewellery stall, though she couldn't buy it. She'd arrived that morning having hitched a lift all the way from Marrakesh with a crazy-eyed South African in a Land Rover. Mohammed had the fine hands of a concert pianist, and when he took hers and slid the amber stone onto her middle finger, she'd felt as if she was holding hands with an old friend. 'Welcome,' he said. 'Welcome. Welcome.' She looked at his deep, gentle eyes and they sat together all day, into the evening. That night he brought her through hot, narrow streets to his sister's home, where she slept on the floor in a room full of children and elderly ladies who wanted to touch her clothes and hair. His sister spoke a bit of English and explained that the rest of her family lived in caves above the city. Some days later, Mohammed took her to his home. They drank mint tea brewed on a wormwood fire, and he introduced her to his enormous family, so many beautiful wide-eyed children. Someone taught her to bake charred *shrak* bread, and they slept on a mattress outside the caves, with whispering juniper trees and sheep that snuffled along the ridge all night, bleating calmly to one another beneath an extravagantly starry sky. For

the first time since Sally Morgan's death, Astrid felt peaceful. She
helped on Mohammed's jewellery stall and stayed for almost a
year. He had wanted to marry her, dear man, and perhaps she
would have accepted had she not been married already.

She decided she must get up, go down the escalator to try to
find the boy, and borrow his phone to call Mrs Baker. Mrs Baker
would say she'd never find him in the crowded terminal, but
Astrid had faith; when you needed a friend you generally found
one, even when the odds were stacked against it. Sometimes, in
fact, you found a friend when you didn't know you needed one.

This had been the case with Mrs Baker. When Astrid let herself into Charlie's Hove house, over two decades ago – 1999, the
millennium looming – she'd found a solid woman in man's work
overalls mopping the kitchen floor, bum swaying. At the sound
of the door closing, Mrs Baker stopped and stood bolt upright.
Gilbert, who was just a pup, shot in and slid across the wet floor,
crashing nose first into a cupboard. Mrs Baker turned and lifted
her chin. 'Who are you?' Her eyes were wary.

Astrid felt indignant. 'I'm the owner of this house.'

'Well, I'm the cleaner of it and that dog's messing up my
floor.' Some of the tension in her face, Astrid saw, had released.

Astrid stayed there all afternoon. There was something reassuring about Mrs Baker's silent, methodical activity. She didn't
respond to Astrid's attempts at conversation, she gave one-word
answers and continued to work with absolute focus, as if she
was alone. She polished taps, bleached stains, vanished smears,
whisked the tenants' dust from lampshades, slat blinds, skirting
boards. She ignored Gilbert, who rampaged about, lawless,
chewing, peeing on rugs. Astrid saw that here was a person
who would not be flustered or distracted, a person who could
get things under control, and keep them that way. For the first

time since she'd found Charlie lying face up by the pond, she felt safe.

As Mrs Baker was putting away the cleaning things, Astrid tried to open the kitchen window and found it jammed. Mrs Baker was washing her hands by then. Astrid rattled the handle, and it came off in her hand. She looked at it, and suddenly felt that she might weep. The past months had really been a bit much, with Charlie's son coming up to the windmill with that dreadful little man, demanding money, complaining that his father should have left everything to him, the eldest son; threatening her, telling her things about Charlie's working life, the murkiness, things she'd managed not to discover in the twelve years they'd been together, not because she was stupid or naive, but because she simply didn't want to know. And now this, a broken window handle. Everything felt fragile and cheap – ready to fall apart.

Mrs Baker dried her hands, reached out and took the handle from Astrid. She fiddled with it then opened a kitchen drawer and took out a silver tape measure. From her overall pocket she plucked a screwdriver with which she unscrewed the belt clip on the tape measure. Astrid watched her deft hands. 'What are you doing?' But Mrs Baker didn't explain. She slotted the flat clip down behind the window handle which seemed to bypass the lock. The handle gave a click and turned. Then she unscrewed the whole thing from its frame and bent over it on the counter-top. Moments later, it was all back together. She opened the window, and closed it again, smoothly.

This time it was Astrid who had no words.

Mrs Baker screwed the belt clip back onto the measuring tape. Her face had remained neutral throughout, but there was some-thing softer around her eyes. The setting sun lit up her ruddy skin forming little sparks on the tips of her salt and pepper curls.

'Have you got any other cleaning you want done?' she said.

Her tone was matter of fact, but Astrid sensed an urgency, not a desperation exactly, but hope, perhaps, and this surprised her.

'No, unfortunately,' she said, 'I have to sell this place, it's going on the market tomorrow. It belonged to my late ...' She never could think what to call Charlie. 'Boyfriend' sounded undignified – she was about to turn sixty – husband inaccurate, 'partner' wrong. 'He's died.'

Mrs Baker looked at her properly for first time. 'I'm very sorry to hear that.' Astrid felt a plummeting in her stomach, and a sense of exposure, as if Mrs Baker had lifted a bandage to reveal the awful bruise of Charlie's absence. She looked out the window. It would not do to weep in front of a stranger. Self-pity really was unbearable. In the distance, the setting sun stained the undulating sea a rich deep carmine. She cleared her throat. 'He had a heart attack. He was only sixty-two. He provided for me in his will, but his son's in trouble, and so I thought if I sold this house then I could ...' She stopped herself. Mrs Baker didn't need to hear the details of Charlie's financial dealings or his grasping son, or the horrid little man he'd brought to the windmill. 'Luckily, I also own a windmill,' she said, then an idea popped into her head. 'It needs a clear-out actually. I thought I might put paying guests in it.'

Mrs Baker frowned.

'I suppose I should really phone up the agency, shouldn't I?'

'No need for that. I can come. When do you want it done? Tomorrow?'

Astrid wrote the address on a scrap of paper, with her name and telephone number. Mrs Baker looked at it. 'Miller?' She raised an eyebrow. Astrid laughed and shrugged. Mrs Baker shoved the paper into the pocket of her overalls. Her features had grown more lively, as if there was a smile inside her that she wasn't going to release.

'And your name is . . . ?'

The brown eyes rested on her face a moment. 'Baker,' she said. 'Mrs Baker.'

They shook hands. Mrs Baker's felt leathery and warm.

'Do call me Astrid.'

Mrs Baker nodded but didn't offer her own first name.

At eight o'clock the next morning, Mrs Baker strode into the courtyard with a canvas knapsack on her shoulder. Astrid had been listening out for a car bumping up the lane and was upstairs when the doorbell jangled on its wire. Gilbert went wild. She rushed to the front window and looked down at the courtyard. A September mist draped over the hawthorn hedges and the walled garden, blotting out the Downs, erasing the lower floors of the windmill. As she flung open the window a spider's web on the clematis trembled, jewelled; she leaned out and called down. 'Mrs Baker? Just a moment – I'll come down!'

Not counting the undertaker, only two people had come to the windmill in the four months since Charlie died, and Gilbert, fired by the memory of that visit, shot out, snapping and yapping, when Astrid opened the front door. Mrs Baker, in sturdy boots, paid him no attention and after a few moments, he lost interest, and dashed off after a squirrel. Mrs Baker put down her knapsack. Her cheeks were rosy, mist droplets clung to her curls. The soles of her boots were caked in chalky mud.

'Did you come up on foot? You should have said, I could have picked you up!'

Mrs Baker narrowed her eyes and Astrid had a sense of getting it all wrong; she must calm down, she realised, behave more like an employer. 'The windmill,' she said, 'is over there.'

Mrs Baker's eyes crinkled slightly. 'So I see.'

'Well, yes, I suppose you can't really miss it.' Astrid waved a hand, vaguely, and laughed at herself. She realised, then, that Mrs Baker hadn't been admiring the architecture but thinking of the cleaning task ahead. 'Do you want to come up and have a look? I'll just get my boots on.'

Mrs Baker's eyes widened as they adjusted to the dim interior of the windmill. She took in the peeling walls and gangrenous windows, the dust and debris and things – all of Constance's things, and some of Charlie's too. 'It's perfectly habitable,' Astrid said. 'It just needs a good clean. I used to live in here myself. That was twelve years ago now, but it can be quite cosy and . . .' She tailed off. People, she knew, had different standards. When Charlie rescued her after the Great Storm, he'd seen the way she'd been living – the ripped sofa and the Calor gas heater, the tiny outside loo and the tin bath that she had to fill from the stove – and called her a hippy, a vagrant, a tramp. He'd take care of her, he promised, give her light, plumbing, warmth, the mod cons that a woman like her – a goddess! – deserved. Being in property (he was a builder, or a developer, or something of that nature, she'd never fully got to the bottom of what he did; he liked to keep his work life separate from home for reasons that had, later, become abundantly clear), Charlie had known how to renovate the cottage and the granary, and quite a few Sussex workmen seemed to owe him favours. Looking back, she didn't know why she'd allowed him to move in and take charge like this. She must have been very lonely or bored or lost – or all three? She couldn't quite remember. But she'd never quite shaken the feeling that she'd betrayed the windmill by moving into the cottage with Charlie and that, somehow, it resented her for this. The walls, she noticed now, were mottled, some areas streaked with moisture, the plaster puckered in places like scar tissue. None of this had ever really bothered her.

There had been winters when the wind raged and tore and grappled with the tower. She'd plugged the windows with cotton wool and kept the musty old tapestries over them, but she'd felt the cold leak in anyway, through the bricks, the floor, the cap. At night the wind had whistled round the upper floors, gusting down the stairs, and tinkling the grain bell. On squally days, when you came in, if you weren't fast, the wind would sweep in too, like a vandal, knocking over pictures and vases, flapping tapestries.

Mrs Baker rested her hands on her broad hips. 'Is there running water up here?'

'Of course. There used to be, anyway, I assume it still works. There's a tap in the courtyard if not,' she added.

'What about a toilet?'

'There's a little outdoor privy on the other side, but you're welcome to use the cottage loo.'

'How much are you going to charge people to stay in here, then?'

Perhaps it had been a mistake to ask for help. 'I shall deal with the logistics later, Mrs Baker,' she said. She found that she rather liked how the name sounded, planted like this at the end of the sentence, a humorous formality, the little finger lifted, camply, from the fork.

Mrs Baker was looking at a broken rocking chair which, Astrid thought, could be a prop from a Hitchcock film. The taxidermised stoat peered at them from its seat. Mrs Baker's gaze moved from the chair and rested on it. 'He looks like Tony

Blair,' Astrid said, and Mrs Baker's lips twitched, a brief smile. Her eyes travelled to the trunk containing Constance's belongings – the letters, tapestries, coffee pot, photo album, ceremonial swords, books. A table lay on its side next to the iron bed. The brown velvet sofa, its fabric faded to a flesh-colour on the arms, its seats gnawed by rodents so that it sprouted horsehair, sat in the centre with blankets and cushions strewn. Sometimes Astrid would come and sit on it with Gilbert to get away from Charlie, and sometimes just to be alone; hours would vaporise. Time in the windmill passed differently, she found.

Charlie had dumped things in the windmill too, over the years. Mrs Baker's left boot was planted quite close to an iron saw with some missing teeth, a coil of old rope and a bucket of old Formula One keyrings. There were bits of milling equipment, too, a couple of battered wooden sieves, and some pieces of the original mechanism that had been brought down to take weight off the upper floors: rusted hooks and chains, a massive wheel with cogs the length of Astrid's forearm, and one of the smaller millstones leaning on the wall, its granite surface scored and pockmarked.

'Do you want to see the upper floors?' Astrid lifted Gilbert and tucked him under one arm.

Behind her Mrs Baker cleared her throat. 'This might be more than a day's work.'

'Oh, the upper floors are fine, don't worry.'

She turned and saw that Mrs Baker was standing still, no doubt weighing up whether to follow or flee.

'The stairs are perfectly solid, except for a couple of places at the very top, but I can tell you where not to tread.'

Mrs Baker, she saw, was standing on the trapdoor to the tunnel – Astrid prayed that it would hold her weight. She never

liked to stand on top of the trapdoors, just in case. 'Let's go up.'
She went over to the canine funicular, popped Gilbert on his
cushion and secured the dog basket door. He peered out with a
resigned expression. She pulled on the sack hoist chain and his
basket began to ascend, jerkily, towards the first trapdoor. She
didn't need to use the funicular for just one dog, of course – she'd
originally devised it out of necessity for Dixie Belle's litter – but
she rather wanted to see how Mrs Baker would react to the
sight of a dachshund rising through the windmill. 'I adapted
the sack hoist,' she explained 'The millers used to attach a heavy
bag of grain to this chain, and the wind power would lift it
through the windmill, pushing open these trapdoors, up to the
Bin floor – that's three floors above us. Look, Gilbert's demon-
strating.' The brass door knocker she'd attached to the top of the
dog basket pushed the underside of the first trapdoor so that it
lifted, allowing the basket to pass through onto the Spout floor;
the trapdoor flopped shut behind it on its leather hinges, making
a loud bang, raining dust and bits onto their heads.

Mrs Baker shook off the scatterings but said nothing, as if it
was entirely normal to watch a miniature wire-haired dachshund
rise through a windmill in a modified sack hoist. Astrid was
pleased by this reaction: Mrs Baker could remain impassive in
the face of the unexpected, she was not a fusser.

The oak treads on the ladder stairs were worn into two smooth
declivities by a hundred years of millers' feet, but Mrs Baker
was sure-footed as she followed Astrid up to the Spout floor
where Gilbert was waiting calmly in the funicular. His black nose
pressed on the grille as they came up, sniffing. Astrid opened
the basket, and he hopped out. The Spout floor did need a good
scrub, there was dust and cobwebs everywhere, but the only
objects were a cracked butler's sink, a small table with a wonky

leg, a couple of chairs, some empty shelves and a bugle. Astrid picked this up and peered into its horn. She had no recollection of ever having owned or used a bugle. Where on earth had it come from? She left it where it was. 'This used to be my kitchen,' she said. 'It was rather basic, but perfectly good.' She coaxed Gilbert back into the funicular and pulled the chain again, transporting him upwards towards the next trapdoor, and the Stone floor.

Mrs Baker climbed silently behind Astrid but as she got to the top, she let out a muted cry. The Stone floor probably did look a bit eerie. Only one curtain remained, a faded claret velvet that trailed from a brass pole above the lectern and the stone altar, a rectangular slab of marble set on a mahogany table. Next to the altar was a smaller spindle-legged side table on which the big wooden crucifix lay, like a weapon.

'Is this a *chapel*?' Mrs Baker had lost some of the calm neutrality. She looked alert, now, as if calculating whether Astrid might be about to produce a dagger and sacrifice her on the altar. Astrid tried to sound light as she knelt to release Gordon. 'Isn't it fun? The woman who turned the windmill into a home – her name was Lady Battiscombe – dug this altar stone up in the village churchyard, or her friends did, one night after a wild fancy dress party in the twenties. They must have lugged it up the hill. I believe she even had it consecrated by a bishop.' Astrid went over and touched the pockmarked marble. 'It's probably medieval.'

'What is?'

'This stone.'

Mrs Baker was looking quite confused.

'Henry the Eighth didn't approve of altars – there are saints' relics sealed inside them, you see, bits of a saint's bone or fingernails or whatever. If you crawl and look underneath you can see a little circle – that's the cavity for the relic.' Mrs Baker was standing very still and frowning, as if her brain was working fast. Astrid felt that she was babbling. Then it struck her that Mrs Baker might be offended. 'Are you a churchgoer, Mrs Baker?'

'I was raised Baptist,' Mrs Baker said, with some finality. 'No relics.'

Astrid had a sense that they were going down a difficult path, so she took Gilbert to the window. The mist was rising off the Downs and the long grass on the closest slope was still bursting with wildflowers – a childhood song popped into her head. *Daisies are our silver, buttercups our gold; this is all the treasure we can have or hold.* It was written by the woman who wrote *Mrs Miniver*. How odd, Astrid thought, the miscellaneous facts that skitter into one's mind. *Mrs Miniver* then made her think of her mother, who would have appreciated the drama of the windmill, the wild winds and bright flowers, the scattered flints and sheep's wool tumbleweed; the expansive sky.

Behind her, Mrs Baker cleared her throat.

'Sorry.' Astrid turned. 'Do you know, I've been here almost twenty years and it still stops me in my tracks.'

Mrs Baker looked through the window, too, and nodded and Astrid could tell that she understood. For a moment, they gazed out together, as if this was their kingdom.

'Two more floors – Bin and Dust.' Astrid decided not to bother with the funicular, and tucked Gilbert under one arm.

The heady feeling was stronger on the Dust floor. The air felt thinner forty-four feet up, and the light was so clear, everything very bright, with the tapping of the wind against the sweeps and fan stage and little gusty draughts coming through the cap. Mrs Baker had lost some of the wariness – perhaps she felt it too, the space, the beams of light, how small they were against something huge and unfathomable. Mrs Baker shoved her hands in her overalls, and craned to look up at the domed cap. 'It's built like a church,' she said.

'It is,' Astrid agreed. The cap was still in reasonable shape – Charlie had overseen the repairs eleven years ago, the summer after the Great Storm, and they seemed to have lasted. She remembered standing under the tower that hot day in July as the men levered off the cap with a cherry picker so that they could rebuild it, replacing the burned-out panels. It had seemed a brutal act, like brain surgery, violent and unnatural and terribly risky, exposing secret spaces. The windmill had looked somehow helpless, Astrid couldn't bear to watch – she had to turn away. And then, as so often happened during moments of heightened emotion or stress, she saw Magnus. He was leaning on the five-bar gate, partly concealed behind the chassis of the builder's van, watching her intensely and with such longing, as if to say, *What in God's name are you doing here? You belong with me, and you know it.* He lifted a hand, tentative, not quite a wave.

Charlie must have felt her trembling against him and put his arms round her and pulled her closer. 'It's all right, my love.' He patted her ear, her hair. 'They'll put her cap back on again, get her all fixed up, good as new, you'll see.' She always hated the way he called the windmill 'she'. When she'd extricated herself and looked back at the gate, Magnus was gone. Charlie moved away then, marched over to the builder's van and one of the men yelled out, 'Watch it!' There was a clang, a thud – she couldn't look.

Despite Charlie's assurances, the windmill had never been good as new, not even close. Other than repairing the cap with English oak, the renovation had been superficial: sweeps patched back together and reattached, the crack in the north wall 'stitched', new windowpanes to replace those shattered by the storm. The glass had been a palaver to install; the panes had to be puttied from the outside, because otherwise the wind could shove them inwards. She remembered the glazier at the top of the ladder, shouting down, precarious: 'The wind's her best friend and her worst enemy!' It had seemed to Astrid that the windmill's worst enemy was internal, though, because when all the workmen had gone, the woodworm continued to gnaw through timbers and beams, drilling runnels into applewood, hornbeam and beechwood cogs, across oak floorboards and stair treads; the rust continued to work through the remaining mechanism, the iron hooks, chains and wheels and up the cladding, and the damp seeped up the crumbling bricks, loosening mortar and putty, mottling and puckering the plastered interior.

Mrs Baker had moved over to the window and was peering down. Somewhere on the lower floors something scurried and skittered, then gave a brief chesty rasp – just a breeze perhaps, puffing through the remaining mechanism. Astrid beckoned Mrs Baker over to the hatch and heaved it open so that they could climb out, onto the stage. The wood creaked beneath them, and Astrid wondered, suddenly, whether it would take their weight. Mrs Baker moved to the edge, clung to the rail. She imagined a shudder and crack, the stage detaching, tipping. The fan wheel spun and whirred and rattled and down below, the bright chalk path spooled along the ridge of the Downs, east to west, and beyond that, the glittering sea.

It was easy to imagine the windmill in full grinding. The air inside would have swirled with dust, and it would have been so loud – a symphony of creaks and squeaks as the iron driveshaft turned the wheels, the rapid percussive thuds of the cogs and teeth, locking and releasing to turn the shaft, and the millstones below – the rhythmic swish of grain coming down the feeder, spreading out between the granite slabs, crushed in sandpapery huffs. Perhaps the miller would step out here sometimes, onto the fan stage, to suck in air; John Dean once told her that millers had a terrible life expectancy, many of them died of lung disease from breathing in dust all day.

Mrs Baker was standing her ground, holding the rail, and Astrid felt as if this solid, taciturn stranger had passed some kind of test, though she didn't know what the test was, exactly, or who had set it. 'You must go downstairs backwards,' she said, climbing off the stage and ducking back inside. 'Never forwards.'

Floor by floor, they circled back through the windmill together, holding on to the ropes, moving silently down each ladder staircase.

They cleared the ground floor that day, scrubbing and scraping, and at lunchtime Astrid went to the cottage and made her best cheese sandwiches: a generous squirt of salad cream, sliced mini gherkins, grated Sussex cheddar, ploughman's pickle and lots of sandwich spread. Mrs Baker ate it sitting on the old millstone, boots planted apart, her overall sleeves rolled up to show solid freckled forearms. Astrid noticed a ghostly line in the calloused flesh of her ring finger.

'Do you always work for the agency?'

'Mostly.'

'I hope you won't get in trouble for coming here today?'

A shrug. 'It's not up to them.'

In someone else, such conversational dead ends might suggest dullness, but Mrs Baker hummed with intelligence. There was an alertness about her, too, as if she was keeping herself a few steps ahead of anything Astrid might say or do. Two lines scored the gap between her brows, two more bracketed her mouth. Her red cheeks, seen close as Astrid leaned to take the plate, were laced with broken capillaries.

She was the stronger woman by far. Astrid tired well before her and flopped onto the sofa. She opened the letter tin. She hadn't looked at the letters in years. She pulled one out of the Outrage bundle.

*F. Layton Burgess, Chairman*
*Claycombe Parish Council*

*10th September 1920*

*Dear Lady Battiscombe,*
*We at the parish council are dismayed and disgusted by reports of your guests singing lewd songs as a walking group of local ladies passed the windmill yesterday. The ladies were, naturally, distressed. When they asked your guests to desist, they were treated to an obscene nursery rhyme, and then the spectacle of a man emerging from the windmill in a woman's peasant dress, brandishing swords.*

*These ladies were on a public footpath, minding their own business. Such activities have no place in civilised community. If you cannot think of your community, then I urge you to think of your child.*

*We have discussed this matter fully at an extraordinary meeting, and the village is in full agreement that, should anything of this nature happen again, we shall not hesitate to alert the law. The Mothers' Union has also been notified.*

*Yours sincerely,*
*F. Layton Burgess, Chairman*

Astrid put the letter back and took one out of the Walter
bundle.

*Windmill Hill*

2nd June 1920

*Dearest Walter,*

*How I wish you felt as I do about the windmill. If only you'd been able
to return, you'd have seen it differently. The weather was certainly
foul, and your visit home so very brief – I only wish you'd agreed
to stay overnight instead of rushing back up to London with Rufus,
because the next day was clear and very beautiful here. We could
have had a long walk, through golden buttercups and skylarks, and
you would have loved it so much.*

*It was sad to have seen so little of you on your visit, but I do
know that the trips to the shipyard were necessary and there are so
many people for you to see in London. Is it strange to me how hard
it is to design a small battleship. I had never really thought about
this properly, until you explained it. I had somehow imagined that
it was just a matter of general shrinkage.*

*I'm also sorry about the confusion I caused by coming back here,
but of course it was pointless for me to twiddle my thumbs in London
when you were away with Rufus and there is so much for me to
do here. For a start, you're right, I must tackle the mice – they are
rather taking over, despite Miss Jones's ingenious system of traps
and baiting.*

*I am disappointed that you did not take to Mr Banks. He can be
taciturn, but he is an excellent man, and has helped me enormously.
I did not feel he disrespected you. He has strong pacifist ideals,
certainly, but he is not judgemental. I'm glad you approve of Daphne,*

*though not surprised that you found her a little peculiar. She can certainly be direct and doesn't tend to bow to convention in dress or manners, but I am glad you appreciated her. She asks me to tell you that she'd like to paint you and Rufus together – some kind of tableau involving exotic birds.*

*I now wish you could have come a bit later, as she has just invited a friend of hers, a Portuguese, to the windmill in July. He runs a 'canine travelling circus' and plans to construct a wire from the Spout floor to a pool. The dogs, beagles apparently, dressed in knitted pirate costumes with cutlasses between their teeth, sit in a basket which comes shooting down the wire. They leap off at the end into a water feature, where they swashbuckle. Apparently, they love it, and beg to go again.*

*I hope your return voyage was safe and as comfortable as possible, and that you have what you need for the final stages of this interminable build. Do send news when you can. Tell me how New York was? I'm rather jealous.*

*Your C*

'You want to get old papers and things inside the house.' Mrs Baker glanced over Astrid's shoulder. 'It's damp in here.'

By sundown, they'd only managed to clear the ground floor, but they'd done a decent job of it. Furniture had been wiped clean of spiders' webs and dust and mouse droppings, rugs beaten and rolled, tapestries folded back into the trunk. Charlie's junk was piled out in the courtyard – organised into scrap, tip and charity; the floorboards were scrubbed, the flaking walls wiped down with bleach. Mrs Baker's overalls were more grey than blue, now, and there were cobwebs in her hair. Astrid felt shattered – she hadn't worked so hard in years. Charlie had barely allowed her to lift a finger. But Mrs Baker seemed no more tired than when she'd arrived at eight that morning. She tidied away the cleaning products, emptied the bucket and wiped her hands down her overalls. The birds laced the air with evening songs, and far off across the slopes sheep bleated to one another.

'Will you want me to come back and do the upper floors?'

'Would you?'

Mrs Baker nodded and gave a slight shrug.

'Please do – please. Tomorrow? Could you? But I should pay you now for today. If you'd come to the cottage, I'll get my purse . . .'

Her purse was in the hall and as she pulled out banknotes, she saw that Mrs Baker, who had remained on the threshold, was looking at the sky. It was pink, the light fading – two bats shot out of a hole in one of the oaks and swooped low across the courtyard, hunting for insects. A blackbird warbled, and around them the Downs gave off their ancient and expansive evening scents; the leaves exhaled and the chalk dust settled. Down in the woods a magpie squabbled with a jay, and rooks cawed.

'Where do you live? I can drive you home.' She pointed at Gloria. 'I've got Charlie's car.'

Mrs Baker shook her head. 'No need.'

'But there won't be any more buses now.'

She didn't reply. She took the banknotes, counted them, and folded them into her breast pocket, then bent to tie her bootlace. Astrid felt, suddenly, that if she allowed Mrs Baker to walk off down the hill, she would vanish for ever. 'But I can't let you walk.'

Mrs Baker picked up the knapsack.

Astrid felt a sort of panic. 'Why don't you stay here tonight? I've got a spare room, the bed's all made up. It would be no trouble. Then we can start early tomorrow on the upper floors.'

Mrs Baker looked away, across the courtyard, as if weighing this idea on some internal scale. She glanced at the sky again. There was no wind, and a deep, hazy stillness was falling around them. From up in the windmill's cap, the barn owl let out a haunted screech as it set off on a twilight hunting expedition.

'I've got eggs, I can make us an omelette – you must be so hungry. Come in, come in.' Astrid turned and walked, decisively, down the hall, hoping that Mrs Baker would follow.

Mrs Baker's face didn't exactly fall as she entered the kitchen, but somehow it registered dismay.

'I'm not much of a housekeeper.' Astrid laughed. 'I'm a bit disorganised, I'm afraid. Charlie was the domestic one and since he died, I've rather . . . well . . . I'm not a hoarder, though, I just like to keep things.'

Mrs Baker stared.

'But I could probably do with some help around the house too, if I'm honest.' She started to laugh again but Gilbert had stuck his head inside an empty baked bean tin and started running along the bottom of the Rayburn, panicking, and making a terrible clattering. It took a moment or two to catch him and by the time Astrid got his head out, Mrs Baker was at the sink, tackling a frying pan.

Astrid felt a rush of relief. She hadn't realised how much she missed having another person in the house. She got out the eggs, opened a bottle of wine, then found herself telling Mrs Baker about the Great Storm, and Charlie's rescue mission. She described how she'd crouched on Constance's iron bed with the tower rattling and shaking and howling above her. Things were flying around outside, smashing against the walls and the cap making tremendous clangs and cracks – planks, scrap metal, tree limbs shooting past. She'd smelled burning – a terrifying smell – and had forced her way outside, hardly able to stand up against the wind, which was deafening. A hunk of corrugated iron from a distant farm bounced off the bricks inches from her head; a slice of tarpaulin had plastered itself to the tower. The force against the fettered sweeps was causing such friction that enormous sparks shot from the teeth of the brake mechanism, burning scarlet holes in the cap. Astrid watched as, after more than three decades of restraint, the sweeps tore themselves free from their shackles with a guttural screech, and began to spin; slowly at first, then faster and faster – out of control.

The cap was smouldering, but she had no bucket, no hose, no telephone – there were no mobile phones in those days. Then she heard a terrific crack, a splintering, and a sweep was off – she saw it cartwheel across the lavender garden and bounce over the far wall into the wild darkness. Then there was an almighty crash behind her as the elm toppled across the entrance to the courtyard, blocking the lane. No fire engine could get to the windmill any more, even if she'd been able to call one. She feared she'd be injured, perhaps killed, if she tried to get down the hill to the village and she realised she had no choice but to stay with the windmill. She clawed her way back inside the tower. On the upper floors, she heard glass smashing; the grain bell clamoured. It struck her that the saftest place would be the tunnel – if she didn't burn or suffocate down there.

From his house in the village Charlie had seen a patch of the Downs lit up as if someone was letting off a giant emergency flare and thought, immediately, of the 'windmill woman'. He woke a friend, and they drove up, battling the last part of Windmill Hill on foot, two big men hunched against the gale with ancient trees crashing down around them; they feared the worst. He told

her later that the windmill had looked like a giant screaming
Catherine wheel, with red sparks shooting from its cap. It had
seemed like a catastrophe at the time, but really it had saved
her. It was almost as if the windmill had summoned Charlie to
fetch her.

As Mrs Baker listened, she took a bowl, cracked four eggs into
it, and began to whisk. Then she poured the eggs into a pan
she'd heated. 'You tell a good story,' she said over the hiss and
bubble; Astrid thought she saw a smile.

The spare room had been Charlie's study. As they got to the
bottom of the staircase, Mrs Baker paused at the pulley and
basket. 'Another dog lift?'

Astrid nodded, and to demonstrate she loaded Gilbert into
the round basket, strapped him into the harness and began
to hoist. 'I don't need it with just one dog, of course, but I've
trained him anyway, just in case. I call this one the Dickinson,'
she said, 'after the reclusive American poet, Emily, who used to
lower gingerbread to the children.'

Mrs Baker's expression remained entirely blank.

Astrid looked up. Gilbert's small nose was poking over the
edge of the basket. 'It's the same principle as the canine funicular: a miniature dachshund's legs are too short to cope with
the spiral staircases in here or the ladder staircases in the windmill . . .'

Mrs Baker peered up at the basket, suspended above them.
'Did you think about getting a bigger dog?'

'Ah, but I didn't choose my dogs, they chose me, or the uni-
verse chose me for them. I found my first, Dixie Belle, in the
woods near here – the poor dear was just wandering around, no
collar, nothing. She turned out to be a pregnant runaway – and
thus a dynasty was spawned.'

The study was a bit of a mess. Charlie's word processor dominated the desk, his typewriter sat on the wardrobe and his papers were everywhere; she hadn't sorted anything out. His clothes still hung in her wardrobe, his shoes were under their bed, his coats in the hall. The spare bed hadn't been slept in for a while, but it was made up and hopefully clean. It was dark outside now, a starless, windless, suspended night. The owl gave its sad, hoarse screech, and Gilbert watched calmly as Astrid drew the curtains. He'd accepted Mrs Baker in the house without objection. There was something about her that discouraged fuss.

Astrid turned and saw an expression of profound relief on Mrs Baker's face, as if the tension had been released from around her mouth and between her eyes. She looked exhausted, but younger; softer, and less intimidating. 'Do you know,' Astrid said, 'I don't think I even caught your first name?'

There was a pause. 'Eileen,' she said, quietly. 'It's Eileen.'

It was such a sad-sounding name, a cry of anguish. Astrid decided that 'Mrs Baker' suited her better; solid, firm, practical.

It took a few days to clear the rest of the windmill and get rid of all the stuff, and then Mrs Baker started on the cottage, and then they decided to whitewash the interior of the windmill, and somehow – though neither of them could quite pinpoint how – the weeks turned to months, and then years; Mrs Baker never left.

Mrs Baker always said that she had only stayed for those first few nights because she'd felt sorry for Astrid, bereaved and alone in a filthy and chaotic cottage, surrounded by her dead man's belongings, but Astrid had sensed from the start that something wasn't right. The look of relief on Mrs Baker's face as they stood in the bedroom that night had haunted her for quite some time.

She hadn't quite articulated it to herself then, but looking back, she had sensed that Mrs Baker was in deep trouble and had nowhere else to go. It would be another ten years, of course, before she found out why.

*Windmill Hill*

*18th June 1920*

Dearest W,

I woke at dawn today, wrapped myself in a shawl and went out in the morning mist (I walk such distances now, I am as strong as an ox). The calls of pipits and skylarks were magical, and the rising sun saturated the landscape in glorious pinks, with deep cerise cumulus in the east, and indigo streaks overhead. The mist rose to reveal the carpet of wildflowers and truly I felt that I was in paradise. But then, suddenly, I heard a faint whining, whooshing sound, and I looked up to see ravens moving overhead – they seemed to come out of nowhere, a black mass riding low and fast on the tail wind, and I lost the sense of wellbeing and was suddenly very nervous. I thought I must come home and write to you immediately. Are you well and safe?

It has been such an age since I heard from you. Are you cross with me still, about my 'antics'? Let us not quarrel any more, dear, let us be friends again. We have always been such good friends, haven't we? I keep thinking of the summer we met – after your father died and your mother sent you to us. I was terribly jealous because you and Sheridan were inseparable. And then Sheridan played the attic ghost trick, and you were so terrified, poor dear, and I saw the fragility in you – and after that you and I were firm friends. I know we have been so much apart lately. We live in this world quite differently now, don't we? But you will always be my dearest friend. Shan't we be kinder to one another?

The air, as I write, is musical; I have spotted bullfinches, goldfinches, linnets and greenfinches here, and every morning I wake to the *rhythmic coo of woodpigeons. Sometimes at night I am woken by the screech of our resident barn owl, up in the cap, and the badgers can be quite noisy, whickering and chirruping – fighting sometimes, too, like mad dogs.*

*Talking of which, I (or rather Daphne) have decided to hold an impromptu summer solstice costume party for some of my new acquaintances – there are so many who find my windmill intriguing and wish to see it. One of Daphne's friends is bringing some musicians who are visiting from Paris, so there will be jollity. It was Daphne who insisted that we dress up. She has designed our costumes: I am to be a Druid, in a white robe, leather belt and speckled bird headdress with fluttering wings, and she my Druidess, in a magnificent headdress with antlers and a strange bird nest feature. She and Miss Jones (who has declined to dress up) have been sewing all week. A friend of Daphne's is bringing a 'ceremonial high priest' (real or make-believe, I honestly haven't dared ask), and Mr Banks is coming as an oak. You would adore all this – I know how you love a costume party. I wish you could be here too.*

*Do write again, a more forgiving note perhaps, when you find the time. I know how busy you are, and how the responsibility of your ship weighs on you so very heavily. I shall be glad of your triumphant news.*

*Your C*

*PS. I forgot to say that no, I have not yet been back to Smythe Square, but I shall try to go next week and check that all is well with the house.*

# Chapter 11

All the planes were grounded, the monitor was a line of red. She saw the Edinburgh flight, but no time was given. She had no way to contact Nina to tell her this, unless she saw the loping boy again, or asked a stranger for a phone. The need for a Jim Beam had become rather urgent. She spotted a bar and, tugging the carry-on case behind her, pushed through the crowded terminal towards it.

There were a lot of people in the bar, but she wormed through them, bellowing 'Excuse me!' as if she had somewhere urgent to be. She found herself next to a tall black man in a well-cut suit. He glanced down at her. He was awfully handsome, broad-shouldered, a little grizzled at the temples. The barman happened to be passing and she called out, projecting from the diaphragm, 'Do you have Jim Beam?' She felt the man turn to stare down at her. She kept her eyes forward. She could see the top of her face and hair in the mirror behind the optics. She barely came up to his shoulder. He wouldn't dare object to a little old lady pushing in.

'I'm waiting, too, actually.' His voice was deep, firm and controlled. She pretended not to hear, lifted her chin, adjusted her scarf and waved at the barman. 'Hi! Barman? Jim Beam?'

The man leaned down. 'I'm waiting to order, too,' he said, more loudly.

She craned to look up at him, pretending surprise, touching her ear. 'Sorry – were you talking to me? My dog ate my hearing aids – both of them, can you believe it? It's a wonder they didn't kill him, those little batteries, absolutely lethal. But I suppose he sicked them both up somewhere – though nowhere I could find.'

She watched the man's irritation slide towards bafflement and then a smile spread over his face. The barman appeared.

'This young lady would like a bourbon,' the man said. 'And I'll have a black Americano.'

'My flight's delayed,' Astrid said. 'I have no idea why.'

'Well, yes, everything's grounded. There's a . . .' He looked over at the monitor and she didn't catch the end of his sentence. She needed to sit down, she felt suddenly drained, but the stool was high, and she'd never get onto it with one arm. He seemed to read her mind and leaned towards her. She waited for him to take her elbow – after a certain age, people did that, it was most annoying – but he held out an arm. 'Need someone to lean on?' His biceps felt like chunks of granite under the soft wool of his jacket as she hauled herself up, wincing.

She really must find the painkillers, though right now it wasn't her wrist but her back that was agony. Different bits of her body were behaving like tantrumming toddlers, warring for attention. She put her handbag on the bar and dug around in it with her good hand. She felt the man trying not to stare as she pulled out gloves, tissues, reading glasses, the windmill keys, a ziplock bag containing something white – a spare pair of pants. Mrs Baker must have slipped them in, just in case. She tried to shove them back into the bag and knocked the keys which slid across the shiny surface. The man shot out a hand and caught

them. The keyring was a large yellow plastic thing shaped like
a chicken with the words *Cluck off you motherclucker* stamped on
one side. One of the Letters from Beyond clients had left it in
the windmill, and she'd taken such a shine to it that she'd pretended to know nothing when they phoned to see if they'd left
it. She saw the man read the chicken as he handed it back; he
smiled. She managed to find the packet of painkillers, then, but
with one hand she'd never get the foil out. Again, he reached
out a huge hand.

'Can I help?' He pulled the pill foil out of the package. 'One
or two?'

She held up two fingers. 'You are kind.'

'Even with two good hands these packets are hard enough
but with one . . . My mum used to have trouble too.'

'It is rather a torment.'

'I'm not sure top doctors recommend co-codamol and bourbon,
though.'

'Well, they should, it's a magical combination, let me tell you.'

The barman set the drinks in front of them and held out the
card reader. Astrid turned away to pop the pills into her mouth.
In the mirror she saw the man tap his credit card. She waited
a beat, then turned, 'Goodness, you didn't pay, did you? You
naughty man. How *terribly* kind of you.'

He smiled and nodded at her wrist. 'Broken?'

'Slightly.'

'What happened?' He pushed Jim Beam towards her good
hand.

'I fell.' She took a slug of Jim Beam, felt it snake down her
throat, smoky and warm. 'Off a horse.' A horse sounded more
fun than a collapsing garden table. She felt his eyes on her and
added, 'So careless.'

There had been a moment, just a split second when they'd known it was all about to go. There was a sinister cracking and Nina looked stricken, and then the whole construction lurched sideways and came thudding onto the ground with the sound of splintering wood. Astrid must have been projected sideways and backwards, which was a mercy because it meant her legs weren't trapped between table and bench. She remembered Gordon leaping through the air like a cartoon dog, his curly ears like wings; her coffee cup arched above her.

She must have stuck out an arm to break the fall. It was a miracle that she hadn't broken a hip. Mrs Baker, meanwhile, had been shot in the chest with a sawn-off shotgun. At least, that's what it looked like. She'd flopped back onto her bottom, legs in the air, and the sponge cake had upturned on her breast leaving a gruesome jam stain. Other than this, though, she appeared to be unscathed. Nina's leg was trapped under the table, and she was struggling to free herself but, being young and bendy, she got out unharmed.

At first, Astrid thought she'd broken her spine. The pain was acute. Too afraid to move, she felt Gordon's wet nose on her cheek, and then Mrs Baker and Nina were looming over her, blotting out the sky. Nina pulled out a phone. 'I'll call an ambulance.'

'No ... no ... I just can't seem to ... I'm absolutely all right, really, I just ...'

She summoned all her courage and somehow managed to roll onto one side, her lower back shooting pains down her leg. But as she leaned on her arm, she felt a sickening jolt, and she knew it was bad.

'Don't move,' Mrs Baker said.

Nina crouched next to her. 'Your back might be damaged.'

'My back's been damaged for years, now help me up.'

Hendricks appeared then, and stuck his nose into her left eye, and then Juniper was trying to climb onto her face, dribbling pee. Mrs Baker swept all three dogs off and, with her help, Astrid managed to get into a sitting position. She held out her good arm and Nina took it, Mrs Baker was behind her, and she felt hands hoisting her armpits and then, somehow, she was on her feet. She didn't dare touch her wrist; it felt very odd and sickening, as if it no longer quite belonged to her. 'So stupid!' she cried. 'Stupid, stupid, stupid!' The table was in ruins, cups and saucers scattered on the scrubby grass, the sponge cake had plopped over, the Battenburg was smashed next to it, and the dogs were now feasting on the marzipan, rapturous. The coffee pot must have just missed Nina, or bounced off her, and was upturned behind her on the grass. Nina's jeans were ripped down the side of one knee, but other than that she seemed fine, and Mrs Baker, despite the appearance of blood and gore, was uninjured.

There was a slightly absurd moment as they got into Gloria. Astrid got in the front seat out of habit while Mrs Baker let the dogs into the back, but then they realised that Nina probably shouldn't be in the back with Hendricks, so they had to get Hendricks out and Nina in, and Hendricks started snarling and baring his teeth, and then Astrid decided she must go in the back seat with him, and somehow Nina and Astrid ended up in the back together, with all three dogs on the front seat.

It struck Astrid, as they drove off down the hill, that she hadn't been to A&E since the night forty-five years ago when she, Rohls and Magnus had followed the ambulance as it sped Sally Morgan through country lanes. She remembered the dark trees flashing by with Rohls at the wheel of the Bentley, erratic, shouting, and Magnus sprawled semi-conscious in the back. She felt Nina touch her shoulder.

'Are you cold, Astrid? You're shaking. Here.' Nina took off her duvet jacket and tucked it over Astrid's knees.

There was a retching sound from the front seat. 'Oh, dear God,' Mrs Baker snapped as the smell of vomited marzipan floated back.

Astrid felt Nina's hand take her good one. 'We'll be there soon,' she said. 'They'll give you very good painkillers.' She held tight to Nina's hand trying not to yelp as Gloria bumped down over the chalky potholes. She wished she'd had the foresight to have a Jim on the way out.

'Where are you trying to get to today?'

Astrid came back to the present – the bar, the man, who glanced at his phone, took a swig of coffee, then looked up, expecting an answer. Astrid picked up the bourbon. 'Edinburgh,' she said. 'I'm going to see my ex-husband. He betrayed me forty-five years ago and he's still trying to destroy me even though he's dying. I'm attempting to stop him. What about you?'

There was a moment of silence, then he gave a belly laugh. 'Shit!' He picked up his cup, clinking it against her glass.

'What about you?' she said again. 'Where are you going?'

'Well, I'm supposed to be speaking at a medical conference in Frankfurt. My soon to be ex-wife isn't there, she's in London. She's trying to destroy me, too, though, as it happens.'

'Oh dear. Poor you. It's no fun, is it? Are you a doctor?'

'I am.' He nodded and held out his hand. 'That's why I'm so good at opening pill packets. Emmanuel Olowe.'

She put her hand in his. 'Astrid Miller. What sort of doctor are you?'

'Reproductive.' He saw her confusion. 'I'm clinical director of a fertility clinic.'

Astrid thought of the Formica table in Switzerland, the woman's mottled forearms, the crucible of dried blood. She knew that what happened to her that day had damaged her, inside. She was in her early thirties when she met Magnus and until then she'd never had the slightest desire to be a mother, but practically the first time he undressed her it was as if her biological self had risen and seized the controls. Magnus was dying for children, lots of them, and they'd never used contraception, even when she was playing Lady M, and it would have been disastrous to be pregnant. On some level, perhaps, she'd known that it couldn't happen.

If things hadn't gone so wrong, then maybe she would have seen a doctor like Emmanuel and found out what was damaged inside. She had a sudden urge to ask him what might have happened in there – could the woman have taken something else out along with the foetus, or ruptured something perhaps? But of course, it was a moot point now and it might not be appropriate to ask a stranger something like this in an airport bar. A doctor like Emmanuel might perhaps have fixed whatever was broken but there was never any chance, and, as it turned out, that was a blessing because if she'd had Magnus's baby, she'd have been in a far worse situation when he abandoned and betrayed her.

She'd not used contraception with Mohammed either, or anyone else for that matter, because she'd always known that if Magnus couldn't make her pregnant, nobody could. And by the time she met Charlie she was in her late forties, far too old to reproduce. Sometimes she imagined what might have happened if Magnus had been the infertile one, and she'd had Mohammed's baby. She might still be living as a Bedouin with lots of little grandchildren and a big, dear family. It was an odd thought, quite pleasant, but entirely theoretical. The only life that felt real to her was the one she was meant to have had with Magnus – the

one that had always played out in the background – a chaotic
north London home with an overgrown garden, gnarled fruit
trees that the children would climb, and dogs, of course, lots
of dogs, and an enormous kitchen table where friends would
come to eat and drink. And she would have kept her career.
Some women of her generation did – Judi Dench had a daughter,
Maggie Smith at least one child, maybe two; Sheila Hancock,
surely, several. Her generation could – did – have it all.

Emmanuel's phone rang, and he gave a rueful smile. 'Sorry,
talk of the devil – I'll have to . . .' He turned away. She couldn't
hear what he was saying. She remembered that she needed to
borrow a phone to ring Nina, and Mrs Baker. Her scarf was
falling off, but she didn't dare let go of the bar. She felt unstable
perched on the stool now that Emmanuel wasn't watching her.
She wondered how she'd get down if he left. She really must
ring Nina, who might be on her way to the airport already, not
realising there were delays. It would be the second time, in fact,
that poor Nina had had to hang around waiting for her.


They'd been in A&E for almost four hours before she was seen.
Mrs Baker kept saying that Nina should go, but Nina had insisted
on staying, which was a rather good thing, because hospitals
made Mrs Baker extremely edgy. At first the three of them sat
in a row of uncomfortable seats listening to a conversation next
to them.

'But Mum,' the large woman next to Astrid shouted out, 'you
were sectioned!'

The mother, Astrid noted, was around her own age and looked
terribly unwell, with skin the colour of a greyhound. 'How did
that come about?' the old woman said, in a wavering voice.

'You went mad at the old vicarage, Mum, remember?' The

daughter looked just as unhealthy as the old woman, really. There were dog hairs on her black baggy clothes, a white stripe down the roots of her hair, blotchy pale skin. It was impossible to know which of them needed the medical attention. 'You went ballistic, Mum.'

The mother, Astrid realised, smelled faintly of pee. At least, she hoped it was the mother.

'You had a lovely room there,' the daughter continued. 'But it was that spirit obviously. It's a shame because that was such a lovely place.'

'There was something there, definitely.' The mother sounded matter-of-fact.

Mrs Baker leaped to her feet, wild-eyed. 'I'm going to check on the dogs.'

'She can't stand hospitals,' Astrid explained to Nina. 'Bad associations.' The daughter and mother stared at them for a moment, then resumed their discussion of the spirit world.

Nina said, 'I get it. Hospitals always remind me of my mum. She had breast cancer.'

'Oh dear, how dreadful. Did she die from it?'

'Yes. It was four years ago now.' Nina looked a bit hollow and lifted her Costa coffee cup. 'That was partly why I moved to Edinburgh. I needed a fresh start.'

'Well, it's kind of you to stay here with me,' Astrid said. 'Mrs Baker wouldn't have left me on my own, but she'd be unbearable if she stayed in here.'

Nina smiled, took another sip of coffee, then lowered the cup. 'So, since we're probably going to be here a while, would you be up to talking about Magnus, do you think?'

'Magnus? Here? Now?' Astrid had almost forgotten that this was the reason Nina had come all the way from Scotland.

'No. Of course. Now's not a good time. You're in pain—'

'As long as you stay positive, Mum, it won't attach itself to you!' the daughter next to them bellowed. Astrid tried not to turn and stare; she had a feeling that she could easily be sucked in. Perhaps the distraction of talking about Magnus might not be such a bad thing. She looked firmly at Nina. 'What do you want to know?'

Nina nodded. 'Okay. Right. Great! Well, so, let's see. I think I told you that the final draft of the memoir's due to be submitted to the publisher in just a few weeks, didn't I? And that Magnus is very sick and—'

'Too sick to know what's in his own book.'

'It's more than that – he didn't have much involvement in the memoir, even before he got sick. He'd basically left the whole thing to Dessie and the ghost writers – he really didn't want anything to do with it. So, it's been Dessie's project from the start. Dessie's obsessed with his father's legacy. It's him who hired me, not Magnus. He's very . . . well, he's a details man. It's been going on for quite a few years now, and he's fired at least three previous writers. He's currently suing the one before me for taking materials out of the archive. The memoir is quite . . .' She paused, as if reining herself back in. 'I'm really not supposed to talk about it, that's the problem. I've signed all sorts of confidentiality agreements. Dessie's American and, well, do you know him? He's very . . . I think he's quite litigious.'

Astrid had only met Desmond once, in an Italian restaurant in Soho in the mid-seventies when he was a small boy, just five or six years old. She and Magnus were recently married and the boy's mother, a terrifying Scandinavian model with gappy front teeth, was in the process of moving from a commune in Greece to California. She used to vanish with Desmond for months, sometimes not telling Magnus where his son was. It was all terribly distressing. Astrid had been prepared to love the boy, but he was quite off-putting, watchful and solid, his square face darkened by the Greek sun, his peculiar, bulbous eyes monitoring everything. She'd felt such pity for the child. When his mother didn't come back, they'd taken him home to their basement flat. She didn't reappear for ten days, during which Desmond glued himself to Magnus, mostly in silence. When the mother finally reappeared, without an explanation, she took him off to LA. Astrid read in a newspaper some years later that Magnus had tried, and failed, to get custody.

'He'd definitely fire me if he knew I was here,' Nina was saying. 'He isn't your biggest fan.'

'Who? Desmond? Why? What on earth has he got against me?'

'I think he blames you for breaking his parents up, and maybe also for what happened to his mother.'

'His mother? Magnus had already left her when he met me – I barely knew the woman. What happened to her?'

'Unfortunately, she killed herself when he was a teenager.'

'Well, that's ghastly, but how is it my fault?' Astrid remembered the model's unhinged bug eyes and gappy mouth. How very odd that Desmond should blame her for his mother's problems. But, she supposed, pain was more manageable when you created a villain on which to pin it.

'I think Magnus was pretty absent throughout his childhood,' Nina was saying, 'and that's a source of a sadness, maybe for both of them. Perhaps also a lot of guilt for Magnus. I think that's why he's been so hands off, you know, letting Dessie do this thing. Dessie's extremely passionate about his father, he's very protective. He moved Magnus out to Northbank last year – that's Dessie's house in the Borders – but it's quite isolated up there. It's a bit sad really. It's incredibly lavish and beautiful,

Dessie renovated the whole thing from top to toe, but it's also really empty. Magnus has a live-in carer, who's very nice, but he's had no visitors in all the time I've been there and—'

'You live in Magnus's house?' Astrid recoiled. It hadn't occurred to her until this moment to wonder where Nina lived.

'The accommodation came with the job; it was a condition of it actually. But I don't live in Northbank itself. I live in the gatehouse, it's five minutes' walk down the drive. I have to go up to the house every day to work in the library, where the archive is. Dessie's paying me a lot of money to live there and do nothing but finish his book.'

Astrid imagined Nina and Magnus laughing together and Nina winkling information – morsels, stories, titbits – out of him for the book. Her wrist hurt – quite a lot. She felt sick. Gordon would be anxious, he hated the car, and Junie would need a pee, her bladder wasn't good, and Hendricks would be baying at pedestrians. She looked around. 'Where on earth is Mrs Baker?'

'Astrid.' Nina leaned closer, talking gently. 'I don't get to talk to Magnus. Not at *all*. I've been at Northbank since August, that's three months, and I've only met him twice. Dessie doesn't want him bothered with the book. He has a whole wing of the house to himself, so our paths never cross. I only spoke to him properly for the first time two weeks ago and that's when I contacted you.'

'Really?' It was all getting more and more bizarre. She needed Mrs Baker to make sense of it. Her chest felt fluttery and odd.

'Dessie was in New York – he's in New York a lot, thank goodness – and I came out of the library and found Magnus on the sofa, waiting for me. He wanted to know how the memoir portrays you. He said he'd got suspicious that Dessie had read him out a different version of the chapter about your marriage – specifically about what happened at the hunting lodge.'

Astrid felt the waiting room spin.

She felt Nina touch her shoulder. 'It's okay, Astrid. We don't have to talk about this. I'm sorry.'

Astrid looked into Nina's anxious face. 'What does this book say about me?'

Nina hesitated. 'Are you sure you want to know?'

Astrid held on to Nina's arm and tried not to keel over.

'Well, okay, it sort of paints you as the jealous wife. It says you were jealous of Magnus getting the role in *I Am Me*, and you were threatened by Sally Morgan – you were out to destroy her, essentially.' Nina squeezed Astrid's hand. 'But Magnus told me this isn't how it happened. He got quite agitated about it. Then he looked like he was going to collapse and Mrs McKittrick – that's his carer – came rushing in. Before she took him off, he told me to come and find you. He said . . .' Nina looked into Astrid's eyes. 'He said you're the love of his life, Astrid.'

'Why would he say that?' Astrid shouted. 'He abandoned me!'

The old woman and her daughter swivelled in their chairs – Astrid had almost forgotten that she and Nina weren't alone in A&E. 'He abandoned *me*,' Astrid said to them. 'And lied, to protect himself – and then he made me lie for him too.' The mother and daughter looked at her for a moment. The old woman nodded. 'They do that,' she said. 'Bloody bastards.'

'You know, Astrid, I'd love you to tell me what really happened,' Nina said, 'but right now I think we should probably stop, honestly. You've had a shock, you're in a lot of pain, it's distressing to have to think about all this, and it was so long ago, you probably don't remember much anyway.'

But Astrid did remember, unfortunately. She remembered absolutely everything.

# Chapter 12

There had been a full moon on the night they stayed at the Tudor hunting lodge. Rohls' driver collected them in a Bentley outside the theatre after the Saturday evening performance and Astrid had slept for over two hours with her head on Magnus's shoulder. He shook her awake as they were coming down the drive and as she opened her eyes, she saw a huge mottled moon dangling over a line of bare trees. She remembered her father getting her out of her bed one night to show her the December moon. They stood at her bedroom window together, looking down, and he told her it had a special name, the 'Long Night Moon'. She remembered noticing how it floated, pale and perfect, on the surface of the lake which, just a week later, would open and swallow him up.

As they rounded a corner in the drive the Tudor hunting lodge appeared in the moonlight, black bricks crosshatched on red. It was moated, and girdled by oversized topiary cut into surreal *Alice in Wonderland* shapes that dwarfed them as they got out of the car. Magnus squeezed her hand – *He's going to love you, don't worry*. But she had no interest in what Rohls might think of her. It seemed to her that Hollywood, at that time, was a collection of drugged-up, priapic egotists who were somehow persuading studios to hand over millions of dollars for their vanity projects. Hollywood was Magnus's dream, though, and always had been, ever since he was a child in Leith taking refuge at the flicks; she knew she must support him. He peered up at the hunting lodge. *How the fuck did we get here, Aster?*

Rohls appeared at the front door, cigarette in hand, framed by two massive Buddhas. He had to stoop to avoid the lintel. As he took Magnus by the shoulders and pulled him into a hug, his eyes travelled up and down Astrid's body. He wore an Aran jumper – she remembered this particularly because later, as they followed the ambulance through the country lanes, she noticed that its cream cuffs were rusted with Sally Morgan's blood.

'Hey? You look a bit zoned out there? Are you okay?'

Astrid opened her eyes to see the line of optics, her own white hair multiplied to infinity and the man's face, this Emmanuel, this fertility doctor, staring at her. It was rather disorientating, going backwards like this, her mind jolting through the past and round to the present again.

'You had a bit of a wobble,' he said. 'Pills and booze tend to do that.'

'Is that a medical diagnosis?'

He laughed. 'Yes. Yes, it is.'

She peered out at the busy terminal. People were crowded beneath monitors, some motionless, staring, others agitated and barking into phones. A young couple at a table nearby was arguing, chins out, the man jabbing a stubby finger at the woman. Two armed police officers walked past purposefully with chests puffed. There was a subtle feeling of escalating aggrava-tion, as if public order was about to unravel. 'What on earth is happening?'

Emmanuel looked surprised. 'You mean the delays? There's been a drone sighting – didn't you know?'

She felt a stab of fear. 'Are we under attack?'

'Oh no, no, no – more like an, um, you know, an incident, someone fooling around. Nothing to worry about. It's just the planes have to stay grounded till they sort it out.'

'Has there been an announcement?' Her hand flew to her ear.

'It's probably nothing,' he said. 'Really. Just some idiot. If drones get tangled in a turbine engine, they can do a lot of damage, so the airports have to be really careful. Last time this happened, they grounded hundreds of flights and it all turned out to be a hoax.'

'A hoax?'

'Or some kind of mass insanity. Lots of people thought they saw a drone, even police officers. But there was nothing. I'm not sure anyone ever got to the bottom of it.' He laughed again. She liked his ready laugh, open-mouthed, booming, full of heart. She remembered seeing images of distraught people stuck in Gatwick for days, missing weddings, funerals, graduations, holidays. There had been a piece of mocked-up footage on the BBC News of a drone drilling through the wing of an airbus, causing catastrophic damage. She tried to push this image out of her head. She really didn't need a reminder that she was soon to be inside a lump of metal held together by nuts and bolts, kept in the air by spinning blades, burning gases and, perhaps, collective delusion.

Emmanuel's phone pinged again. 'Sorry.' He began to type with his huge thumbs. A group of young men came into the bar, bellowing, chanting, shoving; a stag night perhaps. One of them jolted her cast, causing a nauseating shot of pain up her arm. Emmanuel didn't notice. He picked up his briefcase. 'I'll have to go somewhere quieter.' He moved away.

Astrid felt as if she'd been abandoned on a mountainside
with a pack of wild animals. The young men were so loud and
their energy tightened the air. They *were* stags, clashing antlers,
bumping chests. They weren't aware of her, couldn't see her –
she was entirely invisible to them. They could knock her off the
stool, trample her without noticing. She wanted to get away, out
of the bar, but the floor was a long way down and she was not
sure, not sure at all, if she would be able to make it on her own.

10th August 1920

Dear Walter,

It seems you have not had time to reply to my last two letters, but although it is late evening, and my body is weary, I am not sleepy, so I will tell you what's been happening here.

I have been avoiding the village since the solstice party, which was a tremendous success until some local busybodies appeared, objecting to the bonfires, and claiming that the high priest was a Satanist (he was, in fact, a barrister from Richmond). It all became rather heated. Some of the villagers stormed off to find the Watch Committee, but a couple stayed, and were persuaded to have some wine. By the end of the night the headmaster of the village school was dancing the can-can with a Parisian flautist. At one point, two stags, a bishop, a Hungarian acrobat and a very drunk swan – all covered in mud – came staggering up the hill with an altar stone they'd dug up from the churchyard. Daphne feels we must install it in the windmill as a 'conduit between worlds'.

I must try to sleep now, I suppose. There is a storm coming, violet clouds are thickening over the Downs. On the slopes I can see the sheep have gathered in huddles, like piles of beige stones, and it is windless suddenly, everything has gone eerily still. The night, I fear, will be unruly.

Your C

# Chapter 13

She couldn't see Emmanuel any more, but surely he wouldn't just leave her? She needed his phone, apart from anything else, to call Nina. The knowledge that Nina would be there to meet her when she got off the plane felt terribly reassuring. Nina had turned out to be such a comforting person. After A&E, she'd ended up staying the night at the windmill. By the time they left the hospital it was late and they were all hungry, so Mrs Baker drove them down to the seafront for fish and chips. But then Gloria had the usual starter motor problem, and Mrs Baker had to open the bonnet and tinker. It all took a very long time, and the tablets kicked in, and Astrid fell asleep on the back seat covered in coats and blankets.

She woke up in the dark, hot-water-bottled by dogs, on an incline, bumping around – Gloria was climbing the final slope to the windmill. She could see nothing but her body could read the track like braille: each chalky bump, each dip, hollow, puddle and flint. Nina was in the front seat next to Mrs Baker and they were talking loudly over the engine and the roar of the heating. Astrid heard Nina say, 'He never stopped loving her.'

'That's why he buggered off to Hollywood, is it?'

'We didn't really . . .' Astrid didn't catch the rest of the sentence, but heard the last bit: '. . . the love of his life.'

Brainblood Hall, Astrid remembered. The tabloids had called the hunting lodge 'Brainblood Hall'.

'If she was the love of his life, why didn't he stand up for her?' Mrs Baker's voice was louder, strident. 'Why did he leave her alone to crack up?'

'I don't know. I think he's trying to put it right now . . . Problem is, I can't talk to him about it any more. Dessie says he'll fire me . . . honestly don't know . . . don't want to be part of something that might . . .'

'Walk away then.'

'I've thought about it, believe me,' Nina said. 'It hasn't been easy working for Dessie. The whole thing feels wrong but I can't just leave.'

'Why not?'

'Well, I haven't got any money. I get paid when I submit the book and if I leave now, I won't get anything and then . . . my own . . .'

'Don't you have family?'

'Not really. I have some cousins in South Africa . . . them twice, when I was little.'

Mrs Baker said nothing, but Astrid knew she'd be softening. If anyone knew what it was like to be alone in the world, it was her. 'No friends? Boyfriend?'

There was a pause. 'I was with someone, but not any more. And I only moved to Edinburgh four years ago . . . kind of lost touch . . . London and . . . in a way.'

Astrid heard the heartbreak. She knew the signs: shrinkage, self-inflicted isolation. She wondered what had happened to poor Nina in London. She wished she had the strength to sit up and join in the conversation. There was no good relying on Mrs Baker. It wasn't lack of interest, it was just that in Mrs Baker's world curiosity was risky, secrets the norm. Gloria rattled up the last, steepest part of the hill, emitting sinister fumes. Through the window she saw the windmill, silhouetted by the full moon. Mrs Baker was saying something about bedding. She closed her eyes and heard Nina's voice but didn't catch the words. Mrs Baker turned off the engine. 'That's Astrid's story to tell.'

Or not tell. Astrid wasn't sure how she could put it into words, even if she'd wanted to. The Tudor hunting lodge had smelled of damp carpet and hashish, she remembered that. There was a tiger spreadeagled by the huge stone fireplace, a relic of empire, skin flattened out with a stuffed wedge head and glass eyes. Astrid was so transfixed by it that it took her a moment to notice Sally Morgan curled on a sofa, a doll-like thing with fine, bright hair cascading over a fur coat several sizes too big. She was even tinier than she looked on screen, her face more delicate, younger, prettier, in the firelight.

After Sally had floated, silently, up the stairs ahead of them to show them their bedroom, an octagonal oddity with a canopied bed that smelled of mildew, they all went back down to the fireplace and drank red wine. Rohls, with his legs out and his ankles crossed on the tiger's head, talked about the meetings he'd had in London for *I Am Me*. Magnus was to fly out the following week to start filming in upstate New York. They talked about the script, and Rohls' detailed vision for Magnus's character. Astrid, who had done two performances of *Macbeth* that day, was almost delirious with exhaustion, but Rohls and Sally Morgan were functioning on American time.

In the early hours they ate game stew in a back kitchen. Rohls talked about how they'd film certain scenes, and about Magnus's character's motivations in each. Sally Morgan made no attempt to join in. Her pupils were enlarged, she ate nothing and swayed back and forwards, very slightly, almost imperceptibly. When Magnus spoke, Rohls listened with narrowed eyes and nodded through cigarette smoke. A pair of pheasants dangled by the window next to Astrid's head, females with blue baling twine passed through their nostrils, gathering their beaks together from a hook so that they seemed to have been caught mid-song, throats stretched. She could smell their sweetly rotting flesh. She reached out to touch the feathers, russet and gold, subtle flecks of amber.

She ate but was too tired to drink. Magnus and Rohls consumed everything in large quantities, and after they'd finished, they all went back to the fireplace. Rohls tossed logs on the fire, took a poker and jabbed the embers until the flames rose up and roared, illuminating the tiger's glass eyes. He took a bottle of scotch, sat in the biggest armchair and sloshed the whisky into four glasses. Sally Morgan watched him intensely all the time, as if trying to calculate whether he was real, or an aspect of a wider hallucination. Rohls talked on and on about Borges and Nietzsche, and her cigarette dripped ash onto the fur.

Magnus was obviously very, very drunk. His hair stuck up, his eyes were pink and heavy-lidded. Astrid felt sorry for him, that in a week's time he was going to have to go to upstate New York and make a film with this egotistical, inflated bore. It struck her then that they were on the threshold of an alternative existence, one that would change them in a way they could not yet fathom. She felt terribly sad, suddenly. Sally Morgan tried to stand up, swayed, and sat back down, too close to the fire. Sparks fizzled onto the coat. Astrid smelled singed fur but did nothing. She must go to bed and end this unpleasant evening.

The alcohol seemed to have had almost no effect on Rohls, and when Astrid said that she was going up, he looked at her, curiously.

*Tired, honey? I'm not. You want to know why?*

*Perhaps you haven't been on stage at the National today?*

*That's funny.*

Rohls took a drag of his cigarette, and hinged his jaw to cut a smoke ring.

*You're funny, Astrid. But no. I don't get tired. You want to know why?*

Astrid didn't, but felt sure that he was going to tell her anyway.

He began to say something about how the blood supply to his brain was superior to hers – he called it the 'heartbeat in my brain'.

Sally Morgan struggled unsteadily to her knees.

Rohls was saying that the human skull is formed of two plates which are open at birth. *We're literally open-minded.* The skull doesn't fully fuse until we're about twenty-one years old – this pre-fused brain is the source of energy and creativity but when the skull closes up we grow depressed, neurotic, stuck, we begin to die inside.

*If I hadn't met the countess, I'd probably have killed myself by now.*

Astrid glanced at Magnus who was nodding, drunkenly, but she wasn't sure he was taking anything in. Rohls was saying that it was the countess who owned the hunting lodge, they'd met in Amsterdam.

*She's enlightened, a spiritual person – she's a visionary. She changed my life.*

He put down his whisky and leaned forwards, elbows on his knees, speaking just to Astrid now, understanding that she was the doubter in the room, the one to persuade.

*I'm on a permanent high because of her. I had depression my whole life and now it's gone. You want to know why, Astrid?*

Expecting a lecture on psychedelics, Astrid didn't.

Rohls got up, and came over to her chair in one swift move. He leaned on the armrests on either side of her, and bent so that his face was close to hers; she could smell his gamey breath, cigarettes and whisky and something else, a sort of rancid, buttery stench that must surely be rising off his soul. With one hand he pulled back his hair and showed her a dent in his forehead, the size of a newborn's fingerprint, close to the hairline. She looked at it and started to laugh.

'Astrid. Astrid?' Mrs Baker's voice tunnelled through the memories. 'Astrid. We're home. Wake up.'

She couldn't quite open her eyes. She heard the creak and slam of Gloria's front doors, and there was a blast of freezing air. Gordon hopped off her lap, and she felt the other two dogs tunnel out from under the coats.

'Nina's stopping here. Too late for her to get a train now.'

Astrid managed to sit up and open her eyes. 'Splendid.' Her mouth was dry.

'I could always sleep in the windmill; I could go down the tunnel to get in?' Nina sounded hopeful.

'Only if you want hypothermia,' Mrs Baker said. 'There's a big enough sofa in the snug, I'll make it up for you.'

The next morning when Astrid came down, Nina and Mrs Baker were in the kitchen, eating toast and marmalade. Juniper was sitting on Nina's lap, licking toast crumbs off her fingers. Gordon was over by Tony Blair, looking disconcerted, and Hendricks was in his basket, head on front paws, monitoring Nina. When Gordon saw her enter the kitchen, he flung himself across the tiles, wagging and yelping and making little delighted leaps.

'You had quite a lie-in,' Mrs Baker said. 'I'm driving Nina to the station in an hour.' The Kit Cat clock informed her, smugly, that it was ten past ten. Astrid hadn't slept that long, or that well, in years. There was something to be said for a doctor's tablets.

She felt a bit jealous, though, that Mrs Baker had been up, chatting to Nina all this time without her. It struck her then that she really didn't want Nina to leave. 'But you can't go yet! I haven't shown you the lavender garden. And we haven't really talked, have we, not properly?'

'We could do both?' Nina said.

'Don't you want to eat?' Mrs Baker said to Astrid.

'I'll eat when I'm dead.'

'You really won't.'

It was impossible to get her silver puffer coat on with her wrist in a cast, so Astrid had to wrap herself in blankets against the biting wind. The dogs shot across the courtyard and up the slope. She shouted after them, but they ignored her, and vanished behind the fallen altar. 'So rude!' The wind punched her eardrums, making her jaw ache, stiffening her lips.

'I'll get them!' Nina took off, before she could be stopped, her jacket flapping, her dark ponytail whipping from side to side. Astrid watched, struck by her energy which was different, freer and more youthful than when she arrived. She held her cast close to her chest as she picked her way across the courtyard; she didn't want to stumble. The nurse had told her that a blood clot forms a callus over the fracture and then the bone starts to grow again, knitting over the weak spot. She pictured the fibres fusing themselves back together – extraordinary, really, even at her age, this capacity for healing and regeneration.

The dogs were scrabbling like maniacs at the altar, but Nina wasn't trying to stop them, she was leaning over it to peer into the windmill. Astrid didn't have the energy to stop her now. Nina was no threat, she felt sure of that. When she got to the windmill, Astrid ran her fingers over the underside of the marble and found the little circle where the hole for the relic had been carved and plugged.

'Look,' she said. 'Nina? Under here – you can feel it – the little cavity we were talking about, cut into the stone for the saint's relic. That's how an altar is consecrated, you see: the bishop puts in the relic and seals it up and does something elaborate with oils and prayers, and then it's holy – or magic, or whatever you want to believe.'

Nina knelt down and craned her neck so she could peer up at the underside of the altar. She traced it with her fingers. 'Which bit of the saint is it, do you think?'

'I like to imagine a fingernail, I think.' She told Nina, then, how Constance's friend Daphne had brought people to the windmill – bohemians, musicians, poets, painters – and one night in 1920 there had been a solstice party, and some of the guests went down to the churchyard and dug up the altar. 'I've no idea how they carried it all the way up the hill.'

'Didn't the village want it back?'

'I'm not sure they ever worked it out. Perhaps they didn't know the stone was buried in the churchyard to begin with? There may even have been a bishop involved that night . . .'

Nina listened, nodding, as the wind rattled and bashed at the fantail above them. 'How do you know so much about this?' she said.

'I have letters Constance wrote to her husband, Walter, when he was in America, designing a tiny battleship. There's a whole tin of them, in there.' Astrid nodded into the windmill. 'There are some from outraged locals, too, and a few from her very bossy sister-in-law. They're quite interesting.'

'How amazing to have her actual letters – I mean, to hear her voice like that. God, I'd really love to read them.' Nina stood up and leaned over the stone to look into the dark interior. 'Won't they get ruined, with the door broken like this? Won't the rain get in?'

'You sound just like Joe Dean – the millwright. He keeps coming up here and telling us to get it fixed. The thing is, Nina, there's no money, none at all.'

'Could there be grants and things? Have you looked into all that? I'd be happy to help you research it if you like.'

'That's terribly kind of you, Nina, but I have no money to pay a researcher either.'

'Oh no, you wouldn't have to pay me! It's just a bit of googling. I could do it right now, honestly.' She got out her phone and began to tap at it.

The dogs were digging madly under the stone again. It was astonishing what they could pick up on, the tiniest scent. They'd scrubbed and bleached the marble slab the day after the Awful Incident, and three seasons had come since then, surely there couldn't be anything left to sniff out. But there was obviously a lingering trace of something: Alan, probably. Or a bloodstained slipper.

A gust of wind shook the fan stage, and Nina looked up from her phone.

'The lavender garden's more sheltered,' Astrid said. 'Come on, it's this way.'

'A Heritage Lottery grant might be an option.' Nina held up her phone as they got to the gate. A seagull's feather, whipped by the wind, danced in front of them, twirling circles, trapped in a tiny twister, and they both stopped for a moment, transfixed.

'*I am a feather for each wind that blows.*'

Nina looked at her. 'Is that from *The Winter's Tale*?'

Astrid realised she'd said it out loud. 'Goodness, Nina, you know your Shakespeare.'

'Oh no, not really, but I just watched it – your one, the 1976 RSC production that was televised by the BBC. You were honestly magnificent. I went online and found theatre reviews, too, of your work. Critics were in raptures about you – not just for that *Winter's Tale*, but for pretty much everything you ever did. I can't believe you played Ophelia at Stratford, straight out of drama school – that's incredible.'

'I *was* rather good. But how on earth did you see my *Winter's Tale*? Good Lord!'

'It's online.'

'*The Winter's Tale* is on the web? Goodness. So, people can just watch it now? Anybody?'

'Yes. Anybody in the world. It's on YouTube. It's got loads of views. The comments say how amazing you were – people asking what became of you, that sort of thing. I'll show you if you like.'

'What? Good Lord, no. Oh no, I don't think I'd like that.' The idea of watching herself was a very bad one; she'd be forced to think about what she'd lost. She had stopped thinking about all that many years ago, and she definitely wasn't going to start up again now.

They came into the walled garden and followed the brick path that Constance had laid almost a century before. Mrs Baker had coaxed life into the lavender years ago, patiently cutting and propagating seeds, but lately there had been neglect; the bushes were gnarled, stiff and woody, the purple flowers hardening to dust – the scent was still powerful, though, when you rubbed the heads between your fingers.

But Nina barely looked at the lavender. 'You were as good as Judi Dench, or any of the other great actors of your generation,' she said.

Astrid didn't object because she felt that this might, in fact, be true.

'Do you miss it at all?'

'Miss the theatre? Oh no, no. Well, I did for a while, but not any more. I still adore Shakespeare, of course, even though his women all end up mad or dead.' What she did miss about acting, she thought, even now, was the relief of not having to be herself all the time. Being an actor was such a glorious escape from the self.

'Was there no going back to the RSC after . . . ?'

'No.'

'Magnus blames himself for that, I think.'

The wind was picking up and Astrid suddenly felt very cold; above them the windmill gave a low moan, and the fan stage trembled. She hadn't gone out on it for years and looking at it from below, seeing its rotten stays, she thought how lucky she was that it hadn't collapsed when she was standing on it, bringing her down forty-four feet to chalk and flint.

Nina seemed to notice that Astrid was shivering; she reached over for the slipping blanket, pulling it up around her shoulders and tucking it securely at her neck. 'It's freezing out here. Should we go back to the cottage? We could talk there?'

But Astrid wanted to know more about Nina, and if they went back to the cottage, then Mrs Baker would muscle in and make them get organised, and start finding bags and hats and things, and get them all into the car far too early. She was always ridiculously early – though this might be because Astrid was always ridiculously late, so she had to compensate. Mostly, they balanced each other out.

'What did you do in London?' she said to Nina. 'Before you moved to Edinburgh?'

Nina cleared her throat. 'I was a film editor.'

'Well! Were you really? How fascinating, Nina. What did you edit?'

Nina looked up at the Stone floor window and squinted for a second, as if she'd seen something. Then she looked back at Astrid. 'I started out doing documentaries, and then I worked on a couple of dramas. My last job was a series for the BBC called *Dark Sister*.'

'*Dark Sister*? You worked on that? But we watched it! The whole country watched it – it was awfully gripping. Didn't it win lots of awards?'

Nina nodded. 'It did really well. Bill – the director . . .' She paused, blinked, cleared her throat. 'He got a BAFTA for it. He's in America now, making bad movies. He took his whole, um, family out there.'

Astrid saw her give the tiniest wince as she said the word 'family'. 'Ah, Bill is the one who hurt you,' she said.

Nina's eyes widened. 'How do you know I was hurt?'

'I heard you say something about a disappointment to Mrs Baker, in the car last night.'

'Ah, right, I thought you were asleep.'

The dead wood on the lavender bushes made them look scrawny, but in early summer they'd swell again into fat purple bobbins, sending out signals to the bees and butterflies, filling the air with their rich, uplifting scent. Astrid wanted to tell Nina this, but she felt terribly weary. They walked down the path between the bushes and Nina, perhaps sensing Astrid's flagging energy, moved closer, speaking clearly. 'I don't know if you heard me say in the car . . . but, well, I got a sense from Magnus that he feels awful regret, genuinely, about what happened. I think he never really got over losing you.'

Astrid looked away. She didn't want to hear this. 'Do you know, I feel a little off, actually. Let's go back to the cottage now, shall we?'

'Of course. Yes, but Astrid—'

Astrid steered towards the gate, speaking loudly. 'Now, Nina, you really must tell me how you ended up at Northbank. How on earth did you go from film editing to writing Magnus's book for him?'

Nina was by her side, and seemed to realise that the diversion was necessary, and that she must talk. 'Right. Okay. Yes, well, it was chance, really. A friend of a friend lived in Edinburgh, and I was looking for work. I'd been doing some freelance journalism, film reviews mainly, and they offered me six months filling in for someone on a Scottish magazine. I didn't want to work in TV any more, but I had no money, so I left London. When the magazine job ended, I was actually doing a bit of academic tutoring, and whatever freelance articles I could drum up. And then I wrote an article for the *Scotsman* about Thelma Schoonmaker—'

'Who's that?' They were walking by the wall, now, sheltered from the worst of the wind. Astrid felt fluttery and out of breath, so she stopped. Nina's eyes were bright. 'She's one of the greatest American film editors. She's collaborated with Martin Scorsese for fifty years now – she did those massive films: *Raging Bull*, *The Age of Innocence*, *The Wolf of Wall Street*. She's had a huge impact.'

'Do you know, I don't think I've ever thought much about a film editor's job.'

'Nobody does, really. But a good editor can make a film. You're basically sitting in a room for sixteen hours a day with the director, and together you figure out what shots work best – you know, whether one scene is flowing, or a character's dominating, or underplayed, or which look or cut best conveys a certain feeling or mood. It can be incredibly subtle. I could show the director an image or a cut and connect it to something else and it'll change the entire meaning of the film. I could move a cut by two frames and change a character completely.'

'Goodness, what fun!'

'Kind of. It's intense, though. I remember a journalist once asked Thelma Schoonmaker what a nice lady like her was doing working on such violent films. Do you know what she said?'

Astrid looked at her, curious. She'd changed. She'd grown more upright and forceful, less polite. 'What?'

'"They aren't violent till I cut them."'

They both laughed at this.

'A lot of the great editors are women – it helps to have no real ego. That's why it's called the invisible art.'

'You loved the work, Nina – I can see that. Why on earth did you stop?'

'Well, I stopped loving it, I suppose.' She looked away. 'I'd just had enough.'

'So, did Dessie find you through your article about Thelma Shoo . . . ?'

'Schoonmaker. Yes, he did. He was trying to find a new writer, I think he'd just sacked the last one, and he wanted someone who understood the film world. I had quite a few reservations, but he was offering me so much money, including a tiny percentage of the royalties, and I couldn't not take it, even though I've never ghostwritten anything before. But it was only for a few months, so, at the start of the summer I moved to Northbank – it's been a very odd experience.'

'Working for Desmond?'

'Well . . .' She glanced at Astrid. 'Yes. Definitely. I mean, he's in the States a lot – he flies over from New York all the time and I never quite know when he's going to appear, and when he does he always wants to have dinner with me which is incredibly uncomfortable.' She moved forward to open the gate. 'He's a foodie and tries to wow me by shipping in Shetland oysters and things – it's sort of excruciating. I think he was hoping for something more. I've had to . . . manage him. Quite carefully.' She really did look stronger, Astrid thought, and more energetic, too, as if the wind was feeding her vitamins. 'Dessie' – she gave a grim smile – 'is very much not my type.'

'Oh dear, yes, I can imagine. What is your type?'

Nina laughed and closed the gate behind them. 'I was supposed to be asking you questions, Astrid, not the other way round. I thought actors were supposed to love talking about themselves?'

'Oh no, I don't think so. Or maybe that comes later, with fame, I don't know. Most people become actors because they want to escape themselves. We're more interested in other people and what makes them work – that's probably why we want to act, you know. The last thing we want is anyone finding out how boring we really are.'

'I don't think anyone could call you boring, Astrid.' Nina pushed back wild strands of hair and looked up at the windmill. She said something, but a gust of wind circled the tower, and swept her words away.

Astrid reached out and caught her sleeve. 'What?'

'Oh, nothing.' Nina looked round, and there were tears in her eyes, but perhaps it was the wind. They were coming underneath the windmill, now, and then the wind was on the other side and the tower sheltered them.

'What happened to make you leave the film world? Was it this Bill?'

Nina looked up at the rust-streaked tower and narrowed her eyes. 'Well, yes. It was in a way. A bit of a cliché, but I sort of lost faith.'

'In him, or in the job?'

'Both?'

'But why?'

'Well, I suppose I did a lot to make *Dark Sister* what it was and after a success like that people would expect a director to want to continue to work with the editor. I did too – I mean, I assumed we'd be a team – but Bill was trying to make his marriage work, so he didn't fight to bring me out to America with him. He went off to make the movie and left me behind. And I suppose because of the situation with his wife, he didn't talk me up to anyone, either – he just sort of left me out in the cold. So I think everyone assumed there was something wrong with me, or my work, or both, and, so, well, when I found myself editing adverts for nappies . . .' She shrugged. Astrid saw then that she'd been badly hurt, badly treated and had, like a winter shrew, responded with shrinkage. Somehow, she'd let herself get so small that she'd ended up in an isolated gatehouse on the edge of a Scottish estate, writing an old man's life. A gust slammed against the other side of the windmill which braced and rattled. Astrid heard, or perhaps felt, the windowpanes shudder against their puttied edges.

Nina said, 'I suppose you might know a bit about what that feels like.'

'Abandonment and betrayal?' Astrid nodded. 'I do, rather.'

Another gust roared up over the Downs, and this time it swept all the way around the base of the windmill and caught the edge of Astrid's blanket, almost whisking it off. Nina grabbed it, rearranged it.

'Was this Bill the love of *your* life?' Astrid said.

Nina closed her eyes for a second, took a breath, then opened them. 'I thought so, at the time, but since all the MeToo stuff, you know, I suppose I've seen it all quite differently. He was my boss – he was older, a very experienced director, he had the power to fire me. And we were stuck in an editing suite together, really intensely and creatively, just the two of us for weeks on end, and he was very charming and magnetic and I suppose I was extremely naive, in retrospect. But it doesn't matter now. I really don't want to go back to the TV world. I did miss the actual work for a while, but I just don't want that kind of life any more, those kinds of people. It isn't me. It's not who I am at all.'

'You and I were both collateral damage, weren't we,' Astrid said, 'for ambitious men?'

Nina looked intensely at her and nodded. Then she said, 'This might not help, I know, but I really think Magnus regrets whatever he did to you. He definitely doesn't want to hurt you again. He really wants this memoir to tell the truth about you.'

'Oh, nonsense, Magnus wouldn't know the truth if it bit him on the arse!' She felt so cold, dry-mouthed, shivery.

'You're freezing, let's go back inside now.'

'We need to get the dogs. Gordon! Gordon!'

'You know,' Nina said. 'I was thinking in the night that maybe I shouldn't keep doing this book. I mean, maybe Mrs Baker's right and I should walk away and let Magnus sort his own story out.'

'But what about the money? What will you live on?'

'I'll survive. I can always go back to tutoring kids.'

'No, you mustn't do that. Take the money at least.'

'But I don't want to make you relive all this. I can see the memories are really painful for you – and I can't promise that Dessie's going to allow the truth to be written, even though Magnus wants it. Dessie's a total control freak and he's never going to let his father look bad. He's deeply invested in his legacy. And I definitely don't want to be responsible for writing any more lies about you. To be honest, I don't even know if I'll be allowed to talk to Magnus again, when I get back. At the end of the day, it's Dessie who decides what version goes to the publisher next week, and he's hell-bent on making his father look heroic.'

Astrid peered up into Nina's kind, anxious face. It was ridiculous that she should feel responsible for any of this, when really it was these two men, father and son, who were organising all the lies. Nina was simply trying to do the decent thing. Magnus was the only one who could rectify this situation. He could put his foot down and insist that the book give the true version of events; he could stand up to his own daft son. But he wouldn't do that because his remorse was fake. Nina had fallen for it, but who wouldn't? He was a world-class character actor, after all.

She wasn't sure why he'd said she was the love of his life, though. That was just unnecessary. Magnus wasn't a cruel man. But then, perhaps he'd become so. Hollywood warped people, it generated fakery – though if Magnus was now entirely fake, then surely he wasn't fake any more, but genuinely rotten?

The fluttery sensation in her chest intensified. Thinking about Magnus really wasn't doing her any good. The doctor had counselled against stress. Better to stop thinking altogether. She began to move away from the windmill, but her foot caught on a flint, and she wobbled. Nina steadied her, took her good arm again. Astrid toed the flint. It was gnarled, the size of a man's fist. 'Do you think there's something inside it?' Astrid said. 'I always hope I'll break one open and find something exciting. An amateur archaeologist once found an entombed toad in a flint, not that far from here. The toad was dead, of course, but intact and entirely perfect.'

They rounded the windmill to find Mrs Baker bending at the fallen altar, bum in the air, grappling with dogs. She stood up and turned, one wriggling under each arm. Hendricks' tail was just visible as he tunnelled further beneath the slab of marble. Gordon saw Astrid and began to wag and yelp to get to her.

'You know,' Nina said, 'I don't think it would take that much to move this out of the way. It's a bit wedged, but I think two strong people could probably shove it out, or haul it out, maybe, with a rope and a car. Then you could prop the door shut or something. It would stop the rain getting in?'

'I was just telling Nina about the entombed toad!' Astrid had a feeling that she'd been too open with Nina, had said all sorts of things that Mrs Baker wouldn't approve of. She leaned to Gordon, who licked her face, giving little delighted squeals. She yearned to hold him but was hampered by the cast. She turned back to Nina. 'It's in a little museum in Brighton, it's really not far. We could all go and see it.'

The wind flattened one side of Mrs Baker's hair and then the other. 'She's got to get her train, Astrid. We have to leave here in half an hour.'

'But the toad's a must-see.'

'The toad's a hoax,' Mrs Baker said. They moved off, back down the grass to the courtyard with the wind shoving them from behind.

'Says who?' Astrid wanted so badly to hold Gordon, but it wasn't possible with one arm. She felt debilitated. The fantail shuddered again above them.

'The bloke who found the toad is the same one who found the Piltdown Man,' Mrs Baker said, as if this settled things.

'The Piltdown Man?' Nina looked confused, but game.

'Near here. Skull fragments, a jawbone, some teeth, that sort of thing. The missing link for civilisation, so he said.'

Nina nodded, uncertainly. 'So, the Piltdown Man was an archaeological hoax too?'

'That's right,' Mrs Baker said, over her shoulder as she stepped up to the front door. 'Took all the London experts forty-odd years to work out that it was an orangutan.'

'Just because the Piltdown Man was an orangutan doesn't mean the toad was a hoax,' Astrid pointed out. 'He could have had some genuine finds too, the poor man. There have been plenty of other cases of entombed toads, you know – from all over the world.'

'God help us.' Mrs Baker rolled her eyes as she pushed open the front door, letting the dogs gallop off down into the hall.

'But Nina's interested, aren't you, Nina?'

Nina nodded, slightly too vigorously.

'The Tibetans believe that entombed creatures are lost souls, stuck in little circles of hell, and they release them by breaking the rock and—'

'You've got her on her specialist subject now.' Mrs Baker walked off towards the kitchen. 'You're never going to shut her up.'

Nina looked as if she was trying not to laugh. 'Have you two lived together for a very long time?' she said to Astrid.

'For ever,' Astrid said. 'Well, since the millennium. Which was my sixtieth birthday. I was born on New Year's Eve. Charlie used to call me Hogmanay. I'd quite forgotten that. Hoggers. So awful. It drove me quite mad.'

Nina was still smiling as she followed Astrid into the kitchen.

'We aren't a couple, though, you know, Mrs Baker and me. Not in *that* way.'

Nina nodded, frantically, and looked earnest again.

Mrs Baker said, 'I came up here to help her after Charlie died.'

'Well, you two seem very in tune.'

The Kit Cat clock stared at Nina then at Mrs Baker, then at Nina again. It was definitely speeding up, Astrid thought.

'Most of the time I want to throttle her,' Mrs Baker said.

'She's joking.'

'I'm not.'

Astrid took her seat by the Rayburn and Gordon sprang onto her lap. Nina was zipping up her backpack, getting ready to leave. It felt rather nice, the three of them in the kitchen. She didn't want Nina to go. *When shall we three meet again?* She wanted to slow time down and keep Nina for longer. She remembered reading somewhere that even the tiniest unit of time contained a story, complete in itself; even the space between the ticks of a clock could be divided into a beginning, a middle and an end. It was ten past ten and Nina would soon have to leave: the beginning of an end, or, perhaps, the end of a beginning.

*Windmill Hill*

*12th August 1920*

Dear Walter,
Your letter is so unexpectedly harsh that I must sit down to reply
immediately.

No, I do not long for a more 'conventional existence' and I
am surprised that you should ask me this. Perhaps it is a fatal
stubbornness on my part, as you say, or, yes, some lack of femininity
in me, but there it is, I am perfectly happy with, as you call it, the
'bohemian' life. I have, in fact, never been happier. I have solitude
when I choose it, wide skies, mile upon mile of downland on which
to wander. I do not have to keep things clean and neat. I wear
comfortable clothing, much of which I buy in men's outfitters (in
fact, I should probably mention that I have cut all my hair off, too).
And from time to time, I have encounters with free spirits – some of
whom have broad and emancipated minds. For the first time in my
life, I am in the company of diverse and interesting people, and I
am thankful for this, and everything that comes with it – red wine,
canine circuses, violins, spiritualists.

It is all just a bit of fun, Walter. Have you forgotten what that is?

If Miss Jones is as unhappy as you suggest, then she is free to
leave. I impose no restrictions on her, I am not her gaoler. But to be
frank, Miss Jones is having the time of her life too: there is so much
to disapprove of, and so much to do. She has never been more alive.

I am sorry you find this behaviour unbecoming, but you are
thousands of miles away and as unresponsive as a stone, so really,
how I live is none of your concern. It is almost as if you are jealous.

You say I talk too much about Mr Banks and Daphne, but I

*have seen you with Rufus. I am not naive, Walter. You yourself are perhaps a little more 'bohemian' than you care to admit – and I firmly believe that there is no shame in that, no shame at all. The shame lies in the mendacity, the double standards, the pretence.*

*Oh, there is little use in these fraught exchanges, really, is there? When you eventually do return then we shall perhaps find it easier to discuss our future and agree on a sensible way to live.*

*C*

*PS. You will have just received a letter about the windmill which I suggest you disregard.*

# Chapter 14

The terminal was hellishly crowded. Had airports always been like this? Some people were striding around though she couldn't understand why, as no flights were leaving. Others had given up, and sat, head in hands, on uncomfortable seats, or perched on their bags on the floor, staring at phones. Society, of course, was divided in this way: those who became active and defiant in the face of adversity, and those who gave up, feeling, perhaps, that they'd got what they deserved. She had once loved to travel, but of course most of her wanderings had been overland, hitchhiking or on buses. It had been decades since she'd set foot in an airport, decades since she'd been anywhere at all, in fact, other than the funerals, and the odd day out along the Sussex coast.

The pain in her spine had faded, fortunately, thanks to the Jim Beam and the tablets. She'd like to order another, but she had a feeling that airport drinks would be very expensive and perhaps unwise, physically. She tried to summon up an internal Mrs Baker, a voice of restraint, but she couldn't, not quite. Mrs Baker had been so unlike herself lately, so very unrestrained. Only a few days before Nina came, when they were coming into the kitchen from a stroll around the garden, she'd startled, theatrically, then turned and stared through the open kitchen door. The clock's eyes switched to the door, then back to them, shocked.

'What?' Astrid cried. 'Good Lord! What now?' She followed Mrs Baker's gaze to the shrouded hall. The fur on Gordon's neck ruffled and he gave a low growl. 'That dog knows there's something here,' Mrs Baker said. 'Look at him. That's a spooked dachshund.'

Fear is catching, of course; Gordon was staring, ears pricked, his body a quivery tube of muscle. She bent to pick him up, but he remained rigid. Pain shot across her lower spine, leaving a queasy residue. 'You've whipped him up,' she said, crossly. The shadows in the hallway looked purplish, as if the air had been bruised by someone passing through it, someone who really should not be there, but often was. And then, suddenly, all three dogs were yapping like demons. 'Oh, good God, stop it!' Astrid shouted at them all. 'Stop this racket!' She pressed her hand over Gordon's snout, but they all carried on.

Mrs Baker went into the kitchen.

'You're being quite absurd!' Astrid hurried after her. 'It's the draught from the front door.' As she turned to shut the kitchen door, she caught the scent of lavender in the chilly hallway.

She spotted Emmanuel over by the entrance to the bar, still on the phone. His face was very serious. She felt light-headed. She could hear Mrs Baker: *What do you expect, you SOB, drinking in the middle of the day?* Nina would probably be leaving for the airport any minute now. She really must use Emmanuel's phone to warn her of the delay.

She wondered how Nina really felt about her coming to Scotland. Astrid had announced the plan just as Nina was getting into Gloria to go to the station; Mrs Baker had gone back into the cottage for Astrid's shawl.

'Look, Nina, I've decided to come and confront Magnus myself. I won't have you lose your job, or the payment. I'm going to come to Northbank and talk to him – I shall insist on being taken out of the book.' Hendricks shot past them, back up towards the windmill.

'Oh. Wow. Okay.' Nina rested one hand on the car door. 'That's . . . But the thing is, Astrid – the problem is Dessie. If he finds out I came here and shared the contents of that chapter with you, he won't just fire me, I honestly think he'll sue. I've signed all sorts of confidentiality things.'

Astrid felt disappointed – she'd expected Nina to leap at the idea. But then Nina was thinking out loud. 'But no, no, you should come. You should definitely see Magnus. He'd want that too. You could come to Northbank when Dessie's not there. I know he's got to be in New York next weekend to pick up an award on Magnus's behalf – maybe you could come then? Is that too soon? But there's Mrs McKittrick, too, she might tell him, I suppose . . .'

'Mrs McKittrick?'

'Magnus's carer.'

'Perhaps you could give Mrs McKittrick the morning off?'

'Yes, unfortunately, that's not really up to me.'

'Look, all I need is half an hour alone with Magnus, Nina. Surely we can just say I saw the interview in the *Sunday Times*? You don't have to be involved in any way.'

'Yes.' Nina seemed to gather herself together. 'Yes. No, absolutely, you're right. You must see him – you must. We'll figure it out. I know he'd be—'

'Hendricks!' Mrs Baker bellowed across the courtyard. Astrid and Nina turned. Hendricks stopped digging and emerged from the stone, ears flapping. He had something in his mouth, it looked like a rag. Above him, the windmill seemed to be leaning over to see what he'd dug up.

Emmanuel was coming back, smiling at her. She'd ask for his phone. He was such a gentleman. Not that being a gentleman meant much, really. Magnus had been a gentleman, until he wasn't. In fact, as far as she could tell, for a good few years after they'd divorced, Magnus had been the opposite: a womanising hellraiser. In the eighties, whenever she'd stumbled across an interview with him or seen him on the television, on *Parkinson* or *Wogan* or in the news, he'd seemed like a total stranger. He'd even looked different: leaner, slightly dead behind the eyes, always too tanned, wearing ridiculous outfits. At times she'd wondered if he was, in fact, having some kind of prolonged nervous breakdown but she hadn't allowed herself to engage with those thoughts too deeply.

Emmanuel had stopped – he was back on his phone. He turned and walked away again.

Magnus was the past, she told herself, though he'd always had a bad habit of popping up in the present. At the height of his success, she couldn't open a newspaper or magazine without finding his pale eyes staring back at her, and even now there were replays of his films on the television, and sometimes his voice would float out at her from Radio 4, electrifying the air. She had never adjusted to these encounters; to the plummeting sensation in her chest when she heard him, or the inevitable emptiness she'd feel afterwards. That could take a very long time to pass.

Nothing was as bad as the time she'd encountered him in

Brighton, though. That had been very real. It was Christmas, in the contented first years of the twenty-first century after Charlie died, and before Alan came, when there was still money. She and Mrs Baker had been shopping in the Lanes and they'd quarrelled, she remembered, about a pair of purple velvet shoes that Astrid had wanted, and Mrs Baker said belonged in 'a tart's boudoir'. Mrs Baker had stomped off, leaving her with the dog, and she heard Magnus's voice calling her name. A rush of energy ran up her spine. She turned to find him standing just feet away. He looked older, though his skin had a Californian lustre. His eyes were the same: the irises a pale grey ringed with darker blue. He stepped forwards, started to speak, but someone spotted him, yelled out his name, got between them, and then someone else, and then another and another, and in seconds a crowd had gathered, pressing in – it all happened instantly, shards to a magnet – and Magnus was staring at her over all the heads, his eyes pleading with her not to leave. She hurried away, shaken.

Later, she discovered that he'd been speaking at the Brighton Festival. It seemed an odd choice for a film star, though of course that had been, in retrospect, the fallow period of his career, before he got the Marvel role.

Her chest felt very strange now, sort of draughty. This trip to Edinburgh was obviously a colossal mistake. How on earth would she face him again? She couldn't possibly walk into his home and confront the fact that he was dying – *dying* – let alone try to talk him out of doing something he might not actually be doing at all.

She hadn't even been back to Scotland since he took her to his mother's funeral almost half a century ago. They'd travelled up overnight on the *Flying Scotsman*. It must have been just after he was cast in *I Am Me* because he was keyed up, buying drinks for strangers, telling stories, magnetic even in grief, or perhaps especially in grief – everyone was drawn to him. A woman trying to get closer to him elbowed Astrid in the face, and her eye came up purple and swollen. Magnus worried that his siblings would think he was a wife-beater and took her down Princes Street to buy sunglasses which she kept on throughout the funeral, even though there was no sunshine, it being winter in Leith, and when they left, she overheard Magnus's eldest sister, a terrifying pub landlady, calling her 'that London poser'. Funny how something as small as a pair of sunglasses can change the story – and that was the nice sister, too, the one who'd looked out for Magnus when he was little. She wondered what had happened to all those siblings; there had been so many, each more gigantic and alarming than the next. He was the baby of the family, so they'd be old – probably all dead by now, or senile. So many people were these days.

After the funeral they went into Edinburgh and a fog had rolled in, and he gave her his coat, a pea coat, and then he came down with a terrible chill. She had to nurse him on the train and put him to bed in the Hampstead flat; she thought it was pneumonia, but the doctor said it wasn't, and she realised it wasn't the cold that had driven him to bed, making him shiver and sweat, it was grief – not just for his mother, but for his childhood, all that instability and neglect. She hadn't thought about this in years, how sensitive Magnus could be, and how she had adored this. She hadn't been able to remember the good things about him, she hadn't allowed herself.

She felt light-headed. Emmanuel was right about bourbon and pills: bad idea. But she always had lacked discipline. She remembered the headmistress at Roedean, her final school, bellowing at her, 'Your mind is chaotic, Miss Miller, you have no discipline *what*soever.' Not just her mind, as it turned out since she was then expelled for meeting a boy outside Electricity House, in Brighton – they were apprehended by the physics teacher.

She needed the loo. She looked down, resting her elbows on the bar. There were curly dog hairs on her sleeve, a sprinkling of small question marks. She experienced the lack of Gordon as one might a phantom limb: his little damp nose and anxious trusting eyes, his body like a furry, heated beanbag, weighing on her lap. She looked round for Emmanuel, but he was gone.

She glimpsed herself again in the mirror. It was like looking at a crone from one of the ridiculous Disney films she used to make Mrs Baker watch after Mellie died and Alan tracked them back from the funeral – all that was twelve years ago now. She should have worn something more colourful and vibrant. It had taken her a while to decide what to wear. She wasn't used to it – she often didn't bother to get dressed at all. Mrs Baker had given up objecting, and she'd actually been tempted to wear her nightdress; it was thick flannel, a lovely Liberty print, practically a vintage frock, and really quite cosy when worn with lots of jumpers and two pairs of leggings. But it wouldn't do for the outside world, she did know that. When she'd pictured herself sitting in the same room as Magnus, all her possible outfits had seemed ill-advised.

She'd decided on the special velvet jacket, for authority. But now she saw herself in the airport lighting, she realised that black was awfully draining. The accents of amber helped, the Syrian necklace. She needed a scarlet lipstick. If only she had the energy, she'd go and buy one. Power dressing, they used to call it in the eighties. Shoulder pads. *A red lip*. She pushed aside an intrusive image of Alan's lips, open, his bleeding mouth and shocked little eyes. She must not – absolutely must not – think about the Awful Incident. She must be strong and never think about it again.

She wondered what Magnus would make of her now, wrinkled, diminished, crooked-fingered, the body he'd once adored thickened and sagging around its dodgy spine; one arm, pathetically, in a sling. For years she hadn't much minded about ageing; there was no point in dwelling. *Better than the alternative*. In fact, whenever she did think about her ageing body, she felt it had done rather well, all told. The one inheritance for which she could genuinely and unreservedly thank her mother was an excellent bone structure. But now she saw herself through Magnus's eyes: a crone. He used to tell her that she was most beautiful to him first thing in the morning when she'd just woken up, with no make-up, no artifice. What would he think of her morning face now? Withered and wild. He'd be appalled, repulsed.

Then again, he probably wasn't looking so hot himself. Cancer could have such a ravaging effect, even on a man like Magnus. Nina had called him frail. Astrid hadn't thought about the physical reality of this, what it would be like to see his once magnificent body wilted and sickened, hooked up to an oxygen tank. *Sans teeth, sans eyes, sans taste, sans everything*. Best not to think about that, either.

Someone was making an announcement over the speaker system, but she couldn't decipher the words. Her skin felt clammy. She tried to undo the buttons of her jacket but it was so fiddly with one hand. She wasn't used to wearing proper clothes. Mostly these days, when she really had to get dressed, she just wore stretchy things – leggings, tunics, jumper dresses she found in Help the Aged or British Heart Foundation. She always made Mrs Baker drive to Lewes because the quality of the goods in charity shops was so much higher there. She still had some decent clothes hanging in the wardrobe, from the days when she interacted with people, but most of the zips and buttons didn't do up any more. Her favourite party dress still fitted as it was a loose cut, but she'd decided that it probably wouldn't do. 'Judi Dench does Baby Jane' was how Mrs Baker had reacted when Astrid had put it on to go to the dentist a couple of years previously, after she'd developed the ghastly toothache.

'N.D.Y.,' she'd muttered with a swollen tongue, shoving her feet into the sparkly floral wellingtons that Mrs Baker most despised.

'N.D.Y.?' Mrs Baker had looked at her. 'You might not be dead yet, Astrid, but I'll kill you myself if you wear those bloody wellies.'

One button had fallen off the jacket, she saw, leaving a star-burst of threads. Then she noticed Emmanuel. He hadn't left! He was standing by the entrance to the bar. He must be hot in that wool jacket, but perhaps he was one of those people who didn't notice temperature. Magnus had been like that too, he'd get more and more snappish, unaware that the problem was physical and easily solved. She'd learned to make the necessary adjustments: 'Here, take off your coat,' or 'You must be freezing, put this on.' She remembered thinking it was something to do with the childhood neglect; his mother had never told him to wear a coat or take his jumper off. Astrid had liked to fuss over him, and he'd accepted it gladly. He'd looked after her in other ways. Until he didn't.

She hadn't been terribly good at loving people after Magnus. Loving people involved cranking up the very mechanism that needed to remain shut down. Charlie used to say, 'You're com-pletely unreachable.' Poor Charlie, he was solid, a protector, but he never quite got her, or knew how to deal with her. He used to say she had 'black moods', when she'd go up to the windmill and shut herself in, sometimes for a few days, but she didn't feel dark when she did that, she'd just needed to be inside the windmill, alone. She kept blankets, pillows, books in there. She had her kettle, her bath. Nothing much had changed since she lived in it – it had always been draughty, chilly and a bit dilapidated. The day after the Great Storm, Charlie had driven her up the hill from his house, with the dogs – it would have been Dixie Belle and Bombay, in those days – to assess the damage. They'd had to climb under the fallen elm. The cap was burned up on one side, there was a massive, charred hole, and the sweeps had been torn off. She could see one, smashed to pieces, against the lavender garden wall. Up on the Stone and Bin floors several windowpanes were broken, but Astrid was relieved to find that the ground floor, at least, was essentially undamaged. She put down the dogs and turned to say this to Charlie, but his expression was full of sympathy. 'Shit, Astrid.' He shook his head as his gaze travelled round the room. She tried to see it through his eyes: cracked limewash on the bricks, going green in places, flaking, with patches of damp, a plank coming down off the ceiling, a fissure through which you could see the floor above, the broken window she'd never got round to fixing, and of course, the chaos of all her papers and books and unwashed plates – Bombay was licking one – and mugs, wine glasses, her clothing strewn about. The only storm damage she could see was that a picture had blown off the wall and the glass lay in pieces on the floor, and the quilt she'd hung on the washing line – which was strung across the room – had been blown off and must have knocked over a vase of dried lavender; the stalks were scattered. Other than this, it was mercifully intact.

'Shit,' Charlie said. 'The wind must have swept round this

like a twister when you opened the door to get out.' He shook his head again and peered up through the ceiling. 'This place is going to be uninhabitable for a while, I think.'

She had loved Charlie in her own way – loved all sorts of things about him, at least. He was practical and kind, and had earned good money, though there had been other things going on behind the scenes that she'd never quite got to the bottom of, largely because she'd never wanted to. There had been none of the fever or longing or joy she'd felt with Magnus, but none of the agony either. She'd never felt that she couldn't exist without Charlie, which was a very good thing since it was only eight years before she found him by the pond.

She was beginning to feel positively unwell. She knew it wasn't the alcohol, or the painkillers or the airport lighting or the temperature. It was Magnus. The thought of continuing to exist in a world that no longer contained him was unbearable, and she didn't know why. She shouldn't, mustn't, wouldn't think about it any more.

A woman walked past in a blue turban, and it made Astrid think of the indigo blue turban she'd worn in the cover photograph of *Past Lives*. She remembered the regression hypnotist, a heavy, bearded, charismatic man, had asked her to wrap a scarf round her head and he'd used that image in the promotional materials, not because she was famous – she'd only just finished her first season at Stratford then – but because she was his star subject: she'd produced Little Bobby, a Victorian street urchin whose bloodcurdling scream, as he burned to death in a Bethnal Green fire, was the grand finale on the little floppy record that came with the book. She'd found the book after Alan came, when they were putting everything back in the bookcase in the snug. She'd been startled by her own face. She'd never

been conventionally pretty, 'no oil painting' as one of the RADA
tutors had put it, but her young face really had been majestic.

They dug out Charlie's turntable. The little record was crackly
but the scream, when it came, was rather disturbing. Mrs Baker
had pretended to laugh, but Astrid could tell she was rattled.
'I won the final year prize at RADA, Mrs Baker, I know how to
produce a good scream. That was Lady M's scream, more or
less – when she's sleepwalking, trying to get the blood off –
*out, out* ...' She stopped. She almost never allowed herself to
reconnect with Lady M, even though she sensed her sometimes,
lurking inside, *N.D.Y.*

Mrs Baker sensed that Astrid was in a painful corner and redi-
rected her. 'What made you do all that regression stuff then?'

She'd only done it as a lark. Someone in the Company knew
the hypnotist, and it had seemed harmless enough. Her involvement hadn't served her well later, though. When the scandal
blew up, the papers got hold of the turban photo. The *Daily Mail*
called her 'Astral Astrid'. The photograph had contributed to a
public willingness to believe that she could be responsible for
such a peculiar act. It hadn't helped that when printed in black
and white her high cheekbones and enormous eyes had given her
face a disturbing, skull-like quality, simultaneously odd and sultry.

She thought, then, of the Irish chieftain's skull that had sat
on the mantelpiece in the Tudor hunting lodge. Later that night,
when she'd come back into the room and found the three of
them on the tiger skin – Rohls hunched like a succubus over
Sally Morgan, who was naked from the waist up, with Magnus
kneeling behind her, holding her arms to her sides – it had
seemed to be the presiding force. She remembered Sally's terrified eyes staring at her over Rohls' shoulder.

*

She did feel rotten now, quite nauseous. She really needed to find the loos, but Emmanuel still had his back to her. Perhaps he'd forget she was there, walk away, be gone. Nobody wants to be saddled with an old lady. Might she throw up? There was nothing to be sick into except her handbag. She wanted, very badly, to be back at the windmill in her chair by the Rayburn with Gordon on her lap, Hendricks and Junie snoring at her feet and Mrs Baker bashing at some root vegetables.

She had no idea why she'd said that dreadful thing at the drop-off point, about being her employer. She didn't think of Mrs Baker like that, never had, even when she was paying her. She longed to fix the quarrel. What would happen to the dogs if she upped and left? She suddenly remembered the unsavoury visit to Hastings, all those years ago, when Mellie had briefly moved there after a rehab programme. She was supposed to be 'getting her life back together' but didn't seem entirely stable. When Mrs Baker popped out to buy milk, Mellie said, through a cloud of cigarette smoke, 'Can't believe Mum puts up with your dogs, she bloody hates dogs, 'specially terriers.'

'They're miniature wire-haired dachshunds,' Astrid had said, and wondered, then, at the remarkable mother–child bond. This unhappy, whey-faced young woman with scarred arms, self-tattooed hands, fragments of metal through her nose and chin had seemed so very unlovable and yet, every single Saturday Mrs Baker had caught the train to London, bringing food, blankets, clothing she had bought in charity shops and painstakingly laundered and mended. She would return late in the evening, drawn, silent – unwilling, or perhaps unable, to talk about her only child.

Mellie had been dead over twelve years now, but Mrs Baker was still mostly unable to talk about her. The pain and guilt, misplaced as that was, were too intense to put into words. There was an element of trauma, too. Astrid had gleaned that although Alan had never physically touched Mellie, the level of threat in the home had done awful damage. A few days after Alan's first visit to the windmill, when they were having a cup of tea in the kitchen, Astrid had gathered up the courage to ask again why Mrs Baker had felt she had no choice but to stay with him all those years.

'He said if I ever left, he'd come for Mellie.' She looked away, with a shrug. 'I believed him.' Her face grew subtly unstable then and her hand began to shake. Astrid went over, took the Garfield mug, put it aside, then held her hand quietly until the emotions had subsided.

After that, she hadn't pressed her to remember any more. 'If you look back,' Mrs Baker once said, 'all you see is the mess you've made, and it's too late to clear that up, so best not to look.' Where it got complicated, though, was when that mess broke into the present. And this was definitely going to happen if Astrid didn't put a stop to the memoir. Mrs Baker didn't believe that the media would come to the windmill because she'd lived her whole life in obscurity – for the past twenty years, actually incognito. She had no idea what it was like to have your life hijacked by reporters, to see your face in every tabloid, to be shunned by friends and colleagues, laughed at, leered at, loathed; accused of having a famous young woman's blood on your hands.

She fanned herself. Her mouth felt hollow, her gums baggy, as if the remaining molars had loosened in their sockets. She felt sure that if she opened her jaw, her teeth would pour from her lips like gravel. *Sans eyes, sans teeth* ... One of the young men bumped into her again, she seized the bar with her good hand. If the drone dropped a bomb, or terrorists appeared in the concourse, she'd be trampled, she knew it. Nobody would stop for her; nobody would even see her. She straightened her spine. Self-pity was such an unattractive quality – she absolutely must not succumb to it. She was so lucky, after all, to have most of her limbs intact, and all her marbles.

Above her screens flashed out lines of delay. Where *had* Emmanuel gone? If there were official explanations for the chaos, she couldn't hear them. The air seemed to vibrate with trapped energy, a clammy wave passed up and down her body and it struck her that she really was going to faint. The pack of men was barking, howling behind her; she felt shadowy curtains at her peripheral vision, blood pushed against her eardrums, and then everything drew away. Was it her heart? No, it was her head. She felt, briefly, curious, and pictured a vessel leaking trails of bright blood through the grey coral reef of brain tissue. If this was it – a stroke – she'd never see Mrs Baker again, or the dogs. Or Magnus. She'd never see Magnus again. This couldn't be it – she wasn't finished. But the velvet curtains folded over her, anyway, softly blotting out the ruckus.

13th August 1920

Dearest W,

I wrote yesterday in hot blood and regretted it the moment the envelope dropped inside the village post box. I understand that my life here seems strange, but my hope is always that if I tell you about it, you will understand – I have never felt happier, or more myself. I only wish to include you.

So, at the risk of angering you further, I will continue to share my news. I don't think I mentioned, in my last letter, that Miss Jones has been unwell – she took to her bed for several days. She seems better today, if subdued. Our roles were reversed, and it was me (and Daphne) making the beef tea and answering her calls. The doctor says it is not influenza but something more nebulous, perhaps nerves, or exhaustion. I did not tell him that the day before she fell ill, she stumbled across Daphne painting a young male poet (she is recreating The Birth of Venus – the poet was unclothed). It was innocent, but Miss J shocks easily. Before you ask, I have questioned her, and she is adamant that she will not return to London. It did not help that the East Sussex Mothers of Choir Boys group happened to be passing on their annual wildflower walk just as Miss Jones came upon the scene. Hearing her screams, the young man leaped up and, well, you can probably guess which direction he turned.

As I write, Miss Jones is up and talking about making custard. Daphne has gone out to gather eggs. (Did I tell you we have hens now? It was Mr Banks's suggestion. Miss Jones will have nothing to do with the birds, but does delight in the eggs.) We are considering the possibility of a goat too, though you, I'm sure, will say that's too 'bohemian'. Miss Jones is on your side – she says she is too old to milk an animal. I, of course, would not dream of inflicting her on one.

Do send what news you have, so that, in return, I can share in your life. I cannot imagine the responsibility of overseeing the building of this ship and I'm sure this accounts for the hurt tone of your last letter. I do so want to hear more, though I understand that you cannot share details of the build. I am sure that before long you will be triumphant: your 'Small Battleship of Tomorrow' will be celebrated around the globe for ever more.

Until then, your C

# Chapter 15

Her eyelids were leaden, she could only just peer out. A face
came into view. Emmanuel. She wasn't sure where she was,
but she knew she wasn't at the windmill. Her arm hurt. There
were other voices. *Is she okay? . . . She just went down . . . Should
we . . .*

Emmanuel's deep voice, close to her ear. 'Astrid?'

She could move. She was fine. She tried to lift her head.

'Don't move.'

*Needs a doctor.*

'I am a doctor.'

All the voices swirled. *Drinking . . . Middle of the day! . . . Her
age . . . Who's she with? . . . Crashed over . . . Caught her . . . Been
drinking . . . Poor old thing . . . Sad . . . Not me . . . Hit her head? . . .
On her own . . . That man there . . . Travelling alone . . .*

She forced herself to open her eyes and focus on Emmanuel's
face. 'Oh dear!'

'Try to stay still for a moment, get your breath back.' His voice
reverberated, mercifully audible.

'Perfectly all right. Just a tiny little faint.'

Then, her lower spine flaming, she was sitting up, fine, but not
quite anchored. Someone had picked up her scarf. Emmanuel

was peering into her face, one hand on her wrist. She tried to speak, 'N.D.Y., I hope?'

'What?'

'Not dead yet?' She must look ghastly. She smoothed her hair. Had she wet herself? She ran her hands down there – thank God, no. 'I'm really quite all right.' Someone – a young man with tattooed arms, one of the stags – had brought a cup of water.

Emmanuel hovered, his huge hand beneath the cup, ready to catch it if she let go. 'Do you know what year it is?' She did – laughed, told him. 'And who's the prime minister?'

'A dreadful charlatan.'

He laughed and got her to put down the cup and squeeze his hand. Then she drank some water. She felt fine, though her back and wrist were both very sore.

'You need to get to a hospital to be checked out.'

'Oh no, I can't do that. I have to go to Scotland. My friend's meeting me.'

'Sometimes people your age have mini-strokes.'

'Nonsense, I just fainted.'

'Are you sure you won't go and get checked out? It could be your heart, too.'

'At my age, Emmanuel, people only come out of a hospital feet first.'

He didn't object. She saw the ghost of something, a memory perhaps, pass briefly across his face. He helped her up, and over to a sensible chair. She did her best not to wince at the complicated pains in different parts of her body. She really was fine, if embarrassed for causing such a fuss. 'You can all go away now,' she called out to the people who had crowded round. 'I don't need any more help!' And to her surprise, they backed away and dissipated. She realised then that she needed to escape, not just from the bar, but from the airport. If she stayed in the terminal, she would never get out.

'Could you eat something?' Emmanuel produced a Cadbury's chocolate bar and broke off a square.

'Not quite.' She cleared her throat. 'I'm being an awful pest.'

'You aren't at all, really,' he said. 'It's seriously hot in here. I feel a bit like passing out myself.'

'You should take that wool jacket off then.'

He looked at her. 'You're right.' He took it off and hung it on the back of her chair.

'Do you know,' she said. 'I don't think I shall get on an aeroplane today.'

'Yes, honestly, I think that's the right call.'

'I must speak to my friend, she'll be waiting for me at Edinburgh airport,' Astrid said. 'Could I borrow your phone?'

Nina's number was somewhere in her carry-on case. Miraculously, it was next to her chair. She couldn't quite trust herself to bend down and unzip it. She decided to ring Mrs Baker, who would ring Nina. But then Mrs Baker would know something was wrong and Astrid would have to tell her about the faint, and then she'd insist on coming to fetch her. The prospect of continuing the journey seemed enormously difficult, almost impossible, but going home felt worse. It would be a failure of character.

She'd get a train to Scotland, she decided. She'd always liked the train. Could she do that? There was no reason why not. There was a train station at Gatwick. She'd need to tell Nina she'd be late.

Emmanuel said, 'Can someone come here and pick you up?'

'Well, they could, but I wouldn't be here because I'm going to catch a train to Edinburgh. They go from King's Cross, don't they? Or is it Euston?'

'A train? But you'd have to get to Victoria then all the way across London.'

'I know that, but I'm completely fine now. Never better. I really must get going. My ex-husband is dying, you see, and I must see him.' The statement came into focus, suddenly felt real. Her eyes filled with tears. 'Could you possibly unzip my case, that pocket there? I need to get a phone number.'

'I'll unzip it if you eat the chocolate.'

'As the bishop said to the actress.'

Emmanuel was grinning as he bent to unzip her case. Then he straightened again. 'Listen,' he said. 'I'm not going to make it to Frankfurt in time to give my talk. I've basically missed the whole day, so I'm going to get a cab back to work. I can drop you at Euston, it's not far from the clinic.'

She felt a sense of relief, like a physical warmth, as if his big wings had folded around her. He took his phone back and began to look up train times to Edinburgh.

# Chapter 16

She couldn't imagine what the taxi would be costing. Emmanuel said his clinic was paying. He must be doing awfully well in fertility. As they crossed London there was plenty of time to talk. His mother had died eighteen months previously, he said. She'd fallen in her bathroom and couldn't get up and had had to wait over four hours on the tiled floor, wedged between the sink and the loo, until an ambulance came. He was on a transatlantic flight at the time and only got his sister's messages when he touched down later that day. He hadn't been able to say goodbye because, at that time, nobody was allowed into the hospitals. His voice cracked as he said this. She reached out and took his hand. He looked surprised but didn't pull away.

It was difficult to thank him properly, and as his taxi drove off, she felt guilty, though she didn't quite know why. It was almost as if she'd abandoned Emmanuel, as if he'd needed something from her that she'd been unable to provide.

At the ticket office, she asked for a return to Edinburgh. When the man told her the cost, she thought she must have misheard. 'But I'm a pensioner!' Eventually he had to write the amount down on a piece of paper and slide it under the glass. She stared at the figure and told him, briskly, that it was absurd, she did not have that sort of money. She couldn't put it on the credit card. Mrs Baker would be livid. She needed to think.

There was a terrible sense of defeat as she sat down on the bench, with her carry-on case next to her. She could go back to Gatwick and see if the planes were running but she'd have to get herself all the way across London on the underground, and she didn't have the energy for that. Or the money. She felt a wave of despair. And then, at that exact moment, she noticed that the Edinburgh train was sitting right there, on the platform nearest to her bench. The barrier was partially open – as if it was simply waiting for her to notice it, and get in.

A Sikh ticket collector materialised as she was walking through the gate and asked to see her ticket. She tapped her ear. 'I'm so sorry, I didn't catch—'

'Ticket, please!' he shouted.

She put her head on one side. 'No, so sorry.' She shook her head. 'My naughty dog ate my hearing aids and I really can't hear a thing, the background noise in the station . . . it's completely impossible . . . Could you perhaps write your question down? I'm going to Edinburgh – is that my train?' He ushered her through, pointing at the train in an exaggerated way.

'Thank you, dear,' she said, in her most fragile old lady voice. 'You *are* kind.'

He looked at her carry-on case, then picked it up, and carried it for her down the platform. Then he stopped and said something about needing to look at her ticket to find the seat. She hopped into the train. 'Aren't you clever!' She looked at his name badge. 'Mr Singh. How did you know this was my carriage?' He beamed and lifted her case up after her. 'You're a darling, I shudder to think what I would have done without you.'

She felt untethered as she sat down. If only she had the

dogs – dogs were allowed on trains. She tried to remind herself that although Juniper would be a decent traveller owing to her laziness, Gordon's nerves wouldn't take it and Hendricks would be a liability. She remembered Hendricks nipping a little boy at a station once – it was when they'd gone to see Mellie in Hastings. No, it couldn't have been Hendricks, it would have been his father, Gilbert, in those days. Mrs Baker insisted they travel by train in case anyone spotted them and got the numberplate. At the time, Astrid had felt this was a bit extreme. It wasn't until after the funeral, to which they'd driven, that she understood that Mrs Baker's precautions were entirely realistic. Presumably, when it came to the funeral, Mrs Baker had been too much in shock to consider security.

Poor Mellie. A life wasted. Children could bring such heartbreak. On balance, Astrid was glad not to have had one. Her own mother, in a rare break between marriages, had once said, 'You mustn't have a baby, you'd make a rotten mother, darling, far too scatty,' which had seemed rich coming from a woman who, one Christmas, had sent her new husband's driver to the wrong boarding school.

She thought, then, of Magnus, who'd always wanted a big family. He agreed with the man in the Larkin poem, that 'adding meant increase'. Things hadn't worked out the way he'd hoped because despite three marriages, he'd only ended up with one child, who to all accounts was a litigious nutcase. Charlie's children weren't exactly delightful, either, come to think of it. She hadn't heard from either of them in over two decades, thank goodness. The son had been particularly bitter, protective of his mother even though, as with Magnus and the Danish model, the marriage was finished long before she and Charlie had got together. It was a few weeks after Charlie's funeral that the son, all grown up by then, had appeared on the doorstep with a wiry man. It took her a while to realise that they wanted her to sign both cottage and windmill over to them. Sitting in her kitchen, the wiry man crossed his legs, slowly, and explained, in a quiet voice, that Charlie's son owed him a very large sum of money, something about a property investment that had not come good. When she pointed out that the windmill was hers and she'd bought it well before she met Charlie, the smile left his face. He got up and went over to the window. 'Remote up here, isn't it?'

Charlie's son said nothing the whole time, and she'd realised after a bit that he was terrified. He'd got himself into a muddle, that was clear. In the end, she gave the boy all the proceeds from the sale of the Hove house. Charlie had loved his son, and although he'd left Astrid some money and a house, he had also provided well for his children. Even so, she couldn't knowingly allow the boy to come to any harm.

Her mother had been right, she'd have made a rotten parent, absolutely no discipline. But if there was an emptiness inside her now, it wasn't about children – any maternal instincts had been well and truly satisfied by dogs.

Someone was tapping her shoulder. She opened her eyes. A young woman with pink hair said, 'Sorry, I think you're in my seat.' She flashed a ticket.

Astrid gazed up at her.

'It's my seat, look.' She held out her ticket.

Astrid tapped her ear. 'I'm profoundly deaf.'

The girl repeated herself a few times, then wandered off, sulkily, to another seat and started tapping at her phone. Ridiculous behaviour. The train was half empty.

Astrid wondered if the girl might let her borrow the phone

when she'd calmed down. But of course that would involve admitting that she could hear well enough to talk on a crackly mobile phone on a train. She did need to talk to Mrs Baker though. The notion that they'd squabbled about payment felt a little surreal now. But money had been a struggle for years; perhaps the resentment had ratcheted up, only to detonate outside the airport. How many years had it been since Charlie's money ran out? It had been after Mellie's funeral, of course, twelve years now.

Astrid had never intended to tell Mrs Baker that Alan had appeared at the windmill. It was only a day after the funeral, it would be too much for her, but it had been a shock to walk into the kitchen, having just picked an armful of daffodils, to find a man by the Rayburn, crouched over Sapphire and the puppies. He was stroking Sapphy's head, and his Harrington jacket was stretched to burst over his back. The Kit Cat clock twitched frantically above him. 'Nice little things,' he said, without looking round.

Sapphire was lying on her side. Astrid could see the pups' tiny tails poking from under her belly as she wagged a feeble greeting. He turned then, and she recognised the face that had made Mrs Baker run from her child's funeral. It was broad and tanned by the Spanish sun, perhaps almost handsome once but turning jowly now. His hair was cropped but sparse on top, and his skull gleamed through it here and there. He looked older than Mrs Baker, though Astrid remembered that he was a few years her junior, only nineteen when they met.

'What kind is it then? Sausage dog?'

'She's feeding.' Astrid stepped forwards. 'Please don't touch her.' She dropped the daffodils on the table but kept hold of the scissors.

He stood up, unhurried, and she saw that he had a pup in each hand. They mewled and squirmed, little paws paddling the air. Sapphire looked up at her babies, no longer wagging her tail. 'Please put them back,' Astrid said, sharply. 'They're feeding.' Alan wasn't very tall, which surprised her as she'd always imagined an enormous man. She hadn't noticed at the funeral because he'd been sitting down – she'd only seen his face. When Mrs Baker spotted him she was on her feet in an instant, heading for the crematorium door before Mellie's wicker casket had even been lifted onto the catafalque. He was heavy and muscular, barrel-chested, in a jacket that was too tight, the jacket of a younger man. She wondered if he'd just come back from Spain and taken it out of storage, or perhaps borrowed it.

'Look at my manners,' he grinned. 'I'm Alan, Eileen's old man. I saw you at Mellie's funeral yesterday but you two rushed off before I could say hello. Too much for her, was it? Can't blame her. People look to the mother, don't they, when a child goes wrong. I'd shake your hand but . . .' He held up a puppy.

Astrid glimpsed the tawny patch on the belly: Juniper. 'Please put them down,' she said. She could hear Gilbert yapping frantically somewhere in another part of the cottage.

Alan shrugged. 'Not much of a litter, is it? Where's all the others then? Stillborn, were they?'

'She only had three, and yes, one was stillborn.'

'Only three?' He looked down at Sapphy and tutted. 'That's a bit pathetic. They go for a fair whack, don't they, these little dachsies.'

'They aren't pure bred.'

He looked at one pup, then the other. 'I quite fancy a dog again. I had a big old Mastiff in Spain, savage bastard – excuse my language, sorry. They say it's how you treat them, don't they, but that dog, he was bad from the start. It's the Spanish blood. Couldn't trust him as far as you could spit him. But I loved that dog like my own child. When he got himself run over I cried like a baby.' He nudged Sapphy's basket with a boot, which was polished, and incongruously expensive-looking. 'What about Eileen, though? What does she think of this dog breeding lark? Not a dog lover, old Eileen. I'm surprised she puts up with this little lot.' He looked right at her for a moment, holding her gaze for too long, then looked down at the pups, which mewled and wriggled in his fists.

'Give them to me,' Astrid snapped, holding out her hands.

'I wouldn't leave her alone with them for long if I was you. You can't trust a woman who runs off without a word after twenty-seven years of marriage, can you? Heart of stone.' He lifted Juniper to his nose. 'Ain't that right, little 'un? Heart of stone.' He puffed air at her tiny nose, making her startle and squirm.

'Give them to me.' Astrid stepped closer and reached for the pups. His aftershave smelled smoky, citrussy, high-end.

'Almost eleven years without a word,' he said. 'Not a word. Not a fucking word.' He held the puppies to his chest. 'Thought she'd died. How long has she been up here then? She thought she could vanish, I suppose, like in the films.' He looked right at her. 'What is she then, an old lesbo now, up here with you?'

'Mrs Baker works for me.' Astrid made a grab for the pups.

'Mrs Baker?' He gave a nasty laugh, whisked his hands up so that Astrid couldn't reach the pups, then spun round, thumping his shin against Tony Blair, and dropping them into the sink. She couldn't remember if the washing-up bowl had water in it. She lurched forwards, but he held her back, hand flat on her breast-bone, a fat vein pulsing in his neck, the anger triggered, perhaps, by hitting his shin. 'When I was a kiddie, my mum used to make me drown the pups when one of our bitches had a litter. They were always having litters, worthless little tarts. Quickest way' – his breath smelled of cigarettes – 'is you fill up the bowl and dunk 'em, hold them under till the wriggling stops.' His scalp was shiny, his aftershave overpowering. 'Of course, you can put them in a sack in the river, but my ma wouldn't let me do that. Made me do 'em one by one. She wanted to toughen me up, mad cow.' He gave a throaty laugh. Astrid took a step back, then ducked past him and whisked the squirming puppies out of the sink. There was no water in the bowl, but they were damp and shivery. She cradled them to her chest and turned. Alan was gone.

He was over in the doorway, blocking her route to the phone in the hall. She knelt at Sapphire's basket. Her hands shook as she tucked the damp puppies up against their mother's warm flank. They rooted and began to suckle. She stroked Sapphire's head, whispered reassurances, trying not to convey anxiety, using old techniques, her breath, her diaphragm, absenting herself from fear. Gilbert, she noticed, was still yapping. She realised she'd been aware of the sound since she walked into the kitchen.

'I want my wife back,' he said, from the doorway.

'Well, she doesn't want you.' Astrid lifted her chin. 'She's not your property. You must leave her alone.'

He looked surprised. He seemed to be weighing up whether to lose his temper and she sensed the rage trapped and quivering inside his body. Then he relaxed, grinned. 'Where is she then?'

Astrid raised her chin. 'She's gone to Asda.'

He bellowed out a laugh. 'Asda?'

'She doesn't want to see you.'

His smile vanished. 'How do you know what she wants? You don't even fucking know her name.'

'I certainly do.' She glared back at him. 'I also know why she chooses not to use it.'

'It's going to take more than a fake surname if that's what she's thinking.'

'She doesn't want to see you. Why can't you just leave her alone? She's just lost her daughter.'

'Mellie was a daughter to me too. I raised that kid.'

Astrid remembered something Mrs Baker once told her about Alan forcing his way into the bathroom when Mellie was in the shower, aged thirteen. He'd stood with the curtain pulled back and stared at her body. When Mrs Baker challenged him, he was indignant. 'What? I was just looking. I'm allowed to check how my own girl's developing, aren't I?'

'She wants nothing to do with you,' Astrid said. 'And this is my house. I'd like you to leave.'

'Well, I can't do that, sorry. She's got my slippers, see, and I want them back.'

'Your *slippers*?' Astrid shook her head. 'Is this a joke?'

He leaned on the door frame and continued to stare. 'I wouldn't take the piss if I was you.'

'I don't have the faintest idea what you're talking about.'

The veins in Alan's neck were huge now. He still hadn't blinked. He looked hyper-alert as if he was measuring the situation from all angles, calculating what she might, or might not know; what he might do to make her tell. She felt that if she moved in the wrong manner, or said the wrong word, he'd spring across the kitchen.

She summoned Lady M, felt her heart harden, her body expand, grow more upright, muscular, taller; she lowered her chin, her voice. 'What will it take to make you go away, Alan?' she said. 'For ever.'

By the time Mrs Baker got back, an hour or so later, Astrid was calmly seated by the Rayburn with Gilbert on her lap. She'd found him shut in the hall cupboard, very shaken. Sapphire was exhausted, the pups tucked against her, safe and sleeping.

She said nothing about Alan, but she couldn't stomach the Welsh rarebit that Mrs Baker listlessly made, and it was all she could do to stay sitting down in the snug after supper, she felt so agitated. At bedtime she moved the dog basket upstairs. Mrs Baker followed her down the hall. 'They'd be better off by the Rayburn where it's warm,' she said. 'Plus, they'll keep you awake all night.'

'I want them next to my bed. Sapphy's a bit off.'

Mrs Baker looked at her a moment but said nothing more.

Astrid was awake all night, not because of the puppies. Sapphire kept whining and turning in circles, and then she had awful squits on the rug.

The kettle blew up the next morning, as if it had stored the tension of the previous day and as Mrs Baker hunched over it, she said, calmly, 'He was up here yesterday, wasn't he?'

Astrid was standing behind her, holding both puppies. She bent down and rummaged in the cupboard for the kibble jar.

'When I was at Asda.' Mrs Baker reached over with one hand and plucked the kibble jar out, then, neatly sidestepping Tony Blair, went back to the plug. 'He was here, wasn't he?'

'What? Who?' Astrid's throat felt as if someone was squeezing it. She was an appalling liar – Mrs Baker sometimes laughed about it, saying that for a trained actress she was useless, and she'd reply that all actors are dreadful liars because it was their job to tell the truth.

'Astrid?'

'Yes?'

'What did he want?'

She held the pups close to her body, and said, quietly, 'He said something about wanting his slippers back.'

Mrs Baker's body went very still. After a moment, she said, 'How did you get rid of him?' Astrid put the puppies down next to Sapphire, who hardly moved. Then she put a handful of kibble into each dog's bowl, arranging it neatly with her fingertips. When she looked up, Mrs Baker's face was ashen. She seemed to read Astrid's expression, gave a brief nod. 'How much did you give him, Astrid?'

'What?'

Mrs Baker's voice was hollow. 'Because whatever it was, he'll have spent it already – last night, gambling or paying off a debt. It'll be gone.'

Astrid laughed. 'It really won't, honestly.'

'No, Astrid. Listen to me. No matter how much you give him he'll come back. He's always coming back.' She looked down at her work boots, which weren't securely laced. 'I suppose he followed us back here, from the crematorium. I didn't spot him. I don't know why he waited a whole night, before he came up here.'

Astrid was about to say something reassuring but Mrs Baker gave a quick nod, as if she had an invisible interlocutor in her head.

'Right. He wanted you on your own. He knew he could scare you, get some cash out of you first ... He'll have you pegged as the one with the money. Then when he's extracted what he can from you, he'll come back for me.'

'He won't, Eileen! Honestly. You mustn't worry any more, really. He won't be back.'

'Yes, Astrid, he will.'

'But he won't. Honestly. I gave him enough to make absolutely sure of that.'

Gilbert came over, wanting kibble, wagging his tail, claws clicking on the tiles. Astrid had a sense that she'd made a terrible mistake, but she wasn't sure why. 'How much?' Mrs Baker's voice was almost weary. 'How much did you give him? I'll pay you back.'

'Don't be ridiculous!'

'How much? I've got a bit saved up.'

'I won't take your money. Stop being silly.'

'He's coming back here, Astrid.' Mrs Baker sounded odd, preoccupied, as if her brain was working on several levels at once, her voice simultaneously flat and intense.

'He really isn't. And he didn't even ask me for the money. All he wanted was some slippers. So bizarre. I told him you didn't have any of his things.'

Mrs Baker shut her eyes, nodding. The eyes of the Kit Cat clock flicked to and fro, to and fro, and the pipes behind the Rayburn gave a shudder. Astrid tried to laugh. 'He can buy a new pair now anyway.'

Mrs Baker didn't move or speak.

'What are these slippers? Why is he so . . .' Astrid was distracted momentarily by Sapphire, who hadn't lifted her head. Usually, she'd be over as soon as the kibble jar rattled.

Mrs Baker turned away, dodging the stoat; her hands moved over the countertop briskly as she tidied away the delicate screws and fuses, putting it all back in the electrics tin. 'The only way to stop him coming back here is for me to leave,' she said. 'So that's what I'm going to do. I'm going to have to go.'

'What? What on earth are you talking about? I've just told you, Eileen, he isn't coming back.' She went and reached for

Mrs Baker's arm, grabbing at the scratchy wool of her dressing gown. 'He didn't ask me for money, I gave it to him of my own free will. He won't come back because there isn't any more and he knows that, I showed him my Nationwide passbook.'

Mrs Baker shook Astrid's hand off her arm and braced herself on the countertop. 'Oh, no, Astrid. You didn't.'

'I did. That's how I know he won't be back, don't you see? This is exactly why I did it. I can't have him terrorising you like this. I won't have it. I had to put a stop to it. And we made an agreement, he and I, so you mustn't worry any more. He knows there's no more money, he won't come back and bother you. He gave me his word.'

Mrs Baker turned, then, and gave her an anguished stare. 'But *Astrid*, Alan's word means nothing. Nothing at all. And he won't believe that someone who talks like you hasn't got other bank accounts, other assets – you own a bloody windmill!' She clutched her head. 'But it's not even about money – that's just him taking what's dangled in front of him. The money's just a bonus. It's the slippers he wants.'

'What on earth is it about these slippers?'

Mrs Baker went and sat, heavily, on a kitchen chair. She put her hands over her nose and mouth, fingers straight up over her eyes, then she peered out between them, circled the middle fingers over her eye sockets, pressing hard, as if trying to clear her vision. Astrid felt as if everything in the kitchen – the dogs, the clock, Tony Blair – was waiting for an answer. Mrs Baker's fingers stretched out the corners of her eyes then she pulled her hands down her cheeks as if trying to shed her skin. She took a deep breath in through wide nostrils. 'I took them the night he went to Spain. He'd done a robbery up in Essex, a big house – some rich businessman who collected historic slippers or whatever. It was all over the news, the papers called them the 'Slipper Gang'. Alan kept this one pair, I don't know why. Handmade, velvet things, used to belong to Cary Grant – some kind of trophy. When he was upstairs getting his passport, I put on my Marigolds and lifted them out of his bag.'

'And that's when you ran?'

'I was supposed to go to Spain after him, a day later – he left me a ticket – but I went to a B&B in Hove. I signed on at the agency next day, and I was cleaning your house the day after that.' Her shoulders slumped. 'Your Nationwide account, though, Astrid? That's everything you've got left. What are you going to live on now?' She leaned forwards, elbows on knees, as if she might be sick. Her striped pyjama bottoms rode up showing sturdy shins above her boots, pale, freckled skin. She shook her head. 'I can't leave you here with nothing, and I can't pay you back that sort of money. My God, Astrid, what have you done?'

'Now, you must stop being so silly. You won't pay me a penny! I don't want that. I owe you far more than money. You saved me, after Charlie died. I don't know what I'd have done if I hadn't walked into the Hove house and found you there. It was my decision to give Alan the money, and it's only money! I've thought it all through. I won't be able to pay you wages any more, not for a while, but we've got my pension. Honestly, we'll be absolutely fine. We don't need much to live on. You'll stay here, we'll grow more vegetables – we'll expand the vegetable patch right up to the end of the lavender garden, the way it used to be in Constance's day. We'll get chickens, like she did, maybe a goat . . .'

Mrs Baker didn't seem to be listening. She was staring at her scuffed work boots, loose-laced. The unblinking eyes of the Kit Cat clock flicked from side to side, more rapidly than ever.

'We can be like *The Good Life*. I loved that show, didn't you? Everyone adored Felicity Kendall, but Margo was my favourite – Penelope Keith, such a fine actress, such *pathos*.' She took the bowl of kibble over to Sapphire who sniffed at it, and laid her head down again.

'Astrid.'

'What?'

Mrs Baker gave her head a little shake, blinking. 'Why in God's name are you talking about seventies telly?'

'I'm just saying we can get by, here, together. We'll make this work. We'll turn the windmill into a B&B, you know I always meant to do that. You really mustn't worry.'

Mrs Baker sprung up. 'Hang on. Did you write him a cheque? You can stop a cheque.'

'I made it out for cash. Anyway, stopping a cheque surely *would* be the quickest way to get him back here.'

'He's coming back here, Astrid. Get that into your head.'

'You must stop talking like this.'

Mrs Baker stared at her. 'I can't even go now because I'd be leaving you here with nothing.'

'No. You can't go because I can't possibly manage without you. Imagine what would happen if I tried to fix a kettle. Can you see me trying to wire a plug? And I'd be living on beans on toast again – do you remember when I boiled that rice and I looked into the pan and the steam scorched half my face. You called me Phantom of the Opera for a week. It would be chaos here without you, and you know it.'

'But Astrid—'

'Right. That's settled then. You'll stay. I won't be able to employ you as such, but we'll find ways to supplement my pension, and you'll get yours soon anyway, and everything'll be marvellous, really it will. If Alan comes back here, Gilbert will go ballistic – remember what he did to that man from the windmill committee? He'll go bonkers and we'll call the police, and hand him in with Cary Grant's slippers.'

Mrs Baker shut her eyes, then turned and walked out of the room. The eyes of the Kit Cat clock swivelled to follow her, aghast. Astrid hurried out into the hall in time to see Mrs Baker vanish into the snug. 'Eileen, wait!' she called. 'What are you doing?'

'I'm going,' Mrs Baker's voice boomed back, 'to fetch his slippers.'

It must be some kind of post-traumatic stress, Astrid thought. His reappearance must have triggered a panic response in Mrs Baker, not least since she was already reeling from the funeral. She rushed into the snug. 'Eileen,' she said, as calmly as possible. 'Could you sit down for a moment? Just sit down?'

But she was hauling the bookcase on its castors, exposing the entrance to the tunnel. Her usually ruddy cheeks still had a tinge of grey, her jaw was set, but she didn't look panicked, exactly; she seemed more grimly determined than frightened. She stopped with one hand on the hatch door. 'You know,' she said, 'it was you saved me. If it hadn't been for you coming to Hove, and getting me up here to clean the windmill, and letting me stay on, I'd probably be dead now.'

'What are you talking about?'

'You knew I'd slept there, didn't you?'

'What? Where?' Astrid shook her head.

'At the Hove house.' She looked drained, suddenly, very pale. Astrid was struggling to keep up.

'Hove was only going to be the first step. I'd been trying to get away for years – my plan was to get Mellie clean, so we could go together. I knew if I disappeared without her, he'd go for her because that's how he'd get me to come back. But when I saw the slippers, I realised they were freedom.'

'The slippers set you free?' It all felt a bit surreal.

'Yes, for God's sake, Astrid, aren't you listening? Those slippers he took from the Essex job, they could put him in jail for life because they link him to the Slipper Gang. Forensics, everything. And I've got them.'

'But why on *earth* didn't you give them to the police back in 1999?'

'Because I needed them for insurance. They're what was keeping Mellie out of Alan's hands all these years.'

'But jail would have done that, surely?'

'Not necessarily. He'd just be sitting there planning what he's going to do to us when he gets out.'

Astrid tried to absorb the realisation that in the decade or so that Mrs Baker had been living at the windmill she would have always had one eye on the hill, knowing that the next car to bump up it could contain Alan, or one of his acquaintances. No wonder she'd seen off trespassers with the captain's ceremonial swords.

'I sent him a message saying those slippers were with a third party, and if he ever went near Mellie again, they'd be given to the police. But now Mellie's gone' – her voice broke – 'and he knows where I am. All he has to do is throttle me, and it's over. The only reason he didn't do that yesterday was he saw his chance to get some cash out of you. He knows where I am, and now he'll be back for me – and the slippers. He probably thinks you're the third party.'

'The slippers,' Astrid said. 'Where are they now?'

Mrs Baker nodded at the hatch door. 'Inside that silver coffee pot, up in the windmill.'

'Then it's time.' Astrid had finally caught up. 'We must take them to the police immediately.'

# Chapter 17

Astrid looked at the window. It was dark outside now and rain-drops tadpoled down the glass, which held the carriage on its trembling surface. Trains offered time to think but she did not want time to think. It was thinking that had got her into this situation, hurtling north to confront Magnus.

She must catch someone's eye, borrow a phone, but nobody was paying her the slightest attention. An old woman travelling alone was invisible, a ghost.

Sometimes, of course, invisibility had benefits. It certainly had when they'd gone to the police station the day after Alan first came to the windmill. It had taken them a while to get any attention at all, and then they'd been told to wait on uncomfortable chairs – a woman with a lot of peroxided hair was shouting at the officer behind the desk, something about her husband. Astrid was only half paying attention. She was worrying about the dogs who were locked in the car. They couldn't be left alone at the windmill now as there was no way of knowing if Alan might be back, but Sapphire was still very listless and wan, poor darling, eating nothing, and the puppies really shouldn't be wriggling around in the car unsupervised when they were only eight weeks old. They'd probably chew their way out.

Mrs Baker had fetched the coffee pot from the windmill. The slippers were in a ziplock bag, a bit squashed, but even through the plastic their quality was obvious: soft leather soles, a quilted lining, velvet exterior and a crest embroidered in gold thread. 'Huntsman, Savile Row,' Mrs Baker said. 'Made to measure. I looked them up once.'

'If they weren't so valuable, we could sell them.'

A big lad in a lanyard finally came out and introduced himself, but Astrid didn't catch his name or rank. He was absurdly young, clearly a junior, sent out to deal with the batty ladies. Mrs Baker stepped forwards but said nothing. She seemed to have become distracted by the woman who was still shouting at the front desk.

'We have some information for you,' Astrid stepped up.

'About?' He sounded bored.

'You've got him in there with Alan fucking Stonehouse!' the peroxide woman screamed. 'Stonehouse did Shoreham last night, not my husband! He had nothing to do with it!'

Astrid looked at Mrs Baker, who had frozen.

The young policeman's eyes flicked to the blonde woman too. Her dress was stretched round her bottom and breasts like a bandage, riding up at the thighs. She bellowed, 'He's got nothing to do with Stonehouse and you lot know it! You've got no fucking reason to be keeping him here.' She noticed them staring and turned. 'What? What you fucking staring at?'

Mrs Baker galvanised, shoved the slippers into her handbag, and seized Astrid's arm. 'My friend's not herself,' she said. 'It's the change of life – she gets ideas. I need to get her home.' Before Astrid could say anything more, Mrs Baker had tugged her out of the station, into the car park. She looked back. The young officer was striding, shoulders back, towards the woman at the counter who tossed her hair and jabbed a finger at him. They were forgotten already.

Back in Gloria, Astrid was baffled. 'What on earth happened? Why are we leaving?'

'Didn't you hear what she said? They've got Alan in there. He's in custody for a Shoreham burglary last night.'

'Good God!' The shouting woman's words sank in. Stonehouse. Mrs Baker was reversing out of the parking space, the car belching oil and fumes. 'But he would have to have done it right after he left the windmill. Can that be right? Are you sure she said Alan Stonehouse? She did, though, didn't she?'

They'd pulled out of the car park and were driving away from the police station, very slowly because it was a 20mph zone. 'Good Lord, Eileen. We almost—' Mrs Baker was fiddling with the radio and found a local news; she held up her hand. There was some burble about a large emergency presence at Brighton Pier, cause as yet unknown, and then there it was: there had been an armed burglary near Shoreham in the early hours of the morning. Gunshots had been fired. A police helicopter was deployed. A thirty-three-year-old woman was believed to have died at the scene and a fifty-nine-year-old man, the homeowner, was in hospital. He'd been beaten – they were getting reports that his tongue had been severed. Astrid and Mrs Baker, and probably the whole of Sussex, took in sharp breaths and covered their mouths. The victim was known to the police. A source said the property had been under police surveillance for some time.

'But . . . but . . . but . . .' Astrid was well out of her depths now; the sensation was both alarming and heady. 'But why? Why on earth would Alan do that? I'd just given him all that money!'

'This wouldn't have been about money, Astrid. Alan knows some nasty people. He'll have owed someone a favour. He'd have been in the pub, someone would have found him, got him to go with them. That bloke in hospital, the thing about the tongue, he'd be a snitch.'

Astrid swallowed and looked back at the dogs, suddenly afraid that they'd be gone but they were still there. Gilbert looked thrilled, but Sapphy was curled on the floor, very still, nose in paws, her pups rolling around her in the footwell. Astrid undid her seat belt and leaned back to stroke her head – she gave a faint wag. She scooped up the pups, bringing them onto her lap to give Sapphy a break.

She turned back to Mrs Baker. 'But this means they've got him, doesn't it? They've got him, Eileen! He'll definitely go to prison now, for years, won't he? They've caught him red-handed; a woman was shot – a man was beaten. And we've still got the slippers.'

Mrs Baker said nothing. Her jaw was set, and Astrid saw that her throat had gone blotchy, always a sign of stress.

'If he ever gets out, we'll take them back to the police, and they'll lock him up again, for the Slipper Gang robbery. It's over, Eileen. It's over.'

Mrs Baker's hands gripped the frayed leather steering wheel, knuckles white, skin stretched over bones. Astrid remembered, then, that they'd essentially just walked into a police station and announced their connection to a known criminal. 'You don't think the police will come for us, now they know we know him?'

Mrs Baker shook her head. 'They don't.'

'But didn't you say you're his wife? When we first went in?' Astrid had been distracted, worrying about Sapphy, wondering if she'd have the squits or the pups would chew Gloria's seats. She hadn't really heard what Mrs Baker said when she approached the desk.

Mrs Baker glanced at Astrid. 'I didn't give my name,' she said, as if that should be obvious. 'I just said I wanted to talk to someone about the Slipper Gang.'

'Did I give my name?' Astrid couldn't remember what she'd said.

'You didn't give him anything. No one was paying any attention to us anyway, they were too busy staring at the woman with the big—'

'They were!' Astrid laughed. 'They couldn't see anything but the boobs, could they?'

'I should imagine they'll think we're a couple of middle-aged curtain twitchers from Shoreham – that's if they even give us a thought.' She could hear the cogs of Mrs Baker's mind slotting into place. 'They know all the men involved. If that Shoreham house was under surveillance, they don't need witnesses. And even if they remembered I said something about the Slipper Gang . . .'

Astrid reached over and squeezed her solid forearm. 'We've vanished into thin air.'

Mrs Baker's hands had relaxed a bit on the wheel as she turned off the main road, and as they drove down the narrow lane which wound along the foot of the Downs, Astrid felt as if they were in a film, *Thelma and Louise*, making an escape. But of course, Thelma and Louise had gone off a cliff. Then again, Thelma and Louise were young and pretty, and so had been noticed and hunted down. If they had been menopausal and badly dressed, they'd have got away with it. She started to laugh. They'd outwitted both Alan and the police, but of course, it wasn't wits, really, it was luck – or perhaps something bigger and less fathomable, a higher power that had reached down just in time to sweep them from harm's way.

Mrs B. A. A. Saxon-Savage
Chairman
Mothers of Choir Boys, East Sussex Chapter

Lady Battiscombe,

I am writing to you in the strongest terms, following a highly distressing incident which took place yesterday morning as we, the East Sussex chapter of Mothers of Choir Boys, passed your windmill on our biannual 'Wildflower Wander'. As we reached the entrance to the footpath by your windmill, we were treated to the unspeakable spectacle of a young man entirely unclothed save for a long, blond wig.

We do not expect to have to negotiate such monstrosities on our precious Wildflower Wanders. This is wholly unacceptable. We shall await your sincerest apologies, and your absolute assurance that this sort of thing will never – and I repeat, never – happen again.

Whilst some of the group managed to find humour in this outrageous display, many of our ladies were so upset that they had to turn around and go immediately home.

You should know that I have also informed the Bishop of Lewes.

Yours truly,

Mrs Beatrice Saxon-Savage

Chairman

# Chapter 18

A taxi from Edinburgh to Northbank would be astronomical. She'd have to put it on the new credit card, though how they'd ever pay that off was anybody's guess. There was no point in worrying about it, though. It was important, Astrid thought as the train shot up through Northumberland, not to be bitter about money, or the lack of it. They had so much to be thankful for, and looking back, the paucity of funds had made life richer, and more interesting. They'd always managed to avoid absolute destitution; their attempts to make a living had been varied, variable, sometimes chaotic, occasionally stressful, but also, on balance, rather fun.

The day they got back from the police station they both felt quite shaky. Mrs Baker went and put the slippers back inside the coffee pot and took it up to the windmill again and when she returned they sat in the snug drinking Jim Beam and watching reality TV shows that expelled people, one by one, for not being good enough.

'I'll sign on for some cleaning work tomorrow,' Mrs Baker said, in the ad break. 'We're going to need more than your pension to live on.'

Astrid had one eye on Sapphire, who really hadn't moved all day, and had refused even a digestive biscuit soaked in warm milk. She must phone the vet, but of course there was no money for vets any more. 'Surely we can think of a better way to make a living?' she said.

'There's nothing wrong with cleaning houses.' Mrs Baker sloshed some more Jim into both their glasses. 'We're not exactly an employer's dream, are we? I left school at fifteen and you're a seventy-year-old unemployed actor.'

'Which means we have life skills. There are all sorts of things we can turn our hands to.'

'They want qualifications these days, Astrid, not hands turning to things.'

'My cousin Festus – he was the one who first got me into acting – used to make a fortune as a life model.' Astrid stretched her feet towards the fire. 'He had no qualifications whatsoever except that he was terribly fat. They loved him. They don't want conventional lookers at art schools.'

Mrs Baker gazed at her over the rim of the glass. 'Really, Astrid? Is that all you've got?'

'I could be a mystery shopper. I always fancied that. You get a buttonhole camera, like a spy, and you have to casually sidle around. Or sales? I'm so good at sales. Did I ever tell you that I used to demonstrate blenders when I was at RADA? I was the top seller. They were terribly unforgiving in the end, even though I'd warned them about the lid. They refused to have me back – didn't even pay me that day's wages.'

Mrs Baker looked almost as exhausted as Sapphire. She was staring at the TV, but not really listening to it or to Astrid. She'd been through so much in the past few days, with Mellie's funeral and the shock of Alan's reappearance. All the horrible memories must be crowding back. But distraction seemed like a good idea, so Astrid kept talking. 'My best money, not counting the years at the RSC, was from the automatic writing. I had these pretty little business cards made up: *Letters from Beyond, magic from within.* I could revive it. What do you think?'

'Revive what?'

'Letters from Beyond – my pen, Mrs Baker, was a conduit from the spirit world.'

Mrs Baker muted the TV. 'Are you trying to tell me you used to be a *medium*?'

'Oh Lord, no, nothing as grand as that, no, no, no. I just used to write people letters from their dead loved ones.'

'As Madame Savoy? You said you were done with her, all that drunken groping.'

'Oh Lord, no, I'm not reviving Madame Savoy, I'd rather starve, no. I'm talking about something I did before I even met Charlie: automatic writing, channelling the spirits through my pen.'

'You were a con artist.'

'I certainly was not! I never claimed to be psychic, I just tried to tune in, you know – or perhaps tune out. I let my hand travel over the page, and somehow things just came out. It's quite hard to explain without sounding peculiar, but on a good night the words would just flow. They always seemed to make sense to the people who came, too, that's the funny thing. Anyway, I could do that again, I used to rather love it.'

'If you're winding me up, Astrid, I'm really not in the mood.'

'All I know is that the letters seemed to make people feel less sad. That's all that matters at the end of the day, isn't it? I gave succour. It was quite lucrative, too, you'd be surprised.'

'What, people *paid* you to do this?'

'Oh yes.'

'And that was here? When you were living in the windmill?'

'Yes, before Charlie came. I used the Stone floor.'

'Wasn't that a bit risky, you up here on your own?'

'Oh no, my clients were mostly potty ladies, nothing worrying ever happened.'

'*They* were potty?'

Astrid was affronted. 'Automatic writing has a perfectly respectable history, Mrs Baker. A lot of famous intellectuals have dabbled in it, W.B Yeats, Arthur Conan Doyle, to name just two, though their wives did all the actual writing, and they took the credit for it, but still—'

'Astrid,' Mrs Baker said. 'Stop.' She put her hand to her forehead. 'Please. I can't ... Just stop for a minute. I can't hear myself think.'

'I'm simply saying that it was decent money, and the outlay was minimal, a few silk scarves, a pack of joss sticks, a bit of deep breathing, a bottle of sherry and a nice pen. I've still got my silver fountain pen somewhere. We could advertise in the *Fortean Times*. I was lucky, you see, my clients were all rather well off. I hit a rich seam, thank goodness, because I had no money when I came here. I'd spent it all on the windmill, which was a questionable decision, in retrospect, but there we are. I wasn't at my best at that point, as you know.'

'Where *did* you get the cash to buy this place? Family money, was it?'

Astrid stared into the fire. 'No, no. There was none of that. Or, well, there used to be, originally – my father's family were very well off. But after he died, my mother gave it all away to her subsequent husbands, funding their ventures and scams. Her problem was optimism, you see, she saw the good in them, even when it wasn't there.'

'Then how *did* you buy the windmill?'

Astrid had never confessed this to anyone, partly because

nobody had ever asked, not even Charlie, and partly because she'd hidden the truth out of shame. 'It was from Magnus,' she said, quietly.

'What, the divorce settlement?'

'Oh no, I took nothing when we divorced. It was after that. When I got back from my travels my mother died, suddenly, and I was a bit, well, rootless, I suppose, sofa surfing, that sort of thing, for quite some time. I even had a period in someone's bothy in Stromness – do you know, there's a place up there called Twatt?'

'Astrid. The windmill money?'

'Well, yes, Magnus was famous by then, I think he was living in Malibu. I suppose someone told him about me and one day his assistant appeared at the friend's house where I was staying and she gave me the keys and deeds to the flat in Hampstead that we'd rented when we were together. She came on a pink scooter, I remember, quite chic, Italian – not her, the scooter. She was from Cheadle – his assistant. He married her a few years later. What was her name? I think of her as Chervil, Chervil from Cheadle, but that can't be right, can it? Cheryl?'

'Sorry, Astrid.' Mrs Baker cut her off. 'Your ex-husband gave you a flat in Hampstead?'

'Well, it was 1980, Hampstead was shabbier then, and it wasn't huge, it was only a basement. He was just making a point, of course.'

'A point? What point?' Mrs Baker shook her head, flabbergasted.

'Well, we fell in love in that flat. It was our only home together. He wanted to show me his life had moved on and mine hadn't. It was a gloat. He didn't even write, or phone. Just sent the deeds and keys on a pink scooter with the pretty little assistant.'

'But you took it?'

'I know. I was weak. But, well, would *you* have said no to a flat in Hampstead?'

'No one has ever offered me a flat in Hampstead, or anywhere else.' Mrs Baker thought for a moment. 'You don't think it was romantic, though, sentimental or whatever?'

'What? Good God, no. We'd been apart for almost five years by then. He was entering his hellraising phase. Do you remember him? There were photos of him living it up in Malibu, all those parties with glamorous women. I think he was working with Scorsese at the time. And anyway, he got married again a year or two later, to Chervil with the pink scooter. No, I'm ashamed to say I knew it was a bitter gesture, and I took it anyway, and that's the truth. If I'd been a stronger person, I'd have sent Chervil packing, but I'm afraid I wasn't strong. Never have been. And I had nothing. My career was ruined, my mother dead, and five years on people were still recognising me, and shouting lewd things. So, yes, I'm not proud of what I did. But at least I didn't live in the flat. I sold it straight away and bought the windmill.'

Mrs Baker was staring into her empty glass.

'Have I gone down in your estimation?'

She looked up, surprised. 'What? Bloody hell, Astrid, who am I to judge anyone? I stayed with Alan for over twenty years.'

'But you had no choice about that, you had to protect Mellie. That's not weak, it's the opposite, it's incredibly strong. It's self-less. It's noble.'

'Noble?' Mrs Baker gave a hollow laugh. 'I let her down, though, didn't I? All those years I was trying to keep him off her, and she got messed up anyway.' She put her head in her hands and her shoulders began to shudder, gently. Astrid rose, spilling Gilbert off her lap. She crouched down and took Mrs

Baker's rough hands in hers, squeezing them tight. 'You did nothing wrong, Eileen,' she said. 'Nothing. You mustn't think like this. You did everything you possibly could to protect Mellie. You can't blame yourself that she got in with a bad crowd, that happens to lots of young people. You were a loving, devoted mother, that shaman said so at the funeral. Mellie never blamed you for any of her problems – she worshipped you.'

'I failed her.' Mrs Baker pulled her hands away and fumbled in her sleeve for a tissue. Out of the corner of her eye Astrid saw Gilbert at the dog basket, nosing Sapphire. 'I couldn't protect my own child.'

'If there was damage, Alan did it.' She looked into Mrs Baker's tired, blotchy face. 'He damaged you too, you're his victim too.'

'I'm nobody's victim!' Her chin went up. Astrid knew she'd said the wrong thing. Mrs Baker's eyes were pink-rimmed and bloodshot – she looked as if she hadn't slept for weeks. 'I didn't mean – I only meant—'

'You meant well, Astrid, I know that, but I don't like that word. I'm not a victim, I'm a survivor. I learned how to control his temper, I knew when to shut up, when to speak, when to submit, when to vanish. He had me cut off totally, I had no friends or family or money but I stayed because ... well ... you know all that ... I can't ... but I used to fantasise about retaliating. God, I did. Once, when he was passed out drunk, I sat there and held a kitchen knife against his throat for an hour. I knew his secrets, all the stolen goods he'd brought into the house, all the crimes. I had them all filed in here.' She tapped her head. 'I was planning my exit for years. Years.' She cleared her throat, looked away, her jaw clenching. It was the most she'd said about her past in all their years together. Astrid noticed that her hands were shaking, and she understood suddenly that Mrs

Baker wasn't vulnerable, she was angry. What she'd taken, for a moment, as fragility was, in fact, rage, contained for decades and now shoving its way to the surface.

Mrs Baker put down her glass, carefully, as if she knew she might crush it. 'That's enough about him,' she said. 'I don't want to talk about him any more.' She took a breath through flared nostrils. 'Anyhow,' she said. 'How did you find them?'

'Find who?'

'The clients. The Letters from Beyond clients.'

'Oh, them. Oh yes . . . well . . . they came to me.' And because she knew that she needed to talk again, she pulled up the footstool and told Mrs Baker how it all happened.

It was soon after she'd moved into the windmill, and she was sitting on the sofa one day, doing the crossword, or perhaps writing a letter, when a man's voice simply popped into her head. She felt herself slide out of the way and the voice filled her mind, took her over – but he wasn't talking to her, he was talking to himself. She had a pen, so she started to write down everything he said. He was expressing an awful regret that he hadn't kept his little girl safe – he should have watched her, he should have kept her from harm. The voice only lasted a few minutes, then was gone. It wasn't frightening, or threatening – it simply felt as if he'd strayed into the wrong room, and had stepped out again when he realised his mistake.

A few days later, she found herself asking the woman at the village shop what Constance's child had died from. She and the shop lady had never spoken before, except to say, 'Good morning' or 'Thank you.' The woman stared at her for a moment. 'You don't know? All this time you've lived up there?'

'Know *what*?'

'The windmill killed her. One of the sweeps hit her on the

back of the head.' She tapped the back of her own head, quite hard, then folded her arms in disapproval.

At that moment, the bell jangled and Clarissa Pelham-Hole burst in, with clumps of mud flying off her riding boots and a moth-eaten velvet coat swinging behind her. Astrid had never spoken to Pelham-Hole before but had occasionally seen her sweeping through the village in a rusted Daimler, an imposing person in her sixties with an elderly, panicked-looking Labrador on the passenger seat. She lived in the Georgian vicarage. 'You look ill,' she boomed at Astrid. 'What's the matter?'

Astrid, who'd lost all restraint by then, told Pelham-Hole and the shop lady, who was rapt despite her disapproval, about the man's voice, and how she'd written all his words down.

'Automatic writing,' Pelham-Hole barked. 'You've had a visit from Mr Banks.'

'Father of that poor little girl.' The shop lady nodded. 'Illegitimate,' she added, in a whisper.

'Banks was in charge of the Battiscombe estate,' Pelham-Hole continued, bossily. 'Fathered Lady B's child. Didn't you know?'

'Well, yes, I did know that.'

'My ma knew her.' She shook her head. 'Lady B. Barking mad, of course, living up there for years as a recluse with that ghastly maid, Miss Smith.'

'Miss Jones.'

'Absolute Rottweiler.'

Not long afterwards, Pelham-Hole appeared at the windmill, Labrador by her side. Astrid, who was up on the Stone floor, heard a thwacking sound and looked down to find her striding towards the windmill, swiping at the daffodils with a stick. She seemed to have a deep hatred of them.

It turned out that Pelham-Hole's aged father had recently died of a stroke. He'd hidden vital financial papers in the house – the family had searched everywhere but couldn't locate them. 'I thought you could try your automatic writing.' She decapitated another daffodil. 'Find Pa and ask the bugger where they are.' Astrid began to say she didn't know how to do that but Pelham-Hole gave her a no-nonsense look. 'I'll pay. Fifty pounds?'

They went up to the Stone floor. Astrid tried to make her mind blank, but nothing happened. She could feel Pelham-Hole's eyes boring into her, so she started to write anything that came into her head, and as she did, she began to hear a bumbling, stiff and slightly apologetic voice. All he had to say was that he wished he'd been nicer to the dog. He didn't say anything about any papers. Astrid slid the page to Pelham-Hole, expecting an explosion. She read it and bowed her head. Astrid waited to be shouted at and glanced nervously at the stick. Then she realised that the woman's broad shoulders were shaking – she was weeping. The Labrador put its nose on her lap, and she buried her face in its fur and sobbed. The Pelham-Holes never located the papers, but after that, well-off ladies started coming to the windmill in droves.

Mrs Baker nodded. 'Clarissa Pelham-Hole died ages ago, though, didn't she? The vicarage belongs to that bloody banker now, doesn't it? Bankers don't want automatic writing. You'll never get rich loonies like Pelham-Hole's lot, not now.'

'Perhaps not.'

'A bed and breakfast would be better.'

Astrid was a bit disappointed. Having told the story, she felt it might be fun to revive Letters from Beyond. Charlie had put a stop to it in the end; he couldn't stand what he called 'the mad poshos' coming in and out. But she'd rather enjoyed herself, while it lasted, and had missed it for a while.

'That's what you were planning, originally anyway,' Mrs Baker pointed out. 'To put paying guests up there.'

'But that was a decade ago, I was only sixty. And the windmill's in an even worse state now.'

'N.D.Y., Astrid. We can clean it up, just the ground floor. If we make that good, get the electrics back on, stick some of those old rugs down and get a new mattress, some curtains and whatnot, it'll be fine. It won't take much. They'd have their own entrance. We can do up the outdoor privy, and I can take them up their breakfasts on a tray. People like something different, don't they? I read about yurts the other day. People are paying a fortune to stay in them, glorified tents, a hundred quid a night.'

Astrid imagined erecting yurts behind the windmill.

'Oh, oh! We could do Bedouin tents – lanterns, music. It could be magical.'

'We don't need tents, Astrid, we've got a bloody windmill.'

It struck Astrid then that Mrs Baker needed, above all, to be busy. She needed a project. She'd be up there the next day with a mop, a bucket and her toolkit. Perhaps there was room for compromise. 'How about Letters from Beyond *and* a B&B?' she said. 'What do they call it? Upselling? When you ask if they want chips with that . . . you know what I mean. We could call it Bed, Breakfast and Beyond? I'll write letters, and they'll stay the night in the windmill. They'll put up with the bad plumbing and draughts and odd noises because it'd be part of the spiritual experience.'

Mrs Baker weighed this up, then to Astrid's amazement, gave a nod. 'Beyond Bed and Breakfast.'

'Genius!'

'It might work.'

But Astrid wasn't listening, because she'd noticed something about the way Sapphire was lying in her basket, a stillness beyond normal stillness, and, just as she had when she found Charlie by the pond, she knew.

**8th January 1921**

DEEPLY REGRET TO INFORM YOU THAT SHIP WAS
LOST AT 13.17 HOURS WITH ALL HANDS INCL. YOUR
HUSBAND CAPT. WALTER CHARLES ARTHUR BISWELL
BATTISCOMBE. I SEND SINCERE CONDOLENCES.
CONFIRMING LETTER FOLLOWS. DO NOT HESITATE TO
TELEGRAPH ME IF I CAN BE OF ANY ASSISTANCE.
    VICE ADMIRAL ROBERT E. ELKIN

# RETURN TO SENDER. RECIPIENT DECEASED

*Windmill Hill*

*8th January 1921*

*Dearest Walter,*

*By the time you read this, your maiden voyage will be over. You will be extremely happy and relieved, I know, and feted by all. I send you my heartfelt congratulations.*

*I have thought deeply about whether to write this letter. I did not write it before as I wanted to be sure. Then I delayed, because it seemed cruel to spoil your triumphant time after all the struggles you've endured. However, I feel certain that it would be even more distressing for you to return to Smythe Square to be confronted with a very difficult reality, and without warning. I must therefore tell you, Walter, that I am expecting a child. The father, you will perhaps surmise, is Mr Banks.*

*I know you will find this news difficult and distressing. I am deeply sorry for the pain it will cause you, and the embarrassment. You will be very angry, but I hope you will understand, too, that lately I have longed for a child. We have always been such good friends, you and I, but there are so many things we have never said to one another, aren't there?*

*I know you will agree that our lives have grown more and more separate, not just while you have been in America, but before that too. This does not, of course, excuse my actions but I hope that you will, one day, understand them, and perhaps forgive me.*

*I shall not write any more now as I do not know what else I can say to you except that the child will be born in late April. I shall* have Daphne and Mr Banks to help me. I do not intend to leave the windmill.

Of course, we shall speak about all this in full when you return. I hope that you will play a part in this child's life, I so want him to know you.

Do send word when you get to Smythe Square, and I will come immediately – or as soon as you wish.

C

P.S. Miss Jones, though understandably dismayed, has agreed to stay on.

# Chapter 19

It was never good to think back to a moment of loss. She'd never know whether it was Alan who gave something to Sapphire, some slow poison, or whether it had been the shock of him threatening the pups. It could, of course, have been nature misfiring as it had with dear Sloe, Gilbert's mother, who had died young too, out of the blue of a heart condition. But Astrid's gut told her that it was Alan. They didn't have the money for the vet to open her up and confirm this, even if they'd wanted to. They laid her to rest in the family plot up behind the windmill, beside Gilbert's great-grandmother, Dixie Belle, his grandmother, Bombay, and his mother, Sloe.

Beyond Bed and Breakfast did work. Sensible people might want good plumbing and insulation, but an advert in the *Fortean Times* does not attract sensible people. An early guest wrote an article for *The Paranormal Review* about watching an invisible hand flip the bible pages up on the Stone floor. After that they were inundated.

Not keen on strangers, Mrs Baker kept to the background, cooking breakfast, doing laundry, keeping the books. Astrid was front of house. She dug out her old kaftans and enjoyed herself immensely. People wanted to hear about the history of the windmill, so she told stories, wildly embellished, about Lady Battiscombe, Miss Jones, Daphne and the Bloomsbury group. She described pagan ceremonies, solstice costume parties, spiritualists and canine zipwires; she told how one night they had dug up the stone altar from the far end of the churchyard, without anyone finding out, and had carried it up the hill in a gypsy cart, or in a donkey cart, or on the back of the strong man from a visiting circus. She told them about Walter, too, and the Lost American Boys, and how Constance felt burdened by guilt for the captain's terrible 'battleship of the future', which, being small, had fatally lacked ballast. And she told them, too, about Constance's love affairs with both Mr Banks and Daphne, and about her poor little girl who was knocked down by the sweep, killed instantly, days before her fourth birthday.

As the guests departed, she'd urge them to go to the village churchyard and find the lichen-covered cherub.

## Anemone Hope Banks
### 29 April 1921 – 25 April 1925
#### 'Beloved daughter of the wind'

The guests, naturally, saw ghosts everywhere. Some swore that they saw a weeping woman walking in the lavender garden in the moonlight. Others were woken by wails swirling round the windmill above them, or, when they were coming to the door, saw a pale face looking down from the Stone floor window. Some saw monks dancing in the woods, or thought they heard a horse and looked out to see a gypsy caravan vanishing down the hill. Many were woken in the dead of night by the tinkle of the grain bell or laughter outside, and some said that as they lay in bed

268 LUCY ATKINS

on the ground floor, they heard a woman's voice whispering in
the tunnel below them, '*Get Out.*'

Subtlety was key. You couldn't take anything too far. And
atmosphere was everything. She performed Letters from Beyond
on the Stone floor, with pillar candles on all the windowsills,
scarves and joss sticks and the crucifix nailed to the wall.
Sometimes the words flowed so that she could hardly keep up,
and sometimes she struggled to think of a thing to write, but
mostly the guests were happy with whatever words she produced, and she saw that grieving people would inject meaning
into the most banal sentence, find a loved one's idiom in the
most generic phrase, providing it came from the nib of a silver
fountain pen in an incense-filled windmill after dark.

They kept Beyond Bed and Breakfast going for several years,
and made enough to live on, though not to repair the windmill.
Looking back, her seventies had been a happy, busy, vibrant
time. Alan was sent to jail for a minimum of ten years for the
Shoreham burglary, and the slippers were safe in the coffee pot,
in case they should need them when he got out.

The windmill, however, was not happy. Its plumbing grew
increasingly erratic, its water supply sometimes ran brown, or
not at all, and in winter it was bitterly cold on the ground floor
no matter what they did with paraffin heaters, electric radiators,
Persian rugs, tapestries and plastic sheeting over the windows.
The floorboards were unsafe, too, and the trapdoors definitely
weren't secure. They told guests they must on no account go
higher than the Stone floor, but nobody listened – paranormal
enthusiasts are not obedient people. One hefty visitor trod on
the trapdoor on the Bin floor and it cracked under his weight;
he saved himself from plummeting through it by clinging to the
canine funicular. Astrid sometimes felt that the Last Man had

been the windmill's way of putting a stop to all the disturbance, as if it had pinched the wind through its windows and cracks and hollows at just the right pitch to suggest the plaintive moaning of a devil, in order to drive him out.

Astrid felt her head judder and opened her eyes. For a moment she had no idea where she was. She seemed to be nowhere, in fact, locked into a dark shuddering cell with a white-haired spirit staring at her. Then she realised that she was looking at herself in the blackened window. The train. She was on the train, rattling up the north-east rim of England.

She smoothed her hair. She very badly needed a phone so that she could tell Nina her time of arrival, and check that Mrs Baker hadn't absconded. They had spoken briefly on Emmanuel's phone in the car, but the conversation hadn't gone well. When Mrs Baker picked up, Astrid had felt a wave of relief. She tried to explain what was going on.

Mrs Baker sounded upset. 'You're *what*?'

'I'm in a doctor's taxi, I'm on my way to Euston to get a train to Scotland.'

'Whose taxi?'

'Emmanuel, he's a fertility doctor. I'm speaking to you on his phone.'

'You're in a taxi with a fertility doctor?'

'You must tell Nina I won't be on that flight. I might not be in Edinburgh till early evening. Emmanuel saved me. There's been a drone attack, you see.'

There was silence.

'Hello?' Astrid pulled the phone away, peered at it. Then Mrs Baker's faint shouty voice floated up. 'What do you want me to say? You've lost the plot completely, Astrid. You need to turn around, wherever you are, and get yourself home.'

Emmanuel glanced up from his papers and she put the phone back against her ear. 'I'm simply keeping you abreast of my movements,' she hissed.

'Well, don't!' Mrs Baker snapped. 'Not if you're doing stupid things.'

'Fine! I shall be home tomorrow, as planned, either by plane or train. Please tell Nina I'll be arriving by train, now, not plane. I shall find my way to Northbank. Goodbye.'

As she handed Emmanuel his phone back, she thought she heard Mrs Baker's voice, but it was too late. He smiled as he tucked it back into his coat pocket. 'Everything okay?' Astrid nodded, though she wasn't sure. The streets of London flashed by, tall buildings, black cabs, and bicycles, so many bicycles these days, parts of the road portioned off for them, and faces, numerous faces, most of them strained or determined or grim. She felt worse having heard Mrs Baker's voice. An insurmountable distance, not just geographical, seemed to have sprung up between them.

It wasn't the first time they'd fallen out. They'd known each other so long, been so intensely in each other's company, that they were capable of enacting entire elaborate disagreements on multiple levels, sometimes without uttering a single word. Astrid would often take herself off to the windmill to calm down on the horsehair sofa, with quilts and cushions and books. She'd light the stove, listen to the radio, brew tea, her mood soothed by the familiar creaks and moans, the damp air, the thud of the wind against the cap and the rattle of the fan stage. She was usually the first to apologise. She knew how infuriating she could be to live with – chaotic, messy, scatty, impractical. 'You're on another planet!' Mrs Baker would cry as she turned off the gas or saved the bath from overflowing. 'God only knows what you did before I came.'

'Well,' Astrid would say, 'I had Charlie, and before Charlie I lived in squalor.'

It struck her that this was the first time in years that she'd properly had to fend for herself. It was exhilarating to have out-witted a ticket collector and illegally boarded a train to Scotland. Mrs Baker would be appalled; she was rigidly law-abiding. This suddenly made sense because of course Mrs Baker had never been able to risk coming to the attention of the police, who might link her back to Alan, or even alert him to her where-abouts. Alan had contacts everywhere, she said.

Perhaps they did need a break from one another. It couldn't be healthy to be so close quartered. For more than two decades they'd hardly been apart, though that wasn't necessarily from choice; not counting the windmill, neither of them had any-where else to go, and even if they'd wanted to go somewhere else, there was no money for it.

Perhaps Mrs Baker really would leave. Astrid remembered her saying, about Alan, how she'd known when to stay in a room and when to vanish. Living alone at the windmill didn't bear thinking about, even with the dogs. It would be impossible – but not for the reasons Mrs Baker probably imagined, all the economies and practicalities of running a home. She might find a way to stretch her pension, tape up broken glass, fix taps, remove mice and spiders, unblock drains – she might even remember to turn off gas rings and bath taps if she knew nobody else was going to do it for her, and if a kettle exploded, there was always a pan for boiling water. But she'd be lost without the friendship – the dreadful reality shows and Jim Beams, the ghost sightings and bickerings; the sense they had of each other's vulnerabilities, and the way they could shore each other up, without even thinking. Sometimes, of course, a little sink hole would open, unexpectedly, that could not be plugged. She remembered joking once, after they'd squabbled for almost an hour about how to make poached egg, that they were turning into an old married couple. Mrs Baker was sitting in her chair by the Rayburn, her big legs sticking out in front of her. 'If you were Alan,' she'd said, 'and I did your eggs wrong, you'd put down your fork, like this' – she laid an imaginary fork slowly on an imaginary tabletop – 'and I'd know.'

'Know what?'

She looked away but the pain was etched on her face, years and years of it.

She'd been at the windmill for eight or nine years by that time and had never directly referred to her life with Alan other than to say he'd been mixed up in things she didn't want to know. Astrid hadn't realised until that moment that Alan had been physically violent.

'Did he hurt you very badly?' she said, quietly.

Mrs Baker leaned over, held her hand out, pointing at the roughened palm. Astrid didn't have her glasses on, but she peered at it and nodded, not wanting to put her off.

'Held it on the gas ring when I burned his sausages.'

'Oh my God, Eileen.'

She tugged her sleeve down and looked away. 'That's just one.'

Astrid didn't know what to say. It was inconceivable that anyone could do this to Mrs Baker, who was so strong and authoritative. 'But . . . why didn't you leave him?' she said, tentatively.

Mrs Baker looked back at her steadily. 'He said if I ever left, he'd come for Mellie.'

'But he'd never have got custody. She's not even his biological child.'

Mrs Baker stared at the floor. 'He wasn't talking about custody.'

The train swayed around a corner, everything tilted, and Astrid felt tears pressing in her eyes. It really didn't do to think about what Alan had done to Mrs Baker over the years. She shut her eyes, but the image of his bloodied face in the rear-view mirror loomed up. He'd looked clownish, pinked up by Gloria's back lights, his face streaked, lips misshapen, shoulders lopsided, one arm dangling. He held up a hand in a sort of desperate plea. There was a moment of indecision, the windshield wipers clunked and Gloria growled, funnelled fumes. Then Astrid shouted, 'Drive! Go forwards! Put it in Drive,' and Mrs Baker wrenched the gearstick, shoved her foot down.

But she was not going to remember the Awful Incident. Going back like this really was ghastly and futile. Memories were so unreliable, after all. One person would remember something one way and another would contradict that memory entirely. She remembered when they were moving out of the family home, she and her mother were sorting things to sell and her mother had tossed a Georgian porcelain vase at her, shouting 'Catch!' She'd bungled it, of course, as her mother knew she would – and it had smashed, creating a mini catastrophe to distract from the major one. Her mother stared at the fragments, laughed, and then burst into tears. Years later when she brought this up, her mother had said, 'Don't be silly, darling, you caught the vase! I remember distinctly feeling you'd risen to the occasion, when you were so terrible at games.'

She forced herself to open her eyes. It didn't do to think too much about her mother, so dear, and so deadly. She longed for someone to talk to, a distraction, but there were only a few individuals in the carriage, nobody looking at anyone else, everyone in headphones. Still, train travel was much more civilised than air. She realised then that she was hungry. It had been a long time since she'd eaten; she'd had nothing all day, in fact, but a square of Cadbury's from dear Emmanuel Olowe. She wished she'd thanked him more fully. He'd been so kind. She would write. Perhaps they would become friends. She thought about Mrs Baker's ham and piccalilli rolls. She'd made them as a midnight snack when Nina came, and they all got back to the windmill, but it turned out that Nina was a pescatarian. Astrid hadn't been able to eat the roll that night, she'd been too woozy from the painkillers and the sleep in the car, and the fish and chips they'd had earlier, but she'd happily have one now. She hoped Mrs Baker had phoned Nina. It struck her, then, that she had no idea if she'd even find a taxi that was willing to take her all the way from Waverley station to Northbank. But there was no point worrying about logistics. It would work out. Things mostly did.

She'd probably have to see Magnus tomorrow, though. There would be no tea or cakes today. She still had no idea what she was going to say to him. She couldn't imagine trying to threaten him with legal action, not really. He'd laugh in her face. He might be horrified when he saw her, white-haired, wrinkled, old, but then, she supposed, he was white-haired, wrinkled and old too. The problem was that old age wasn't linear. People weren't young, then middle aged, then old. Some people were old even when they were young, and Astrid felt no different inside, at eighty-two, than she had at thirty-two. She felt pain organise itself at the base of her skull and straightened her shoulders. Her wrist was beginning to throb again. She needed more pain-killers, perhaps. Pain had a way of making you feel weak when, in fact, you were at your very strongest.

Magnus might assume that she was after his money. There might be reproach. He might have conveniently forgotten how he turned his back on her, how he'd allowed these appalling things to happen not just to Sally Morgan, but afterwards to her. She remembered the last phone call they had. Their transatlantic distance had been intensified by a crackling delay.

*Can't you come back?* she'd cried into the void.

He couldn't walk out on the first day of filming, they couldn't stop the production for him, he wasn't in any position to demand things; Rohls could replace him in an instant, he'd replaced Sally Morgan in only three days; the filming went to three or four in the morning, there was no break in the schedule.

She didn't make a fuss, but he must have heard the trauma in her voice, and the desperation. Earlier that day as she'd hurried towards the theatre, a man had lunged at her. *I'll give you sex games, you cunt.* She didn't tell Magnus about this – the shame was visceral, if illogical. She couldn't speak about it to anyone – everything felt too dangerous and out of hand to organise into words and she knew she needed to keep a distance from it, because that was the only way she could get up on stage every night. Then, over the crackling line, Magnus said what her mother had said: *It'll blow over, it's tomorrow's chip paper.*

She almost put the phone down.

He told her to hold steady, not to feed the fire, to keep her head down, not to talk to the media. He said it would be forgotten in a day or two and he'd come back the first break he had.

She was standing in the hall of their flat, she remembered, where they'd stood just two weeks earlier, after they got back from the hunting lodge. They'd had two hours' sleep, then, and Magnus was having to pack his bags to get to Heathrow. He said he could barely remember what had happened the night before. *She wanted him to do it, though*, he said, firmly.

*What? No, she didn't. She was terrified.*

She remembered Rohls looking at Sally. *You know, I wish I'd done it at your age. Why not? We could do it right now.* Sally's stoned eyes widened, and she gave her head a little shake. Rohls laughed, got up and loomed over her with his legs planted apart, his hands on his hips.

Later, when she was pulling him off Sally, Astrid had seen the erection straining at his trousers.

Next to the phone there was a bunch of roses that Magnus had sent when he arrived in America. The petals were dead already, scattered, and next to them lay a fake bloody dagger, the sort you buy in joke shops; someone had shoved it into her hands as she came out of the theatre. *You weren't that drunk*, she hissed into the receiver.

There was a pause. *What? This line's really bad.*

She left for the theatre, spinning inside with fury and she was still spinning when she got on stage. She gave the best performance of her career that night.

Magnus had turned his back on her in the most profound sense – and on Sally Morgan too.

At one point, after it all blew up, after Sally was dead, and replaced, and Astrid was dealing with the media and members of the public, she'd phoned Magnus at five in the morning his time. No answer. She tried again an hour later. The next day, the *Daily Mail* ran a blurry photograph of him with his new co-star, Sally's replacement. Their heads were bowed together, foreheads almost touching; Magnus's hand was on her arm. She phoned Rohls' assistant who promised to get hold of Magnus. There was no phone call that night. The next day, another tabloid ran a story with the headline *Dead Actress: Sex Game Gone Wrong.* Someone in the hospital had told a reporter that, under her coat, Astrid had been naked from the waist up, whilst Sally was 'starkers' except for a bloodstained fur.

The next night, coming out of the theatre, she was shouted at by a group of irate Christians, and then chased to the tube by some drunk men. When she got home, she could hear the phone ringing in the flat but by the time she got inside, it had stopped. She dialled Magnus's number in New York State; no answer. The *Guardian* had been delivered that morning; her face was on the masthead. *A Woman Scorned.*

Magnus's abandonment wasn't really like her father's, now that she thought about it. When her father had taken pills and walked into the lake, he'd been overcome by a darkness which he must have carried inside himself for a very long time, perhaps always. He'd hidden it so well; he'd only ever been her smiling, eccentric, loving daddy. It wasn't just her he'd concealed his pain from, the shock was universal. 'None of us saw it coming,' her mother always said. 'It must have been a moment of madness.' People used to say she'd got her acting talent from her mother, but it was her father who had the real talent. Her mother was all artifice, fey, insecure, but for years her father had persuaded everybody, perhaps even himself, that he was happy.

Magnus, on the other hand, had never concealed his true self. His sights had always been fixed on a screen career, and she knew he'd do anything to make that happen. When he went along with Rohls and then left the country, he was, at least, being true to himself.

On the last night of her career, she had to turn her eyes away from newsstands as she went in and out of the tube. People nudged each other, whispered, shook their heads and as she hurried, head down, out of the carriage and up the escalator, someone shouted, *Loony cow!* She had to push her way into the theatre through a group of mocking reporters who wanted her to comment on the rumours about Magnus and his new co-star. A man in a trilby came out of nowhere, spat in her face. Worse than any of this, though, was the Company. Everyone was furious or horrified – or, at best, baffled. Some questioned her intensely about what had happened, others couldn't meet her eye. She couldn't cope with the scrutiny, and so she went into herself, stopped talking to anyone. In response they closed ranks, and rightly so, because her sudden notoriety, her position at the epicentre of this ghastly scandal, threatened to overshadow everything they'd worked to achieve.

A *Telegraph* journalist wrote a long, pseudo-intellectual piece about how she was bitter because she was too old for Hollywood and had never been beautiful enough to be a leading lady. She'd been uncontrollably jealous of Sally Morgan, the talented world-class beauty, only twenty-three years old, who was to be working so intensely with her husband and in a drunken rage, perhaps during a 'strange, bohemian sex game', Astrid had attacked the younger actress.

But Hollywood had never been her dream. Her only ambitions had been to master Shakespeare's poetry and rhythms and to play Cleopatra at the National; she never managed the latter, but there had been moments, with Shakespeare, when she felt herself reach a transcendent and heady place. Neither the *Telegraph* article nor any others said that Magnus was her age, and no matinee idol himself. None questioned his role at the Tudor hunting lodge, and Rohls was barely mentioned.

As she sat on stage that last time, Act 5, Scene 1, it was as if the membrane that separated her from the character dissolved. The disorientation and guilt were overwhelming; there was the striking of the clock, the smell of blood, blood on her hands, her robes and she knew she couldn't live any longer with what she had done, the pain was intolerable. She had only the haziest memory of what happened next, but she read, later, an account of it: instead of giving the final scream, then exiting stage right, she'd gone downstage, teetered on the edge, torn her robes, kicked off her satin slippers and climbed into the audience, who thought that it was an avant garde twist to the production, until it became clear that this was not the case.

Afterwards, she thought her life was over, but it really wasn't; it had just been halted for a bit, then had changed tack. She'd been stripped of one identity but eventually she had adapted to being someone different. She didn't mind that sometimes she was unhappy, it was silly to believe that one could be happy all the time. When circumstances called for it, she was perfectly prepared to be sad, knowing that no sadness would last for ever; that no experience was permanent, either good or bad.

The train was slowing into a station. There was an incomprehensible announcement, sudden movement, bags coming from luggage racks, the zipping up of coats, laptop lids shutting.

Others were getting on. A woman took the seat opposite. She looked just like Joanna Lumley – *was* she Joanna Lumley? Astrid peered at her. She was glad not to have Hendricks. Hendricks had a powerful loathing for Joanna Lumley and would stand and bay at the television when she came on. The woman glanced at her with a faint smile, as if she was a member of the royal family. She almost certainly wasn't Joanna Lumley.

Astrid's eyeballs felt exhausted then, as if they'd been switching from side to side like the Kit Cat clock. She closed them and felt Gordon nosing her palm, his warm breath, his damp beard, the warm loaf of his body settling on her lap. She opened her eyes again. It was beginning to feel like an effort to separate the real from the imaginary. The woman, in fact, looked nothing like Joanna Lumley. Her eyes were too wide apart, a bit bug-like. Sally Morgan had had wide-apart eyes too; they dwarfed her delicate features, which were curtained by the fine golden hair. Had she lived, she'd be in her late sixties now – she might have turned out a bit like this woman, bleached and tweaked and painted, with something stricken and immobile around the lips and eyes.

Sally's eyes had looked dazed as Rohls turned his attention on her, took her chin between his thumb and forefinger. *I can do it to you right now.* He bent and touched her forehead with his thumb, a priestly gesture.

*This is ridiculous!* Astrid used her Roedean voice, but Rohls ignored her. Behind them, on the sofa, Magnus looked unsteady. His eyes were open, but not entirely focussed.

Rohls took his thumb off Sally's forehead, looked into her eyes a moment longer then gave a casual nod. *You're going to be so happy you did this, honey. Let the light in, and the devils out.*

Astrid suddenly had no patience for Rohls and his dangerous twaddle, for the needy actress or for Magnus, lying drunk and stupid on the sofa. She got up, went over to him and held out her hand. *Bed.*

Magnus looked up at her but didn't move. He was horribly drunk, she saw, and also, perhaps, fascinated by what was about to take place. *Well, I'm going up.* If she removed herself, she thought, Rohls would stop. He needed an audience. All three watched her leave.

She went into the kitchen and poured herself a glass of water. She was exhausted, her mind felt disordered. She couldn't leave Sally with Rohls. She stared for a moment longer at the strung-up pheasants, necks torqued, then turned and went back into the

hall. The door to the front room was open and she could see
Magnus, still sprawled on the sofa with his eyes closed. Sally was
by the fire. Rohls, thankfully, had gone. Astrid was so tired she
could hardly stand now, she had to go to bed, she had to sleep.
She turned and climbed the wonky staircase. For a while she
walked up and down uneven corridors, confused by the layout of
the house, unable to find their room. She entered a study deco-
rated with long-nosed Inca horses and gold-leaf stars; a peculiar
human skull watched her from a pile of papers on the desk. It
was deformed, she saw, elongated, as if it had been grown in a
tunnel. She backed out and went back down the creaking hall,
where she stopped beneath a seventeenth-century portrait of an
elderly man with a hooked nose. She knew she had to go back
downstairs, she couldn't leave Sally down there until she was
sure that Rohls really would leave her alone.

She heard a high-pitched whine as she got to the bottom of
the staircase. She went to the doorway and saw Magnus outlined
by the fire, kneeling behind Sally, holding her arms. His head
was turned away as if he was unable to watch whatever Rohls
was doing to her. Rohls was hunched over Sally. The back of his
hair curled onto the collar of his pale sweater.

'Are you all right?'

Astrid blinked her eyes open. Joanna Lumley was leaning in,
head on one side.

'Me? What? Why?'

'You made a very odd noise. I thought you'd stopped breathing.'

She was embarrassed then at the idea of this woman, this
nosy stranger, watching her. She must get a grip now. She must
get up, find the toilet. She must eat something – perhaps there
was a buffet car.

'*Are* you all right?' The woman clearly sensed weakness and disapproved.

'Perfectly,' Astrid snapped.

Lumley raised an eyebrow and went back to her magazine.

Astrid glared at her. *Busybody*.

Lumley looked up, sharply. 'Well! I think that's very rude.'

It struck her that she had, in fact, said the word out loud.

The woman was only pretending to read the magazine now, that was obvious. There was an awkward, tense atmosphere between them. She felt she should say something normal. 'I'm going to Edinburgh,' she said. Lumley raised her eyes, briefly, but said nothing. 'I'm going to see my ex-husband,' she continued. 'He's dying, at his son's house in the Borders.' The words suddenly seemed to line up and she felt a falling sensation inside her chest. She remembered the feeling that she could not – did not – exist without Magnus; that her body and his were part of the same engine and that if you cut one off, the whole mechanism would shudder to a halt.

'I'm sorry for *you* then.' Lumley sniffed.

'Oh, don't be. He's a monstrous man.'

She lowered the magazine, raised one pencilled brow.

'He abandoned me. A long time ago.'

Lumley softened, then, very slightly. 'Yes, well, lots of them do, don't they?'

There was a moment of silent solidarity. Astrid pictured Lumley's unfaithful husband, a retired executive, a golfing Tory with a new young wife. She sensed the woman's curiosity, now, and her intrusiveness. 'I don't know why I'm telling you this.' She looked away.

'Well, don't – I didn't ask you to.'

Astrid opened her bag with one hand. She needed the

painkillers. She imagined telling Lumley everything about the night in the Tudor hunting lodge. It would sound berserk. 'I've loathed him for forty-five years.' She found the tablets.

'Forty-five years? Shouldn't you have forgotten him by now?' Lumley made no effort to sound friendly; Astrid felt their horns lock again.

'Forgetting him was impossible, I'm afraid. He's a very famous actor.'

Lumley rolled her eyes. '*Is* he?' She looked back at her magazine.

Astrid gazed at the eyelids, gold and brown eyeshadows creasing into the folds, and thought of the Irish chieftain's skull with its empty sockets. *He's 700 years old.* Rohls held it up, turned it this way and that as he talked about monastic surgeons, shamans, Peruvian knives, enlightenment, intense perceptions, cerebral blood flow, Hieronymus Bosch, Tibetan monks. Magnus was agog – or seemed to be. Perhaps he was pretending? She couldn't tell. It was possible, in fact, that this was the moment she lost him; the moment when she couldn't tell if his interest in Rohls was real or fake.

Later, when the ambulance came flashing up the mile-long drive, Magnus's eyes looked as empty as sockets on the ancient skull.

'I suppose you'd rather not say.' Lumley sniffed. 'How convenient.'

Astrid tried to refocus. 'Rather not say what?'

'Who this famous ex-husband of yours is.'

'Oh, I don't care about that. He's Magnus Fellowes.'

Lumley blinked as if Astrid had puffed smoke in her eyes. Then she laughed, and shook her head. 'You weren't married to Magnus Fellowes.'

Astrid looked away, at the juddering window; her hair was a white dot in the darkness, bone on ink. 'I was an actor too,' she said. 'But I gave it up. Or it gave me up.' Lumley stared back at her magazine, nostrils flared. 'Then I ran a bed and breakfast in Sussex.' It sounded so sensible; she saw herself with a shiny Aga instead of a rusty green Rayburn, a sign saying *Live, Laugh, Love* instead of a swivel-eyed Kit Cat clock; windowpanes fixed by glaziers instead of tights, and no windmill – definitely no windmill. 'Magnus went to Hollywood, of course.'

'I saw Magnus Fellowes play Lear last year.' Lumley spoke very loudly, claiming him for herself, as people always did. 'It was one of his last ever performances. He was magnificent.'

'I can't keep talking to you.' Astrid rested her head back on the seat and shut her eyes.

'My God! You started talking to *me*.'

Astrid sometimes wondered what would have happened if she hadn't lost her grip that night on stage. Would people on trains be talking of her magnificent last performance? Perhaps she'd be in James Bond films, or Sunday night period dramas. Perhaps she'd be a dame. Such thoughts were pointless, she knew, but lately because of all the disruption, all the regrets and what-ifs had started spinning inside her again.

She couldn't understand, looking back, why she hadn't been braver and more defiant. Why on earth hadn't she stood up for herself? She could have refused to protect Rohls and Magnus – she could have exposed them.

She had tried to protect Sally, though. When she seized Rohls' arm he stood up. *You stupid fuck! You could have killed her.* Magnus let go of Sally and stumbled backwards – she heard him retching into a plant pot as she took off her shirt and wrapped it around Sally's bleeding head. Her eyes were at Rohls' groin level and she saw that this act was not about enlightenment, it was about dominance and power – it was an assault.

Magnus staggered to the sofa, lay back down and shut his eyes.

Sally was trembling. She seemed very out of it. Then her eyes rolled back in her head, and she went floppy; Astrid caught her round the waist and helped her over to the other sofa. *Don't you touch her*, she said, to Rohls.

She could have insisted on telling the truth to the police and journalists but somehow – and perhaps this was unconscious conditioning from her mother – she had accepted the subordinate position and shut her mouth. As if she were a 1950s housewife, she put Magnus's career before her own, and then, as everything closed in on her, she pretended that she was all right.

They followed the ambulance through the moonlit country lanes, Rohls at the wheel of the Bentley, surely too intoxicated to drive, haranguing her all the way. *What the fuck were you thinking calling a fucking ambulance? I can't have this blowing up in my face right now and nor can Magnus – or Sally, for Chrissake. Your fucking phone call probably just cost us millions of dollars.*

In the back seat Magnus was hunched down with his head in his hands. She could see that he might vomit. There were a few dark spots of Sally Morgan's blood on the knee of his jeans. Rohls swore at her until they came to the outskirts of the city, when his tone hardened. *You called that ambulance, you handed this to the media. You don't think the paramedics are going to talk? You have to fix this now, Astrid, okay. So, here's what's going to happen: we're going to go and get Sally out of that hospital. I'll get her on a plane back to New York tomorrow, and Magnus will be on it too. He can't be involved in this and nor can I.*

They pulled into the hospital car park. Astrid reached for the door handle.

*You're going to say you did this, Astrid. You hear me? Worst case, it's five minutes of media interest, then forgotten.*

She stopped, half out of the Bentley. *What?*

*You come in there and you say you did this.*

*But I can't! I'm performing at the National!*

*You should have thought of that before you called the fucking ambulance.*

Astrid looked into the back seat. Magnus hadn't moved, his head was slumped on his knees. It wasn't until much later that she realised how convenient his stupor was.

Rohls continued to talk as they crossed the car park to A&E, leaving Magnus in the car. *You're just a stage actress, nobody gives a damn about you, but if it's me and Magnus and Sally fucking Morgan, they're going to be all over this on both sides of the Atlantic – it'll be one big salacious distraction just as we start filming. This sort of thing can jeopardise a movie. It's a million-dollar shitstorm you've started here – the studio could insist on replacing Magnus. Everyone's replaceable, Astrid. Do you really want to be responsible for ending your husband's career before it's begun?*

You tap a memory once or twice, Astrid thought, and it resists and then you think it's safe, it's not coming loose, but if you keep tapping, it will loosen eventually, and bits will start to crumble out, and soon the whole edifice will come crashing down, burying you alive.

She had been sitting in the kitchen with a cup of coffee when she heard on the radio that Hollywood actress Sally Morgan had been found dead in her apartment in upstate New York, where she was working on a new film with 'auteur director' Jack Rohls. It was an accidental overdose of painkillers. She phoned Magnus, but there was no answer.

He rang her back, eventually, in the middle of the night,

weeping so much that she couldn't get any sense out of him. It was two more days before the information, no doubt leaked by someone at the hospital, hit the news. She still remembered the BBC announcer's words. *Shortly before her overdose, the American actress Sally Morgan was subjected to a bizarre act of violence here in Britain, at the hands of the Shakespearean actress Astrid Fellowes, wife of Morgan's new co-star Magnus Fellowes.*

She must stop doing this. She must block off these unhelpful memories. *Stop up the access and passage to remorse.*

'Did you say something?' Lumley looked up.

'Absolutely not.' The headrest purred against the back of Astrid's skull. She was such a long way from home, and acutely alone. She remembered, clearly, the first time she had recognised this feeling. She'd been just a child, nine or ten years old, on her way back to boarding school on a winter night. Her mother's driver was listening to loud jazz on the radio, eating Jelly Babies without offering any to her, and she had understood, suddenly, that she was alone in the world, and always would be. The realisation was frightening at first, even terrifying for a short while, but then it struck her that it might be liberating, and perhaps empowering, not just to comprehend this difficult fact but to embrace it. It wasn't until much later in life, when she was in her fifties perhaps, that she fully understood how contentment lies in the curation of one's solitary space: the careful, imaginative selection of thoughts and memories, and the effective suppression of those that are ugly, or do not serve.

Mrs Baker came down the aisle, then, plonked a ham sandwich and a cup of tea on the table, popped out a couple of painkillers and stuck them into Astrid's good hand. *There you go, you'll feel better in a minute. This'll pass.* Astrid felt a rush of relief and opened her eyes; Mrs Baker vanished.

Lumley was still pretending to read her magazine, *Good Housekeeping*. Astrid moved her diaphragm slowly and tenderly up and down, controlling the flow of air in and out of her lungs. She was perfectly all right. In a minute she'd go and find the loo.

The doors slid open, and a ticket inspector appeared at the other end of the carriage. She imagined the train's brakes rattling and screeching as it came to a halt, and she was escorted onto a patch of the Northumberland coast. They were passing a small station and a clump of bare trees flashed by, waving their limbs. She remembered Magnus coming into the hall at the hunting lodge waving his arms as she dialled the ambulance, *She's okay.* His speech was slurred. *It's okay, Aster, stop. Come back in, she's fine. She's fine. It's just a bit of blood.*

The ambulance dispatcher had wanted a location, but Astrid didn't know where the Tudor hunting lodge was, she didn't even know what county they were in. Magnus seemed unable to locate any useful facts. He swayed, glassy-eyed, beneath a stag's head. There was a pile of letters on the console, the countess's post – Astrid took one and read out the address. Rohls strode across the hall and sliced his hand onto the plungers, cutting the line.

At the hospital, the doctor firmly pretended not to notice that he was treating a famous movie star, but there were suddenly nurses everywhere. Rohls moved to the doctor's side and nodded at Astrid. *So, I guess my friend here told her it's an ancient procedure, totally safe, you know, the secret of eternal youth.* He rolled his eyes. *The vanity of women, right?*

The doctor, who was about Rohls' age, athletic and tall, turned his chilly gaze to Astrid. *I'm sorry, you consider this a safe procedure?*

Sally lay motionless on the examination bed with her eyes

shut. They'd taken off the fur coat and put her in a hospital robe. Her hip and pubic bones jutted through the flimsy cotton; she looked brittle and sharp but somehow transparent and temporary, too, a sliver of ice. There was a bandage around her head.

*The world's oldest medical procedure.* Rohls oozed Californian bonhomie. *That's what you told her, right, Astrid?*

Their eyes met.

The doctor sounded incredulous. *Putting a dentist drill through a young woman's skull is not a medical procedure.* Beside him, Rohls nodded.

The doctor's eyes flickered to Astrid's chest before he turned away, and began to write on a pad. She had used her blouse to wrap Sally's head and was naked under the coat. She pulled it tighter, folded her arms. She would hear whispers everywhere around. *Sally Morgan. Sally Morgan.*

Sally's eyes opened, suddenly, and she looked at the doctor, then at Rohls, who stepped forwards and pressed his hands over hers. She didn't pull away. She stared at him for a moment without blinking – a look of pure, cold hatred – and then her eyelids closed again. The doctor turned back to Rohls, as if Sally was his pet dog. *Fortunately, the drill didn't get far through the bone. She'll be fine. Take her home, make her rest. And* – his eyes flicked to Astrid – *keep her away from this lunatic.*

Constance Battiscombe was wafting down the aisle behind the ticket collector. Her hair was swept up, her long throat rose from a fringed shawl; she held her chin high and touched the seat handles, one by one, as she passed them, her tall body swaying with the movement of the train. Her eyes were fixed on Astrid. The lights flickered, and she vanished and Astrid thought, suddenly, of the toad in its little flint prison in Brighton; a hoax, a fake.

Unreal. Yes. She knew that. But how? How had it been achieved?
The amateur archaeologist, a solicitor by trade, must have been a
brilliant actor to have made all those eminent London scientists
believe something that went against all logic. She thought then
of how she could pull together a theatre of strangers, form
them into a collective entity that she controlled with her voice,
her body, her mind. On a good night, there would be a pause
followed by a single exhalation when the play came to an end;
all those souls had fused into one being. This was not logical
either – it was certainly not scientifically explicable, but it was
real, pure and true.

She closed her eyes. Constance was standing right next to
her now. She felt a chill and smelled lavender; she sneezed and
opened her eyes. The ticket collector was standing above her.
'Oh dear, I absolutely must get to the loo!' she said. 'I'm so sorry.
It's terribly urgent, and I don't even know where the loo is.'
The ticket collector, a motherly Geordie, stepped aside looking
concerned and helped her out of the seat. 'It's that way, pet,'
she said. 'Just at the end there, not far, okay?'

Lumley watched with narrowed eyes.

Astrid fumbled with the toilet door, which had a confusing
opening system. Someone passing pressed a button for her, and
it slid open. She fell inside the cubicle, but the door didn't shut.
It took a while to find the button to shut it, but then it slid over
and sealed her inside, with a satisfied hiss. The yellowish light
flickered and there was urinary stench, the floor was sticky. She
smelled stale alcohol. The person before her must have been
drinking. The image of Alan's face popped into her head – the
boozy acrid smell of his breath as he stuck his tongue out. The
dogs had been yapping and snarling, darting at his legs – as
Mrs Baker wrenched open the tunnel door, Hendricks went for

him and there was the horrible sound of Alan's boot thumping
into his ribs.

'Don't!' she shouted.

Alan shoved his face close, mimicking her. '*Don't!*'

She took the sewing shears from their box on the side table
and waved them at him. 'Get back!'

He swayed closer again – just his face. There was a dangerous
look in his eyes – anger, but also something sadistic; he was
enjoying this, he wanted to inflict suffering. He stuck out his
tongue again, waggling it, mocking her – it made her think of
a Maori haka dance, only more unhinged.

She swiped the scissors across the air between them. 'Get
away from me!' He lurched forwards – she saw his stained teeth
and metal fillings, the greyish coating on his tongue, swiped
again; felt a brief resistance. There was a fractional pause in
Hendricks' yapping.

Astrid peed, hanging on to the rail as the train swayed, but
she couldn't work out how to flush, or how to wash her hands.
She looked around for the escape button. She was stuck – like
one of the shrews inside the tree. She'd been out at the tree
the previous night, after she'd woken Mrs Baker with the silly
screaming, and they'd had their cocoa. When Mrs Baker went up
to bed, Astrid was restless – she knew she'd never sleep, with the
airport looming, the night almost over. The only place she'd be
able to rest was inside the windmill, but of course, she couldn't
get in there, so she took a blanket, and Gordon, and went into
the courtyard. The wind had petered out and a meagre moon
hung over the tower, pale clouds trailing around its peeling cap.
She knew what she'd see if she allowed herself to look up at the
Stone floor window, so she didn't look – she moved on beneath
it. She heard its joints creak as if it was turning to follow her.

As she went down the side of the cottage, a badger bustled out from the bindweed and stared at Gordon, sizing him up. Gordon backed away and the badger decided not to bother and moved back again, down a tunnel into the tangled weeds and brambles. Astrid crossed the grass to the pond where she stopped. Gordon stopped too and looked up at her anxiously, wondering what was going on, and why she wouldn't pick him up. She leaned against the Shrew Tree. She was breathing too fast again. The night air was busy with wintry scents of dead vegetation and damp bark, weed-clogged pondwater, slippery flints and the acres of chalk-land that stretched around them, ancient and booming with life.

The trunk of the Shrew Tree felt gnarled and warped under her fingers. Ever since Charlie died, she had felt as if it had something to tell her – as if, one day, it would speak. The bark felt active, buzzing with energy and intelligence. She found the spy hole with her fingers. It was Mrs Baker who had told her that in days gone by Sussex labourers would push live shrews inside ash trees, seal them with little plugs of wood, and then the tree would become a healing tree, a place to bring sick children, prayers, hopes and fears. Mrs Baker had told her, too, that shrews were frenetic creatures, constantly in motion, eating, eating, eating, and that because they were so manic, they couldn't hibernate, and so in winter they simply shrank – bones, body, brain, everything. She pictured the tiny shrews twitching away in the velvet interior beneath her fingers, just out of reach, their restless spirits feeding the tree's colossal, magical energy.

# PIOUS BUNDLE

*3rd May 1925*

*Dearest C,*

*Your brother has forbidden me to write to you. He is still cross that I came to see you – as I'm sure you can imagine – but I shall not abandon you. I am so very sorry for the state I found you in yesterday, and somewhat shocked too, I confess, by the manner in which you are living. I thought we were accustomed to your choice of lifestyle, we put much of it down to the tragedy with Walter, but things seem to have disintegrated further. As a mother, of course, I understand your distress. However, I know you will eventually accept that God has called your little one to Him, and that there is joy in this. You must not let yourself collapse now, Constance, you must gather yourself, ask for God's strength and move on.*

*Do not worry about Sheridan. Although at present he still cannot see beyond the shame you have brought to the family these past few years, even to pity you, he loves you still, I am sure, and will soften in time. As I said to you – though I am not sure you heard me or took in my words – we must now organise your return to London. I shall make the arrangements to prepare Smythe Square for you.*

*You must also let Miss Jones go. I found her so rude yesterday, so very hostile. Your friend, too, was very fierce. As I was speaking to you about God's forgiveness, she stood behind your chair, glaring at me, and rather gave me the shivers, I confess. Your Miss Jones, meanwhile, was quite abrupt as she showed me to the door and as I said farewell, she stared right through me. When you return*

to Smythe Square I shall lend you my little maid, Teresa, who is
personable and efficient, until we find a permanent replacement.

You must know, dear Connie, that Sheridan will find a way to
forgive you eventually. As for London, everyone will get over this
in time. I shall come next Saturday and accompany you back to
Smythe Square. We can organise for your things to be sent up after,
and eventually for the sale of the windmill. God, and I, will take
care of you now.

Fondest love, dear one,

Mary

*The Grange*

*5th June 1925*

*Dear Constance,*

*I shall try to overlook the tone of your letter, I know you are not yourself. I am sorry that you feel it is impossible for you to leave the windmill. I am sorry, too, that you do not want my help. Sheridan saw my distress as I read your letter over the breakfast table today and has forbidden me to have further contact with you. I am writing to let you know that you shall not hear from me for a while.*

*However, before I do sign off, I urge you to reconsider. It is not reasonable, or seemly, to stay in that windmill, living the way you do, overrun with mice and bats and strange women, bringing more embarrassment to your family and particularly to your poor brother, who has tolerated so much. Think of your little nephews and nieces. It is not too late to save your reputation!*

*I have discovered, by the way, that this woman Daphne is known throughout London as a bohemian who is much too fond of wine. You must cut ties with these women, Constance. You are a widow now, you no longer have an illegitimate child, you could live a perfectly respectable existence. You could, perhaps, take a Grand Tour of Europe for a year or two?*

*Think of your family if you will not think of yourself.*

*Fondest,*

*M*

*The Grange*

27th April 1926

Dear Constance,

I confess that I felt some dismay when I left you yesterday. It is obvious that your health has been in further decline over the past year since God took your child to Him. It was my duty to come to see you on that sad anniversary, but I find it deeply unsettling, the way you live now, in that draughty windmill, the walls covered in artworks of a very troubling nature, with holes in the windowpanes, the wind howling and that blasphemous oratory with its stolen altar.

Your life is chaotic and punishing. You are thin and drawn. I urge you, again, to let Miss Jones go. She seems, with your ghastly 'artist' friend, almost to have taken full control of your life; it is as if your windmill has become the asylum, and those two women your keepers.

Constance, you must come to your senses! Rid yourself of the ghoulish Miss Jones, stop entertaining artists and adulterers. I heard, at luncheon the other day, that there has been spiritualism and sapphic dancing at your windmill. People in London call you 'bohemian' now, which as anybody knows is another word for lunatic.

Your house in Smythe Square is waiting for you. People will, eventually, forget what you have done. Some already feel sorry for you and understand that it was the horror and shock of what happened to Walter and to all those young American sailors that has caused this weakness – and, of course, the loss of your child. I am relieved, at least, to hear that you have finally ended your association with the charlatan, Mr Banks.

I do not wish to be unkind or judgemental, but this is no way to

live. Sheridan feels the same as I. He is prepared to see you, should
you put aside the windmill and return to a civilised, respectable life.
Say the word and I shall send my man to fetch you.

   With deepest concern,

   M

*19th December 1926*

*Dear Constance,*

*Do you plan to live this way for ever? I have not told Sheridan how I found you yesterday; can you not see yourself? You and that dreadful woman dressed like men, you swinging a chisel whilst speaking of your freezing tower as if it were human. The way you live now is quite beyond our comprehension. That windmill seems more real, more alive and certainly more important to you than any of us can be. Miss Jones, meanwhile, is wholly unsuited to the task of containing you, as is your rude friend who is clearly complicit in, and perhaps the architect of, your wicked lifestyle.*

*You are a spectacle. Can you not see that?*

*After you turned me away, my driver had to stop in the village because the motorcar needed attention. He feared it had been damaged from coming down that awful potholed hill. A local approached to see if he could help and wished to know why we had been to the windmill; when I informed him that I was a respectable relative, and that you would be moving back to London, he laughed and said, 'She's only coming off that hill in a box.' I closed the car window and waved him away, but he was laughing his head off. So, you are, Constance, a laughing stock, even in that village. I tell you this out of compassion and not from any desire to wound you.*

*You would hardly let me speak, but I came today to insist, once and for all, that you drop this stubborn fixation, come to your senses and return to normal life. Walter has been dead almost five years, there is really no excuse. People will forgive a certain amount of eccentricity from a grieving widow, but this is simply too much!*

*I wish you to know that, unless you agree to return to Smythe Square, I shall cease all contact forthwith. Sheridan, naturally, feels the same.*

*Our children are still alive, and we must think of their reputations.*

*M*

# Chapter 20

Sometimes, poor hearing could be a blessing. The taxi driver didn't stop talking but she could tune him out rather effectively. She wondered whether Nina would be cross about the missed flight. She must have been waiting back at Northbank for hours, perhaps trying to distract Mrs McKittrick. Magnus would no doubt have gone to bed – it was almost eight o'clock by the time the train reached Waverley and it had taken a while to find her way out of the station. There had been a storm of football supporters on the platform, chanting and hollering and waving beer bottles. Lumley, who had marched away in heels without a goodbye, stopped suddenly, turned and pointed. 'Go that way if you want a taxi.' To Astrid's surprise she was right – emerging onto a quieter street she found a taxi passing, and waved it down. She hadn't much idea how far outside Edinburgh Northbank was, or how much it might cost to get there, but she had no choice, her hitchhiking days were definitely behind her.

The words 'daughter', 'Galashiels' and 'speech therapist' floated back and she made occasional approving noises. The notion of speech therapy made her think, of course, of mouths and tongues, which circled her back to Alan, again, the way his hands flew to his mouth, and he leaned over, spitting strings of bloody saliva, and roaring. Mrs Baker saw her chance, sprang across the room, took him by the shoulders and thrust him backwards towards the tunnel hatch. Hendricks and Juniper were on him, the back of his head hit the low door frame and his body folded in two. Mrs Baker gave him a final shove in the belly with her boot and he went backwards into the tunnel. She shut the hatch, turned the key and wrenched the bookcase back in place while Astrid watched, frozen in shock, unable to move or even speak. There was a thudding on the other side of the bookcase, and they heard muffled roars. Mrs Baker came over, silently took the sewing shears from Astrid's hand, wiped them on her sleeve, closed them, and put them back into the craft box.

She really must stop thinking about the Awful Incident. It made her feel quite dizzy and sick to go back there. *S.O.B.* She must organise her thoughts and come up with a strategy to deal with the present destructive man: Magnus. It struck her, suddenly, that she did not have to be herself when she met him. He wasn't the only brilliant actor. It was Meisner who'd said that the actor's biggest resource was their limitless imagination, and so she would use hers. She would become tall, strong and resolute and fierce, she would alter her posture and voice and insist that he remove her completely from his memoir.

The taxi driver seemed to be asking her something. He kept turning to look back. She tapped her ear and said in her frailest voice, 'I'm awfully sorry, dear, but I don't hear well. My naughty dog ate my hearing aids, can you believe it?' He turned, smiling, his kindly face was plump and jovial but a bit concerned. She'd rather he looked at the road – forwards not backwards – so gave him her sweetest old lady smile then looked away. A few minutes later, he drew up in front of a pair of tall wrought-iron gates. They'd driven quite a long way through the dark countryside by then. She really didn't want to think what this might mean for the fare.

He turned and hooked an elbow over the seat. 'Well, hen, this is you.' She touched her ear, buying time. 'This is you,' he boomed and tilted his head. 'Are you all right? You're looking a wee bit pale if you don't mind me saying so.'

'Oh, yes, I'm perfectly fine, thank you, just a bit tired. I've come all the way from Sussex today.'

'Ach, now that's an epic journey.'

'You're terribly kind, really you are.'

He smiled, and peered up at the gates. The tiny, sharp gatehouse sat behind them, blank-eyed, flinted, windows unlit. It looked pinched and sad, perched on the boundary, peering through the bars at the lane.

'Are you going up to the big house then? That looks like a long driveway. It's cold out there tonight,' the taxi driver said. 'I'd best take you right up to the door, huh? You can't be walking all the way up there with your bags. There's rain coming too.' He sounded protective now, and she felt grateful. 'No extra charge,' he added. Astrid peered up at the gnarled metal gates and the gatehouse. If she told him to turn around and take her back to Waverly, she'd never have to see Magnus again.

But she had to stay tonight. She couldn't possibly afford the taxi fare back to Edinburgh. She was also exhausted, bone tired, drained and even if there were trains in the late evening, they'd get into London in the small hours and then what would she do? She could perhaps wait on the gatehouse doorstep till Nina came home, then turn around tomorrow and go home. But if she stayed, then Nina might make her go and see Magnus. Perhaps she could ask the driver to take her to a local B&B, and avoid the whole thing. But he was out of the car already, big-bellied, wrenching open the gates and then they were moving through them. As they came up the drive she saw some eerie, muddled ruins – the nunnery. Nina had mentioned that there was a ruined nunnery in the garden, a place in which unwed mothers and witchy oddballs would once have been imprisoned for their own protection. A Georgian house rose above it, lights blazing. It was too late to change her mind now. The decision to confront Magnus had been made for her by a kindly Edinburgh taxi driver.

She watched the taxi's tail lights disappear off round the bend between the trees. He had accepted her credit card, tapped it on his machine, but had charged her far less than the amount she'd seen on the meter, which he said was broken. She felt rotten now for not having listened to his chatter. He'd even walked her up the front steps, supporting her elbow. She'd insisted he leave but before he went he pulled on the doorbell. She waved him off, shivering inside her velvet jacket. The air was dense with coming rain, biting cold – *the air bites shrewdly, it is very cold.* Shrewdly. She felt herself shrinking inside her clothes, shrew-like, twitching and shrinking to survive.

Perhaps Nina would come and scoop her up and take her down to the gatehouse. She could have a hot cup of tea, collect herself, sleep and decide in the morning whether to face Magnus or not.

The ringing echoed inside but still nobody came. She'd catch her death if she stood on the doorstep much longer. She wished she'd worn her silver padded coat. Mrs Baker would tell her to try the door, get inside, she did know that. She turned the brass handle – it opened.

'Hello?' she called into a broad, flagstoned hallway. 'Hello? Nina? Are you there?'

She left her carry-on case by the bench beneath a stag's head, and moved towards a broad, curved staircase. A grandfather clock watched, disapprovingly. Her Asda trainers made no sound on the flagstones, and she saw herself floating down the hall: the ghost of Magnus's past, slipping into his house to present him with his crimes.

There was a kitchen to the right: gleaming appliances, a wall of French windows, high ceilings, lights blaring, a cream-coloured Aga. A painting of a pawing bull filled one whole wall – the scale of it all made her dizzy and shrunken. She should have asked the taxi driver to come inside with her. She felt like a trespasser in another world. A fridge, double-fronted, hummed enquiringly, then stopped. What could an old man need from such a stupendously large appliance, such a palatial kitchen? But of course, this was Desmond's home, not Magnus's, built to impress. A huge white clock, its face denuded of numbers, ticked solidly above the lustrous Aga. It was ten past nine.

She went back into the hall and stood at the bottom of the staircase. She had absolutely no idea what to do now. For a moment, she wanted to laugh and then she felt a bit wobbly, as if she might weep. She must locate Nina. Or even Mrs McKittrick – she no longer cared about Desmond finding out about her visit. Or perhaps she could find a phone and ring Mrs Baker, who would tell her what to do.

She felt something in the house shift – she wasn't sure what, or where. She imagined Magnus listening, watching – houses like this surely had surveillance equipment? Was this silence a game? A strategy? But no, Nina was here somewhere, and Nina wouldn't play games. Where *was* Nina? She remembered her saying that Magnus had his own wing of the house. The staircase was vast, curving round on itself, and she didn't have the physical strength to climb it. She needed to sit, or she'd collapse at the foot of his stairs.

She peered through a doorway into a drawing room with cornicing and a chandelier over giant white sofas with tartan cushions and lamps softly illuminating the corners. Everything was still and clean and pale and huge. She heard footsteps thundering down the stairs and whisked round; the staircase was empty.

There was a landing area halfway up, a semi-circular window over it. The sound must be rain drumming against the glass. Above the landing a long, elegant light, two glass orbs on wires, started to sway – but of course, they couldn't be swaying, they were far too heavy for that, it must be an optical illusion, her own warped brain. It was possible that the galloping sound had come from inside her head too. She went back to the drawing room and sat down on one of the white sofas – her lower back shrieked, and she tried to breathe, ignore it. If she waited here, then at some point Nina or Mrs McKittrick or someone else would find her and take charge.

Her trainers sank into the pale carpet. There was a stack of golfing magazines on the coffee table – Magnus had no interest in golf, surely – and beneath that all sorts of curiosities: a fountain pen, postcards, a leather-bound book, a compass. She peered at the objects and thought of the Leith house in which he'd grown up, cramped and dilapidated, rammed with combustible siblings. His mother's coffin had practically filled the living room that day, its ends almost touching each flocked wall. He'd be lonely in a huge empty house like this; it was all wrong for him. She felt a sudden sadness. This wasn't where Magnus belonged. But, of course, she didn't know where he belonged any more. She tried to pick up the compass, but her hand met solid wood. The tabletop was flat and smooth, and she realised that it wasn't covered in objects at all, it was a painting, a trompe l'oeil surface. The notion that even his clutter was fake filled her with dismay.

She looked up. There was a huge collage of photographs above the fireplace – every one of Magnus. In some, he wore tuxedos and held up trophies, in others he stood on beaches or boats with stunning women, or laughed arm in arm with famous actors, singers, politicians. She hauled herself off the sofa and went over to the wall. There he was with Judi Dench, and there with Tony Blair – the real Tony Blair – and there, a still from *Othello*. When did he return to the stage? The late eighties or early nineties perhaps, when his film career had begun to flag. How fitting that he should play the great, selfish manipulator, Iago. Seeing Magnus's life collaged like this, his face creasing and crumpling, his hair fading, what struck her was the unchanging look in his eyes. She had never noticed this in the glimpses she'd caught of his face in magazines or newspapers or on the TV before she switched over, but she saw it now, a sort of desperation. And she wondered whether he'd been lost all these years and she'd never been able to look at his face for long enough to see it. She felt, suddenly, as if she'd let him down, which made no sense at all.

She moved away from the photographs and back to the sofa again. The very idea of guilt was ridiculous. How easy it was to take responsibility for other people's choices. Absurd! Whether Magnus had been happy or not was no concern of hers. This was no good, no good at all. She couldn't wander this huge silent prison with Magnus somewhere nearby, disabled and bitter, or waiting and watching. Where on earth was Nina? She must find the telephone, call her and be rescued. Coming to Northbank was a dreadful, dreadful mistake. She'd expected to feel all sorts of things, but not guilt. Not pity.

She felt positively unwell now and had to force herself to

breathe more slowly. She needed to take control of the spinning feeling inside her chest. She remembered the A&E doctor's parting words: *Don't overdo anything*. There had been guff about scans and procedures; nonsense, all of it. There was nothing wrong with her, she'd told him, that a Jim Beam, three dachshunds and a good night's sleep wouldn't fix.

She noticed a door in the wood panelling, then. It was ajar. Perhaps her eyes caught movement behind it, or perhaps she heard something, because she suddenly knew that it was Magnus.

Her first thought was to flee. But where would she go? To the ruined nunnery? An unfamiliar resolve locked into place. It was no good running away again. She had taken the journey to his door, she must go through it now, alone, and face him.

She didn't have to conjure up a character because, as she walked towards the door, she felt suddenly righteous, and as that feeling spread, she grew more solid and upright.

She saw his wild hair first; from behind, still wavy, surprisingly thick, and white. He was sitting at a leather-topped desk beneath the window of a wood-panelled study. There was an oxygen tank next to him, a blanket on the chair back. He had his head in his hands and was very still – asleep? Dead? No, he was upright. *N.D.Y.* She spotted a whisky bottle by his elbow, a glass half full.

He must have sensed her presence. He turned, and as she saw his face an involuntary spark of joy shot up inside her. His cheeks were sunken under the beard, he was thinner, certainly, more frail looking, but not all that changed; she knew him.

He peered at her across the room then cleared his throat. 'Aster? Oh, dear God. Is that you? My eyes aren't good. It's you, isn't it? Or is this . . . fuck! . . . No, it is you!'

She felt herself pull back and squint. Her vision closed in, as if she was peering at him through a notch in wood.

'Aster? Fuck me – I thought you weren't coming. I thought you'd changed your mind. Are you with Nina? Was that the doorbell? I didn't . . .' She didn't catch what he said. '. . . thought you . . .'

'The front door was open.' She heard the strength and clarity in her own voice. 'Where's Nina?'

'She's with you, isn't she?'

'No?'

'But she went up to Edinburgh to get you off the train. How did you get here?'

'I took a taxi.'

She walked towards him with her shoulders back, her chin up. He gazed at her.

'Fuck me, Aster. It really *is* you, isn't it? Not some' – he laughed – '*strange infirmity*.'

She caught this and almost smiled. 'It's definitely me.'

'Sorry . . . sorry . . . I can't seem to get up right now.' He waved vaguely at his legs. 'Seeing you . . . Will you sit? Please. Here, take that chair, bring it up next to me.' His grey eyes were warm and alight. 'You really made it,' he said. 'It's *you*.'

She felt her chest tighten as she got the chair and sat down. Now that she was so close, she suddenly wasn't so solid inside after all.

'I'm not too good on my feet right now, but that doesn't matter. You're here. It *is* you, isn't it? Are you okay? You look magnificent, though I'm half bloody blind, I'm afraid, so—'

'And I'm half deaf.' She managed to lower herself into the chair. 'So you'll have to stop mumbling.'

He fumbled for the whisky bottle, and she saw that his hand trembled. 'Will you have a drink? I'm not supposed to drink but . . . sitting here waiting for Nina to bring you – we've been waiting hours. Jesus, what happened to your arm?'

She wanted to reach out and steady the bottle, but she wasn't sure her hand would be much better than his.

'Or would you rather a coffee? Though you'd have to make it yourself. I'm supposed to be in my bed – Mrs McKittrick's gone home to fetch something so this is my big chance. She'll kill me herself if she sees me drinking.' He peered at the bottle.

'I suppose I could have a small one,' she said, formally. 'But first I must phone Nina. If she's gone to meet my train, then she might still be waiting for me.'

At that moment, the phone on the desk rang. Magnus turned and picked it up.

'Ah, Nina,' he said. 'We were just talking about you. Yes, she's here. With me. She's just walked into my study.' A pause. 'Yes, yes, I suppose so.' He held the phone out. 'You missed each other at Waverley.'

Astrid took the phone and looked away but felt his eyes on her.

'Astrid? Thank God – I was starting to get worried!'

'I'm terribly sorry, Nina, I had no idea you were going to be at Waverley. I got a taxi.'

'It's okay, you poor thing, are you okay? What an ordeal! I rang Mrs Baker, but there was no way for either of us to get hold of you. I'll ring her and let her know you've got there, unless you want to? But you're with Magnus now, aren't you?'

'Would you let her know I'm safe? Tell her I'll phone her when I'm finished here.'

Astrid watched Magnus reach, unsteadily, for a glass. He felt the edge of it and sloshed in some whisky. She saw him, young and beautiful, standing in a Tudor hallway under a stag's head, swaying, dazed, dead drunk.

She said goodbye to Nina and took the glass, tipping the alcohol into her mouth. It burned her throat and spread through her chest, oiling tight spaces. She was all right, she really was.

'Have you any idea . . .' But he was mumbling again and she didn't catch the words.

'You'll have to speak up,' she shouted.

He was leaning on papers. She saw a pen by his elbow and realised that when she came in, he hadn't been asleep, he'd been reading. It was a manuscript, printed in large font. There were scribbles in the margins. His own life – he was reading about his life, or the fake version of it that Desmond had constructed. She wondered whether all the fumbling about with whisky, the blindness, the Shakespearean quotes, the inability to stand up, was performance – straight out of *King Lear*. He had perhaps decided to dupe her with frailty so she wouldn't make a fuss about his book. 'I just play the cancer card,' she remembered an aged aunt saying once, whilst dying in a lavish Kensington flat, 'and everyone does what I want.'

'How are you, Aster?' he said. 'You look . . . beautiful.'

She tried to ignore this, gestured at the manuscript. 'I'm not here for a catch-up, Magnus. I came to talk to you about your book. I won't have any more lies about me.'

'Oh.' He faltered. 'Christ. Yes. God. Straight to it then. Oh, Astrid, this fucking memoir.' He looked back at her, bushy brows gathered, uncertain.

'*Your* fucking memoir, Magnus.'

His brows tightened. 'But you mustn't worry . . . see, Nina's printed the chapter out for me. It's the first time I've actually read it and it's garbage, obviously. Dessie's very . . .'

'You can't blame Desmond for this. It's your life.'

Magnus looked right at her. 'Dessie actually hadn't let me

see this version of your chapter. I made Nina give it to me. He wants me to come out of the book as a heroic figure, he's very, very protective of my legacy. This is, truly, the first time I've read it.' For a moment, he looked a little bit bewildered, as if he couldn't quite keep up with what had been happening. Despite herself, she believed him.

But Magnus was brilliant at making people believe – he'd won an Oscar for it. He looked earnest and seemed to be breathing a bit too fast. She saw him glance at the tank next to his chair and she suddenly felt that the manuscript might be the least important thing in the room. She looked away, hoping to give him permission to take in some oxygen.

'I'll make sure it's the truth or nothing,' he said. 'I give you my word.'

She told herself that she did care about the contents of the book, of course she did. This was the reason she'd made an eleven-hour journey to his door. It felt both surreal to be in the room with him, and entirely normal. 'What *is* the truth then?' she said. 'I'd like to hear it from you.'

'The truth? God. About . . . ?'

'About what you and Rohls did to Sally Morgan!' she boomed.

'Fuck. Yes. Okay. We really are getting straight to it then. Okay, so look, I mean . . . you know what—'

'You'll have to speak up!' she shouted again. 'My dog ate my hearing aids.' He gazed at her, and she saw a flash of amusement, perhaps fondness – or a combination of the two; she felt heat rush to her face. 'What do you think happened? I demand to know!'

He took a slug of whisky. 'Right. Okay. That night. Well, I held Sally's arms while Rohls tried to drill a hole in her head, and then you – rightly – called an ambulance, and then I – wrongly – fucked off to upstate New York leaving you to take the blame, thereby ruining your career and possibly your entire life.' He took in a rasping breath.

She stared at him. This was not how she'd envisaged the conversation going. 'I've had a very good life, thank you very much. I've had a marvellous, excellent life.'

'I'm very glad to hear that.' He nodded. 'I really am. Very glad. I'm not going to make excuses for what I did, it was unforgivable, leaving you to take the blame. I've tried to avoid thinking about it for years now. I didn't want a fucking memoir, you must know that. Nina would have told you that? She's a good egg, that Nina, I wish my son would have let me talk to her, but look, I'm making a hash of this, I know. What I want to say, what I've tried to tell you so many times over the years, is that I was an idiot. All I can say is at the time I didn't understand what was happening. I thought it would all blow over. I thought the fuss was mainly about Sally's overdose, not about your part in all that nonsense.'

'Nonsense?' Astrid stared at him. 'She died!'

'But it wasn't the trepanning that killed her, Aster. It was the drugs.'

She closed her eyes. This is what he'd told her at the time, perhaps to assuage his own guilt. Because he was guilty; he had been complicit that night, he should have stopped Rohls, refused to hold Sally's arms. A vulnerable twenty-three-year-old in the hands of a man twice her age, a man who controlled her career – her life – was a timeless crime, and Magnus had enabled it. At the very least, he should have walked away from the film. She remembered telling him this, back at the Hampstead flat, as he packed his things. He'd looked at her, hungover and incredulous. *But Aster, if I refused to work with monstrous men, I'd never work again.*

'You were right, though,' Magnus said now, 'Rohls was a vile fucker.'

'So were you, arguably.'

'Me? But I genuinely didn't realise what the media was doing to you, Aster.' Magnus lowered his head. 'I had no idea what was happening back here, until it was too late.'

'I'm not talking about me – I'm talking about Sally Morgan.'

'Oh, that night? I can only remember bits of it – I was incredibly drunk.'

'Not too drunk to hold her arms down.'

'No. No. You're right. Shit, I do remember some bits – I remember Rohls telling me it's a reflex to put your hands up when the drill hits the bone.'

The bore hole had been close to Sally's hairline. Astrid's hand went, involuntarily, to her forehead. Magnus looked shocked, too, and rubbed his forehead, then took another slug of whisky. Then he peered at her, nodding. His breaths rasped, he was ghoulishly pallid. 'I'm sorrier than you know, Aster. For all of it, I really am. But . . .' He mumbled something.

'What?' She realised he couldn't speak up because his lungs had lost their power.

He raised his head and looked right at her '. . . I only ever wanted you.' His eyes welled up. 'Aster? Did you hear what I said? *I only ever wanted you.*'

She felt herself become hot, a sort of fury rising. 'Nonsense! You chose your career over me.'

'What? But I didn't, my God, I really didn't – or I didn't realise I was, anyway. I had no clue you were under that much pressure till you fell apart. I was in upstate New York, remember? They didn't have British newspapers. There was all the trauma over Sally's overdose, and Rohls replacing her with Julie, practically overnight, and then the filming started, eighteen-hour days, and it was crazy. And you were telling me you were fine – on the phone, you really did say that, a lot. I had absolutely no idea how things were at home for you, or what the media was doing. I think maybe Rohls didn't want me to know – remember how his people manufactured those photos of me and Julie to deflect media attention?'

'You abandoned me.'

'It was unforgivable and selfish to let you take the blame and I've regretted it pretty much every day since. But I tried to get to you – I kept phoning you and missing you, and you wouldn't call me back. I had no idea how bad it was, then you just vanished. I tried to get to you, so many times, to tell you . . .' He tailed off, struggling to breathe or perhaps to fight back the tears. 'But you didn't want me in your life any more.'

Astrid tried to organise herself back into a position of outrage. 'The entire world thought I took a dentist drill to Sally Morgan's head. It was so . . . so . . . *mad.*'

'It *was.*'

Their eyes met. Astrid felt the rain lashing at the enormous windows, drumming on the roof of the house; on the lawns and the ruined nunnery, across the Scottish woodlands, and the fields of the Borders beyond. Then she saw, with shock, that tears were running down Magnus's cheeks into his beard. He dashed a hand over his face. She tried to remind herself that he was a fine actor, a national treasure, but she knew what was real, and what wasn't; she knew him. And seeing him like this, full of regret, a broken old man, was unbearable.

'But *you* left me, Magnus.' Her words sounded petulant.

He blinked and shook his head. 'What? No. God no. Definitely not. You left *me*. Don't you remember?'

'What?'

'You tore off your clothes and climbed off the stage and left the country the same night. You didn't tell anyone where you'd gone – for a while, I honestly thought you were dead. I thought you'd killed yourself. It was terrifying. Then someone said they'd spotted you in Marrakesh, so I flew out there from New York, but you'd gone. I found out later you'd gone off to live in a cave.'

'After you helped Rohls to drill a hole in Sally Morgan's head causing her to overdose, then made me take the blame!'

He stared at her, then reached for the oxygen tank, slotting the mask over his face, breathing in and out, looking down at his lap.

'The world thought I trepanned her in a sex game!' she shouted.

He took the mask off again and hooked it on to the tank. There was a long silence. She saw his shoulders were shuddering and she half rose, thinking that he might be having some kind of fit, but he lifted his face and she saw that it was bright-eyed – he was laughing.

She stared at him in furious disbelief.

'Sorry,' he said. 'Sorry. Fuck. I know, Jesus, I know none of this is remotely funny, I do know that, but for a moment there I heard us, and it all sounded completely insane.'

He was right, she realised. There was an element of Beckettian absurdity in all this: the two of them, Nell and Nagg, trapped in their own tiny, futile prisons. A line from *Endgame* popped into her head: *Nothing is funnier than unhappiness.*

'Jesus Christ, Aster.' He shook his head. 'I've missed you. I've missed you so much.'

She looked into his eyes. 'I hated you for abandoning me,' she said, 'But most of all, what I really couldn't forgive you for was your weakness.'

His laughter turned to coughing and his eyes filled with tears again, whether from physical or emotional pain she wasn't sure. He took another swig of whisky and cleared his throat. 'I was weak,' he said, croakily. 'I didn't stand up to Rohls, I told myself Sally wanted to be trepanned – I chose to believe that – because the alternative was to walk away from the film. And I chose to believe you when you said you were fine. I was craven – I probably still am. I hate myself for it. I've got everything' – he waved a hand – 'but my life's basically been empty because I always loved you – I still do.'

Suddenly, and unexpectedly, she believed him.

More spasms came up from his chest. His hand covered his mouth. It was liver-spotted and bonier, but she knew the shape of the fingers, the broad nails. In a vein she saw the perforation from a canula, with a pale rectangle where the surgical tape had held the needle in place. She wondered if he'd unhooked himself from something to be here, upright, waiting for her – expecting her to walk in with Nina but finding her suddenly standing behind him. It must have been quite a shock. She longed for the painful coughing to be over. He put down the oxygen mask and swallowed. 'Is there any way you can forgive me, do you think?'

She looked down at her plaster cast. Inside it, the bone throbbed.

'What did happen to your wrist?'

She shook her head. She wasn't ready for chit-chat or diversions.

'You know,' Magnus said, seeming to understand this, 'a part of me *genuinely* believed Rohls' shit about enhanced consciousness and brain blood and sacred medical procedures. If he'd offered to drill a hole in my head that night, I'd probably have let him.'

'But you let him do it to a fragile twenty-three-year-old instead.'

'Rohls lived to be eighty-five with a hole in his head, and his countess is still alive, I think – I heard she's campaigning to have trepanation available on the NHS.'

'Sally didn't get to be old, though, did she?'

'Sally would probably have overdosed at some point. The extent of her addictions came out at the time, but I suppose you missed all that because you were living in a Bedouin cave?'

'Sally Morgan overdosed after Rohls assaulted her. You can't possibly think the two aren't linked?'

Magnus frowned, nodding. 'No, no, I do know that, you're right. I didn't want to admit it at the time, but I do now – I've made a note about it here, in fact.' He tapped the manuscript. 'At the time, I chose to believe it had nothing to do with the trepanning, because I suppose I couldn't really handle that.' He looked stricken and she saw that he had finally forced himself to take responsibility for what he'd done. He rested his head in his hands, breathing heavily. After a bit, he looked up. 'I did you wrong – both of you. You and Sally. I let my ambitions take over.' He paused. 'But is there any way you can forgive me for it, Aster, do you think? I've missed you so badly, so very badly. There's been a hole in my life – in my heart – all these years. You were the only thing I ever really wanted, and I blew it. Spectacularly.'

'You wanted fame.'

'I wanted *you*.'

'You chose fame!'

He shook his head. 'It didn't feel like a choice. I mean, I didn't know I was choosing. Rohls had handed me the golden ticket, I couldn't not take it. Remember how I struggled for a break? You were there, picking me up every time. I didn't want to end up a frustrated, miserable drunk, dead at forty like my father, or mad like my mother.'

'You seemed to do a splendid job of being drunk and mad in Hollywood instead.'

He gazed into his almost empty whisky glass. 'I know. That's the irony, isn't it? I lost myself after you left me, you must have seen that. When you vanished, I just lost myself. I stopped drinking that way years ago, though, believe it or not.' He held up his whisky glass. 'I take the odd dram when Mrs McKittrick isn't looking, but it tastes like shite since the chemo.' He gave a haunting cough, fumbled for a handkerchief, and took another painful breath.

She turned away; his frailty was unbearable. There might be a freedom, she realised, in letting go of all this anger, this right-eousness. Magnus was flawed, but he wasn't monstrous. She didn't feel so righteous any more – she didn't even feel that angry. She'd clung to her story of betrayal for forty-five years, selected memories to fuel it and kept others out; how exhausting that had been, and how self-defeating.

'I've had a big life.' He tapped the manuscript. 'It's all here. But it all feels kind of fake.' He peered at her perhaps trying to decipher her expression. 'You're rightly wondering why the fuck I wouldn't read my own memoir, aren't you? But the truth is, I couldn't face it. I did have Dessie read me out the chapter about you so I could check he did right by you – and what he read me wasn't the version Nina's given me here, I can tell you. But I won't read the rest of the book. Seeing my life laid out like this, with a beginning, a middle and an end just makes the void more obvious. I did an awful thing. I lost my way with Rohls that night, and I don't think I ever found it again.' His voice shook. 'I was meant to spend my life with you, Aster.'

'But you left me!' She felt like the chorus, dumbly repeating the refrain.

'Astrid, I didn't. God Almighty, woman.' He was breathing faster again. 'How many times can I say this? I would *never* have left you.'

The feeling that there had been a monumental mistake was suddenly unavoidable. She felt sick. *My old brain is troubled.* Her heart was troubled too, she knew, but perhaps it always had been.

'I tried to find you. Have you forgotten?' He reached for a pot of pills next to the manuscript. 'I waited for you in Hampstead that time, the letter I sent you, with the deeds, remember? I said I'd be there the following day – I remember, vividly, that it was two p.m. I had a bottle of champagne on ice. I was so sure you'd come. And you never showed up. Don't you remember? I said in the letter that if you didn't come, I'd know you wanted nothing more to do with me and I promised to leave you alone.'

'What letter?'

'I sent it with the deeds? Don't you remember, I got Cheryl to bring them?'

'Cheryl?'

'My assistant, at the time.'

Astrid thought of the blonde on the pink scooter, so sweet and friendly. 'Chervil.'

'What?'

'She didn't give me a letter. She just gave me the deeds and the keys.'

They looked at each other.

Magnus gave his head a shake. 'But ... okay ... whatever ... I came to that lovely old windmill of yours too, but you know that, of course.'

'What? When?'

'You saw me, come on. It was after that huge storm in 1987 when your windmill almost blew away. I was in London when

I saw the news about the south coast and I thought about what might happen to a windmill in a hurricane, and I was scared for you – I broke my promise and drove straight down that morning. You weren't there, your man said you were at his house, down in the village. Told me the windmill was private property. He was pretty aggressive. He wouldn't even tell me where his house was.'

'Charlie?' she said. 'He never told me you'd come.'

'I had to go to LA after that,' Magnus continued, 'but I came back again later and it looked pretty bad still. I remember there was a cherry picker up there, and they were winching off the cap. You were with your man that time too.'

'What time?'

'When they were taking off the cap. You saw me, Aster. I know you did. I was standing at your gate, and you looked right at me and your face kind of crumpled, and I thought, *God, it's okay, she still loves me*, but then you turned away and sort of buried yourself in his arms. You chose him, not me. It broke me, honestly. That moment, I think it broke me.' He lifted both hands and pressed his temples.

Astrid remembered seeing Magnus by the gate as the windmill cap was coming off; the subtle brown butterflies, gatekeepers, dancing next to her, as if someone was tugging them on tiny threads.

'I came back another time after that. Your husband told me to fuck off then too.'

'Charlie wasn't my husband.'

'He wasn't? Well, he said he was. He told me you never wanted to see me again. He wasn't messing around. He even described what he was going to do to me, or what he was going to get his associates to do to me, if I came back.'

'*Charlie*?' It was hard to absorb this, it wouldn't quite land.

Magnus was struggling to get the pill pot open, but she was no good to him, not with one hand. She lifted her whisky glass and saw that it was empty.

'And you didn't reply to my letter either, so I . . .'

She leaned closer. Her head buzzed. 'What letter?'

'I wrote to you, you know I did! The only love letter I've ever written; it was about ten pages long.'

She shook her head. 'No, no, no, you didn't write. When?'

'After I came up there. You wrote back and told me to leave you alone. You must remember.' Magnus sounded frustrated. He coughed again, bent over, his hands pressing his forehead. 'You wrote me that horrendous typed, formal response saying you were happier with him than you'd ever been with me, thank you very much, and you never wanted to see me again. After that I just . . .' His mouth trembled. 'Well, I thought it was fair enough, I suppose.'

The hands of the carriage clock on Magnus's desk seemed to be speeding up, moving round its face in tight circles, backwards – they were definitely moving backwards. 'I never wrote to you!' she shouted. The wood-panelled walls sucked up the sound.

He looked startled. 'What?'

'It must have been Charlie.' Her heart seemed to have come loose, like the hands of the clock or the sweeps of the windmill. 'But I was happy with him. And I'm happy now. Very. My life has been very happy.'

'How? I'm not talking about me, I'm not that much of an egotist, I'm just wondering how you could be happy without your career? You lived for the stage. You were magnificent, you—'

'So what?' She cut him off. She was not going to allow him to undermine everything. 'I've had a wonderful life, thank you. I have a very dear friend who looks after me. I have my beloved dogs. And I have a windmill! I wake up on the South Downs every morning. You might think that's a small life, compared to yours, but I don't think it is – I've done lots of interesting things. I've had a magnificent, meaningful life. I wouldn't change any of it.'

He nodded. 'I'd forgotten this about you. You always were brilliant at being happy. You're so much more self-sufficient than I ever could be. Despite everything I've done, I've never managed to live well. I suppose I needed you for that.'

She gazed down at her wrist which throbbed inside its cast. 'If you really wanted me more than you wanted your career, then you'd have given it up for me. You could have walked away from Hollywood. You knew where I was.'

'I wish I had,' he said. 'If I could go back and do it again, I'd give it up and come to live with you in that windmill.'

Mrs Baker, she thought, might have a thing or two to say about that.

She realised, then, that Magnus might have loved her, but he would never have been able to walk away from Hollywood, and if she'd stayed with him, she'd never have bought the windmill, or met Mrs Baker – would never have been able to offer her sanctuary – and she would never have had her beloved dogs. There had been highs and lows, many of each, but the bedrock of her life had been the deep friendship; constant, accepting, solid, anchored by domestic routines and objects: coffee pots and stoats, knitted jackets, kettles, clocks, taps, cups of tea, and the deep, wordless understanding they had between them. She wouldn't change that, she really wouldn't.

Whatever her feelings for Magnus might be, and at that moment they were too dangerous and chaotic to classify, she knew that her life would have been infinitely poorer without

Mrs Baker. And she'd definitely take the South Downs over the Hollywood Hills any day. Under different circumstances she could have been happy with Magnus, she knew that – they'd been truly happy before Rohls appeared – but she could never, ever have lived in Hollywood.

'There was that time in Brighton too, in the Lanes,' he was saying. 'When you walked away. I married my third wife after that. Fucking disaster.'

'Stop, Magnus. You must stop, all this regret . . .'

He said something she didn't hear.

'What?'

'I kept divorcing people because they weren't you!' he boomed, then bent over, coughing.

'Going back like this isn't helpful.'

He cleared his throat and gave an empty laugh. 'I know. Honestly, if this fucking memoir has shown me anything, it's that going back there is a *really* bad idea. *But Then Again* could not be more ironic.'

She laughed then, despite herself. Too Few to Mention. If they'd both mentioned their regrets a bit earlier then they'd still be together now, facing his death side by side. The thought was vertiginous; she stopped laughing, felt her head swim.

'But I promise you one thing. This book's going to tell the truth about you. I do love my son, I wasn't a good enough father when he was a kid, I was absent, caught up in all the noise, constantly working. I left him to his insane mother, and I've tried to make up for that. I mean, I basically do anything he wants – I even gave that *Sunday Times* interview because he told me to, and I hate fucking journalists, loathe them – but that stops here, now. I won't let Dessie put out lies about you.'

'How can you possibly promise that?' she said. 'You might

die before this book is published. You probably will.' She sat up straight, despite her painful spine. 'I won't have it, Magnus. I won't be in this book. You must take me out. Erase me entirely.'

He had the pill lid off, finally, and shook two out into his palm. '*Erase the troubling thoughts*,' he said.

'Stop it.'

'What?'

'Stop quoting Shakespeare at me.'

'I can't help it. Don't you do it all the time, quote Shakespeare? It drove my third wife mad.'

'You've been quoting Shakespeare at me through the media for years.'

He looked at her, then laughed. 'You noticed!'

'The last one was a low blow.'

'What do you mean?'

'*Nothing is but what is not.*'

'But that was . . . that was me telling you that I've lived a kind of parallel life with you, in my imagination, all these years – not always consciously, but in a way the only thing that feels real to me is *that*.'

'What?'

'You!'

'Take me out of your book, Magnus.' It came out as a kind of yelp. It was too painful, too destabilising, to allow his words to settle inside her.

'I've made notes for Nina, here.' He tapped the manuscript. 'I'll show them to you. She can write it up this way and submit it to the publisher next week. I'll write a covering letter insisting it's my version or nothing, and I'll talk to Dessie. Tomorrow we can sit down, the three of us, and look at it. I've got it all here.'

'But even if you do that, people could still come to the windmill, they might still want to ask me about it. And I can't have that, I cannot, I will not have reporters coming to my home! Certainly not now!'

His brows knitted. 'Has something else happened, Aster?' After all these years, it seemed, he was still so attuned to her that he could hear things she wasn't saying. Suddenly, she longed to tell him everything about the Awful Incident; how, as they had driven away from the windmill that night, Mrs Baker had stamped on the brakes, and brought the car to a halt.

The windshield wipers had flipped and for a moment they'd sat side by side, in the fume-filled Mercedes.

*Why have you stopped? Go, Eileen! Drive!*

*We have to go back, he'll wreck the windmill.*

*He'll wreck us! We'll go back to tomorrow when he's sobered up.*

*He's no better when he's sober.*

*Then we'll wait till he's gone.*

*He'll be back.*

*Eileen. Just drive! Put it in Drive.*

'You're scared, Aster. What happened to you?' Magnus said. 'What's happened to scare you like this?'

'What? Nothing. It's complicated. It has nothing to do with you.'

He nodded and popped the pills into his mouth, then reached for the oxygen. He put the mask down without using it. 'I get it.' He pressed both his hands on either side of his skull again.

'Does your head hurt?'

He ignored the question. 'I hadn't thought about it like that till now but there's always a possibility that the media's going to pester you about me. So, no. Okay, you're right. It's fine. I'll scrap the fucking book. I won't do it. I'll pull out of the contract, I'll tell Dessie – I'll write the publisher a letter tonight. If the

book's going to hurt you in any way, Aster, if it *could* hurt you,
then I won't let it happen.'

She hadn't expected this. He understood, even without
knowing the facts. He got her, of course he did, he always had.
She felt something in her heart shift, as if things had rearranged
themselves to make room, perhaps, for forgiveness; not just of
him, but of herself. He took one hand away from his head and
reached out. It hovered for a moment in the air between them,
and then she lifted her own good hand and put it into his. She
felt his fingers fold around hers and all the whirring pieces inside
her seemed to settle, and, just for that moment, everything was
exactly where it should be.

# Chapter 21

Nina was on her knees by Magnus, talking on the phone to the ambulance dispatcher when a hefty middle-aged man rushed in. He shoved Astrid aside, almost knocking her over, and loomed over Magnus. 'Dad? Shit. Dad? Can you hear me? Are you okay? Dad!'

Astrid managed to get up and out of his way, nursing her arm. She felt dizzy from the jolt, and moved back, feeling for the seat where, moments before, Magnus had been sitting and holding her hand. Dessie glanced up, over his shoulder, and in the square face and weird, compound eyes, she saw the strange child. He went back to loosening the top buttons of his father's shirt. 'It's okay, Dad.' His voice shook. 'You're doing great.'

Magnus really wasn't. She couldn't see his face any more because Dessie was between them, but as he'd looked into her eyes, his left cheek and eyelid had dropped, lopsided, and his lips too, as if someone was pulling downwards on a string attached to the bottom corner of his mouth. For a moment she'd thought he was fighting back tears again, but then she understood that something was profoundly wrong.

Nina got up and came to her. She was still talking quietly to the dispatcher, giving details of the driveway. 'No, he isn't speaking.'

She reached down and took Astrid's good hand. Astrid looked up into her kind eyes and felt very glad that she was there.

Dessie looked over his shoulder again. His eyes were bloodshot. 'Who the *fuck* are you?' He stared at her for a beat then grabbed a cushion and slid it under Magnus's head. 'There, that's better, Dad. Don't move okay. The ambulance is on its way. Nina's just talking to them now. You're going to be okay, Dad.'

Magnus's legs were oddly arranged on the carpet, crooked, one shin tucked under the other calf. A tartan slipper had come off, his socked feet were limp.

Desmond turned to Astrid again. 'What happened here? What the fuck happened?'

She tried to answer but her throat and chest were constricted. Nina squeezed her hand, 'Desmond's just got in from New York.' A woman with short, greying curls and a sensible cardigan appeared in the doorway. 'Dad's collapsed!' Dessie shouted at her. 'Where the fuck were you?' The woman muttered something about going home for some clothes and hurried to Magnus's side.

'He sort of keeled over,' Astrid said, to nobody.

Something in her voice sparked recognition – Dessie twisted to look at her.

'Dessie, this is Astrid Miller.'

'*Astrid?*'

She looked back at him. 'Hello, Desmond.'

'What *in the name of fuck* are you doing here?'

'Now then, Dessie.' Mrs McKittrick's voice was soft. 'Let's stay calm for your dad till the ambulance gets here.'

'What have you done to him?' Dessie's face was contorted.

'Dessie, please.' Nina squared herself between them.

'What the *fuck* is Astrid Miller doing in my house?' he shouted at Nina.

Astrid looked at Nina and then at Mrs McKittrick. 'He took two pills,' she said to the women. 'Just before he collapsed. And he'd had a glass or two of whisky, I'm not sure how many he'd had before I got here. He didn't seem drunk, though. His face went lopsided – he'd been holding his head a bit before that.'

'You gave him whisky? Dad can't drink,' Dessie shouted. 'You stupid cunt!'

'Dessie, for God's sake.' Nina seemed to grow taller. 'Can't you see she's upset?'

'Get that cunt out of my house.'

Astrid wanted, very badly, to lie down next to Magnus, to hold and comfort him as best she could until the ambulance arrived, but Desmond was an immovable lump of fury.

'Now then, Dessie,' Mrs McKittrick said, as if to a tantrumming child. 'It won't help Dad if you get agitated like this. Let's all calm down now.' She'd knelt on the other side and was, Astrid saw, taking Magnus's pulse. Her expression was grim.

Magnus's other hand lay loose on the carpet by Desmond's knee. She noticed the curl of his palm, closed her eyes and felt it cup her face. Then the background noise in the room seemed to increase, as if her hearing aids had been inserted, miraculously, and were operating selectively, at preternatural levels: she could hear each raindrop as it hit the window and burst, each tick of the carriage clock articulated into syllables, the busy rub of wool fibres under Dessie's knees and, stranger still, the halting swish of blood as it squeezed in and out of her failing heart.

The rug was thick wool, a gentle green, and Magnus's hand looked casual, resting on it – she could almost imagine that he was lying on the grass after a picnic on the Heath, full of French bread and ham and red wine, the drifting clouds reflected in his beautiful pale grey eyes. And she heard a rasping series of breaths and then there it was, the soft lifting of his departure – and then nothing, a trembling silence. Magnus had gone.

Dessie began to howl like a little boy.

# Chapter 22

'Are you okay, yourself?' The paramedic came over. She had no memory of getting out of the study, onto the drawing room sofa. Nina must have guided her. The paramedic got down on one knee. 'You're looking a wee bit pale yourself.'

Dessie was in the study still; she could hear him talking in a hollow tone, though she couldn't hear the words. Magnus's legs had been straightened. His feet looked sort of formal now. Someone had removed his other slipper, straightened his trousers.

The paramedic said, loudly and clearly, 'Shall I take a wee look at you? Could I do that?' She gazed into his kind face. His skin was gently dimpled from long ago acne, and he was maybe Nina's age, not much over forty, but going grey, eyes puffed up from long nights managing other people's worst moments. He took her good wrist in his hand and, after a moment or two, produced a stethoscope, with an encouraging smile. 'I'll have a wee listen for a moment if that's okay?'

Nina hadn't left her side. 'It's okay, Astrid, you're just looking a bit shocked, that's all.'

'Well, I am a bit shocked.'

'What happened to your wrist?' the paramedic asked.

'I was attacked by a picnic table.'

He smiled. 'Do you mind if I just pop a few stickers on your chest, and take a little reading of your heart, with my fancy machine?'

When he'd finished, he did up her buttons for her, respectfully, and then said something she didn't catch. Nina leaned in. 'He'd like to bring you to the hospital to get your heart checked out by a doctor, Astrid. Would that be okay?'

'Absolutely not.'

'There's some irregularity.' He sat on his heels. He was patient.

Nina said, 'She just watched the love of her life die.'

He turned to Astrid. 'That's why you need to be checked out at the hospital. Hearts don't really like shocks.'

'I had all that done a week ago,' Astrid said. 'When I broke my wrist. I know what's wrong with me.'

Nina was having none of it. When Astrid refused to get into the ambulance, she said she'd drive her to the hospital, and Astrid simply didn't have the energy to object. She didn't much care where she was, anyway, a hospital, a car, a sofa.

As they wound their way through the dark, rain-lashed lanes, she felt that nothing was real any more, as if they were spinning through a surreal landscape, perhaps an obscure part of her subconscious, and soon she'd pop back into her body and she'd find herself back at the windmill; Mrs Baker would make cocoa and tell her to go to bed, and they'd let the dogs out, and she'd knock her shin on Tony Blair and the clock would twitch its tail and flick its eyes. Everything would be fine again, everything would be normal.

'You must be completely exhausted,' Nina said. 'You're probably in shock, like the paramedic said. We should have given you something sweet before we left. I might have a Kit-Kat or something in the glovebox.' She leaned over and rummaged. Astrid thought of the Kit Cat clock, the Rayburn, the cluttered kitchen. 'I want to go home,' she said.

'Of course you do. Of course. Don't worry, we'll get you home.' Nina lifted herself off the seat and reached for her phone which was in the back pocket of her jeans. She handed it to Astrid. 'Here, why don't you phone home now?'

Astrid gazed at the device.

'You need to put in the password. It's 1111.'

At the sound of Mrs Baker's voice, Astrid felt her throat close and her mouth wobble. 'Nina?'

'It's me, Eileen,' she said. Then tears came.

Nina pulled over. She reversed so that the back of the car was against a five-bar gate and took the phone because Astrid couldn't stop weeping. She explained what had happened, while Astrid looked in the rear-view mirror and tried to get a grip. A cow had come to see what was going on. Its curious head loomed over the gate and its fur and eyes were tinged crimson by the tail lights. Another came, then, from the side, lifted its tail and let out a stream of shit. Then another, and more. People were wary about bullocks and bulls, all the showy males, but not cows. Cows looked harmless, but if threatened, they could be deadly – they could gang up and trample people to death. She'd almost experienced this on the Downs, once. A herd had closed around her in the corner of a field, staring and stamping cloven feet, heads lowered, blowing at the dogs, churning the mud, and she'd had to shove herself and the dogs, painfully, through a hawthorn hedge to escape. After that she was always careful to skirt cows, and to have an escape route planned out.

Nina was telling Mrs Baker not to drive up to Scotland. 'I'll bring her home myself,' she said. 'Tomorrow . . . No, honestly, I don't mind at all. Please. I'd like to. I don't think I can stay here, and I haven't actually got anywhere else to be . . . Yes, really. I promise. Please try not to worry, honestly, she's going to be fine. It wasn't an emergency. He just said she should get it checked out . . . We'll call you as soon as she's seen the doctor, okay?'

More cows had come. They blew at the tail lights, staring through the rain, steaming breath, steaming shit. The wiper cleared the back windscreen intermittently, but more rain fell. Gloria didn't have a back wiper, and when Alan had lurched up behind the car that night, his outline was warped by raindrops. She'd felt Mrs Baker warring with herself in those moments – instinct telling her to put the car into reverse. Astrid, too, had imagined the heavy old Mercedes crushing Alan's body into the chalky track, but then she closed her hand over her friend's.

*Eileen. Just drive! Put it in Drive.*

There was a moment's hesitation – Astrid wasn't sure if she was going to reverse over Alan – then Mrs Baker put the car in Drive, and they jolted forwards, leaving him hollering and swaying in the rain.

As they bumped away down Windmill Hill, Astrid looked back. The rear windscreen was too wet and it was too dark to see him any more, but as they rounded the corner, plunging steeply down towards the village, she thought she glimpsed, in the wing mirror, a low dark lump – Alan – crawling through the rain towards the verge.

It wasn't more than a couple of hours before they'd steeled themselves to go back, thinking he would have sobered up a bit, perhaps been cowed by his injuries. Their intention was to get him off the hill; take him to the hospital if he needed medical attention, or call the police if he remained violent. But when they got back, there was no sign of him. They got out of the car and walked up and down the track in the freezing rain, shouting his name, but Alan had vanished.

They returned to the windmill in trepidation, knowing that he could have staggered back up the hill; he could be waiting for them in the windmill, or inside the cottage. The coffee pot was lying in the courtyard, rain pinging off its sides, surrounded by broken glass. Above it, they saw that the Stone floor window had been smashed. Mrs Baker went over and picked up the coffee pot. She looked inside it; the slippers were gone.

The worst damage seemed to have been done by the altar stone. Alan, in his rage, must have tipped it off its table, and from what they could see it had smashed through the floorboards on the Stone floor into the Spout floor, presumably bringing Alan with it, and then bounced down the ladder steps to the ground floor, ending up on its side, wedged in the front doorway.

Astrid had never allowed herself to picture what had happened to Alan that night. He must have hauled his bruised and broken body off the track, through a gap in the hedge, and down the sheep field into Tangled Wood, finding shelter in the hollow holly tree. If he was thinking at all, he was probably trying to take a shortcut to the village for help.

A few days after the police had dismantled the white bivouac, and all the vehicles had driven away, one by one, Mrs Baker brought an *Evening Argus* up from the petrol station. They read the front-page report together. Someone in the police had obviously been talking.

The body of a sixty-eight-year-old man, Alan Stonehouse, which was found in the woods up on Windmill Hill, had been beaten and the tip of his tongue partially severed, according to a 'police source'. These injuries suggested that Mr Stonehouse had been an informer, and that this was a gang-related recriminatory

attack. Police found 'evidence' on him that linked him to a particularly brutal crime back in the 1990s by the so-called 'Slipper
Gang'. An Essex businessman had his throat slit during a violent
burglary, jewellery and objects worth over a million pounds were
taken, including a famous pair of slippers which had belonged
to the actor Cary Grant. No members of the Slipper Gang were
ever caught. Police believed that the planting of evidence on
Stonehouse's body was likely to be a message: a warning to
others who might consider informing. Stonehouse, who had
recently been released from jail after serving twelve years for
his part in the infamous Shoreham burglary in 2010, had not
died of his injuries. The cause of death, the newspaper said, was
'hypothermia'.

It was odd, Astrid thought, how Alan had become 'the body of'
as if his spirit might still be hovering somewhere, waiting for an
opportunity to come back. She wondered, then, where the body
of Magnus Fellowes was. Perhaps still at Northbank waiting for
the undertaker to arrive. This made her think of something that
had happened not long after she first arrived at the windmill –
something she hadn't thought about in years. There had been
the sound of tyres on the chalk path one summer's evening, and
a tentative knock on the door. A tall, thin young man stood on
the threshold, wearing a black suit that was several sizes too
large for him. 'I've brought the hearse,' he said.

It felt like a continuity error. 'Am I dead?' she asked. She
saw the hearse, parked in the courtyard. It took them a while
to work out that he'd come to the wrong windmill – he was
supposed to be collecting a body from another mill twelve
miles away. As omens went, it had felt pretty heavy-handed
and for a while Astrid had lived with a sense of dread. This
had, of course, turned out to be entirely misplaced, because

here she was at eighty-two, alive and well. Or maybe not well, exactly, but certainly *N.D.Y.*

The body of Magnus Fellowes might need an autopsy. She couldn't think about his skull being opened, or his chest – they wouldn't do that to him, surely? He'd had terminal cancer, he had been expecting to die, though not, of course, from a stroke.

Had she killed him?

Of course she hadn't.

She waited for the monstrous fact of his death to sink in, but it hovered at the back of her head somewhere, just out of reach. She had lived without him for so many years, perhaps this new, definitive absence would turn out to be no less of a presence. But somewhere deep down, perhaps in her soul, she felt something new: a profound sadness, a deep lack.

'You'll need an operation on your heart,' the doctor said, after all the tests had been done and her chest had been prodded and listened to and scanned all over again. It wasn't an emergency, there was medicine for now, but she needed an operation to open a valve, and soon. No surprises there. It was exactly what the doctor in Brighton had said, though she decided not to mention that.

Nina explained that Astrid lived on the south coast.

The doctor, a glamorous redhead, talked of referrals. 'Your heart,' she said, 'will have been compensating for years without you even knowing there was something wrong. But then at some point it will have started to send out signals.' Dizzy spells, tiredness, shortness of breath; a sense of things misfiring, spinning; palpitations, insomnia. The notion that her heart had been signalling to her made her think of the language of windmills. The miller would stop the sweeps in certain positions to communicate life events to the community – celebration, sickness, rest. One position, she remembered, the St George's Cross, and was a sign of mourning among windmillers. It was known as 'Miller's Pride'.

'The heart can compensate for a really long time,' the doctor explained. 'But at some point, it can't keep it up any more.' She looked solemn. 'If we don't get in there soon and fix it, it will fail.'

# Chapter 23

Astrid never saw Desmond again. He was engulfed by grief, and by his father's extensive funeral arrangements, the international media outpourings, the obituaries and news reports and retrospectives of Magnus's career, and, of course, by the memoir. The day after Magnus died, Nina left Astrid resting on the sofa in the gatehouse and went to find him. She told him that she wasn't prepared to write anything defamatory about Astrid, and showed him the big font chapter that she'd printed out for Magnus. Magnus had scribbled in the margins, correcting events, adding details. She told Dessie that she intended to submit this version to the publisher, or nothing. He fired her on the spot.

She told Astrid what had happened as they drove south that day, and on that long journey, they made some decisions about what to do next.

Nina wrote the article on her laptop in the snug, monitored by three curious dogs. When it was finished, she read it out to them as they sat at the Rayburn. The article told the story of what happened to Sally Morgan in the Tudor hunting lodge. Nina quoted Astrid in several places. It was not a stretch, Nina wrote, to link Sally's fatal overdose directly to this trauma. Four decades before women could hope to be listened to, Sally hadn't

been able to accuse Rohls of assault – she had perhaps not for-
mulated it this way, even to herself. But the pain and shock had
turned inwards, and she had numbed herself with more and
more opioids. Astrid, meanwhile, had put her husband's needs
above her own, taking the blame. What the press did to her was
inexcusable. These events had ended not just their marriage,
but Astrid's career.

Nina also described Magnus's regret, using the words he wrote
in the margins:

*I was weak and I let Sally Morgan down, I not only failed to protect
her that night, I facilitated the assault. I also betrayed my wife. Astrid
Miller was my only true love and I have felt her absence like a winter,
all my life.*

Mrs Baker looked up from her cup of tea and swallowed the
mouthful of flapjack. 'Like a winter?'

'Sonnet 97.' Astrid gazed at Gordon who shifted uncomfort-
ably on her lap, probably because Mrs Baker had put him in the
lurex striped party jerkin – she was in charge of dressing the
dogs while Astrid had one hand, and made strangely flamboyant
choices.

'So, Astrid, it's up to you now.' Nina closed the laptop. 'Whether
I send this to the *Sunday Times* or not.'

'Will it stop the memoir?' Astrid said.

Nina shook her head. 'I don't think so.'

'Won't Desmond sue?' Mrs Baker said.

'It doesn't say anything defamatory – it just tells the truth
and I can prove that, because I've still got the manuscript that
Magnus wrote on.'

'Dessie will be incandescent,' Astrid said. 'He'll combust!'

'He probably will, but he'll get over it. And most of the book
is about Magnus's glorious career and all the famous people

who adored him. The section about you is actually a very small part of the overall book.'

'Small but deadly,' Astrid said. 'Put that on my tombstone.'

Nina laughed, and glanced at Mrs Baker. 'The article's not just about Magnus, though. The wider point is how powerful men have always tried to control and silence women.'

'But Rohls got away with it,' Mrs Baker said. 'At the end of the day.'

'He did, but he won't be revered any more, or celebrated once this is out. I can't say outright that he killed Sally Morgan, or I will get sued, but I do think the article asks the reader to make that link.'

As she listened to Mrs Baker and Nina discuss the finer points, Astrid realised that the fury she'd carried around inside her all these years had lost its power. Like the second slipper that Hendricks had tunnelled under the altar stone to retrieve, it had been stripped of significance – a scrap that could, at last, be put away.

It was highly unlikely that any reporters would bother to come to the windmill. As Mrs Baker had always maintained, nobody would care about an old has-been who was, a million years ago and for just a few seconds, married to Magnus Fellowes. But they did care, nowadays, about men silencing women – there were hashtagged phrases, women told their stories, abusers were exposed; there were long-awaited reckonings and sometimes even justice. If any reporters did track her down and make the trek up Windmill Hill, perhaps she'd rather enjoy adding her voice to all this.

The answer to any residual fears about intrusion, she realised, was perfectly simple: they needed Joe Dean to come up and move the stone and fix the windmill door back on.

It wasn't just the fury that had dissipated, she realised, but the fear. It had been with them for so long – draped over their home, filling up the dark spaces – and she could feel it lifting now, like the dawn mist that blanketed the Weald in summer, rising off the fields and river and villages slowly at first, before vanishing all at once, as if someone had whipped it away.

They phoned Joe Dean and he was up the hill within the hour. They heard his van battering up over chalky potholes. He rang the doorbell and Nina went to answer it while Astrid tried to find a blanket to use as a coat, and Mrs Baker attempted to control Hendricks.

Gordon and Juniper got out in the courtyard and Gordon ran in circles, yapping, round Joe Dean's black Labrador, which looked mildly perturbed, then wandered away to pee on the wall.

'I've got my tools,' Joe said. 'Shall we go and have a look?'

Astrid heard Nina say, 'I could give you a hand if you want?'

It was a bright, cold, gusty day, frost crunching underfoot, the sky clear and huge, china blue. The windmill looked down, curiously, as they all approached.

'Are you feeling strong?' Joe turned to Nina. 'Because I reckon if we both climb over and shove it from that side, it'll dislodge. If it's too heavy, we can stick a rope round it and pull it out with my van but I think we might be able to move it ourselves. Then I can fix this frame and hopefully get the door back on.' He clambered over the stone and began to inspect things. The hinges were bent and warped, but the aged oak door was intact, one corner trapped between the stone and the door frame, so that it jutted out.

Astrid and Mrs Baker stood well back with the dogs, and watched as the two young, strong people clambered around and began to shove at the stone with their shoulders. Astonishingly, after a few goes, it creaked, then shifted, then flopped out with a thud onto the hard, chalky earth, freeing the door, which almost fell onto Nina's head – Joe caught it just in time, propped it back up and then the two of them hung on to each other's arms and laughed for quite a while. Astrid and Mrs Baker exchanged a look.

They all stood at the fallen altar, which lay upturned on the crisp grass. The square of stone, cut into the medieval marble slab, had crucifixes carved into each corner, and one in the centre. You could see the circle that hundreds of years ago had been cut there for the relics, re-sealed, then anointed. There was a deep crevasse in the ground where the edge of the marble had dug itself into the chalk all these months, and there were tunnelling marks from the dogs' claws too, but nothing incriminating, nothing else hidden except for nuggets of chalk and flint, a few scurrying beetles and a worm or two.

Later that day, Astrid and Mrs Baker took up a flask of tea and more flapjacks. Joe was bashing at the door frame which looked more intact now; he was explaining something to Nina about the mill's original mechanism. Nina was listening, cross-legged on the stone, wearing a woollen hat – Joe's. The Labrador lay next to her with his nose resting on her knee. He looked up when they approached, but didn't move; Gordon galloped towards him, letting out small yelps of delight.

'We were just talking about Constance's stuff,' Nina said to Astrid. 'I know you want to keep everything in there, but I do wonder if it's worth drying things out a bit before we store them back inside the windmill? It would be a shame for things like the letters and the rugs to be damaged.'

Astrid thought about this as Mrs Baker handed tea to Nina and Joe. She noticed, with amazement, that Mrs Baker had given Nina the Garfield mug.

She wasn't sure, any more, whether her policy of leaving things inside the windmill, allowing them to moulder and disintegrate, was the right one. Perhaps Constance's belongings should be brought down to the cottage and dried by the Rayburn; perhaps the books should be read again, the letters and photographs shared. Mrs Baker said, 'I'd definitely bring those rugs and tapestries inside now, Astrid, while you've got some help. We could put electric heaters in the ground floor for a while too, maybe a dehumidifier, dry it out before we put everything back.'

Joe looked inside the windmill. 'It's not that bad in here, really,' he said. 'I've seen much, much worse. I mean, the Stone floor needs some significant repairs, and the broken stairs are going to have to be rebuilt, but the ground floor isn't too bad at all – it's quite heartening really.' He reached out and touched the dog basket. Astrid saw him frown slightly, puzzled, run his hand over the chain and peer up at the trapdoor. 'Did you adapt the sack hoist when you lived in here, or was this a Lady Battiscombe invention? It's a good way to get heavy objects up and down between the floors.'

'That's my canine funicular,' Astrid said. 'I adapted the hoist myself.'

'Miniature dachshunds don't do ladder staircases,' Mrs Baker explained. The corner of her mouth twitched, and she looked away.

Astrid saw Joe and Nina's eyes meet. 'That' – Nina turned to Astrid – 'is ingenious.'

'Well, you have to shut them securely inside the transporter basket, of course, so they don't fall out, but it's perfectly safe because the trapdoors are on those leather hinges – once the basket's through the door it falls shut again, so even if by some bizarre accident the chain broke or something, they'd only fall a short distance. And I've cushioned the inside of the basket too.'

Joe cleared his throat, nodding vigorously. 'Well, the mech-anism's designed to be safe. The miller wouldn't want a heavy sack of grain falling on his head.'

'Nor I a dachshund,' Astrid said. 'Or worse still, a basket of them. I was forced to design the canine funicular when my first dog, Dixie Belle, unexpectedly produced puppies, you see.'

'Dixie Belle is a great name.' Nina was smiling.

'A very popular American gin – my father's favourite tipple. He drank it with a twist of lime. My poor Dixie was a stray, and I thought she needed a glamorous name. I found her wandering in Tangled Wood, shivering, starved – completely bedraggled, poor darling. I assumed her belly was distended, like a poor little famine victim, so her puppies came as quite a shock. I mean, I could happily carry one dachshund up and down in the wind-mill, but not five, so I was forced to design the funicular, and it's lasted all this time – I should have patented it. Do you think—'

'You were saying, about fixing up the windmill?' Mrs Baker broke in, looking at Joe.

'Right, yes.' Joe nodded. 'So, I don't think the cap's leaking, which is very good news. The wind tends to come up from the other side, obviously, that's why they're designed with the front door on this side – so not much water has actually got inside. I agree with Nina, though, it's a bit damp. I'd try to dry it out if it was my stuff.'

Nina got up then, and dusted off her jeans. She and Joe both looked at Astrid. 'What do you think, Astrid?' Nina said, gently. 'Shall we bring things inside?'

They carried the tapestries and rugs, letters, photo albums and books down to the cottage. It was almost dark by the time they'd finished. Nina began to spread things out over kitchen chairs

and the table, and next to the Rayburn. Joe moved Tony Blair
to make room and noticed the hole and the stopcock. 'I could
make you a cover for that,' he said to Mrs Baker. 'With a handle
so you can get to it.'

Mrs Baker looked at him for a long moment, and then
shrugged. 'If you like.'

Joe's dog sniffed at the stoat, then licked the empty dog bowls,
picked up a sock from under the chair, and went to chomp on
it by the Rayburn. Gordon followed him over. 'Gordon's in love,'
Astrid said to nobody in particular. 'I've never seen him like
this before.' Hendricks and Juniper ignored the other dogs and
curled around each other in their basket.

Nina was over at the table, looking closely at one of the biggest
tapestries. 'Have you ever had these valued?'

Astrid glanced at Mrs Baker, who went to chop some onions
for a soup. Nina ran her fingers over the design, a luscious green
garden scene, with red birds and louche flowers. 'I think this
might be very old.'

'Well, yes, probably,' Astrid said. 'It does stink a bit, doesn't it?'

'No, I mean, I edited a BBC documentary once about tapestries,' Nina said. 'I might be completely wrong, but this looks
an awful lot like the seventeenth-century Flemish Verdure tapestries we had in the programme.'

'Goodness, surely not?'

'One went in an auction for over a hundred . . .'

Astrid didn't catch the last words because Nina's head was
bowed. 'Over a hundred pounds?'

Nina turned. 'A hundred thousand pounds.'

Mrs Baker put down the onions.

Nina crouched over the tapestry. 'I mean, I don't know, obviously – I might be totally wrong, but it really could be worth

getting them valued. It's possible the windmill has been holding treasures for you all this time.'

Nina slept on the sofa in the snug again that night, and the cottage felt more peaceful than it had in years; perhaps ever.

Dessie's attempts at litigation came to nothing, since Nina was able to show the *Sunday Times* lawyers the original corrections in Magnus's handwriting. Nina's article caused a stir on both sides of the Atlantic, with several other women coming forward to add their accounts of abuse by Rohls in the 1970s and 1980s. Astrid finally told her own story and, for the first time in forty-five years, people were ready to listen. Dessie had no legal grounds to sue anybody, least of all Nina, who had simply done her job, quietly and without missteps, until her conscience made her quit. It certainly wasn't Nina's fault that Astrid had read about Magnus's memoir in the *Sunday Times* colour supplement, and decided to travel up to Scotland to confront him.

# Chapter 24

The sun had rolled up and over the windmill and Nina sat now, with her face tilted up to it, laptop open, eyes closed. She had been working on the section about Constance's little girl and her heart was sore. The skylarks' song rose from the hills around her – it sounded as if the grass was singing – and she wanted to get up and walk out over the hills, which were covered in wildflowers now and made her think of the line from Ralph Waldo Emerson, *the earth laughs in flowers*. Joe had been teaching her the wildflower names on their walks and she could identify quite a few now: squinancywort and harebell, lady's bedstraw, scabious, yellow-wort, fairy flax and, of course, the round-headed rampion, the county flower, the 'Pride of Sussex'.

The work on the book took discipline, though, and today she had promised herself that before she walked, she would finish this difficult chapter. Since the *Sunday Times* article, she'd managed to make a small income from writing occasional features and film reviews, enough to keep her going while she wrote the book. It wasn't an easy chapter to finish, unlike the story that went before, which she'd written in the evenings after working on the windmill with Joe, taking odd days out to go up to London libraries and archives.

There had been a golden, carefree period between Constance's arrival in 1919 and her little girl's death five years later. But things fell apart after that. She had just discovered that Daphne, worn out by Constance's unravelling, had left the windmill in 1928, and moved back to London where she drank herself silly and died of liver disease, in her forties. Her paintings were ignored until, a few years ago, three had been included in an exhibition at Charleston farmhouse, and singled out by critics, which had led to her inclusion in a Tate exhibition the following year. Daphne had left a small archive, and Nina had been piecing together references to the windmill in Daphne's letters. One, written to her mother, described what happened to Anemone.

It had been an unremarkable day with a moderate wind, neither bright nor dull, and Constance had released the sweeps, as she often did, because she and Ani both loved to watch them turn. Mother and child were standing together when a rabbit hopped towards the tower, passing under the sweeps. Ani, having always been warned that the sweeps were dangerous – great slabs of shuttered oak powered by the wind – and that she should never walk between them when they were turning, was terrified that the creature would be hit. She tugged at her mother, their hands slipped apart – and she darted off.

After Daphne left the windmill, Constance became even more of a recluse, cared for to the end by the loyal Miss Jones. One of the villagers, at the age of ninety, wrote a self-published memoir in which she recalled visiting the windmill with her father, who was the village doctor. It was overrun by chickens and goats, with an overgrown garden. Constance was outside in all weathers. She wore men's clothing and would bellow at anyone who strayed into the courtyard or tried to approach the windmill. She walked out on the Downs every day, and later, when she got too sick to walk, ramblers on the footpath would hear her coughing in the lavender garden. People were afraid of her. If you met her on the hills, you knew to take a detour.

After Constance's fatal fall down the ladder stairs, Miss Jones stayed on at the windmill for another six years, before going to a nursing home in Worthing, where she died a few years later, in her nineties. It seemed that she never spoke about the painters, poets and performers she'd met at the windmill in the 1920s: the costume parties and canine circuses; the oboe players, Spanish dancers and famous authors; the seances, Ouija nights and pagan rites. Or perhaps she did try to tell these stories, but found them dismissed as the outlandish ramblings of a confused old lady.

The chapter about the little girl who darted between the sweeps was hard for Nina to think about, let alone write down, and she didn't hear Joe's footsteps. She opened her eyes and found him standing at the table, grinning. Nina kissed Joe, then made a fuss of the dog who wagged and wove in and out of their legs, as if knitting them together with invisible thread.

'I met the postman on the way up, and he asked me to give this to "the windmill woman".' Joe handed her a letter. 'I think that's you.' Nina closed the laptop and took the envelope. There was an English Heritage crest on the front. Joe sat down on the other chair and leaned his elbows on the marble top. They'd put in the grant application for restoration of the mechanism and the reinstatement of two French burr stones, the final phase of the renovations.

It had been two years since Nina had driven down to Sussex from Scotland, planning the article with Astrid intermittently dozing next to her and Magnus's chapter sitting in her laptop bag. She had not been back since. Thanks to the auction of the Verdure tapestry and the coffee pot – which, it turned out, was the work of one of the finest silversmiths of the nineteenth century and took just over two thousand pounds – the bricks were now repointed and tarred, the staircases, floors and broken windows renovated. The fan stage had been dismantled, repaired and reattached, the remaining two sweeps restored, two more built new and the rotting planks in the cap replaced, without having to take it off. The stone altar had been returned to the village church.

When Astrid and Mrs Baker had asked Nina to stay, and then agreed to let her live inside the windmill, she hadn't cared about the draughts, the structural instability or the damp because, perhaps for the first time in her life, she had a sense of belonging. Joe and a plumber friend came up one weekend soon after she arrived, to repair the heating system and strengthen the Spout floor (she did agree to avoid the Dust and Bin floors until they'd found funds for restoring the joists and floorboards). Then, together, he and Nina installed a little kitchen on the Spout floor and, using the sack hoist, hauled the tin bath up to it too. When this task was done, they climbed up to the Dust floor – taking great care where they trod – and stood at the top window side by side looking down. The sky wrapped around them, a delicate wintry blue, with putty-coloured clouds tinged the faintest raspberry at the edges. As the clouds moved, their shadows chased across the turf and the winter light recalibrated so that the colours shifted from pea green to olive to velvety brown. 'These hills change all the time,' Nina said. 'Moment to moment.'

'They do, but they also stay the same,' Joe said. 'They've looked pretty much like this since the Neolithic people first cleared the forests.'

Some days, the wind was overwhelming, and it seemed

hell-bent on destroying all their repairs. It howled up off the
sea and over the hills to wrench at the sweeps, punch the windows, clatter and shake the fan stage. When Nina came in, if
she didn't close the door fast enough, a tornado would swirl
in with her, flapping the curtains, blowing papers into the air,
knocking over picture frames. Joe accepted this with equanimity.
'It's the windmill's job to withstand gales. It calls the wind up
here, and sometimes it's too much, and it gets battered and torn
up, and then we have to fix it. But the wind isn't something to
be feared, it's just part of being here.'

Even so, Nina noticed that he was always checking this and
that, making little adjustments, screwing things in, sealing up
cracks. 'If you don't pay attention,' he said, 'it starts to feel
neglected, and that's when the trouble begins.'

At night, when Joe was away working on another mill
somewhere, Nina lay alone in Constance's iron bed listening
to the same gales and gusts that Constance would have heard,
and the millers before her. She felt the adjustments of the tower,
the creaks and shifts of the wheels, the rattle of the fan stage,
the tinkle of the grain bell and the strain of the sweeps against
their brake. Sometimes the barn owl's screech woke her, or the
spooky, Hitchcockian scream of a vixen down in the woods, but
in the morning, there would be birdsong and the distant bleat
of sheep, and it would be paradise again.

When the wind was right, they'd call Astrid and Mrs Baker out
from the cottage and, with the dogs yapping in circles – Juniper
gone now, but the new puppy tiny and joyful, shepherded by
Hendricks, who was tolerant and grandfatherly, with Gordon, as
ever, trailing after Joe's Labrador – Joe would climb up and release
the brake and the three women would stand back, clutching the
dogs tight, and watch the sweeps turn. Each pass swished hard

and close to the grass, before sweeping up, and back and round again; the oiled mechanism whirred, almost purred, as the shaft rotated, the cogs met, locked, and released. Astrid was maybe a bit slower since her heart operation, but when Mrs Baker fretted that she was getting cold or tired, she'd laugh. 'I've never felt better in my life, Mrs Baker. Do stop fussing. I'm positively radiant with health.'

It was only on certain nights that Nina was woken by the sudden violent clang of the grain bell, or the sound of soft-soled feet waltzing overhead, or a faint coughing down in the lavender garden. When she told Joe about these noises, he reminded her that the wheels inside the windmill were made of applewood, hornbeam and beech wood and as the wind changed direction, the metal teeth would push against one another, so she was probably hearing dry timbers and gnashing iron. The bell, of course, was shaken by the swirling draughts.

'But all our insulation . . .' she said.

He pulled her close and folded his arms around her. 'You can't keep the wind out of a windmill no matter how well you insulate it. All we can really do is be here, and care for it, and patch it up after a bad storm hits.'

Nina mentioned the sounds to Astrid one day, too, as they were sitting by the Rayburn drinking tea. Mrs Baker was outside somewhere, hauling potatoes out of the ground. 'I used to hear her coughing and dancing all the time,' Astrid said. 'And ringing that damned grain bell. She liked to flip the bible pages too. And I'd sometimes glimpse her standing at the end of the tunnel. Have you been down there?'

Nina nodded, vigorously.

'Once or twice, I saw her move away from the top of the stair-case too, as I was coming up from the tunnel. And of course,

Mrs Baker saw her for a while inside the cottage. Neither of us sees her any more, though, not since you came.' Her eyes were bright, and as was often the case with Astrid, Nina couldn't tell if she was being serious.

After she'd read the English Heritage letter, she handed it to Joe. He read it, whooped, and hugged her. The dog jumped up, almost knocking them both over.

Above them, the windmill gave a resounding creak as if it was leaning over to see what the fuss was about, watching as the two laughed and threw their arms around each other. And then the other two were coming out into the courtyard, calling up in high voices; slower, these two, creaking and crooked, followed by the four little dancing or waddling spots of life; and the old ones were coming up to the younger ones, and then everyone was shouting and laughing and failing to notice that the wind had picked up, coming in off the sea, rushing over the ridge of the Downs, clear and hard, carrying salt and complicated scents of wildflowers with seagulls cresting in, and over, clouds travelling fast, faster, onwards, past; and the power builds and hums, the muscles strain for release and at last familiar feet run up inside, and there is the pinch and heave as the brake lets go – the surge as the fantail finds the wind, and the cap creaks, turns, and the sweeps catch the edge and harness it – and then everything inside starts to move: teeth lock, gnash, wheels turn, ropes strain, the shaft begins to rotate, slow at first, then speeding up, oiled, smooth, and the sweeps start to spin. The ones below look up in admiration, perhaps awe, and there is the muscular sensation of catching the wind properly, now, so that the sweeps move faster, spinning backwards through time and space, free and strong, purpose enough even without grain to grind or mouths to feed, timeless, universal: the joy of the wind.

# Acknowledgements

Thank you dear Stef Bierwerth and Judith Murray, for everything you do. Thank you also Kat Burdon, Ella Patel, Hannah Winter, Jon Butler, David Murphy, Lorraine Green, Andrew Smith and everyone in the brilliant Quercus team.

Thank you Mick Herron, Rachel Wooller and Mark Sparrow, your thoughts and encouragement were completely invaluable. Thank you also to kind and generous friends who helped in so many ways: Penny Boreham, Andy Smith, Kate Brooke, Andrew Billen, Ruth Sessions and Father Richard Peers.

I am also very grateful to Steve Tempia and Thomas Stark Holland for talking to me about film editing, Iestyn Arwel for actor insights, Joanna Jones, for stories of Audrey Hepburn and more, and to Simon Potter of the Sussex Mills Group, for patient explanations and a tour of Jack Windmill. Any errors or inventions are all mine.

A dog treat for miniature wire-haired Hugo, and another in memory of beautiful Small, my original muse. My love and thanks, of course, to Izzie, Sam and Ted and above all to John, for everything.